NOT WANTED ON THE VOYAGE

Timothy Findley

VIKING

VIKING
Penguin Books Canada Ltd., 2801 John Street, Markham, Ontario,
 Canada L3R 1B4
Penguin Books, Harmondsworth, Middlesex, England
Viking Penguin Inc., 40 West 23rd Street, New York, N.Y. 10010 U.S.A.
Penguin Books Australia Ltd., Ringwood, Victoria, Australia
Penguin Books (N.Z.) Ltd., 182–190 Wairau Road, Auckland 10, New Zealand

First published by Penguin Books Canada Ltd., 1984

Printed and bound in the United States of America.

CANADIAN CATALOGUING IN PUBLICATION DATA
Findley, Timothy, 1930–
 Not wanted on the voyage

ISBN 0-670-80305-7

I. Title.

PS8511.I573N68 1984a   C813'.54   C84-099283-1
PR9199.3.F548N68 1984a

FOR THESE ESPECIALLY
Mottle and Boy; Maggie and Hooker —
and the horses who
shared the days.

And for
The Two Hundred.

ACKNOWLEDGEMENTS
Among many, I must thank especially David Staines, whose expertise and help in the making of this book were absolutely crucial; Phyllis Webb, whose poem, *Leaning*, was the book's initial impetus and who — along with E. D. Blodgett — heard me out on the subjects of cats and unicorns; and Keith and Catherine Griffin, who let me use their barn as my ark and their animals as my multitude. As always, I owe countless thanks to Stanley and Nancy Colbert — and all thanks and more to William Whitehead. My gratitude, also, to the Canada Council for support received during the course of this work.

NOT WANTED ON THE VOYAGE

Against Despair

And you, are you still here
tilting in this stranded ark
blind and seeing in the dark.

PHYLLIS WEBB, *Leaning*

PROLOGUE

And Noah went in, and his sons,
and his wife, and his sons' wives
with him into the ark, because
of the waters of the flood . . .

Genesis 7:7

∞∞∞∞∞∞∞∞∞∞∞

E**VERYONE** KNOWS it wasn't like that.

To begin with, they make it sound as if there wasn't any argument; as if there wasn't any panic — no one being pushed aside — no one being trampled — none of the animals howling — none of the people screaming blue murder. They make it sound as if the only people who wanted to get on board were Doctor Noyes and his family. Presumably, everyone else (the rest of the human race, so to speak) stood off waving gaily, behind a distant barricade: SPECTATORS WILL NOT CROSS THE YELLOW LINE and: THANK YOU FOR YOUR CO-OPERATION. With all the baggage neatly labelled: *WANTED* or *NOT WANTED ON THE VOYAGE.*

They also make it sound as if there wasn't any dread — Noah and his sons relaxed on the poop deck, sipping port and smoking cigars beneath a blue and white striped awning — probably wearing yachting caps, white ducks and blazers. Mrs Noyes and her daughters-in-law fluttering up the gangplank — neat and tidy — dry beneath their umbrellas — turning and calling; *"goodbye, everybody!"* And all their friends shouting; *"bon voyage!"* while the daughters-in-law hand over their tickets, smiling and laughing — everyone being piped aboard and a band playing *Rule Britannia!* and *Over the Sea to Skye.* Flags and banners and a booming cannon . . . like an excursion.

Well. It wasn't an excursion. It was the end of the world.

3

∞ *Mrs Noyes went running — headlong down the darkening halls — her skirts and aprons yanked above her thighs — running with the blank-eyed terror of someone who cannot find her children while she hears their cries for help. Smoke was pouring through the house from one open end to the other — and at first Mrs Noyes was certain the fire must be inside, but when she reached the door and saw the blazing pyre, she knew it was not the house but something else — alive — that was in flames.*

She paused only a second — long enough to throw up her arms against the heat and to wrap an apron around her head because the air was full of sparks the size of birds and her hair was dry as tinder-grass — and then she was running again — racing through the streaming smoke and she was desperately trying to find out what it was that was making the high-pitched wailing sound that was — and wasn't — a cry she recognized. And she also tried to see and to count the shapes that were moving with her through the furnace — (for it seemed a furnace now) — and whether they were human shapes — her sons — her husband — her daughters-in-law. . . .

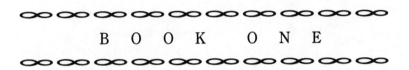

B O O K   O N E

And God looked upon the earth,
and, behold, it was corrupt;
for all flesh had corrupted
His way upon the earth.

Genesis 6:12

∞ ∞ ∞ ∞ ∞ ∞ ∞ ∞ ∞ ∞ ∞

NEWS OF THE messenger's arrival spread like wildfire.

First, she had been seen far down the valley, using the shape of the river's course to find her way. Boatmen striving against the current paused to point and stare at the marvel of her colours. Rising on the updraught — her strength beginning to flag — the messenger made a desperate search for landmarks below her and, at last, found the dusty signals of carts and horsemen; the road curving around the hill. Journeymen labourers, making for the top, paused mid-climb as she began her ascent. The newly invented *para sols* of wide straw hats gave people the look of mushrooms walking on the road — and the messenger thought of food. She was hungry but also disciplined and, though she had flown all night and through the morning, she had paused only once to drink from a barnyard pond at dawn.

Now the journey was nearly over. The sun beat down on her narrow back and cast her shadow like a blue running beast on the track below. Carters, horsemen and labourers all threw back their heads and — shading their eyes — looked up to see her pass. Some — though she could barely hear them — cried to her; *"where have you come from? Where are you going?"* But others, who knew the meaning of her colours, asked no questions. The answers, in times like these, could only be troubling and thus were better left unknown.

At the top of the hill, the pine tree, the crude stone terrace and the altar with its wide, stained surface told her she had arrived at the end of her journey. Dropping lower towards the ground, she could also see the dry mud path leading to and from the compound. Broken walls and clustered buildings, sheep pens and cattle yards made patterns below her. Smoking chimneys showed her where the kitchens were and the kitchen gardens. The steaming dung heap; the conical, woven beehives; the orchard; the bath house and the yellow lawns dying for lack of rain all led her forward till, at last, she saw the walnut tree with its great black arms and its twisted leaves — the one last sign she sought: the emblem of the family living there.

Spent to the point of dropping, the messenger made a final effort to announce her presence. Hovering above the compound, she clapped her wings together till they made a sound as loud as banging doors and breaking glass. And when the noise had reached its climax, an old man rose from an arbour beneath the walnut tree and made his way to the open place above which she hung. When the messenger saw his startled look of recognition, she knew he must be the one she had flown so far to find. Slowly, the old man raised his arm in salutation, after which he offered his heavy sleeve as a place for her to roost.

∞ No sooner had the messenger deposited the missive in Doctor Noyes's hands than she flew up over his head, gave a great cry, and fell at his feet like a stone.

∞ Everyone came running: Shem, with his scythe, from the hill and Mrs Noyes from the kitchen; Emma and her dog from the scullery; Japeth — blue and dripping — from the bath house and Hannah from the orchard. Only Ham was missing — off in the cedar grove, waiting for Mars to appear.

"What? What is it?" said Mrs Noyes, whose voice was hoarse as usual, from yelling at Emma.

Doctor Noyes had still not broken the seal. He was staring at the pink and ruby dove on the ground, her wings still shuddering and the dust still settling over her clouded eye. Waiting for her to die, Doctor Noyes mumbled what sounded like a benediction, but he was trembling — fearful — and the words could not be heard.

For a moment, watched impatiently by the others, he simply stood there wanting to shift his feet away from the dying bird — but unable to move.

Finally, Mrs Noyes could bear it no longer and she said; "what's in the letter, Noah? What about the letter?"

Doctor Noyes broke the seal at last and squinted at the open page.

Shem, Hannah, Japeth, Emma, Mrs Noyes and even Emma's dog watched him as he read and re-read each word, his jaws moving slowly over the sentences, one by one. They tried to read his lips, but his beard was so thick and tangled his mouth could barely be seen.

"Well?" said Mrs Noyes.

"He's coming," said Doctor Noyes. "Here."

Emma's finger was up her nose. "Who?" she said.

Hannah snapped; "oh, don't be such a fool!"

The visitor could only be one Being. The pink and ruby dove at their feet was plain as an autograph written in the dust — one of the ten thousand names of God. Sometime within the next forty-eight hours, Yaweh Himself would descend from His carriage right on this very spot.

"Oh dear," said Mrs Noyes — and looked around the yard, distraught, as if she wished there was time to rearrange the trees.

"Oh, my . . ." said Hannah — lifting her hand to her breast and smiling.

But Emma said; "oh no!" and sat on the ground and wailed. It was not the thought of seeing God that upset her. It was the thought of being seen.

∞ All of this happened midafternoon, with the sun just past its zenith. The heat in the yard was intense and almost white, its glare thrown up from the dried-out trampled earth. Doctor Noyes and his family stood at the very centre of this

glare, dazed and seemingly paralysed by the news they had
just received. It was cool, however, on the fringes of the yard
beneath the trees and Emma's dog went over there and lay
with its tongue hanging out. The sound of it panting was all
that could be heard; that, and the sound of insects. Even the
animals standing in the shade of the barns were quiet — and
the sparrows, starlings and oven birds crowded beneath the
eaves, and the fifteen storks on the roof.

A peacock — thinking perhaps this silence was some sort of
cue — suddenly strutted into the dust and fanned its tail with
a snap. Everyone turned in the peacock's direction. Noah,
looking at its feathers, thought of the eye of God and was sure
it was a sign.

The peacock toed the dust and moved two paces forward —
one pace back — two paces sideways in an elegant pavanne.

Noah, as though in a silent dialogue with the bird, gave it a
nod and fingered the letter in his hand. Then he turned to the
others. "There will be a sacrifice," he said. "This evening."

∞ Shem was the first to make the move to depart.

Before the messenger's arrival, he had been haying in the
meadow halfway down the hill and he still carried his scythe.
Its weight on his shoulder reminded him of what he should be
doing. Nothing — not even Yaweh's arrival — could be allowed
to delay the harvest lest the long anticipated rains should come
and ruin it, beating it to the ground. The coming of the rains
would also drive the peasants from the fields and back to their
distant homes from which, he knew, they could never be
recalled. "We have done for you, Master Shem," they would
say. "And now the rains have come and we mean to spend the
rest of our days rejoicing." Even now, they would be lolling in
the sun beneath their hats and snoring, taking advantage of
Master Shem's absence and putting him that much further behind in his schedule.

Shem was Noah's oldest son and had always been called
The Ox. He was the tallest and the strongest of all the children ever born to Doctor and Mrs Noyes and the first of them
to survive. Sandy-haired, flat-faced and pale of eye, Shem did

nothing but eat and work and sleep. He thought of nothing else but these three things and was devoid of wonder. All he asked of life was a plough he could walk behind and a scythe that was sharp enough to shave with. In Shem's perception of things, all food was placed on tables so that he might eat, and all beds invented so that he might lie with his great limbs flung out unencumbered till he called for his wife to service him. For Shem, The Ox, the world was only what he saw and the people in it only lived when they passed through his field of vision.

Shem addressed his father. "What am I to say, sir? What shall I tell the peasants?"

"Nothing," said Doctor Noyes. "Don't tell anyone anything."

"They'll know we've sacrificed," Shem reminded him. "They'll hear. They'll see . . . and it's not a holy day."

Mrs Noyes, who hated all ritual sacrifice, opened her mouth to agree with Shem but Noah was already speaking.

"That can't be helped," he said. "Make of it what they will, a sacrifice is called for and decreed."

"Yes, sir." Shem was already halfway to the gates, where Japeth's wolves were lying in the shade by the water troughs. He was anxious to leave, but Doctor Noyes had one more thing to say.

"I shall want you to prepare the altar," he said.

Shem was somewhat taken aback. He was the eldest son, yet the preparation of the altar was among the least of the honourable tasks involved in the ritual of sacrifice. He had not prepared the altar since he was a boy. Now, it was Japeth's job, since he was the youngest.

Japeth, as if his name had been called, stepped forward clutching his ragged bit of flannel round his waist, smelling still of lye from the bath house and his hair still hanging in his eyes. But his eyes were shining — brilliant with heady expectations.

Doctor Noyes knew full well what Japeth wanted, but he meant to deny it. The occasion was far too important for any part of the ritual to be fumbled. The last time Japeth had been allowed to wield the knife, the cut had not been clean and the beast — though the least of beasts (a mere rabbit) — had almost escaped. Luckily, that had been a trivial event — one of the minor Name Days — so the effect had not been disastrous. But it had told Doctor Noyes enough about his youngest son's ineptitude to warn him against further trust in such matters.

Now Japeth begged; "please, father."

Noah said; "no. You may hold the basin."

Shem's huge, flat body was ticking with impatience. Conversations baffled him. Why not just *do* things? Talk, so the saying went, was "cheap." But not to Shem. To Shem — talk was time and money pouring through your fingers. He wanted to leave and said so.

Noah waved permission. "But remember; no one is to know."

"Yes, sir."

Shem went on past the gates and the wolves all raised their heads to watch him. Their tongues were pale with fatigue from the heat and their chains hung down in the dust.

Doctor Noyes folded the letter and slipped it into the sleeve of his gown, preparing to retire to the privacy of his arbour beneath the walnut tree. He was deep in thought and already turning to go.

"I know what you're going to do," said Mrs Noyes, speaking so quietly out of the silence that Doctor Noyes had to shade his eyes and search the yard in order to see where her voice was coming from.

She was standing by the prostrate Emma, who was still dismayed at the prospect of Yaweh's presence. Hannah had stepped to one side with a faraway gaze and she hardly seemed to be present. She was looking down towards the orchard.

"I beg your pardon?" said Doctor Noyes to his wife.

"I said, I know what you're going to do and I ask you not to do it."

"Oh, do you?"

"Yes."

"Tell me then, what I'm going to do. Exactly."

"You're going to ask Ham to perform the sacrifice."

Doctor Noyes was silent. She was right.

"It isn't fair," said Mrs Noyes. "It isn't just. He's never killed a thing in his life."

Doctor Noyes placed both hands inside his sleeves and held his elbows. He maintained a look of calm and a steady voice. "It is a son's right — and privilege — " he said; "to perform the sacrifice when bidden. It is *law*," he said. "And it will be done."

"But it's against his scientific principles," said Mrs Noyes. "And you know that!" She wished her voice were stronger. She wanted to yell.

"The only principles that matter here, madam, are the principles of ritual and tradition," said Doctor Noyes.

"The only principles that matter here are *yours!*" said Mrs Noyes, "And you will break Ham's heart, if you insist on this."

"Then good," said Doctor Noyes. "He will break his heart for Yaweh. And about time, too. I'm sick of Ham and his science!"

The peacock, still maintaining the display of his tail, now lifted his head very high on his neck and gave a piercing scream.

"You see?" said Doctor Noyes. "By every sign and signal, my decision is confirmed." He smiled but had to draw the smile back against his wooden teeth, which had almost fallen out of his mouth.

"He's only calling to his mate, for God's sake!" said Mrs Noyes.

"How dare you!" Doctor Noyes was livid. "How dare you take the name of God in vain! How *dare* you!"

This sort of rage — more a performance than a reality — was necessary to keep Mrs Noyes in her place. Also, to intimidate the other women, lest they follow her example and get out of hand. There had been too much of this lately — what with Emma's constant refusal to sleep with her husband, Japeth; in spite of the fact that now she had good reason. Japeth had turned blue. And Hannah could get that faraway look of hers — as if she were contemplating something unheard of — possibly dangerous. So they had to be controlled — the lot of them; which was why Doctor Noyes was so quick with his performances of rage and other intimidating emotions. "How *dare* you!"

"I'm sorry," said Mrs Noyes, her voice sinking back to its hoarse whisper. And she was sorry: even contrite. She had meant no harm to Yaweh. It was just an expression — "for God's sake." People said it every day. Or, most people did. It wasn't meant as insult or mockery. It was just that . . . the peacock had been calling his mate. And Mrs Noyes knew that. After all, he was *her* peacock . . . and she held him every morning while he preened his feathers and she fed him from her hand. If she didn't know him, no one did. Nevertheless: "I'm sorry," she repeated. "I apologize."

"To Yaweh?"

"Of course to Yaweh."

"And. . . ?"

There was a momentary pause while Mrs Noyes collected herself. The next thing expected of her was appalling to her and though she knew she must say it, it came very hard from her lips and not at all from her heart.

"And. . . ?" Doctor Noyes repeated. "You apologize to Yaweh. And . . ."

"To you."

The words were barely carried by her breath. But she spoke them.

Hannah looked at the ground, aware of her mother-in-law's humiliation. She sighed and brought her gaze level with the crumbling walls along the side of the yard. There was the orchard. If only she could spend whole days in there. Hannah almost fancied she could see herself, wandering careless beneath the trees, her mind on any other world but this. She would wear a long, thin gown — pulled down to bare her shoulders — and a pair of shoes or sandals so the nettles and the snakes would not be troublesome. She would unbind her hair and let it fall — as it could — to her waist. She would carry books and apples in her hands. She would . . .

"Hannah?"

"Yes, sir."

"The world cannot function without your participation."
This was one of Noah's favourite precepts.

"Yes, Father Noyes."

"You must go about your business, then."

"Yes, sir."

"And madam . . ."

Mrs Noyes lifted her chin in her husband's direction, but
she would not say "yes, sir" and never had.

"You might help that creature from the ground." Doctor
Noyes indicated Emma. Then he said; "why can't you all just
go about your business?" and he raised his hand as if to dis-
miss them from his mind. "Feh," he said and turned away to
go.

Hannah took a step after him and he glared at her, sideways.
What was she up to, now?

"I must go and make the crown," she said.

"Ah," said Doctor Noyes. "Very well, then. Go."

Doctor Noyes now regarded his daughter-in-law with pleasure. Passing him on her way towards the gates, she nodded
at him serenely. The crown, made of meadow flowers and
sweet grass, would be worn by the sacrifice. It was Hannah's
job to produce such things as these — coronets, hats and
baskets, clothing — anything made of cloth or straw or flowers.
She alone was "going about her business," just as she had
been told. The only treasure in the trove.

Mrs Noyes's back stiffened. *Which leaves me with Emma*:
she thought. *As always*. Then, reaching down, she offered her
hands to help the child to her feet. "Come along," she said.
"We have eight days of work to do in one. . . ."

Emma followed her back towards the kitchens and the scullery where all her life, it seemed, had been lived — except that
portion having to do with hiding bloodied underskirts and avoiding bouncing beds.

∞ Once Doctor Noyes had gone to the arbour, this left
the peacock, Emma's dog and Japeth all alone in the sunburnt
yard with Yaweh's pink and ruby dove in the dust.

Japeth pushed his hair from his eyes and bit his lip. His life, of late, had taken on a pattern of disaster and disgrace that left him almost devoid of feeling and emptied of emotion. His wife wouldn't sleep with him; his father wouldn't honour him; his friends all laughed at him and his mother made him sit all day in a tub of lye, while she screamed at him; "scrub! scrub! scrub!!" His ragged bit of flannel slipped from his hips, exposing him completely — top to bottom, stem to stern. But he didn't care. In fact, he thrust himself before the peacock's beady stare and struck a pose with his arms above his head. But the peacock only turned away and strutted into the shadow of the wall and let his tail subside — decidedly unimpressed.

This left Japeth, Emma's dog and the dove.

"It's because I'm blue," said Japeth. "And that isn't fair! I didn't ask to be blue. . . ." Thoroughly dejected, he dragged his flannel back to the bath house.

This left Emma's dog and the dove.

Emma's dog was small and black and hairy. No one could tell, until it moved, which end was which. Emma had called it "Barky" and the name was apt. It didn't do much else but bark and spread alarms that were mostly false.

Barky didn't like the dove. He sensed it was different, somehow, from the other birds that had fallen from the sky like gifts — downed by one of Japeth's arrows or stunned by hailstones. This dove's wings gave off a kind of heat that was unnatural in something dead — and it had no smell except the faintest trace of roses — not at all right for a bird.

Just as Barky was about to retire again to the shade, having made his inspection of the dove, he was summoned.

"Here, Barky! Here!"

Barky went racing off towards the orchard, whence the voice had called — and then suddenly stopped. Whose voice was that? Who was he running to?

"Here, Barky . . ."

It was not any voice he knew. But still, whoever it was knew *him*. And so he went — very slowly.

Which left the dove.

∞ Once Noah had retired to his arbour beneath the walnut tree, he took out the letter and read it again five times. The fifth time he read it, he burst into a sweat. His hands were trembling so greatly that he had to hold the letter forcibly against his reading stand in order to see it at all. The words before him wavered in and out of focus. Yaweh had written at length of His "*. . . sorrow . . . fury . . . horror,*" and His "*rage*" at the state of the world and the human race—none of which, however upsetting, was necessarily news.

But then He had written; "WHAT HAVE WE DONE, THAT MAN SHOULD TREAT US THUS? . . ."

Slowly, Noah sank to his knees.

Why should Yaweh ask such a question? *What have We done? . . .*

Did it matter what He did? Was He not God?

∞ About an hour before the sacrifice, Mrs Noyes withdrew from the kitchen — leaving Emma standing on a box, arms elbow deep in a tub of greasy pots — and she made her way through the darkening house to the porch overlooking the yard. Emma had been wailing about the loss of her dog and it was just too much to bear. When the screen door slammed behind Mrs Noyes, the sound was deliberate and terse as a command. What it said was: *leave me alone.*

She was safe on the porch. Or at least there was a sense of safety. Mrs Noyes knew better than to think that anywhere was safe. But an impression of what safety might be like could be had in this calm cool place that was her own, with its private view of meadows sloping out of sight beyond the yard and into the forest of treetops floating above the unseen valley. It was a kind of cloister for her: even a cell. If Noah claimed a sanctuary in his arbour and Hannah hers in the orchard, then this porch was sanctuary for Mrs Noyes. She could even remove her cap and kick off her shoes and loosen the lace beneath her breasts and . . . breathe. At last!

Summer evenings were the best of times for Mrs Noyes. Her hour alone with the fading world was hoarded like a secret vice and only her cat was allowed to share it with her. (Where *was* Emma's dog?)

Mrs Noyes loved to sit and watch the sun, resplendent in its orange trance above the hills and the mists all rising up together — each from its separate valley — melding into one thick-scented bank above the heat. All the sounds of the birds flying up for one last meal of insects hanging over the yard; the howling of the lemurs in the treetops, calling to their kindred deep in the other valleys far beyond the river; bee noise and cattle lowing — these were the hymns that Mrs Noyes loved in the evening light. And the songs, way down by the road, of the itinerant work gangs — peasants by their campfires, singing of their distant homes . . . Oh, it was grand in the evening, she thought — truly a kind of heaven.

Gliding back and forth in her platform rocker on the porch, Mrs Noyes hoisted her jar of gin and cheered on the singing — whispering lest she be caught — waving her salutations to the sun. What else could heaven be, she wondered, but a world afloat like this? . . . Nothing connected; nothing hard or real to fall against or stumble over; everything distant, everything benign — just as it was in this painless dusk, forever. And if not forever, at least for what remained of this hour before the sacrifice — before the dreaded altar bell would start to ring.

∞ Every evening, Mottyl the cat would sit with Mrs Noyes in the twilight, round and silent in the shadow of the trumpet vine. Perched at the edge of the porch, she would watch the world drift into darkness through the narrows of her one good eye — the other eye being blind from cataracts. Doctor Noyes made merciless puns about these ''cataracts for cats'' — even though he himself had been the cause of them. Or at least, his experiments had.

Mottyl felt safer with Mrs Noyes than with any other living thing, since Mrs Noyes had saved her life repeatedly when Doctor Noyes had threatened it. But this had been in the old days, before Mottyl's kittens had become the object of the doctor's lethal attentions. His arbour was not an arbour only, for all its leafy, Arcadian appearance. It was also an alchemist's study, a theatre of magic and a laboratory — almost anything the Doctor wished it to be.

"Another experiment: excuse me and thank you . . ." he would say, reaching into Mottyl's nest and removing one of her kittens. There was nothing she could do to stop him. She had bitten him and scratched him and bloodied him in every way a cat could find, but in the end he always won the day, no matter where she hid her nest or what her defenses were. She did, of course, have one way to stop him. She could give up having kittens — if she only knew how.

There was another way — and one she had considered. Kittens could be abandoned — left to die of starvation — victims of whatever birds or beasts might come. She had known this to happen when an animal was old, diseased or wounded. In the end, however, it was a plan Mottyl had given up, partly for the selfish reason that her milk would have driven her mad without kittens to suckle. But, more important, there was the undeniable fact: the young were sacred.

Mottyl put her mind to an image of a nest full of eggs. Her friend, Crowe, had such a nest, and if Crowe did not desire it, she need not hatch the eggs. That was how to abandon the unborn: lay eggs and leave them . . .

These thoughts of giving birth and not giving birth were all too pertinent for Mottyl. She was going into heat. It had started yesterday and now — this evening, brooding with Mrs Noyes on the porch — she was aware of the first, faint warnings along her sides and over her shoulders. Heats come and heats go. And no way to stop them. Still, there was the merest chance she was wrong. It could be a fever — illness — or something she'd eaten. Maybe if she tried an emetic — one of those grasses out in the meadow . . . It could be the weather, too; one whole month of cloudless days. Stillness could be the answer: just to lie here, listening to the squeaking of Mrs Noyes's chair.

Mrs Noyes was obviously agitated. Her presence was filled with vibrations; shudders that passed through her fingers as she leaned down to pat Mottyl's rump. Mottyl wondered if perhaps her mistress, too, was in heat — though there wasn't any smell of that. No blood; no bloodied rags . . .

Now, Emma . . . Emma was certainly in heat — and possibly her first. All the child did was wail and weep and hide from her husband and clutch her dog — the atrocious Barky — and scream for her mother. Human beings were very strange in all this — the way they stomped around their houses, banging doors and screeching at one another when a heat was on. Always complaining — always saying "no!" And succeeding — that was the wonder of it all. Emma had so far avoided the mating procedure with total success.

Japeth, Emma's warrior husband, had finally lost all interest in the matter and spent his time in the bath house, sitting in a tub of hot water. As if there was water to spare! And how could a man lose interest? None of Mottyl's suitors had ever lost interest. Certainly never till the thing was done.

Shem and Hannah seemed very satisfied with what they did. Yet, even though they did it with the given satisfaction, somehow they avoided altogether the consequence of children and this was a great, great mystery to Mottyl. Could it be that human beings had a choice in the matter?

What would Doctor Noyes do if Mottyl could say; "there won't be any more"?

No more kittens to kill.

∞ It was now that Mrs Noyes heard the high-pitched bleating that informed her the sacrifice had been chosen. Any minute now, the bell would start to ring and she would have to go.

She closed her eyes and covered her ears — but it did no good. Anything she might have avoided hearing or seeing, she could hear and see in her mind. And what was the difference? Imagination was a curse and she wished devoutly she had not been "blessed" with it. Blessed. Who did the blessing, she wondered.

She lowered her fingers and drank her gin in great, deep draughts. Oh God! It was all so beautiful out there beyond the porch! It made her weep.

"Eh, Mottyl. Come and weep with me. . . ."

The bell began to ring.

She lifted the cat up into her lap and pushed with her feet

against the railing till the platform rocker was moving in a gentle, even rhythm like a cradle for them both — rocking in time to the tolling of the bell.

Mrs Noyes was afraid of her anger and she did her best to subdue it in the twilight. She was afraid of all the things she wanted to say — and might: the things she wanted to do and couldn't. She was afraid of her ignorance: her fear of all the things she didn't know, but felt. She was afraid for the lamb and for herself—and for Ham and for Mottyl—even for Emma and Emma's dog. Indeed, she was afraid for everyone . . . even for Noah. If she was ignorant, he knew too much. Or appeared to. There wasn't anything he didn't claim to know and this, it seemed to Mrs Noyes, was dangerous. Especially now, what with the order of all their lives in such disarray — the imminence of Yaweh's arrival and the whole world in chaos.

Loathe to leave the haven of her porch—but knowing that in just a few moments she must rise and obey the bell—be witness to the sacrifice — Mrs Noyes counted over the season's mysteries and catastrophes.

Here it was the end of summer and though it hadn't rained, it had already snowed. Or so it had seemed. Small white flakes of *something* had fallen from the sky and everyone had crowded onto the porch to watch. Doctor Noyes at once had proclaimed a miracle and was even in the process of telling Hannah to mark it down as such, when Ham went onto the lawn and stuck his tongue out, catching several of the flakes and tasting them.

"Not snow," he had said. "It's ash."

Ham, after all, had the whole of science at his fingertips and Mrs Noyes was inclined to believe that it had been ash — but Doctor Noyes had insisted it was snow — "a miracle!" And in the end he'd had his way. Hannah had been instructed to write: TODAY — A BLIZZARD.

After that, a great hot wind had risen and blown all the stuff away — whether snow or ash — and nothing had been left for evidence. Still, the image had been unforgettable, disturbing — everything white in August.

The whole year had plainly not been like any other. Just a few weeks ago, the dragons arriving from the north had chosen to end their migration openly along the roads instead of skulking through the woods, the way they usually did. And one of them had gone so far as to come right into the garden, crashing through the wall and lumbering into the pond. Not even Doctor Noyes could tell why the dragons had suddenly chosen to walk this way on the roads. In ordinary times, anyone who wanted to migrate south had done so through the sky — or by following the rivers. No one had ever arrived through the garden.

There was definitely something wrong. It was in the air.

"Think of all that white stuff, Mottyl," Mrs Noyes said out loud.

The heat had been hotter; the cold had been colder. One whole troop of fish had risen from the pond and walked down the hill and into the wood — and the ostrich had given up flying. Earlier, during the summer solstice, the sun had stood still for two whole days and a storm of meteors had pelted the dung heap and killed all the middenites. And this very day, as reported by Ham-the-Skywatcher, the morning star had fallen all the way to the earth. And more than that — as if that wasn't enough — Hannah-the-Orchardwalker had told Mrs Noyes there was a *cormorant* sitting among the apples.

"What does it mean, Motty? What can it mean?"

Could it really be "miracles" — the way Doctor Noyes kept claiming? Or what? They certainly hadn't felt like miracles, the events she was counting over in the twilight. They were sinister events: unpleasant and stomach-churning. Awful — not awesome. Even to recall them, sitting safely in her rocker, made her shudder — the shudder passing through her fingers into Mottyl, who got down at once and sat further off. She didn't need any more shudders.

Not all the problems were natural — or even supernatural. Some were being created willfully, and this made them all the more disturbing. The fires, for instance, burning in the Cities were larger than usual. Stoked by the over-zealous and tended by drunks, their smoke sometimes obscured the moon. According to the itinerant workers who said they had seen it with their own eyes, the Festivals of Baal and Mammon were getting out of hand. They said that a human sacrifice had been approved and chowder had been made of the meat.

The peasants—who wandered from valley to valley seeking work — were notoriously unreliable sources of information. But other evidence was there for anyone who lived downstream to see. Tinsel, confetti and Chinese gunpowder from the Cities polluted the rivers. Loin cloths and feather ticklers were washed up on the banks below the Noyes compound. Sunday last, the sky had turned bright red at noon and the Hymn to Baal could be heard fully ten leagues away.

And then there was Japeth.

Japeth Noyes was the youngest of her sons and the family's resident malcontent. Not that he'd always been that way. As a boy, there was none more trusting and none more eager to find all the pleasures of life. But time and experience were slowly eroding both his trust and his search for happiness. He was giving up—albeit, not altogether—and turning more and more to violence and petulance. Still, of late, he could not be entirely blamed for feeling at odds with the world.

About two weeks ago — driven to distraction by Emma's refusal to sleep with him and by his own inability to force the issue — Japeth had taken off along the road, heading for the Cities. His leaving was not unlike the stories told in fairy tales of lads who, unhappy at home, set off to conquer the great world as dragon slayers and giant killers. Japeth's quest was to find his manhood once and for all — and, returning, to slay the dragon of Emma's virginity and kill the giant of his shame.

But things had not worked out that way. Japeth had crept home, naked and blue and almost silent.

Coming back from however far along the road he had actually got, the boy was apparently in shock and he refused to speak of what had happened on his journey. He just kept mumbling "soup"and "chowder" and "thank you — but no — I'd rather not." His body was covered with a kind of dye, the smell of which reminded Mrs Noyes of sheep dip. It would not wash off, no matter how many times she forced him to scrub and no matter how much lye she put in his soap. "It looks as if our son is going to be blue for the rest of his life," she had told

Dr Noyes. "And his hair! Have you seen his hair?" It was flocculent as lamb's wool.

"Maybe he had it curled at the Festival," said Doctor Noyes, who was more amused than distressed by his son's appearance.

"*Japeth?*" said Mrs Noyes. "Japeth would never do such a thing. His friends would laugh him out of the Club."

It was true. Japeth hid when his friends came to call. He would not go with them, even across the river to kill the wild pigs — and this had been his favourite sport. He chained his wolves to the gate and retired to his hammock. Nothing was as it should be. Somehow, the order of things had become unhinged.

∞ They climbed the hill in time to the tolling of the bell: Ham and Hannah; Emma and Mrs Noyes.

Up past the latrines, the bath house, the ice house, the terrace of sunflowers and into the grove of cedar trees — where Ham stopped cold and turned aside from the path.

Mrs Noyes caught her breath — afraid that he would not go on — for though her sympathies lay entirely with her son, she was fearful of the consequences of his refusing to perform the sacrifice. Noah might do anything to punish Ham: deny him food — lock him in the ice house — even harm him. She could not tell how far her husband might go. He was so distraught — what with Yaweh's impending visit and the mysterious contents of the letter, which apparently were shocking, though Noah would not disclose them. Still — she said nothing but only watched as Ham moved further beneath the trees.

The cedar grove was where he watched the stars — winter and summer — charting their courses and the turnings of the constellations. This was Ham's sanctuary and he had spent over half his life up here, alone with his thoughts and his notebooks.

Hannah sighed, impatient and overaware of the time. "The sun is very nearly set," she said; "and the sacrifice . . ."

"Be quiet," said Mrs Noyes. "Be still."

Hannah was carrying the wreath she had made — the collar for the chosen lamb. All the woven flowers were blue and yellow, braided into long dry grasses and sweet-smelling lamb's ears. She held it up to her nose and turned away to look at the path going on without them up the hill.

Mrs Noyes watched her son, who sat down — silent — on a stump. He looked as pale as his shirt and his reddish hair was lifeless. He pressed his hands against the wooden surface he sat on until his knuckles turned white — and he lowered his head and stared at the ground.

Emma said; "it's dark already, here." And Mrs Noyes said, again; "be quiet. Wait."

"I want Barky," said Emma.

"I said *be quiet*," Mrs Noyes hissed. But her eyes never left her son.

Ham was the second of all the children to survive. It had not been easy to get him here — all the way to manhood — and the effort showed in his curious staring eyes and the pallor of his skin. But he was strong, now, as most survivors are who have passed through plagues and fevers: strong in the sense of stamina and immunity. Ham had lain ill and burning so often in his childhood — his blankets soaked with perspiration — that Mrs Noyes had thought he would be consumed by fire. But he got through it all alive — emerging with a love of life so great that he could not bear to kill. It was for this love that he was paying now, since his father's terms of reverence were God first and all else after.

At last the bell began to toll with greater agitation. The sun was descending and the light was fading on the hill. Mrs Noyes moved a few paces closer to her son — saying nothing, but telling him the time had come.

Ham stood up and shook out his hands. They were numb. He was neither tall, like Shem, nor sleek like Japeth. He was bony and angular and lithe: resilient — but rawboned, with large hands and feet. When he started up the hill in front of Mrs Noyes, she thought his neck was the longest, thinnest neck she had ever seen — and that his back, for all the boy's youth, was old.

Once they emerged from the trees, they could see the altar and the pine tree above them — and the silhouettes of Noah,

Shem and Japeth — Japeth holding the lamb on a leash, the leash pulled tight against his leg. Shem was pulling the bell rope, while Noah stood like an icon — robed in white — with the ceremonial knives and basins laid out before him.

"You're late," he said.

"We know that," said Mrs Noyes.

The bell fell mercifully silent. Shem stood away to one side, totally expressionless, probably already half-asleep.

Japeth delivered the lamb to the altar, where Hannah's wreath was placed around its neck. It was frightened — but not alarmed. It had no notion yet of why it was there and none of the implements of death held any meaning for it. Seeing Mrs Noyes, who had taught its mother how to sing, it greeted her with a cry of recognition and *Mrs Noyes went at once and kissed it on the forehead and picked it up and held it and carried it all the way down the hill in her mind and gave it back to the field from which it had been taken*. . . .

In fact, Mrs Noyes looked askance, unable as always to let the animal see her eyes, for fear it would think she was the cause of its betrayal. Which she was — because she could not put her hand out to stop the blow. She could not even say *no*. And so she said nothing and looked away at the sky.

Noah summoned Ham — and handed him the knives. There were two of them: one for the throat — a second for the belly. The throat knife was curved. The belly knife was long and straight and serrated.

Noah said; "you know why this is being done?"

Ham just stared at his father — hating him. "Yes," he said. "For Yaweh."

"Hold the lamb thus," said Noah — and showed him how to pull the head back and then; "you draw the knife thus — not straight — but using the curve. The cut must go from ear to ear."

Ham took his father's place and held the lamb. He held it very tight against his diaphragm — pressing his own body hard against the altar stone and hard against the lamb. He spoke to it — with his eyes closed.

Noah held out his arms in the ritual position — and Hannah draped the linen cloth, pure white, between his wrists — its long embroidered tails hanging down towards the ground.

Mrs Noyes stepped forward then and placed the silver basin — older than Noah himself — in her husband's hands.

Noah raised the basin to heaven and began the long recitation that ended with God's tenth name.

Japeth stood closer, now, with the secondary basin into which the heart of the lamb would be placed, together with its liver and its kidneys and its testicles.

Emma stood just behind him with the shroud — already dipped in oil of cloves — in which the butchered body would be wrapped and burned.

Shem raised the silver hammer, prepared to let it fall against the stone on the instant of God's tenth name — the name which no one but Noah must hear. And when the hammer struck — Ham must also strike.

Everyone stood waiting — tensed against the moment: praying and not praying — watching and not watching.

The sky turned orange; yellow; white.

God's tenth name struck the air — and, obscuring it, the silver hammer struck the stone.

Ham raised his arm and gave a cry.

All in one movement, he wielded the knife and lifted the lamb, already dead, above his head.

Blood poured onto his head and through his hair and down his face and over his breast. Hannah gasped and even Noah opened his mouth — amazed. But it was only when her son had lowered the drooping head of the lamb towards the silver basin in his father's hands that Mrs Noyes saw what he had done.

A shining moon-shaped wound had sprouted on his arm where the arm had pressed against the lamb — and the blood that flowed into Noah's basin was as much his son's as it was the slaughtered beast's.

Mrs Noyes sank to her knees.

The deed she had not dared, herself, had been done.

∞ The following morning, Mottyl was suffering from heat restlessness. It was a fretful kind of agitation because she had no control over it — and no control over the consequences. Her scat had a lush and all-pervading smell she could not hide. No matter how deep she buried it, its gasses filled the air. Her traces, too, were disturbing. Smacks of blood had begun to appear and the smell of these, together with the high aroma of her scat, disturbed her.

Her age did not improve the situation — neither did her blindness nor her fear of Doctor Noyes. To be so old and to be so afraid for her children not yet even conceived was very hard on her. But there was nothing to be done. Nature was at work and she had to accept it. For the discomfort, however, she tasted several of Mrs Noyes's herbs in the kitchen garden and wandered as far as the fifteenth clearing seeking emetic grasses — but nothing helped.

Even her *whispers* were in an uproar. Usually, they spoke in calm, even tones. Monotonic and reassuring. Mottyl had learned as a kitten to accept these instinctive, enigmatically perceived commands — and to obey them as she did any other of her physical senses. But not today. One minute they told her not be alarmed and the next minute they told her to go and hide in the tallest tree she could find.

They also told her it might alleviate the itch that was slowly spreading along her flanks if she were to go and find a goat and rub up hard against its legs. What she got for her obedience to this advice was an enthusiastic kick, which sent her flying through the doorway into the dust of the barnyard. The goat was apparently not the answer.

Try rubbing up against those fence posts, said her *whispers*, as Mottyl stood up and shook the dust from her back. But this advice was also a disaster. Rubbing against the fence posts produced only hot, dry flushes and blue electric shocks and, finally, a temperature and headache.

Why must every heat be different? Why weren't there hard and fast rules like the rules for birthing and the rules for butchering mice?

Mottyl crept inside the house to Mrs Noyes and asked for some attention to distract her from the mounting fever that worsened even as she toyed with the slippered feet beneath the kitchen table. Mottyl was twenty years old and still — according to Doctor Noyes — she wanted much too often to be lifted up into her mistress's lap as if she were a kitten. "Please lift me up," she cried at Mrs Noyes, whose head and arms were out of sight beyond the fringes of the oilcloth. "Please lift me up, I don't feel well. . . ." But Mrs Noyes was unmindful of the floor and its inhabitants. Even a string of marauding ants had failed to catch her eye, in spite of the fact the string had reached the sugar sack and was slowly turning white with stolen granules. "Please . . ." said Mottyl one last time. But nothing was forthcoming; neither words nor the hoped-for sympathy of an extended hand.

The fact was, Mrs Noyes was trying her best to prepare an appropriate meal for the Guest who was on His way. She was shelling peas and cutting the eyes out of potatoes. Now, it appeared, the Guest would not arrive until tomorrow. Maybe even the day after. Pink and ruby doves had been flying in all morning with bulletins and communiqués concerning the state of the progress and the size of the retinue. "Twenty are coming. . . ." said the first dove. "Now we are ten leagues north of you and veering east. . . ." "Fifty are coming," said the second dove. "Horses, mules and a caravan!" ("And a caravan?" said Mrs Noyes. "I can't feed a *caravan!*") ". . . now we are sixteen leagues, west-by-north-west. . . ." And finally, "forty are coming . . . *south.*"

It was a nightmare.

Worst of all were the endless stipulations regarding the menu. So much fuss about what could not be eaten. Nothing with liver, kidneys, sweetbreads or tripe. Nothing with flanks or breasts or tenderloins. Nothing with fat and nothing with gristle. Consommé, soup and chowder were absolutely forbidden. Endless it was, and Mrs Noyes began to fear the next dove would come with a directive ordering up a banquet without food. Finally she settled on devilled eggs, cole-slaw, creamed peas

and carrots, pickled mushrooms and potato salad, sliced toma-
toes, green onions, cucumber fingers, celery stalks with ched-
dar cheese and garnishes of basil, dill and parsley. Peaches for
dessert and jugs and jugs of frosted chamomile tea. "And if
that doesn't suit His E-for-Eminence, let Him eat hay!" she
shouted at Doctor Noyes. Doctor Noyes, whose concerns regarding the visit were somewhat different than those of his
wife, retired after that and went to sit in the arbour. He remained there for several hours.

∞ Mrs Noyes got up and went to the door of Japeth's
room. "Aren't you going to help me?" she said. "Can't you
get off your back for a change and help somebody?"

"Mumble — mumble — mumble . . ." This was all the reply
that Mottyl could hear from under the table.

"And where might Emma be?" said Mrs Noyes. Emma's
duties were supposed to include the peeling of vegetables
as well as the washing of dishes. "Maybe she, at least, will
help. . . ."

"Mumble — mumble — mumble . . ."

"Oh, the lot of you!" said Mrs Noyes. "No one to help me
— and I'll be blamed when things aren't ready!"

Japeth said nothing.

Door slam.

Mrs Noyes came back and crossed the kitchen floor to the
larder.

"Emma!" she called, but not in any specific direction.
"Emma! Emma! *Em!*" to the world at large.

Mottyl watched the slippered feet as they reached the inner
sanctum of the earth-chilled, gloomy pantry.

"Emma! Childie!" This was Mrs Noyes's endearment for
the girl, who was just eleven years old. "*Childie? . . .*"

Not a word and not a mumble in reply. Probably the child
was looking for her lost dog.

"Well, then — let them all eat hay," said Mrs Noyes. And
Mottyl watched the slippered feet stand tip-toe, heard the sound
of stone crocks shifting on the shelf and saw the feet, at last,
relax. Lids were lifted — something was poured and a great,

long sigh was heard. Presently, the feet returned and took up their place beneath the table. With them came a familiar scent that wafted in the air on the wings of the song that Mrs Noyes had begun to hum. It was a heavy, acrid smell—repellent, if it had not been sad. Mrs Noyes was into her drift again, which always ended in evening tears.

Mottyl got up and walked away with her tail drooping down. She wandered into the yard and across the lawn in search of some high, sweet grasses tall enough to hide her from the sun. Daily life that had been so simple, familiar and even a joy — barring Doctor Noyes and goats — had become a thing of complications, mysteries and pains.

For a while Mottyl lay and listened to the birds with her eyes wide open and her chin between her paws. The blind eye's clouds let nothing in but light. The good eye — though failing — let in the whole world. Meadow larks and bobolinks rose and fell in the sky — one song climbing while the other plunged with flight. It was all very peaceful—all very pastoral — all very calm; almost the image of an old-style, ordinary afternoon.

Mottyl slept, though she did not know she slept. Her eyes were not quite closed and the lizards, passing through the grass, took on the size of giants in the dreams she had begun to watch, but could not tell were dreams. Her shoulder muscles moved spasmodically, throwing off flies and imagined birds that came to carry her away. Her tail flicked back and forth and her claws, of their own free will, dug in and clung to the earth as if she might be going to fall. In the end, deep sleep descended and all the while she lay there, stilled and shaded and dreaming, Mottyl failed to hear the real grass parted and the real feet passing down towards the darkness of the wood. And the trailing of a long thin gown of feathers.

∞ That afternoon and that night were among the strangest in all the history to date of Doctor Noyes and his family — including Mottyl the cat.

To begin with, Japeth's wolves began to howl in the dust by the gate. This was round about three o'clock when the heat was at its worst. The women, Emma included, ran from the house and stood in the yard to watch. The wolves, being tied with long hemp ropes, could not escape into the shade. Japeth — risen blue and naked from his hammock — took one look at them and began to curse. Doctor Noyes came from his place in the shelter of the arbour and stood with the latest of Yaweh's missives wet in his sweating hands. He turned quite pale at Japeth's choice of words — some of which had never been heard in the family compound before. Perhaps they had been picked up along with the blue dye during the boy's adventures on the road.

Japeth's fury was centred on the fact that no one had put down water for his beasts. His over-favoured wolves, in their brass and copper collars, sleek from their diet of venison and live rabbit, had been left to perish of thirst. And this was all the fault of the women.

Hannah and Mrs Noyes remained more or less unmoved by Japeth's ranting but Emma, who was all of five feet tall, with hair that reached below her waist, ran and stumbled, blinded by her flying hair, to the pump beside the house and immediately began to work it like a person bent on dousing all the fires of hell. Nothing, however, would come of her pumping — even though she pumped so hard her feet were leaving the ground. "I can't, I can't," she cried. "There's nothing there. The well is dry!"

"Nonsense," said Hannah. "Really, you are so stupid, child. All it needs is priming." And she strode very calmly to the nearest rain barrel, dippered out the last of the water and poured it down the pipe until it covered the leathers. "There," she said. "Pump."

Emma pumped four pails of water in less than a minute and then, not daring to look in Japeth's direction, she hurried over to the trough that sat between the trees on the garden side of the gate.

"It's full," she said when she got there and was about to pour the first pail of water.

Hannah marched across the yard and inspected the trough. Turning to Japeth, she folded her arms and glared at him. "Not only full of water, my lord — but full of frogs and toads. Are your wolves so afraid of frogs and toads they will not drink because of them?''

Japeth blushed — creating a new and not unattractive hue of violet along his blue-dyed arms and neck.

"My wolves aren't afraid of anything," he said. "Certainly not any old frog or toad. Maybe the water is bad. Maybe . . .''

Hannah bent down. She put up her hand for silence. Something bright and curious floating on the water had caught her attention. It was a long, bronzed feather of a kind she had never seen, lying like a crested moon at the centre of the trough. Before she caught it up with the ends of her fingers, Hannah watched the feather for a moment — floating as it was, serenely, on the surface surrounded by the multitude of drowning toads and struggling frogs. All of these creatures were trying to clasp the feather and to climb on board in order to be saved by it, and when it was removed beyond their reach, they turned to watch it disappear as they might have watched the end of the world.

Hannah stood up — feather in hand.

"Maybe your wolves are afraid of feathers," she said and held it up for everyone to see.

Emma said, "Oh, how beautiful it is!"

Hannah carried it away. It appealed to her. She put it in her pocket.

Noah turned to his blue son and gave his final opinion of the situation. "Maybe the frogs and toads have flavoured the water, Japeth," he said. "You never know. Certainly, I would not appreciate the taste of a toad in my drinking water. Why not remove them?"

This seemed to settle the matter. Emma was told to remove the amphibian intruders — and to replace the old water with new. When this was done, each wolf in turn was led by Japeth to the drinking place.

Mottyl, spying from the grass, watched the tall blue figure of Japeth crossing back and forth on his hunter's legs between the water trough and the gate — and each wolf, run on run, crouching in the servile position of deference offered only to their leader and to Japeth. Each wolf ran with him, one by one and then again in pairs. But no wolf drank. Not even when Japeth fell to his knees and lifted up the water in his hands and drank it as an example. Not even when he lowered himself until, like a wolf, he leaned across the water with his chin dipping down and drank as an animal drinks, with his mouth wide open, drawing the water in with his tongue. Not even when he bathed his face in the trough and offered it to be licked by the wolves — not even then would they drink. Instead, they cried "we cannot" and "we will not" and returned to their places by the gate.

When they cried *"we cannot"* and *"we will not,"* Mottyl shivered. The wolves had never made such a sound — in her experience. Never before had they seemed so mortally afraid. She wondered what it could possibly mean.

Doctor Noyes, who was busy folding up and deploying yet another personal and confidential missive deep in the pocket of his sleeve, made a guess that, for all anyone could know, might have been correct. He said to Japeth, still on his knees by the shimmering trough; "I can only suggest that your wolves are suddenly and unaccountably afraid of water."

"Wouldn't they tell me if they were afraid?" said Japeth.

"*Haven't* they told you?" said Noah. And with that, he turned away and returned to his arbour.

Mrs Noyes went back into the house. Emma, who had been hiding lest she be made to peel the hundred potatoes Mrs Noyes had blinded with her knife, attempted to slip away into the shadows of the trumpet vine, but was apprehended by Hannah, who turned her towards the kitchen. "But I still have to sweep all the floors! How can I do that if I have to peel a hundred potatoes, too?" said the child. "By lamplight at midnight, if need be," said Hannah, and pushed her through the door.

Mottyl watched intently as Hannah walked away and took up a place on a bench that was, oddly, full in the sunlight. Hannah even glanced at the sky — and adjusted her position so the sun could pour more fully over her face and shoulders. Humans were very curious in this, their worship of the sun by showing him their faces. But none was more curious than Hannah Noyes, the wife of Shem.

Leaner than any woman Mottyl had ever seen, harsher of countenance, certainly more intelligent than her husband — able to converse with Doctor Noyes on nearly every subject — Hannah Noyes was a total mystery. Nothing of love or friendliness or joy had ever passed her lips or moved her expression. Moving against her skirts, Mottyl had never felt anything there of pleasure or warmth. Never the descending hand and never the stooping call for a bowl of cream or a plate of entrails. Nothing. What was there was dry as the grass with which Hannah wove her hats and baskets; tense as a willow branch curved with the weight of snow. Even now as she sat in the sun, Hannah wanted something for which she was waiting, and Mottyl, perhaps because she was a hunter, could guess at what it might be. Watching Hannah through the grass, she perceived precisely how the woman felt. It was the same way Mottyl felt hanging frozen and breathless above the kill.

Hannah reached into her pocket and withdrew the feather. Mottyl could not quite see what it was until Hannah lifted it up — arm's length — into the sunlight and watched its pale, bronze patina turning and reflecting all the colours in the sky and earth: blue, red, yellow, violet, orange and green. Hannah seemed both delighted by the feather and astonished at its performance. Mottyl was equally astonished — and not a little alarmed. What kind of bird had the feather come from? It must be huge, since the feather itself was almost as long as Mottyl.

And then Hannah did what anyone will do with a feather in her hand. She stepped up onto the bench and launched the feather into the air.

But it would not fall.

It neither rose nor fell, but stayed at arm's length directly over Hannah's hand, stilled as a stone.

Stepping down off the bench, Hannah turned away for a moment, unbelieving — guessing that when she turned again, the feather would surely have fallen.

But it had not — and it did not.

It would not budge from its place in the air till Hannah rose again onto the bench and took it in her fingers and went away with it towards the orchard. And as she passed the prostrate wolves still lying by the gate, they recommenced their howling.

∞ They come and they go; Mrs Noyes was thinking. Good times and bad times — one and then the other. Sometimes it's the weather — other times, people. Last night, Ham and the sacrifice. This night — Japeth and the wolves. An evening like this, straight out of Paradise — and a boy like Japeth, slamming all the doors in hell because his wolves won't drink. Good news and bad.

Poor old Japeth! A person goes out for a walk along the road and comes back blue and speechless. Terrified. All because of strangers. And this is the boy who always put so much faith in other people . . . never said no to a single request. Trusted everyone: took the hand of a demon, once — led it straight to the kitchen. I had to give it lemonade to cool it off. Almost melted the glass and left a burn mark on the chair. Tramps and vagabonds — hucksters and hawkers — priests selling foreign religions. . . . "Mama — here's another man who's hungry!" Japeth with his imps and crazies. Not like Shem and Ham. Shem only brought home toads and pebbles: "Mama — look at this!" Ham had all those scientific discoveries. . . . but Japeth brought home missionaries — and now he's blue from head to toe.

What's the world coming to?

"Eh, Motty?"

Mottyl was sitting up on the railing — looking beyond the yard towards the trees. She was itchy now, as if she had rolled in nettles.

Mrs Noyes drank from her jar and corked it.

"You want me to scratch your back?"

Mottyl jumped down and clambered into Mrs Noyes's lap.

"Look at all those stars," said Mrs Noyes. "And the sun barely gone behind the hill. . . . Next thing you know, the moon will shine at lunch-time!"

The sky was a pale, translucent shade — more green than blue and the mist that hung above the valleys was filled with light. It was through this mist that Mrs Noyes was looking at the stars. Except . . .

They could not be the stars. Not possibly.

Unless the stars had sunk below the hills.

Mrs Noyes leaned forward, her hand on Mottyl's shoulder. "Motty?"

Mottyl had closed her eyes and was deeply contented — purring against the scratching fingers. All she could think was — *don't stop now*.

"I do believe," said Mrs Noyes; "the Faeries are coming up towards the house. . . ."

Mottyl opened her eyes.

Mrs Noyes said; "get down. I'm standing up."

Mottyl was almost dumped on the porch as Mrs Noyes struggled to her feet and lurched towards the railing, drunker than she had imagined.

"Look at them! Motty! Look!"

Mottyl clambered back to the railing and peered through the double dusk of her murky eyes and the evening light. There was certainly something there very like the stars — but smaller — and moving. It could be the Faeries. Mottyl had seen them before, of course, but that was down in the wood where they belonged.

"Is it them?" said Mrs Noyes. "Can you tell? . . ."

Mottyl could not tell.

"Oh — if only you could see," said Mrs Noyes. "If only someone else was here. Noah never believes me when I tell him about the Faeries — and there they are — right there!"

Mrs Noyes was so excited she ran out into the yard.

By now, it was a certainty: the lights they were watching were indeed the Faeries and Mottyl could hear them. The noise they made could not be mistaken for anything else.

Now they were streaking over the lawn and towards the yard.

Mrs Noyes was flapping her apron — waving her jar and calling to them; "go show yourselves to Noah! *Please* go show yourselves to Noah!"

All to no avail.

Mottyl leaned far out from the rail and peered towards the sky.

A shriek of lights passed over her head and on above the roof with a speed that left the cat and the woman quite breathless.

"Oh, dear," said Mrs Noyes — and then, her voice fading; "come back. . . ."

Mottyl jumped to the earth and went and stood with Mrs Noyes in the centre of the yard, both of them looking back at the house and up at the chimneys.

The storks were gabbling — apparently having been disturbed just as they were settling into their nests. Now they all stood up on their chimneys, waving their beaks at the invaders — who had disappeared.

Mrs Noyes had just said; "where did they go?" when the Faeries came rushing back — zipping over the roof and around the chimneys, setting the storks to snapping at the air. Mottyl had never heard them move so fast. They were usually far more sedate than this — unless they were being chased — and, instinctively, she turned to see if there was anything over the lawn that might be following them.

Nothing.

"Maybe they want to tell us something," said Mrs Noyes. "DO YOU WANT TO TELL US SOMETHING?" she called.

The Faeries raced around the chimneys, first one and then the other.

"What is it?" said Mrs Noyes. "WHAT IS IT?"

The Faeries hovered — shimmering — over the roof as Mrs Noyes, the storks and Mottyl watched. And then they began to make a noise like bees — shimmering brighter and brighter as the buzzing grew louder. The storks started gabbling again.

"Maybe I shouldn't have shouted at them," said Mrs Noyes. "They appear to be angry."

But it wasn't anger that made the Faeries buzz. They were merely getting ready to make their next move.

The Faeries flew up higher, and now that the sky was somewhat darker, their lights could be seen more clearly. For a moment, they hung in a mass — very bright — and their voices could be heard quite distinctly.

Watch.

Even Mottyl could see them, from her one good eye.

Very slowly, the mass of light began to separate — almost, it seemed, to disintegrate. And then it re-formed — in the curious shape of what appeared to be a knot.

Hardly thinking what she was doing, Mrs Noyes — her mouth hanging open and her eyes never leaving the shape of the knot in the air — set down her jar and brought her hands together, using her thumbs and her forefingers to imitate the shape — the thumb and forefinger of her right hand locked like a chainlink through the circle of the thumb and forefinger of her left hand. "Yes," she said. "All right . . ." not even knowing she was speaking.

Now, the figure was dissolving, and the Faeries were moving into a mass again and the noise they made was mellowing — fading — and Mottyl could no longer hear it.

In a moment, the mass of light began to move away from the house and over the yard towards the lawn and then, beyond the lawn, back through the mist and down towards the wood.

Mrs Noyes was left with her thumbs and fingers locked in imitation of the knotted figure and, all at once, the air seemed chilly.

She shivered.

"Mottyl? Did you see that?"

But Mottyl had gone.

Mrs Noyes said; "damn! It isn't fair. Now no one will believe me." She bent down and picked up her jar and, drinking from it, wandered back towards the porch and her chair — looking up at the sky distractedly and almost tripping on the step.

Once seated, with the jar in the cradle of her arm, she put her thumbs and fingers together again and made the shape of the strange design.

What could it mean? She would have to ask Ham. She did

not dare even think of asking her husband. If Noah were to ask her why she wanted to know such a thing, she would have to tell him the truth. She could hardly say she had seen the design in the dust at her feet. And the truth, as always whenever the Faeries were involved, would be thrown out the window along with Ham's seven stars and the phases of the moon. And she, as always, would be thought a fool.

∞ Mottyl had gone through the yard and over the low stone wall and across the lawns and was now on her way through the fields, going down the hill. The Faeries had gone on before her.

Someone had given birth in the meadow and several birds had come to eat the placenta. Mottyl could smell the afterbirth, but could not make out the shape of what had been born or of its mother. It was either a cow or a deer that was standing there, but the grass was so high and the light so poor that only the bulk of the beast was visible and only a pair of flickering ears where the newborn lay. Mottyl stopped and waited until she could make the identification. Not that she was in danger from a cow or from a deer, but only that she was interested. Anything just born was of interest. And there might even be some tidbit of afterbirth that she would find tasty. . . . On the other hand, what with all those birds — whose occasional shapes in the air above the feasting ground were sometimes very large — it would perhaps be wiser to walk around the event and pass it by. Nevertheless, the news of the event itself was tradeable. Crowe, for instance, would enjoy that placenta and might well offer, in exchange, the latest news about fallen nestlings.

Mottyl waited, her nose pushed forward, her head weaving lightly from side to side in order to garner as much from the breeze as the breeze would tell. But there was still an oppressive heat along the ground and the only real movement in the air was a very slight draught created where this heat departed from the grass. Mottyl sat up on her haunches like a rabbit, so that her head was above the draught — but the flavours were all of the meadow and the placenta and nothing of the beast itself. Not that it mattered if it were a mere cow, but if it were a water buffalo . . .

She drew back onto all fours and started to move towards her left, where she knew there was a groundhog straddle leading down to the edge of the wood. She had met this groundhog — whose name was Whistler — on several occasions and knew him to be very old and bad-tempered, though his stories — if you could persuade him — were intriguing.

Whistler had once — at the height of summer — invited her into his burrow when, in passing, she had complained of the heat. But Mottyl had had to back out even before her tail was in the tunnel. Being underground was too alarming. Her host had been put off by this and had told her she was rude and unadventurous. It was — after all — cooler underground than anywhere above and Whistler had only meant to offer shelter from the sun. If the flavour of his burrow was not to her liking . . .

"Oh, no," Mottyl had protested. "Believe me. It is only the confinement." And she had stayed at the entrance to his burrow, baking through the noonhour, just to show him she was not offended, while he had told many stories, lying in the damp earth below her.

It was then that she had come to like Whistler, because most of his stories told of escapes from beasts and demons of whom she, too, was afraid. Tales of escape were like currency and everyone hoarded them. They, too, like the news of a birth or a death or an injury, were tradeable — though the trade was confined to those who shared enemies. A four-footed escape meant nothing to a bird — just as a winged escape would mean nothing to Mottyl or to Whistler. Once they had become friends Whistler had not only given Mottyl permission to use his everyday straddles — but he had shown her where his secret straddles were — the ones which led to bramble patches and holes in the wall.

Later, Mottyl had been able to reciprocate by leading Whistler during the drought to drink at the pond in the Noyes's yard. Whistler had been alarmed at the prospect of going all the way to the river because the drought had left him ill and weak. He was very grumpy and he kept complaining that Mottyl was leading him straight to his doom in the jaws of Japeth's demon wolves. But she finally persuaded him to climb the hill by saying; "the only demon living here is Doctor Noyes."

∞ Mottyl stood up. It was such a lovely evening — calm, with a high, bright sky and the air was filled with apple scent and the smell of grass and trees and birth. It was obvious now it had been a cow. And now that the sun was really gone and the night was coming on faster, the earth itself had begun to give off the darker smells thrown up by worms and the creatures of the night who came up out of the ground.

The cow, having fed on the placenta, was drifting with her calf towards the edge of the wood, where the calf would be warmer. And a porcupine was hurrying down the fence row, praying that no one would see him, while the hawks who had fed on the afterbirth gave way to the ravens. The field was slowly changing hands as Mottyl made her move on the wood, through the dark.

∞ On the edge of the wood, where the fence had been battered by fallen branches, there were groves of catnip and chamomile. Mottyl could not resist and paused to browse. Standing with her hind feet planted in the chamomile, she leaned way up to reach the younger leaves and flowers of the catnip — rubbing her chin against the fence rails and crushing the leaves so their juices would flow. The air began to fill with the most pleasurable smell she could imagine. Long, flickering sensations bounced against her nerve ends and for the first time in days she could not have cared less that she was in heat.

Sometimes, Mottyl would linger as long as half an hour or an hour near the groves of catnip, getting almost as drunk as Mrs Noyes. But this could not be one of those times. She was interested in hearing the gossip of the wood and eager to hear some news of her acquaintances there. Did they know of Yaweh's impending visit, and if so, what did they make of it?

∞ The floor of the wood, some animals believed, was haunted by the dead; though not in any morbid way. It was a case of reverence and respect. Parts of the wood were holy— other parts were treacherous. Some of the holy places served as sanctuary, and a beast who was ill or injured could be safe there, though absolute safety was never guaranteed any- where. Only a fool would think so. But the sanctuary places offered more safety than anywhere else and were known to be anathema to dragons. This was because of the mushrooms growing there, whose smell—though pleasant enough to any- one else—caused dragons to vomit and to take on headaches so violent the dragons could hardly move. It was also thought that perhaps the mushrooms were the source of the healing that so often took place when an animal went into hiding. Bro- ken limbs, torn flesh and bleeding that would otherwise not stop had all been known to mend in sanctuary, while other animals—whose wounds were far less serious—had perished on its doorstep. So the mushrooms, over time and for what- ever reason, had come to be thought of as the spirits of the dead, whose bones had gone down under the leaves and into the earth.

The treacherous parts of the wood were far more numer- ous than sanctuaries: bogs, quicksands and pits — patches of nettle and hornets' nests — sudden grids of razor sharp stones and sudden faults, which opened beneath your feet and burnt your pads with red hot coals. But worst of all were the dragon wallows. Sometimes, the dragons would bury themselves in a wallow, with only their eyes and snouts sticking out — and these were so covered with the dye of red earth that a person did not see them. Dragons could lie in wait forever, and even the quickest beasts of all—the lemurs and the monkeys—had been caught that way, by straying into what they had thought was an empty and harmless wallow.

Mottyl's enemies were no more numerous than the ene- mies of many other creatures, though some creatures had fewer. Like anyone, Mottyl had a healthy fear of dragons and of demons. And anything whose scat had the smell of meat or whose voice was either a bark or a yip or whose wingspread cast a shadow larger than her own — all these were enemies. But enemies were a part of nature and a person had to accommodate their existence. Going into the wood, for instance, a person's wariness doubled automatically — just as it did in an open field or walking into a room where Doctor Noyes was in residence. In the latter case — as with dragons and demons — it would be fair to say that wariness tripled.

This night — when Mottyl had already seen the Faeries up by the house — she saw them again as she entered the wood. They were moving through the trees — feeding, perhaps, on gnats and other insects — and their lights were very bright. Their enemies were things like bats and cobwebs. A spider, with its trappings, meant instant death to the Faeries, who suffocated in their webs.

Mottyl wondered why the Faeries were so busy. On most occasions, they were far less excitable; phlegmatic, even — and one often found whole groups of them peacefully at rest, their lights dimmed and their voices stilled. But not tonight. Tonight — they were everywhere.

It was the lemurs who were considered the guardians of the wood — and no one came or went beyond the fences without being inspected from the lemurs' trees. Either you were allowed to enter or to leave the wood in silence — or under a barrage of screaming. Mottyl was always allowed to pass in comparative silence, though one or two lemurs would say "hello" and — depending on what sort of signals Mottyl was giving off — there might sometimes be playful teasing or a chase. But this was only in the daytime. In the night-time, everyone who entered the wood was treated with the utmost caution and sincerity. No one ever joked or took chances in the dark.

Tonight, the lemur who passed her was a ring-tail called Bip. Mottyl had known Bip all his life, and she remembered his mother. Bip was now about six years old, and he was sitting on the lowest branch of a cottonwood tree, with his tail wrapped round the branch beside him. He jumped down and, with a delicate twitching of his sharp muzzle, sniffed Mottyl thoroughly, fore and aft.

"You're in heat."

"Thank you for the news."

"Not in full heat, though, if I may say."

"You may say. It's true. I'm only in about two or three days — and finding it very dreary."

"It's not the best of times for it. I'm glad that Ringer isn't in heat." (Ringer was Bip's mate.) "There's definitely something wrong around here. Have you felt it?"

"Yes. You can feel it with the people, too. They're all very nervous and high strung. Have you heard about Japeth?"

Yes. Bip had. The wolves had been howling about it. "Blue, is he?"

"Yes. And the Faeries are behaving strangely." She told him how they had come up and flown around the house.

Bip was not surprised. The Faeries had been no better behaved in the wood: flying too close, for one thing — colliding with birds — almost pushing Bip from his branch.

"Who's in the sanctuaries?" Mottyl was curious.

"There's a bear in one. Not one of ours. A forest bear. Came across the river with a broken leg. A couple of deer and some mice in another and that's about all. The usual. But there *is* something else. . . ."

Mottyl could tell Bip was apprehensive.

He picked a flea from his stomach and ate it. "It's just a . . . presence." He looked off over Mottyl's head.

"Like a ghost, you mean?"

"No. Not like a ghost. More like . . ."

"Hello!"

Mottyl's heart nearly stopped—but it was only Ringer, swinging towards them through the branches. When she had reached them, she jumped down beside Bip.

"Where have you been?" Bip wanted to know — and he began at once to inspect her paws and to smell along her flanks.

Ringer told how she had been on the other side of the wood. "I wanted to see if anyone there had anything to add about the new presence. . . ."

"We were just beginning to talk about that," Bip explained. "Has Mottyl heard anything?"

"No." She had decided not to mention Yaweh's visit. The

presence of this other being or creature was too intriguing.

Bip was still putting questions to Ringer. "On the other side of the wood. Did anyone tell you anything?"

"Nothing we don't already know. More about feathers. More about Ham."

"Ham?" Mottyl's ears pricked up at this.

Ringer explained that Ham had been in the wood today. "Just the usual. Turning over logs looking for insects; climbing the trees to look in people's nests. He certainly is nosy. Also, he appears to have been injured. Smell of blood — left arm."

Mottyl explained how Ham had cut himself during the sacrifice — and then; "tell me more about this presence."

Neither Bip nor Ringer replied. Mottyl waited. Perhaps they didn't want to commit themselves. Unfounded rumours — if you were a lemur, and therefore guardian of the wood — were considered irresponsible. Dangerous.

Finally, Mottyl became impatient. "Well?"

Bip hopped back up onto his cottonwood branch and chewed on a leaf. "Please don't tell anyone — but . . ." he leaned over, upside down so his face was very close to Mottyl's. Mottyl could smell the leaf in his mouth; not an unpleasant smell, but foreign to her palate. "Have you ever seen an angel?"

"Of course." Mottyl was almost indignant. "That one who used to hang about the orchard. Sometimes she sat on the gate — sometimes in the trees, eating apples. Carried a sword, but never used it."

"No. I don't mean that kind of angel. . . ."

"Are there other kinds?"

"Yes, I think maybe there are."

Bip held his breath and swung back and forth — and then he jumped down and sat between Mottyl and Ringer.

He was obviously hesitant. "Maybe I'm wrong, but — I think there may be rogue angels, too. The way there are rogue animals."

"The smell is different," Ringer offered.

"Different — but the same." This was Bip.

Lemon verbena — that was the same. And the smell of incense — that was the same. But apparently there was another smell, and Ringer had trouble explaining it. It was "alarming." It was "awful," it was like . . .

Bip hunched down; "rotten eggs."

Ringer looked at him. "Yes. Rotten eggs. And . . ."

"Mud pots . . ."

"The mud pots down by the river flats . . . always bubbling and boiling over!"

Mottyl was alarmed and intrigued. "You're telling me there's something that smells like all that down here in the wood — and you think it's an angel?"

"Yes. And I just wondered if you'd seen anything up by the house."

"Only the Faeries."

"There you are, then. You told us they were trying to tell you something."

Yes. But had it been about an angel?

∞ The following morning, Noah went out and walked on the road. It was still quite early — the air filled with bird song and the dew not dry. The dust on the hem of his robe was heavy with moisture and the old man moved slowly, making for the crossroads where Yaweh would first appear.

To the north he could see the plumes of smoke which told where the Cities were. Every day the plumes changed colours. In the past, when Yaweh had been the object of man's worship, the smoke had been sedate and grey and the fires had been lit only at the ritual hours — the fixed hours of prayer, the consecrated hours of sacrifice. All of this seemed but a moment ago — the time of Noah's youth, though Noah, walking on the road, was now over six hundred years old.

He could remember vividly the old styles of worship: the fathers and the elders, the rabbis and the learned doctors — such as himself — each with his appointed place and function. And the ewes brought forward into the plea-box to witness the killing of their lambs, each sheep allowed her moment of symbolic supplication in behalf of her child. Though, of course, there was never any chance of the lambs being spared, it had still been interesting to hear the cases put by the sheep, some of them very eloquent. Sincere.

And the altars, the cloths and the basins—all the altars carved of the finest, hardest wood and the cloths embroidered—each with its family symbol—each with its monogram—all the great families vying for the finest cloth and the finest embroidery—all the women sewing by lamplight — and the smell of linseed thread and the cotton weave of the cloth. But nowadays, that no good Emma couldn't even use a needle! Well—this latest pilgrimage of Yaweh with all His retinue . . . surely the Fear of God would put the women in their place again. And the young would bow before the Wrath once more, as he had done — as all the young had done in Noah's youth.

He closed his eyes. But oh . . . the basins! Silver basins, copper basins, beaten into suns and moons—the very stars of workmanship! The riches and the joys of worship: mutual consent and congregation and the wondrous hubbub of expectation, silenced only when the Lamb appeared, carried forward, its feet hobbled and made to stand before the anointed and appointed of the Lord God Yaweh, upright and unblinkered, always in the blaze of noon — and the bleating and the moaning and the ecstasy of prayer. Eyes opened wide and watching, each of the acolytes and each of the fathers, each of the elders, each of the rabbis, each of the learned doctors, leaning forward with his basin, leaning forward wielding the sacred cloth — the first blood always caught in the golden cup in those ten blessed seconds while the lamb still stood — alive and dead — before it stumbled, buckled, fell with its blood awash on the altar, streaming into the proffered basins. And the great hymn sung that was now forgotten—all the boys and women singing:

> *Agnus Dei, qui tollis peccata mundi*
> *Miserere nobis.*
> *Agnus Dei, qui tollis peccata mundi*
> *Dona nobis pacem.*
>
> *Lamb of God, who takest away the world's sins,*
> *Have mercy upon us.*
> *Lamb of God, who takest away the world's sins,*
> *Give us peace.*

And finally, each of the fathers, each of the elders, each of the rabbis, each of the learned doctors drank from the golden chalice the first blood of the firstborn lamb on the first day of Festival. . . .

But nowadays, the sons of the father could not even wield the knife — and sacrifice was nothing but a mockery.

As for the present-day Festivals, they were endless—blurred — going on forever so that no one knew where one had ended and the next begun. And the scenes they produced were execrable: abominations of human dignity . . . women flung upon the altars and ravished (some said willingly) before the eyes of Baal. And some repeatedly . . . No, it could not be imagined. Nor the rites of Baal himself, whose incarnation was the Bull — and the chosen woman mounted by him! *Mounted by a bull!* It was monstrous! Monstrous! And worst of all, the men who practised phallus worship, falling on their knees before the priests of Baal . . . no, he could not imagine it.

The thought of all this and the overwhelming prospect of Yaweh's presence made Noah feel quite faint and he found that for the moment he must seat himself on the grassy verge of the road.

Sitting in the sun, he counted over all the details of his preparation for the Lord's arrival. The great Pavilion at the edge of the lawn; the feast Mrs Noyes had created amidst so much unnecessary fuss; the polished silver basin in which to wash God's feet; the instructions to his sons and daughters-in-law; and finally, the choirs of rams and ewes being rehearsed by Mrs Noyes and the sacral lambs being readied for the slaughter. The trouble was that — aside from the flourishes of rage and depression in Yaweh's missive — Noah had no sure knowledge of why Yaweh was coming to visit him. Surely it was not enough — even for God — to say WE ARE IN A TOWERING FURY. . . . WE ARE SPEECHLESS WITH HORROR. . . . OUR HEART IS BROKEN AND WE WEEP WITH SORROW. . . . without some explanation. And then that most mysterious sentence, that most troubling sentence: WHAT HAVE WE DONE THAT MAN SHOULD TREAT US THUS? . . .

"Laudamus te, benedicimus te, adoramus te. . . ."
The sheep were singing in the meadow.
"We praise Thee, we bless Thee, we adore Thee. . ."
Such words as these would surely raise the Lord God
Yaweh's spirits, Noah thought — looking up to see what caused
that shadow. . . .
Oh, dear.
Another dove.
Calamity, yet again.

∞ The heat was at its worst when Mottyl awoke. Her
whispers had already been awake for some time and were
quite bad-tempered.

> *Your other eye will go blind, if you leave yourself about like this*
> *with the sun blazing down.*

I'm sorry. When I went to sleep, the sun was over there.

> *Well, get up.*

Mottyl struggled to her feet — not really wanting to, being
all too aware that the moment she returned to full conscious-
ness, she would also return to the full fury of her predicament.

I smell a mouse.

> *Pay no attention. Move.*

I don't feel well. . . .

> *Do not complain about your condition. Complaints about real-*
> *ity are immature. Be reminded: you are twenty years old and*
> *fully capable of coping with this situation. Now: will you get us*
> *into the shade?*

Mottyl took a sighting on the one absolutely identifiable land-
mark — the fence — and moved towards it, making a detour in
order to avoid a cantankerous armadillo.
It was now late afternoon — a dangerous hour, since many
of the beasts — whose alarms could otherwise be counted on
to track the positions of the universal enemies — were dozing
or asleep. Bip and Ringer were stretched out flat on a cotton-

wood branch, each with all four legs hanging down and only their tails preventing them from dropping. Mottyl could not see them, high in their trees, but she caught a whiff of Bip's markings on the cottonwood's trunk as she passed.

Entering the wood without being challenged had been un-nerving and Mottyl wanted to pause before she went further. She therefore climbed to a fallen and very rotten old tree — where she stretched out to take in the salient smells around her and to sight whatever movement she could. The gloom of the wood was not at its greatest here and something of the dappled light was visible to her — and through it, something of the patterns of shadow and what they might be: the larger trees, the depths of the undergrowth, the hunkered shape of a sleeping cormorant perched against the sky.

What would a cormorant be doing in the wood, so far from the river? Perhaps it was simply one more sign that all was not as it should be. Put together with the rumours of a rogue an-gel already in the wood, it made Mottyl wonder what she might encounter next.

On the other side of the question, if one whole troop of fish had risen from the pond and come down here — why shouldn't there be a cormorant?

By the time Mottyl had come to this thought, however, the cormorant had disappeared.

∞ The quiet was so unnerving, Mottyl did not truly want to move. Her *whispers* were content — the rotten tree was cool, and even its ants and newts were stilled. It would have been pleasant to go on lying there in the benign, filtered light — but it could not be. *A cat in heat is a cat on its feet*, as the saying went and so Mottyl rose and went forward — plunging from the tree into the thick green undergrowth of ferns and pepperoot.

∞ "Who's there?" she called two minutes later, blunder-ing into an unexpected clearing.

"*Mottyl?*"

It was the Unicorn. His voice — a mere, hoarse whisper — was almost as distinctive as his shape.

The Unicorn was so rarely encountered that meeting him was always a pleasant surprise and Mottyl told him so.

"And a pleasant surprise for me," the Unicorn allowed. "Well, well. And you're in heat . . ."

"Yes. And I don't want to talk about it."

"Cheer yourself, Mottyl. The sooner begun — the sooner over. Yes?" And then he answered himself. "Yes."

The Unicorn was not a great deal bigger than Mottyl herself. His nervous habit of talking to himself was well known — and sometimes he could be heard and not seen, as he browsed in the undergrowth. Young and uneducated animals very often thought they were hearing a spirit or a ghost and would tell their parents so — only to be laughed at. "It's only the Unicorn."

As to size, the Unicorn stood not more than fifteen inches at the highest point of its horn — and from tail to horn-tip it was seventeen, maybe eighteen inches long. The horn made up a good six inches of this — and very often the only visible part of the beast was its amber-coloured ornament, cutting a swath through the undergrowth.

Mottyl wanted to know why the wood was so quiet. "It's worrying. . . ."

"There's been a death," the Unicorn told her. "Most unfortunate. Barky, your dog. Done in, we don't know how *or* by whom. Dreadful . . ."

"Oh." Mottyl was distressed to hear it — not because she was friendly with Barky — but because of the troubles it would cause at the house. Emma would cry and slam doors for days. "And nothing to tell us what happened?"

"Nothing."

"He disappeared," Mottyl told the Unicorn; "and we knew he was gone — but not that he was dead. Poor Emma."

"Emma?"

"Emma owned him. Japeth's wife."

"Oh, yes." The Unicorn was silent a moment and then he whispered, looking over his shoulder; "I was browsing here.

Feeling most unsafe. There's a presence, you know."

"Yes. I do know."

"It may well be the presence done him in. It's made life *very* hard to bear. We get about so little, anyway. . . . The Lady won't stir. . . . I have to push about through all this horrible thicket — which I hate — trying to find flowers because, of course, one cannot venture forth to wood's edge or centre, where the large clearings are — when there's a presence about. I feel so perfectly awful about your friend. Are you sad?"

"Not sad — in truth. He wasn't called Barky for nothing, I'm afraid. He made a lot of noise. But — I wouldn't have wished him dead."

"No. No. Well. I must keep going — I'm much too nervous here. If you want to — please walk with me. I could tolerate the company, you know. I'll just take this columbine for The Lady. On the way — I can show you where he is if you feel inclined."

The Unicorn bit off a columbine plant at its base and started forward, the flower in his mouth like a standard, pushing through the undergrowth — with Mottyl following.

∞ Mottyl had known the Unicorn and The Lady for quite some time — though not so long as they had lived in the wood. Sightings were very rare and greetings almost non-existent until they came to know a person. Mottyl had been unwittingly in the Unicorn's presence many times before he had allowed an actual confrontation. The Lady was even shyer. Nothing that moved escaped their notice. Virtually everything and anything might be an enemy, and, as a result, no approaches were ever made to another animal until many weeks and even months of observation had passed.

For some, like the geese and the hens and the peacock, who had never been to the wood, the Unicorn and The Lady were only an idea — creatures whose whole existence was told and embellished by others. Even those like the sheep and cattle and horses, whose daily lives extended all the way down the hill, could not claim to have seen them more than once in a lifetime.

Consequently, legends had grown up around the Unicorn and The Lady — claiming, for instance, that he was silver and she was gold — or that both of them were made of glass and could be seen through like the windows in Doctor Noyes's house. Finding their hoofprints in the earth was considered good luck — and if water had gathered there, drinking it was meant to bring good health. The Unicorn diet consisted almost entirely of flowers — and other legends had sprung up around their feeding beds. Stands of columbines and clutches of wild iris took on the atmosphere almost of holy places, not unlike sanctuaries. "Leave it for the Unicorn" had become a universally accepted axiom regarding the rarer kinds of lily and mimosa.

No one knew where they lived and no one had ever seen their young — of which, however, it was known they had two at a time — no more and no less.

If Mottyl had to put her mind to it and make up the image of the Unicorn after a very long absence from him, she thought of a miniature goat. He was certainly goatish in shape and goatish in colour. The Unicorn Mottyl knew was white — and The Lady was grey.

When they came to the stump of another fallen tree, the Unicorn told Mottyl; "this is where I leave you, I'm afraid. Your friend is that way — as I'm sure you can tell. Dead now over a day . . ."

The poor Unicorn was so nervous he dropped the columbine and, trying to pick it up, he stepped on it, crushing out some of its precious juices.

"Sometimes," he sighed with his oddly mirthless laughter; "I wish we ate trees. There are so many more of them than flowers."

Mottyl sat down to wait while the Unicorn collected the columbine, knowing that if she left him there alone, he might suffer a stroke from the sheer frustration of not being able to pick up the flower and watch for enemies in the trees at the same time. Her presence — though a blind presence — might, in his eyes, at least dissuade the ever-imagined, ever-waiting hunters.

"Goodbye, Mottyl, friend," he finally managed to whisper, columbine in teeth; "I shall — we shall — let us hope we shall all meet again . . . soon. Soon . . ."

He was gone.

Mottyl heard the swish of the ferns through which the Unicorn beat his retreat and she thought how odd it was and sad that a creature with so little cause for fear should be so endlessly afraid. He was like the sparrows she had watched in the winter yards, when her sight was still undamaged and Doctor Noyes was a mere appendage of her mistress. The sparrows — always, always feeding with one eye on the sky and the other on the ground — twisting, twisting — never still — head up, head down — so that every feeding was a nightmare. And she, behind her window — unable to contain herself — leaping against the glass: their enemy. But the Unicorn had no enemies. Or none that she could tell. He and The Lady were respected far and wide. And yet, who could know? Had the sparrows not known that Mottyl was beyond that window? Surely. For they lived their whole lives surrounded by "windows" and an endless dream of breaking glass.

Mottyl knew this must be so, simply because the figure of Doctor Noyes had waited for her beyond a window which only she recognized. Therefore, the Unicorn must be right. He alone — like Mottyl and the sparrows — knew where his own dreaded windows were. And his *whispers* never let him forget.

Indeed.

Indeed.

Be more afraid.

∞ When the Unicorn had pointed out that Mottyl could tell where Barky would be found, he was not alluding to the smell of death. It was the sound of death that would bring her to the little dog. In the woods, as in the fields, the smell of death was universal, since there was always some dead creature in the process of decay.

But the sound of a death was unique. It could be both dreadful and noble — and it brought to the victim a kind of respect that was not enjoyed in life.

It was the sound of flies.

Some had been known — and Mottyl had witnessed this — to achieve the crown of flies before whole death had occurred. This event could be misleading. Certainly, death was accepted under these circumstances, but it could not be said to be welcomed. Death was never welcomed. Sufferance would be a better word.

Sometimes, when the crown of flies accumulated, the afflicted animal — wounded perhaps — was unable to flee. Other times, the crown would accumulate so far in advance of death the victim would become alarmed — go mad, and in trying to escape, bury itself in the earth where it would suffocate — or throw itself into a pool where it drowned because it had no strength to stay afloat.

The crown of flies, for Mottyl, was particularly poignant — and therefore her respect for Barky's crown was profound. It was also deeply troubling to her. This was how her last surviving child had died — after Doctor Noyes had taken all the others. The kitten had been ill from the Doctor's experiments and yet had managed to escape. In his fear he had come to look for Mottyl, still being strongly attached to her smell — since the kitten was only ten weeks old.

But he could not find her.

She had been too busy hiding from Doctor Noyes herself.

Later, in the evening, she found him — the kitten — faraway from the house by an old stone wall.

He was lying in the sphinx position — entranced — and completely obscured by a crown of flies so vast that their noise could be heard a field away.

The sound of it still haunted Mottyl — and here it was again.

Barky's crown was entirely about his head and shoulders. Mottyl sat — as was proper — and squinted at the dog, whose body was displayed in a forlorn position up against a tree. His back was to her, showing that he had tried — as no dog can — to climb.

Only a buzzard will disturb a swarm of flies; but there had been no buzzard for Barky.

The feathers that lay concealed beneath his body—feathers which Mottyl could neither see nor smell—did not belong to a buzzard. They were bronze.

After a suitable time had elapsed, in which the indelible sound had reinforced itself in Mottyl's ears, she rose and with infinite care retreated from the place, leaving the crown to its work.

But she prayed for the dog — by leaving her heat-infested traces nearby. *I, Mottyl the cat, have been here* — this said. *I knew this beast. My prayer is for his release to the buzzards.*

∞ Mottyl had not gone further than four or five body lengths into the underbrush when she heard a great *whoosh* of wings behind her and the sound of a large bird landing in a tree.

Turning, she had to squint against the bright distant sky in order to focus her one good eye. The first thought she had was that her prayer for a buzzard had been answered — and this thought appeared to have been confirmed when she finally caught sight of a large dark shape in the branches almost directly above the place where Barky leaned against the tree he had not been able to climb.

It was the cormorant.

Mottyl instinctively ducked back out of sight — until she realized that a cormorant, however big it might be, was not an enemy.

Still, she was intrigued by its being there and she slowly made her way back to see if she could get a better view of this mysterious bird, whose presence had seemed to be so remarkably coincidental with her own as she had made her way through the wood.

Mottyl caught only one further glimpse of the cormorant as she paused to get round a particularly fat hedgehog who had fallen asleep in her path — and the glimpse revealed the cormorant spreading its wings as if to dry them after a dive in the river. Then the sight of it was lost — forever, as it turned out — beyond the closing fronds of fern and bagwood.

When Mottyl re-emerged in the clearing where Barky sat beneath his crown of flies, the cormorant was gone and in its place was undoubtedly an angel.

∞ "Why don't you come down?" Mottyl asked.

"I'm afraid to come down," said the angel. "There's a dog down there and even though I know the dog is dead, I'm still afraid of it."

"That's ridiculous."

"It may appear to be ridiculous to you," said the angel; "but as far as I'm concerned, this tree is the safest place I can think of right now, thank you, and I intend to stay here."

"I didn't know angels were afraid of dogs," Mottyl offered. "In fact, I thought you weren't supposed to be afraid of anything."

"*Supposed* is a good word," said the angel. "You should remember it when you hear about anyone's habits and foibles. The fact is, I am terrified of dogs, wolves and foxes — and there's nothing I can do about it. Is he really dead?"

"Yes."

"Good."

Still, the angel did not budge.

"Aren't you coming down, now that you know he's dead?"

"I'm praying."

"Then I won't interrupt."

"It's quite all right. I was praying against his being resurrected. . . ." The angel made a fiery gesture with its wide, webbed hand and Barky's corpse was diminished, together with its flies, into a heap of buzzing, black dust. Soon enough, the buzzing ceased, since there was nothing more for the flies to garner.

"Now?" said the angel.

Mottyl crept closer and inspected the ruins of her friend. "Yes. He smells like . . ." She looked up at the angel. "Ashes."

∞ When the angel descended from the tree, she did so by floating to the ground with a graceful, easy manner that was, in fact, so nonchalant that she spent the brief journey — about twelve feet — inspecting her dress.

When she landed and Mottyl was able to get her first truly close up view of the creature, what she saw was the figure of a seven-foot woman with a great, moon-white face and jet-black hair.

Beyond any doubt, this was the rogue angel described by Bip and Ringer. It could be no other. And yet — unlike most rogues, who tended to be hotheads and malcontents and very often dangerous — this creature, rising so impossibly high into the air, was smiling, soft-spoken and beautiful. Though odd. The height was disconcerting and so was the white, white face.

At this very moment, just as Mottyl was making her assessment of the angel, Ham appeared.

He was breathless and had been running, and the effort of the running, Mottyl noticed, had caused the wound to open on his arm and its damp red crescent could be seen through the linen bandage applied by Mrs. Noyes.

"Oh," said Ham. "Forgive me. There you are. Hello, Mottyl."

Mottyl did not reply, but sat down decisively — in the way cats will — to see how these events would now unfold. Presuming that Ham had never met the rogue angel until this moment, she was somewhat surprised to hear them address one another by name.

"You know this cat, Ham?" The angel made an elaborate gesture and folded her hands inside her long sleeves.

"Yes. She belongs to my mother." Then Ham turned to Mottyl. "I only met Lucy yesterday. . . ."

Lucy.

Ham seemed unduly embarrassed and Mottyl wondered why.

I don't think he knows she's an angel.

What makes you think that?

Well — he's treating her like a human being.

Ham was, indeed, attempting to explain the seven-foot woman whose name was Lucy, in much the same flustered manner in which Mottyl had so often witnessed Japeth clumsily introducing his strangers to Mrs Noyes: explanations that were, somehow, excuses — and introductions that were, somehow, apologies.

"I knew there was someone down in the wood. . . ." Ham was saying. "I could see where they'd been walking. . . ."

That was part of it.

"I came down looking for Barky. . . ."

That was another part.

"I fell asleep, you see, and when I woke up . . . this person was crouching above me, cooling me with a paper fan. . . ."

Oh, yes.

Ham's voice droned on. It was all incomprehensible. A seven-foot woman who just happened to be walking in the wood — with a paper fan and — as it turned out — a paper parasol as well. Wearing a long, rose-coloured gown with butterfly sleeves. A woman dressed for a foreign court — whose face was covered with a strange white powder—and whose name was . . .

He cannot possibly know she's an angel.

Lucy. A woman whose hands are enormous and whose fingers are . . .

Webbed.

They were. Webbed. For as Lucy had thrown the ball of fire at Barky, Mottyl had seen the undeniable shape of the long, bony fingers that were folded now inside the sleeves of her gown. Elegant, yes, but unnaturally long and with webbing stretched between them from finger to finger.

Only angels and water birds have webbed hands and feet.

Mottyl shuddered.

She remembered the cormorant. That too, then, had been Lucy.

Suddenly, Lucy was bending down as if to scratch behind Mottyl's ears.

Sotto voce, she said into Mottyl's face, breathing her angel's lemon verbena breath; "not a word, you hear me, cat? Not one word."

And then she stood up and immediately fumbled at her pockets and fumbled with her hands — so that when she turned again to Ham, she was just as he must have seen her first — a white-faced lady of considerable beauty, holding out her white-gloved hand for him to hold.

"Shall we go to the edge of the wood," she said; "all three together?"

And so they went.

∞ At the fence, Lucy paused.

Out over the grass, there was a fluttering shadow.

"What's that?" she said — with a surprising note of trepidation in her voice.

Ham looked up.

"One more dove," he said. "Poor Mama is getting so sick of them."

"Your mother doesn't care for pigeons?" said Lucy.

"No. It's not that. It's just these doves the last few days. Messages from Yaweh . . ."

Lucy froze — upright — standing back beneath the cover of the trees.

"*Pink* doves?" she asked. "And ruby red?"

"Yes. How did you know?"

"I saw one, once." She seemed to have hardened — cooled. "Do you think you might go on alone?" she said. "I must admit to a terrible tiredness sweeping over me. I think I'll just pause here. Do you mind?"

Ham did, it so happened, mind a great deal. So Mottyl went on up the hill alone while Ham and Lucy rested beneath the trees — in the double shade of their leaves and of her parasol.

∞ The dove, looking down, saw a cat walking up the Hill towards the dove's own destination. But the cat was walking very slowly — pausing first to speak with a crow and later to speak with a groundhog.

Could it really be that earthly animals had so few cares that all they did was meander through the fields and gossip with their friends?

What a way to spend your life! Certainly, the dove had no time to pause. Her message was the most vital she had ever carried in her whole career as a Messenger. Yaweh Himself was bivouacked not five leagues distant, and He and His whole train would come up this very hill, after sunrise on the morrow.

This time — it was for certain.

This time — Yaweh would arrive.

∞ Mottyl, down by the wood, was the first to hear the drum and with the drum, the rumble of the great wheels. She was butchering a mouse when the earth began to give off vibrations. At first she thought it might be an earthquake, but the rhythms were too even and the rolling wheels too persistent.

Crowe, who was in the branches above where Mottyl was feeding, called down; "the tree is shaking. Can you feel it?"

"Yes. Fly up and see what it is."

The rumbling and the drum beats were now much louder.

Crowe took off and beat her way through the upper branches until she had reached the sky.

"Can you see? Can you see what it is?" cried Mottyl. "The earth is shaking, Crowe. . . ."

Crowe wheeled higher . . .

"Dust," she called back. "Great tall columns of dust . . . and they seem to be moving on the road. . . ."

"Are they coming this way? Which way are they coming from?"

"From the north . . . from the Cities . . . and yes, they are coming this way."

"Can you see what is causing them? What can be causing them?"

"Something I've never seen before. It's very hard to know. . . . there are horses, I think, with wings! But there's so much dust . . ."

Horses with wings? . . .

"Carriages and cages. . ." Crowe went on calling. "A great

black carriage . . . all its windows shuttered against the dust
. . . and so many cages I cannot tell . . .''

"What's in the cages?"

Mottyl wondered if it was a dragon expedition—if someone
had been hunting dragons and was taking them back alive. She
had entirely lost her appetite and pushed the remains of the
mouse aside.

"Is it dragons, Crowe? Tell me if it's dragons. . . .''

"No. Not dragons, Cat. But I can see the head of something . . . something I've never seen before. A great, long,
golden head — with spots and little horns and ears . . . it has
the longest neck in the world and its head is rising. . . .''
Crowe's voice faltered, hoarse with alarm.

Suddenly, the great bird descended — her eyes wide with
fear. "I do believe," she stammered, between breaths; "I do
believe . . . whatever it is, that beast . . . I do believe it could
raise its head up high enough to catch me out of the air . . .
and its mouth was enormous. . . .''

"Did you see its teeth?" Mottyl wanted to know. Teeth
were all important.

"Would you take time to see its teeth if it was rising out of
its cage at you? I'm not a fool, Cat. Not a fool . . .''

Crowe shifted further along her branch until her wing was
touching the trunk of the tree. "I think I'll just sit here for a
little while and catch my breath."

Mottyl left the half-eaten corpse of the mouse behind her
and turned towards the edge of the wood. The drums and the
rumbling of the wheels had reached a pitch of noise that shook
all the leaves and sent a great wave of sparrows, starlings and
swallows into the sky.

"Don't fly!" Crowe yelled at them, suddenly almost hyster-
ical. *"Don't!* You mustn't fly! *Don't fly!"*

But it was too late. Every bird in the wood had flown and
was in the air above the choking clouds of dust.

"Longneck will get them," muttered Crowe in her corner.
"Longneck will get them . . . just you wait and see. . . .''

Mottyl left her to her muttering and mewing and moved towards the sheet of light beyond the trees. Other sounds had

joined the drums and wheels . . . voices, now, and callings
. . . songs. Yaweh had arrived.

Down on the floor of the wood, a large green beetle had
seized the mouse by its entrails and was dragging it down beneath the moss, and as they disappeared into the pit, the dead
black eyes were staring and the frozen eloquent toes were
pointing at the sky.

∞ Beside the road in the high grass meadow, the rams
and the ewes were crowded against the fence and now they
began to sing:

> *Gloria in excelsis Deo!*
> *Et in terra pax hominibus*
> *bonae voluntatis!*

> *Glory to God on high,*
> *And on earth peace to men*
> *of good will . . .*

Slowly, out of the whirlwind caused by the swirling of the
horses' wings, a large black carriage appeared. Its shutters
were drawn down tight and one of them was ripped, though
some attempt had been made to patch it. The leather skin with
which the body of the carriage had been covered many years
before — the shiny skin which Noah remembered from the very
first time that Yaweh had come as an unexpected visitor looking for sacred champions — had been torn by stones and
streaked with mud from the rivers Yaweh and His entourage
had crossed. It was also spattered with the remnants of ex-
crement, eggs and rotten vegetables, though Noah could not
make any sense of this. The carriage wheels were broken and
old; their rubber rims were worn down to the steel and there
were many missing spokes. The coachman's coat was white
as flour with dust and sand from the whirlwind and his face
was pitted with grit from the roads. His goggles were fogged
and cracked and the wonder was that he had been able to see
at all during the latter part of the journey. He was middle-
aged and fatted with a daily bullock, swallowed with a keg of

ale — the strongest man on earth, as Yaweh was fond of saying. Now, as he stood up to rein in the horses, his coat had turned to cement and the brim of his hat let loose a shower of pebbles.

For a moment there was no other sound but the hissing and clatter of raining gravel, the creaking of ancient harness and the snorting of the horses. Then, at last, silence.

Emma dared to look up and saw the footmen sliding from their box at the rear of the carriage down into the road like two exploding powder puffs. Their faces were those of white-faced clowns, with thumbprint eyes and pencil-thin lips. Beyond them she could see the slowly emerging shapes of the cages Crowe had described to Mottyl — each cage drawn by four mules — or six, according to its size — and each cage framed with gilded rococo designs in chipped white plaster. Inside the cages there were shapes — alive and enormous — with teeth and tails and some, it appeared, with more than one head. There were also banners, barely discernible, drooping in the dust, whose words could not be read except in parts: THE SEVEN DA- -ONDERS! and GREAT MYSTER--S OF LIFE!

Mottyl raced, at this moment, across the road and sat on the lower rail of the fence.

Everyone's gaze, whether openly or secretly, was fixed on the place where Yaweh would appear. The footmen were approaching the door of the carriage and one of them had thrown down a ragged and threadbare carpet onto the road so the feet of God would not have to touch the earth. Emma stole a glance at Doctor Noyes. He was fidgeting with his robe and he seemed to be having a very hard time maintaining his balance where he knelt, leaning forward expectantly in the direction of the carriage. Emma was terrified of Doctor Noyes. Nonetheless, she felt a measure of kindness for him now — a tenderness for his great age and fragility. It was touching, too, she thought — that Doctor Noyes should kneel as deep in the dust as she herself knelt every day before Doctor Noyes in the hour of prayer. The Lord God Yaweh makes equals of us all, she thought, just by putting in a personal appearance. . . .

At last the door was opened, revealing at first a curious glow-

ing flower of light in the dark interior — almost a phospho-
rescence. This was accompanied by the acrid, musty smell of
old, doused fires — the kind of smell found in abandoned houses.
It took a full thirty seconds for Yaweh Himself to materialize
and another thirty seconds for Him to acclimatize Himself to
His surroundings. Apparently the carriage had been closed for
many hours and Yaweh, perhaps, had been sleeping — even
dreaming. Certainly, He seemed to be confused.

The footmen waited patiently to help Him down.

Yaweh drew a small tin box from somewhere in His robe
and opened it. His fingers were not as long as Emma thought
they might have been, though part of the reason for this was
plainly arthritis. The knuckles were huge and the fingers curled
in unnatural shapes. Something was lifted from the box — placed
against His lips and drawn into His mouth. *God sucks lozenges!*
thought Emma, astonished. *Just like Doctor Noyes!*

The box was replaced in its pocket and Yaweh put out first
one and then the other of His broken, twisted hands towards
the footmen. His robe could now be seen by the light of day
and it was black with dark blue facings and, deep inside, where
its linings could be seen in the sleeves, it was red. His beard
flowed all the way to his waist and though it was white, there
were yellow streaks and bits of food and knotted tats. His eyes
were narrowed against the light and their rims were pink and
watery — sore looking, and tender. His lips could not be seen,
though where they were was marked by sweeping moustaches
growing along the upper lip. His nose was like a bone and
strongly hooked and it set Yaweh's eyes very wide apart beneath a broad, high brow that, together with His nose and the
general shape of His head, made Him almost unbearably beautiful, despite His age.

The Lord God Yaweh, who was about to step into the air,
was more than seven hundred years older than His friend Doctor Noyes, kneeling now in the road before Him. Whatever
age this produced, it was inconceivable to Emma. To Mottyl,
it was meaningless. Her Lord Creator was a walking sack of
bones and hair. She also suspected, from His smell, that He
was human.

As Yaweh descended, lifted down by the footmen, suspended until His toes found the carpet, the ewes and the rams began to sing again.

Domine Deus,
Rex coelestis,
Deus Pater,
Pater omnipotens,
Gloria!

Lord God,
Heavenly King,
God the Father,
Almighty Father,
Glory!

And on the final word, just as if on cue, Yaweh fell.

Or appeared to fall, since His chin met the ground.

Everyone stood to offer Him assistance, but at once they all knelt again, since Yaweh had not fallen but had let Himself be lowered by His angels so that He might kiss the earth.

Noah, thinking he should follow suit, leant all the way down and kissed the earth, himself. It tasted of sour stones.

Yaweh rose — or was raised — and the earth had left its mark upon Him — upon His chin and moustaches. Mrs Noyes, deserting her sheep, rushed forward with the corner of her apron raised — spitting on it and preparing to clean God's face the way she would clean the face of one of her children.

Yaweh stepped back, alarmed, and the footmen rushed to prevent Mrs Noyes from touching Him. In the meantime, the Coachman had placed himself directly in the path between Yaweh and all the others. "Not one shall touch an hair of His head!" he cried.

Noah drew Mrs Noyes into her rightful position behind him and slightly to the right.

"I crave the pardon of my Lord," he said. "This cretin here — my wife — is so unskilled in grace, she cannot have known what she was doing. Whatever punishment my Lord decrees, I shall be only too glad to administer twice over. If you would have her hand removed for having dared so much as to reach in my Lord's direction, I shall remove not one, but both, myself. If You would have her blinded, my Lord, for having dared to look upon Your countenance . . ."

But Yaweh waved His hand. "She has been shamed," He said. "That is enough."

Mrs Noyes curtsied sedately, biting her cheeks against a smile. She knew full well Doctor Noyes would never cut off her hands — since without her hands, she would be completely useless to him. Still, for a moment, her wrists ached. Surreptitiously, she rubbed them beneath her sleeves.

Noah stepped aside and indicated his sons and their wives. (Ham — inexplicably and to Noah's fury — was absent.) These presentations were formal and almost silent. Shem had never been a man of words and now he only bobbed his head and muttered, "M'Lord . . ." Japeth attempted to hide his hands and his face by bowing very low — and poor excitable Emma almost found herself sitting on the ground when she attempted a curtsy.

These were such greetings as Yaweh had been given everywhere He went. He seemed to be used to them — and perhaps He was used to worse. Used to having babies thrust in His face and women fainting at His feet and grown men bursting into tears. He was not, however, used to what followed.

As Hannah stepped forward, she did not quite curtsy — but merely bobbed. Yaweh, however, was not so much angered by this as intrigued. What Hannah had done was so obviously deliberate, rather than careless or stupid, He wondered what would happen next. Seconds later, Hannah produced from behind her back a beautifully woven wide-brimmed hat with purple ties and dark blue ribbons and offered it to Him.

"My Lord, I have taken the liberty of weaving this hat, which I beg Him to accept as a safeguard against the weathers of this world, while He is here in our midst. . . ."

Hannah spoke with such clarity and lack of apprehension that Yaweh was genuinely impressed. He accepted the hat, even placing it Himself upon His head. He did, however, allow one of the footmen to tie its ties beneath His chin, which took some moments, since Yaweh's chin was not too easily found beneath the centuries of beard. It was only then, when the hat was firmly in place, that Hannah fell towards the ground in a curtsy of such beauty and grace that even Noah was heard to gasp with appreciation.

More was to be forthcoming.

As Hannah rose, Yaweh offered her His hand and He helped her to her feet. This was unheard of and Hannah blushed.

It was time now to move into the garden and towards the Pavilion. Yaweh stepped unaided from the carpet into the road and made for the gate. As He passed the fence that prevented the meadow from encroaching on the highway, all the sheep burst into song without being told to do so.

> *Domine Deus,*
> *Kyrie eleison.*
> *Rex coelestis,*
> *Kyrie eleison.*
> *Deus Pater,*
> *Kyrie eleison . . .*

Yaweh waved without looking. *Mercy,* at that moment, was not His concern.

At the gates, He paused, waiting for Noah to come abreast of Him. Or so it seemed. But as Noah and his family reached Yaweh's side, they discovered, to their horror, that He was weeping.

Noah said; "my Lord, are You not well?"

Yaweh searched for His handkerchief and failed to find it. Hannah at once produced a clean white piece of linen and handed it to Him and the Lord God Yaweh blew His nose and dabbed at His cheeks. But still the tears flowed.

"It is not that We are ill," He said. "It is not that We are ill. It is the strain of all these weeks of endless, endless touring through the terror of the Cities and then to come upon . . . *this garden.*" He turned to survey it, which brought on more tears until His beard was wet and Hannah's linen inadequate.

Noah looked at Mrs Noyes, who shrugged.

Clearly, the Lord God Yaweh was having a breakdown —

right there at Noah's gate, while the sheep were singing His praises and the wolves were howling in sympathy.

"Your garden is so beautiful," Yaweh repeated, reaching out for someone's hand and finding Hannah's ready to support Him. "So beautiful . . . oh, My dear," He said to Hannah. "Oh, My dear, We have had such a journey — seen such terrors and endured such trials. . . ." He turned to Noah. "Seven times, We have been assassinated. Seven times killed. . . . and you, My old friend, you know as well as We, the desperate methods One must employ to revive Oneself. . . ."

Noah nodded. "Though I have not my Lord's finesse," he said; "I recognize the infinite care with which my Lord must prepare Himself for such events. The revival of the dead — especially if we ourselves are the dead — is among the most exhausting procedures in the Book. And seven times, You say? . . ."

"Indeed," Yaweh sighed. "Seven times dead — plus innumerable wounds. We cannot count the wounds, there have been so many. Here and here and here and here . . ." Yaweh jabbed with His bony fingers at His breast, His arms, His thigh, His neck. "And did you see Our carriage? Swords and axes — rocks and firebrands — vegetables, fruit and eggs and . . ." Yaweh searched for an acceptable word and muttered; ". . . *ordure.* . . ."

Noah shook his head. He did not know how to respond to this. To "ordure."

"We are now the object of the world's derision, My dear old friend. Mocked at and scorned in the streets. *Attacked.* We cannot say . . . We cannot say . . ."

Yaweh again regarded the garden. "But this — this haven. What a joy it is to receive your welcome to this place. Let us go in now."

Noah led God towards the blue Pavilion, cool with its tented walls and bowls of ice. Shem and Japeth remained behind in the yard to organize the watering and feeding of all the beasts in their cages and the mules and the horses and the dogs, while Mrs Noyes and Emma repaired to the kitchen.

Hannah's hand was still on God's arm, which was where He seemed to want it.

∞ When Yaweh and His party had retired to the Pavilion claiming weariness, depression and exhaustion, the day rose up around them like a sheet of fire and everything and everyone fell into a torpor. Noah stayed in the Pavilion, seated beside his old Friend's depressed and exhausted figure, while the Old Man drifted in and out of a troubled afternoon sleep. The smell of dust and lozenges and cobwebs persisted, though Hannah's ministrations — the washing of hands and feet in rose-water and the soothing application afterwards of her own special almond oil—gave some relief. (Later, when Yaweh had awakened, Hannah would spread his couch with a powdery *pot pourri* of rose petals, bay leaves, clove dust and mint. By nightfall, the smells of decay would have been dispelled.)

Michael Archangelis sat in a corner with two of his minions, polishing his breastplate and greaves. Their voices were lowered against their fear of intrusion into Yaweh's rest. The only disquieting fact about the warrior angels was their alertness and wariness. Surely so much vigilance could not be justified here in the safety of Noah's Pavilion. Still, if they had been asked, they would probably have said; "it is just our job. Once you accept that nowhere is safe, you have set yourself on a road with only one direction."

Ever serious, their pallid faces fiercely beautiful beneath their golden hair, these were the only angels whose eyes never rested and whose hands were eternally busy — the long, webbed fingers burnishing, dusting and oiling their armour and weapons, while they whispered of "the populace" and "decadence" and "disrespect" and "harm."

Mrs Noyes, before she retired to the kitchens with Emma, took special note of the fact that in all of Yaweh's retinue, both here in the blue translucence of the Pavilion's interior and out beyond its tented walls, there was not a single female angel— not a single female presence save her own and Emma's. And Hannah's. Yaweh, of course — as anyone knew — had never

taken wives in the formal sense — and, indeed, it had never
been rumoured there was even a single mistress. He seemed
content and supremely comfortable with all his male acolytes
and angels about him. And why not? They had been so impec-
cably trained to minister to His every need — and "their
strength was as a shield" (as the saying went) and their gentleness was the gentleness of ponies and colts. With their long
blond hair drawn back and tied with purple ribbons and their
pale dusty robes and tunics falling with stark simplicity, utterly unadorned, Mrs Noyes was in a quandary as to whether
they were the gentlest creatures she had ever seen — or the
most severe. And still, no women and no female angels. It
was troubling to Mrs Noyes — and she had to admit it — if only
because it meant that Hannah had no rivals in this court. And
already, her senior daughter-in-law appeared to have seized
on this fact with a vengeance.

Yaweh had placed Hannah's hand on His arm and for Mrs
Noyes this had been like a slap in the face: a heart-breaking
demotion. Back to the ever-dominating kitchens — back to
the ever-present ovens — back to the ever-wailing Emma. Back
to the gin.

∞ Out of the heat waves — strolling as easily as figures
floating in a mist — Ham at last appeared with Lucy.

For the last three days they had moved to and fro between
the wood and the house — the harvest fields on the hill and the
kitchen yard — the cedar grove above the latrines and the ice
house cut into the side of the hill below the bamboo forest.
"Here one moment — gone the next. . . ." as Mrs Noyes so
endlessly complained. "Just when I need you most — you de-
cide to fall in love!" she had said to Ham. "And with a *stranger!*"

In the past, it had always been Japeth and strangers. Now it
was Ham.

And yet, with that terrible and wonderful inconsistency of
mothers everywhere in time, Mrs Noyes also rejoiced that
her son had "come out of his long retreat from the human
race." The intense, sweet boy whose love of science had led

him into every pit and to the top of every tree — whose star-gazing had trapped him, even in the depths of winter, with his notebooks high in the cedar grove and whose love of animals had caused him to mutilate himself — this boy had finally found another person: a genuine — if somewhat odd — all-walking and all-breathing woman. Older, of course — but what are years to those in love? Shem's itinerant workers would have a field day and their gossip might even cross the river, to where Emma's family lived — but so what? So what? Did it matter? Could it matter less?

Well — yes. Emma's family were gentle, sweet and moral. And no. It was none of their business who Ham courted.

Mrs Noyes went vacillating back and forth between that "yes" and "no" as often as three times an hour. The trouble was — the Lucy in her mind was a better match than the Lucy she saw — however rarely — in the flesh. Given the romance of daydreams, Lucy's figure — as it toyed with Mrs Noyes's imagination — was glamorous, soft and feminine. Pliable. Adoring of her son. And properly respectful of his parents. But once she appeared in all her seven-foot glory, crossing the lawn or sitting with her knees apart on the fence keeping a wary eye on Japeth's wolves, the image changed so radically — how could a mother not go worrying?

"I met her in the wood, Mama."

Now — really — was that good enough?

"I think I love her."

But he didn't even know her.

"I think she loves me."

Unh-hunh . . .

"We want to be married."

The three-day wonder! (Could she be pregnant *already?*)

"Maybe you could speak to Papa."

Maybe she could speak to Papa! Mama the Icebreaker! Whenever your children get into trouble — out comes: *"Mama, could you speak to Papa?"*

The only one who had never done this was Shem. (On the other hand — how much trouble can an Ox get into?)

Well — she had done it. She had "spoken to Papa."
The answer was *no*. Of course. With the added accusation
that it was all *her* doing.

"If you hadn't coddled that boy, he'd be old enough to recognize a whore when he sees one," Noah had said.

But what a dreadful thing to say! Lucy a journeyman tart? A
whore? A courtesan? No.

And yet . . .

The make-up. The clothes. The sudden appearance. And
those eyes.

∞ Mottyl was alone on the porch when she saw Ham and
Lucy. The Lord God Yaweh and Doctor Noyes were still asleep.
Mrs Noyes, afraid to leave her salads for fear they would wilt
without her, was dozing in the kitchen — gin jar discreetly hidden in her apron. Emma, too, had drifted off, with her arms
hanging down inside a tub of soapy water.

Ham came up first — walking like a happy dreamer — chattering and throwing off information like a waterwheel throwing off spray.

Lucy came up after, laughing out loud — all seven feet of her
visible above the heat haze. Ham did not seem to realize she
was floating in the air behind him and, by the time he had turned,
she was standing on the lawns, just near enough for Mottyl's
one good eye to take her in — the parasol balanced in the air
above her and the long rosy gown with its butterfly sleeves
flashing in the sun as Lucy spun around and flopped on the
grass — still laughing.

"There are fifteen beasts I have never seen before in
Yaweh's Caravan. Fifteen beasts to classify . . ." Mottyl heard
Ham say.

"I recognized them — every one," said Lucy. "Haven't you
ever seen a spotted leopard before?"

She motioned Ham down beside her — and he dropped out
of sight.

Mottyl, intrigued, clambered up on the porch rail in order to
bring Ham back into view. He was lying on the grass — Lucy
seated — the parasol floating above them both. (*Floating —*

floating — like Hannah's feather . . . was Lucy even holding onto the parasol? *If only I could see!*)

There was Ham, whom Mottyl loved — and there was the angel who was so afraid of dogs she killed them. Mottyl should have been content that Ham and the angel were happy. She had much sympathy for Lucy — anyone that afraid of dogs had to be worthy of compassion. And she was likeable enough — even genuinely kind — a great improvement on Hannah, for instance. But there was something wrong — something worrying about her. The fact of her being an angel — and denying it, hiding it from Ham. And, if she was lying about this — then might there not be other lies? Dreadful ones, perhaps, concerning why she was here — and why she was here *now*, in the moment of Yaweh's presence.

∞ Japeth, having finished his host's duties of feeding and watering the beasts in the Caravan — and having shown Yaweh's acolytes the way to the river and the coachmen where the meadows were so that all the winged horses could be turned loose to graze — was sauntering up the hill in the direction of the Pavilion.

But it was not a saunter without purpose.

Japeth had his mind on Michael Archangelis — a figure of glory unlike any he had ever dreamed could exist. The great angel's height — his strength — his golden hair — and his armour presented the most dazzling images of manhood that Japeth had ever encountered.

Only once had anyone come close to matching them — and on that occasion, the manliness had been dark, not golden; terrifying, not glorious.

That once had been on the road to the Cities — the day he had been attacked and almost made into chowder. Those who had attacked him — ruffians and terrorists — had been led by a giant whose stature had not been gigantic, but whose power over his minions had been awesome. All the more awesome for his lack of stature.

He had stood — this man — with his arms akimbo, both hands fisted, thumbs hooked into a wide studded belt. His legs, which were bare, were enormous and his chest had bulged through his open tunic like something with a life all its own. He had tiny black eyes and wild curly hair, from which protruded ears like curled-up bits of bacon, overcooked and black at the rims, as if they were rotting. His teeth — alarmingly white — were nonetheless worn far down towards his gums: the tiniest teeth that Japeth had ever seen.

His minions were dressed in stolen clothes — none of which fitted and all of which were filthy — and some of the clothes were bits and pieces of uniform — red coats and blue jackets and trousers with gold braid stripes. They were pulling a two-wheeled cart with ropes; the cart loaded down with great iron pots and tripods — to say nothing of a vast array of incongruous riches which must have been got from the Cities: silver candelabra — porcelain soup tureens, crystal vases and golden goblets — all of these embedded in great torn swatches of tapestry depicting the murder of Abel by Cain — and loops and bolts of velveteen and satin shot with twenty colours. But the minions themselves had long stringy hair and blackened nails and filthy knees. Some of them — to Japeth's horror — were women.

Japeth — for all his forays with his wolves and all his riding out to kill the wild pig with his friends in the Dragon Club — had never encountered another human being whose whole existence was devoted to violence. He had never seen such men and women as these, who stared at him from the cart they had pulled so suddenly across his path. Never had he smelled such breath as was breathed in his face by these leering women — nor sweat as poured from the grinning men. Nor had he ever been so afraid of another human being as he was of their leader. Strangers were Japeth's trade. But no one had ever touched him with such chilling intent as this Ruffian King whose fingers were blunt, big probes — wandering over Japeth's face and neck with the same independent violence with which the Ruffian's chest had wandered from his shirt.

It had been such a lovely day on the road — and Japeth had only meant to see how far he could venture towards the Cities by nightfall. He was curious, with the dangerous, innocent curiosity of the young, to discover what might be meant by the Rites of Baal—and how a feather tickler might be useful in his vain attempts on Emma's virtue. What was the "two-tongued kiss," for instance, of which his friends spoke so knowingly? Might there not be some kind stranger who could explain the uses of this kiss and of a "monkey-fingered caress" in the breaking of his bride's apparent determination to repel him forever? These, of course, were not questions you could ask of a father like Noah or a brother like Shem. And Ham was innocent as the proverbial babe. As for Japeth's hunting friends, they would have been merciless with their laughter and derision if they ever found out he was a sexual ignoramus and a virgin to boot. There was no help there. From Noah, all he had got was: "obey nature's urgings and do nothing perverted!" Japeth did not even know what "perverted" meant. From Shem, he got no better. "You lie on top and she lies on the bottom." From his friends: "never get in too fast or you'll miss the best part."

Get in too fast?

Get in *where?*

No one would help. He would have to go to strangers.

∞ When the cart pulled across the road, Japeth's stomach turned over. He recognized the gesture from the hunt. It was no different than wolves cross-cutting on a deer.

"Hello," he said. "Nice weather we're having. . . ."

This was what he always said—no matter whom or what he encountered. He would say the same to demons. But he knew by the terrible eyes surrounding him, this time it had not been the right thing to say.

"Nice?" said the Ruffian King. "What the hell is nice about it?"

"Well . . ." said Japeth, lamely.

"I'll tell you what's nice," said the Ruffian King "Our meeting you — that's what's nice."

He had smiled while he was saying this — exposing all his whittled teeth—and it was then the Ruffian King had reached out so bluntly and moved his fingers over Japeth's cheeks.

∞ The Ruffian King and his stringy minions had long ago despaired of finding even the simplest food to sustain them. Outcasts for every conceivable reason — leprosy, crime and depravity being the most prevalent — the band had come together for the simple expediency of mutual survival. At first, they had preyed on travellers only to steal their money. But they found the money impossible to spend. No one would have them in their shops and the Market Police expelled them every time they entered the Cities. Later, they started raiding farms, absconding with chickens, grain and lambs. But winter put an end to that. In the snow, they could get nowhere near the farms without being seen — and, at night, the barns and sheep folds were surrounded by dogs and wolves and even, on occasion, bears. They had become notorious for their violence — but their notoriety had been their downfall. Vigilante groups had been formed to prevent their entry into towns and villages. Posses of horsemen pursued them wherever they appeared. Soon, they could not even steal unharvested wheat, as farmers, more and more, set watches against them.

It was inevitable.

One of their own number had rebelled.

And was killed.

And eaten.

This way, the custom began — and soon there was a new use for strangers met upon the roads.

∞ Japeth, by now, was close to the Pavilion, but the images that filled his mind were so disturbing he was unable to walk any farther. And so he stood on the hill, waiting, while the loathsome events continued to unfold in his mind. He had come to that part of the story most like a nightmare and least like anything real. He had never told it to anyone — though, once, he had walked in the wood and told it aloud to the rocks and to the trees. Putting it into words and speaking the words had given him, at least, a sense that words existed for what had been done to him: that being "marinated" was something that could happen to human beings — that "chops" and "steaks" and "loins" could be cuts from a human body and that "liver" and "heart" and "kidney" — even "kidney pie" — had a human connotation. Wastage, too, such as "offal" and "carrion", and phrases such as "picking the bones clean" had all to do with humankind and therefore with Japeth Noyes.

First he had whispered and then he had yelled the words. Then, unable to articulate, he had screamed till all the birds had flown up and all the animals hidden and even the dragons in their wallows had sunk beneath the surface. And then, by some cathartic means — perhaps because he had come to the end of all the words that could tell his story — Japeth had grown calm and fallen silent.

Even so — in spite of having made the necessary reconciliation between the horror he could not imagine and the horror he had known — he was still unable to confront the central event without feeling ill. Until now, each time he relived it he had to go away quickly into some private place and bring up his dinner and weep and cover his eyes in the hope that, when he uncovered them, his skin would not be blue and the world would be as it was — the world of pristine wonders and the kindness of strangers: the world he had loved as a boy and had thought would be his forever.

But the promise of "forever" had been broken on the road to Baal and Mammon.

Now, on the hill in his quest for Michael Archangelis, Japeth had come to that debilitating part of the story that usually made him sick — and so he sat, with his head between his knees — a blue man weeping in the blue shade of his father's Pavilion, where Michael Archangelis polished his knives and where Yaweh slept.

∞ A fire was started — over in a rocky field by the roadside. Japeth was dragged to the field and stripped. Meanwhile, the women were setting up tripods over the flames, on which they hung the pots. One of these pots, Japeth saw, was already partially filled with a thick milky substance not unlike his mother's corn chowder.

Its smell was unlike anything Japeth had ever encountered before.

It was delicious. Warmly reminiscent of a chicken breast stew he particularly loved. Or a veal concoction . . .

Standing naked in the firelight (it was now coming on to darkness) Japeth had the crazy thought that all would be well. So long as they were engaged in their cookery, the ruffians paid him no heed at all — save for one, who lay out flat beside him, humming off key, while he held Japeth's ankle in a grip of steel.

Comfort soon passed when Japeth saw the Ruffian King approaching. This was not, after all, to be a kindly invitation to join them for supper.

Walking behind the Ruffian King were two of the women, carrying between them a long flat tub that was not unlike a water trough — except that it had a lid. Other women followed these with great, fat jars of crude wine and oil.

Standing before him, the Ruffian King snapped his fingers — and the ankle-holder rose. The women set the troughlike tub on the ground and three or four other ruffians appeared from the slowly gathering darkness. One of them removed the lid. Others took hold of Japeth's arms.

"What are you going to do?" said Japeth. "Please tell me what you're going to do."

"You see this tub?" said the Ruffian King.

"Of course."

"Well, you're going to take a little bath, that's what. A nice warm bath in oil and wine. . . ."

Japeth was lifted, then, by the arms and carried over to the tub. He could not resist. He found himself, more in wonder than in terror, allowing the ruffians to lay him out like a corpse in a box, where they bound both his ankles and his wrists and placed a large unpleasant stone beneath his head.

"That's only so's you won't be drownded," said one of the men — very matter-of-fact and going about his business the way a mother might who was about to bathe her child.

Once he was arranged — full length and helpless — in the tub, the women who had carried the jars of oil and wine began to pour first one and then the other over Japeth's body until he was floating in the stuff. The oil was rancid and the bluish wine so crude it was almost vinegar. It burned his eyes and his privates and his armpits and his lips and, attempting to breathe, he also found its vapours burned his nostrils.

And then, before he was fully aware of what they were doing — the two dark men who had lain him in the tub were lifting up its lid and lowering it down above him: *clang*. And he shouted — but he knew he could not be heard.

∞ Slowly, as his eyes cleared somewhat and adapted to the darkness inside the tub, Japeth perceived the lid was perforated with hundreds of tiny, tack-sized holes — and through these he could not only breathe, but also see some of the flickering edges of the firelight nearby.

Dimly, he could hear the voices of his captors and tormentors singing with increasing drunkenness as they waited for him to marinate. And, every once in a while, one of them would come very near the tub and call out; "we got a ripe one this time" or "the longer we leave'm, the tenderer he'll be!"

Meanwhile, one of the women, who seemed to be the chef, came by from time to time, lifted the lid by Japeth's head and threw in a handful of herbs or a bulb of garlic or a dozen fat onions. At one point, she lifted the lid so high he could see her face — and she looked right into his eyes and grinned. Then she poured a flagon of something unbearably hot and sticky over his head and said to him; "that ought to curl them fancy locks of yours!"

And *clang!*

The lid descended yet again.

Slowly, against his will, Japeth succumbed to a kind of sleep brought on as much by the exhaustion of terror as by the lack of air. And sleeping or dozing, he dreamt of floating in the river and of waterfalls and deep, soothing pools.

When he woke, it was to the rumble of thunder and the thick sound of rain that fell in torrents on his lid.

At first, it did not occur to him the rain might imperil him — because all he could think was: *the rain will put out their fires.*

For the first time since he had been captured, Japeth felt

hope. *They won't eat me raw*; he decided. *If they were going to eat me raw, they'd have done that already.* . . .

But then, all too slowly, he realized he was floating closer to the lid and his nose was touching it. The rain, seeping through the tackholes, was filling his coffin and he would drown.

Why didn't someone come to rescue him?

Surely, having gone to so much trouble — all these hours of marinating — the herbs — the wine — the garlic — they would not let him "spoil" in here.

"Help!" he called — but, at once, his mouth was filled with the dreadful marinade and he realized how very close he was to drowning. Only his nose remained above the liquid.

The thunder was now so close that it came right on top of every lightning bolt — and Japeth was newly afraid of being boiled alive, even without the ruffians' fires, if lightning should strike his tub.

He had seen that, once, when all the fish in an iron pot left out in a storm had been cooked when the pot was hit by a fireball.

His panic now was galvanizing — and he was able to think. With every rush of adrenalin, a new thought came — and each thought compounded the last until he had made a picture of what he must do.

He would rock from side to side — and perhaps this would dislodge the lid. He might even turn the tub till it spilled him, marinade and all, on the ground.

At least, he could try.

The motion of rocking almost did him in — since, with every movement, the pungent liquid sloshed up over his face and into his nose.

Quickly, he learned how to catch and hold a breath before he rocked — and then, with great violence, he threw all his weight to one side and then the other.

At first, nothing happened. But gradually he managed to learn how to use the weight of the marinade as well as his own weight — tipping himself more slowly, so that the liquid had time to gather on the same side to which he had rolled his body.

In the end, he was victorious — though the victory nearly killed him. Forcing himself so far onto his side that his face was trapped beneath the flood of marinade, Japeth was on the point of being drowned when the tub gave a lurch—and spilled him half beneath it on the rain-soaked earth.

It took him fully three or four minutes to recover his senses —and even then, he had to struggle very hard to extract himself from beneath the tilt of the tub. The lid, which had sharp edges, lay beneath him and was cutting into his shins and ribs and shoulders. The effort to be free was a torment.

At last, Japeth knelt — his ankles bound behind and his wrists before him — but he could breathe and he could see.

The field was barren—and all the fires, as he expected, had been extinguished by the rain. The ruffians' cart was abandoned and at first he thought he must be alone. But after a moment's searching of the gloom, he saw the ruffians, crouching in a circle some distance off beneath the trees.

They appeared to be hiding from the storm — and yet they were definitely engaged in some activity, too. Their concentration was absolute, and Japeth seemed to have been not only abandoned, but forgotten.

Using the sharp edges of the lid that had confined him, he was able to cut through the ropes that bound his wrists and then to untie the knots at his ankles.

Naked and blue from his soaking in the wine (though he did not realize the tint on his skin was permanent) Japeth crept to the cart and hid in its shadow. All the while, he kept his eye on the ruffians gathered beneath the trees. They had become more and more engrossed in their activity and he wondered what on earth they could be doing.

When at last it dawned on him that he was forgotten and he was free, Japeth turned for one last look at the ruffians bent in the circle — all of them squatting — all of them
feeding.
Feeding.
Japeth made a circle round the outer limits of the field and entered the wood above the revellers. They were drinking,

too, from the wine jars which had provided Japeth's marinade — and with their mouths full they were laughing and gabbling like geese.

He dared not approach any further than ten or twelve yards, lest he lose the safety of the gloom amongst the trees. But this was close enough to see them clearly and to overhear whatever words could be made from the grunting and the slobbering as their fingers dabbled in the mess before them — seized some bit of something and pushed it hard between their lips.

Their chins and lips and hands and bare knees were covered with a dreadful grease and when Japeth saw what they were eating, he fled.

But before he fled he had heard the words "lightning" and "cooked" and "poor old girl . . ."

He had recognized her, too.

She was the chef, who had looked right into his eyes and grinned as she lifted the lid that final time to *curl his fancy locks.*

And as Japeth fled, the Ruffian King was bending forward, hunkered down like a dwarf, and he was lifting up the woman's hands and sucking the flesh from her fingers.

∞ It was because of this final image that Japeth now had the courage to rise from where he sat outside his father's Pavilion and to seek the one figure he knew could save him forever from all strangers and from all perils.

Michael Archangelis, on greeting Japeth, put his magnificent golden hand on the boy's blue shoulder and said to him; "what can I do for you, lad?"

And Japeth said; "I want to be a warrior. Like you."

∞ Rested and fed, Yaweh sat in a great chair at one end of the Pavilion, fondling his cats.

The chair, raised on its dais, had come with Him in the Caravan. Noah could never have owned anything so grand. Its back was carved with rams and bulls and its arms were carved with calves and lambs. The seat was spread with sheepskins — over which Yaweh's pure white gown, spotted with tomato aspic and covered with cat hairs — flowed all the way to the floor. Other sheepskins were spread beneath His feet and several pillows and cushions supported His back and lifted His elbows away from His tender, brittle sides. Yaweh had such difficulty breathing that He sometimes had to pump His elbows like a bellows in order to force the air into His lungs.

Yaweh's cats were both extremely old and their names were Abraham and Sarah. Abraham was silvery-grey and Sarah, white with blue eyes. They had been with Yaweh so long that no one could calculate their ages. Sarah was indolent and always appeared to be dozing — though her eyes would open from time to time and she would stare at whoever happened to be within range of her sight — in a chilling and often withering way. Many a supplicant had faltered in his speech when Sarah looked at him — and had gone away empty-handed because he could not articulate his request in the blue light of Sarah's eyes.

Abraham, on the other hand, was not so much indolent as spoiled. He was used to being fed from Yaweh's fingers and even had the audacity — though Yaweh seemed not to notice — to feed from Yaweh's own plate on occasion. A silvery-grey paw would appear at table's edge and pull down a chicken wing or a piece of bread and butter into the lap. Sometimes Yaweh would discover the remnants of a crust in His gown and raise it absently to His lips.

Abraham was also extremely horny and Yaweh had to be careful not to pet him too much near the base of the tail. If He did, He would be bitten — in the manner of a love bite which — if you are not a cat — can be painful.

The tables had been cleared and all those who sat in Yaweh's presence had nothing left before them but goblets filled with ice and chamomile tea — which all but Yaweh abhorred.

To one side — the angels — and to the other — the mortals, seated at two separate tables; the angels on Yaweh's right hand and the mortals on His left.

Yaweh's eye was still on Hannah and none had failed to notice this — especially Mrs Noyes, whose place at the table was the most distant from Yaweh. She had taken the precaution of lacing her chamomile tea with gin, and her mind was playing fast and loose with the maddening image of Hannah seated at the table's head, her hair all shining and freshly coiled, and her bodice laced with flowers.

Fine for some — and youth always gets the palm — thought Mrs Noyes, her eyes narrowing and her gaze burning as deadly as Sarah's. I suppose His Majesty thinks *I* could look like that if I were given the time; if I hadn't spent the last three days in the kitchen, while the Orchard Queen was out weaving garlands in the sunshine! . . .

Noah sat nearest of all to Yaweh — his eyes slightly misted at the mere thought that his old Friend sat there before him — and that, after so many years apart, they had broken bread together and toasted one another with . . . (well, it *was* Yaweh's favourite drink) . . . chamomile tea. And at Noah's table. In Noah's Pavilion on Noah's Hill. Astonishing and wonderful. A miracle.

Swept away with such thoughts — Doctor Noyes even turned towards Hannah and was about to ask her to ''write that down in the book'' when he came to his senses.

Yaweh was speaking.

''The company of true friends is as the company of saints. . . .''

Michael Archangelis muttered; ''hear, hear,'' and tapped the side of his goblet with his golden penknife.

Japeth looked across at the Supreme Commander of All the Angels and muttered; ''hear, hear,'' but had nothing, aside from his hunting knife, with which to tap his goblet. When he did so, the weight of the knife's leaden handle tipped the goblet, spilling all of Japeth's tea and ice into his lap. Japeth pushed his knees apart and let the ice slip down to the ground, where it melted at his feet.

Yaweh said; ''We have no truer friend on earth than Noah Noyes — and We thank him for his hospitality. . . .''

Noah nodded and waved his hand as if to deprecate the compliment.

''. . . and We thank him for his friendship. . . .''

More nodding; more waving.

" . . . We thank him for his loyalty. . . ."

Again.

" . . . We thank him for his *love*."

Noah rose to his feet and touched his forehead and his lips in honour of his guest.

"Hear, hear," said Michael Archangelis.

Sarah stared hard at Noah and Noah sat down.

"*Love*," said Yaweh — shifting His pastille lozenge from one side of His mouth to the other — almost losing it in the process — "is the greatest gift that one can offer."

"Hear, hear."

"Its rarity, indeed, raises it far above greatness into the realm of the sublime. It is — We may say to you — the glory of Creation."

"Hear! Hear!"

"Hear! Hear!"

There was extended approbation of these words, with everyone joining in the cries and the tapping of goblets, some with the rings on their fingers, others with the weapons in their hands.

"*Love*," Yaweh's eyes were now ablaze with passionate emotion — "*love* is the one true bond . . ."

"Hear, hear . . ."

"Between God and His angels . . ."

"Hear, hear . . ."

"God and man . . ."

"Hear, hear . . ."

"King and subject . . ."

"Hear, hear . . ."

"Lord and vassal . . ."

"Hear, hear . . ."

"Master and Slave . . ."

"Hear, hear . . ."

There was now a slight pause, as if Yaweh might be counting His fingers to make certain He had enumerated all the forms of love — and in the pause, a very loud cough — the cough from Mrs Noyes at the foot of her table.

Sarah's gaze shifted accordingly.

"But, alas," Yaweh said, His voice sinking to a dramatic whisper; "We must tell you that We of late have witnessed such a paucity of love upon this earth that the only conclusion We can draw is — there is no love upon this earth, saving the love We bask in here and now this evening in this Pavilion."

Everyone leaned forward.

Yaweh's hand rested on Abraham's neck.

"We have travelled in these recent journeys from one end of the earth to the other — and We say to you — *behold, the great world is overcome with madness. . . .*" Yaweh's eyes were lifted to the faces before Him. "Stones and arrows — eggs and ordure. As We have told you, not only have We been reviled and spat upon and jeered — We have also been attacked with fire and swords. Our carriage and Our horses have been mobbed in the streets and We have been overturned. Our angels have bled from the wounds received in Our defense — yet, even so, have We Ourselves been struck by the assassin's sword — not once — but *seven times. . . .*"

Here, Yaweh paused to gather His thoughts and to make some attempt to control His emotions. His focus, in this attempt, now fell on Hannah — and He addressed what followed to her.

"We look upon the shining countenance of this woman and We blush to think what the human race has become. In her eyes and in her demeanour We see so clearly all that was intended in the gesture of Creation. Purity of heart and motive. Devotion and subservience to the greater glory . . ." His voice wound down. "Et cetera. She, though it breaks Our heart to say so, is but one out of thousands; *tens* of thousands, indeed if not one out of the whole human race . . ."

Even Noah was somewhat put out by this "one out of the whole human race" talk, but he quelled his reaction with a quaff of dreadful tea and sat back to hear the rest of what his Friend would say.

"We tell you," Yaweh went on, His gaze now passing from one to the other of His audience; "all that One beholds upon the face of this earth — beset as it is with the stamp of man — is

Pride!'' Yaweh was now so involved in His speech that it spilled from His mouth and He had perforce to use a napkin to catch it and to wipe His beard and chin. ''Pride and lechery; envy and anger; covetousness; gluttony and sloth are, everywhere, all that One sees! The whole deadly canon of wickedness, depravity and horror is all that One beholds! We are assailed on all sides by an onslaught of evil, vice and shame that defies description!''

All who, in the meantime, had leaned a little back, now leaned the whole way forward, fingers twisting and hands enfisted in the tension of the moment. Every mouth was open—every lip was wet with the juices of indignation and wonder.

''Men—women—children: all are the subjects of corruption. None has been spared—and none has been sparing. The very pits of viciousness have overflowed and spilled upon the streets of the Cities, so that One must lift One's skirts to avoid contamination. The hands of sinners reach out to touch One and to drag One down. Their voices call to One from every side. Never in Our wildest moments could We have dreamed such monstrous perversions as One was offered at every turning. . . .''

Yaweh's passions were apparently so violent beneath the seeming calm of His robes that Abraham was driven from his place in Yaweh's lap and all at once the silver cat jumped down and lay upon the floor, his tail twitching in agitation, while his eye roamed the Pavilion, looking for an exit.

''Does this mean, then, the Great Experiment approaches its end?'' Yaweh said. ''Does this mean that what We have proposed has been rejected?''

This was greeted by many cries of ''no! No!'' and ''never!''

Yaweh said; ''your reassurances come too late, My friends. You—and you alone—have heard Our words with any kind of sympathy. Elsewhere—and *everywhere!*—Our voice has been drowned with derision and We have been turned away with gestures of violence and rudeness beyond your imagining. Cries of *'Go Home!'* and *'Get out!'* and *'Leave us alone!'* have been the single order of the day.''

Yaweh wept.

"Thus have We come to you. Thus have We arrived in your midst. Thus do We throw Ourselves upon your . . ."

. . . *mercy* . . .

The word spun round the Pavilion, making those who imagined they had heard it reel with the horror of the image it presented.

They must throw themselves upon *His* mercy.

"Stop!" cried Noah. "Do not say it, my Lord. We will not hear it. Tell us only what You would have us do. But do not speak of our mercy. Only show us Thine."

Yaweh smiled.

He — and He alone — was aware in that moment that the word had not been uttered. He—and He alone—was aware of what He had truly been about to say, which was: "thus do We throw Ourselves upon your *hospitality*." What He wanted — and all He wanted — was a haven, until He had recovered. Now, he surmised, more than a haven had been offered.

∞ Abraham slipped beneath the apron of the Pavilion and took a great draught of midnight air. Above him, the moon was riding on its back through a sea of stars — so many stars, the sky had barely room to show itself. All around him there was the heavy scent of earthly trees and grass; of herbs and meadow flowers and dust. In one direction the warm and almost seductive smell of the barns, with the promise of mice and chicks and goslings. On another side, the smell of angels, mortals, Yaweh and the remnants of the meal just eaten. Somewhere out there — not far, though not so close he could immediately tell precisely where it was — there was a body of water, and beyond it, sheep eating grass. The sound of their bells could be heard, and the smell of their grazing carried across the pond.

Abraham sat down and licked his paws — an act that stimulated precision when the brain had been flooded with a surfeit of information. Yaweh's terrible anger had given off such vibrations that Abraham had been suffused with tingling sensations and most unpleasant shocks: the sky had too many stars in it;

the bits of food he had managed to eat from what fell from his Lord and Master's hand had mostly been vegetable and not at all satisfying; the trees were foreign to him and their scent overpowering; sheep bells were an irritant and wasn't that a female in heat?

The paw licking stopped abruptly.

Abraham scoured the air with his nostrils.

Nothing foreign about the smell of a female in heat. That was universal.

Where was she?

Ah, yes . . .

Right over there.

∞ Mottyl was lying on the edge of her porch, hoping that Mrs Noyes would soon return. Her heat was entering its final, declining state and her discomfort with it was now no more than a running commentary of flickers and spasms that was slowly stuttering down to a halt. There had even been moments, over the past hour or two, when her body had felt almost normal and she had been able to concentrate on the wonder of having survived a whole heat without males. Her *whispers* had fallen to humming pleasantly and she lay, head raised in the dozing position, contemplating a long and pleasant nap in the carpet-seated chair with its unoiled springs and its deeply satisfying sag.

A cat whose scent was only vaguely familiar but quite unthreatening was walking out in the yard. An old cat . . . possibly male . . . possibly not . . . a slim, aristocratic cat, whose belly made an amusing dip in its centre, giving the otherwise trim-looking silhouette a ridiculous air.

Any comments?

No. Not really . . . is, however, definitely male.

Yes, but very, very old. Looks like a rake gone to seed.

A male is a male; be careful.

He looks too old to care. And besides, I'm almost

through this now. No reason he shouldn't come and sit in the yard . . .

You really are crazy, you know.

"Hallo."

"Hallo."

"There's a porch here, where you can rest if you would care to."

"Very kind of you, my lady. My thanks . . ."

"Not at all. I'd enjoy the company."

You fool.

∞ Michael Archangelis was the first to take note of the fact that Abraham was missing. Rather than disturb the proceedings, he rose unobtrusively from his place and went outside to make a search. If Yaweh were to lose His cats, He would be inconsolable.

In time the warrior angel did find Abraham and was able to bring him down from the roof of the porch onto which some mortal cat had driven him. The old male's fur was a bit ruffled, but he looked smug and satisfied. However, before this happened, and all ended happily — Michael was to make another discovery, not of a happy nature.

As he walked through the dust of the Noyes's yard, an object lodged itself between his toes. At first he paid it no heed. It was obviously nothing of consequence and would soon more than likely work itself free. When it persisted, however, riding further and further in towards his webbing, where it could become a major irritant, Michael was forced to remove the thing.

It was a feather of some size.

Absently, Michael lifted this object all the way to his nostrils, very much the way a human being will lift a flower that has just been picked.

For a moment, Abraham was completely forgotten and Michael hurried to the lights of the nearby house. Holding the feather up so the lanterns inside would shine upon it, Michael turned it this way and that with growing alarm and anger.

"Well!" he said aloud, once his suspicions as to the feather's origin had been confirmed. "So this is where he's hiding."

∞ The time had come for the evening entertainments — and the tables were lifted aside. Mead was brought from the cooling house by Emma, who staggered beneath the weight of the great stone jars in which the mead had been seasoned. A fresh set of goblets was provided and the lesser angels and acolytes took each jar from Emma as it appeared, and wandered from group to group pouring out the thick, golden liquid, filling the air with its heavy, honeyed scent. The angels, licking their webbed fingers, smiled with ambiguous seductiveness at this one and that one — angels and mortals alike.

The candles, ensconced in their brilliant glass lanterns, were redispersed, casting new light where there had been darkness through the meal — and shadows where there had been light.

Mrs Noyes was dispatched to produce her sheep and Yaweh beckoned to Hannah, inviting her to be seated on the dais near His feet.

While the sheep were being assembled and the lambs encouraged to be less rambunctious, Noah — who hoped with these entertainments to lift his old Friend out of His great depression — began, as most magicians will, with one or two of his lesser tricks — the showy ones with doves and ducks — that draw such appreciative murmurs of delight, but which, in fact, are the easiest tricks of all.

Having donned his magician's overgown of deepest blue — and having set his magician's tables as near to Yaweh as he dared — and having placed his tall, pointed hat auspiciously upon his head — he commenced.

He performed the *three-doves-three* as his first trick, followed by *six-doves-six* and then, in rapid order, the delightful sequence known as *six-doves-five-and-the-goose*, in which an interloping gander appears first on one arm, then the other and then, from beneath the tall pointed hat, just when it seems that *six-doves-six* have been restored.

This always produces laughter and a confident sense of delights to come — and, indeed, this night in the blue Pavilion, *six-doves-five-and-the-goose* made quite a charming success. The angels loved and applauded it. The acolytes — as children will — squealed with delight — and even Japeth smiled. But Yaweh could not be roused. His lips made a valiant attempt to voice appreciation — but nothing came of it.

So Noah tried again.

This time, he played with fire — quite literally — drawing fire from the air and extinguishing it in a great, translucent balloon (also conjured) only to draw it forth from the balloon in a fresh burst of flames.

Nothing.

Yaweh was so utterly disconsolate that not even *The Rope of Endor* made him smile, as it did all the others.

Noah was beginning to despair, though he knew full well he still had magic up his sleeves and beyond the Pavilion's walls that was guaranteed to dazzle. But *nothing* would dazzle so well as hoped, if Yaweh could not be persuaded in the earliest part of the programme to join in the wonder of it all.

At this precise moment, at the height of Yaweh's spiritual impotence, Mrs Noyes reappeared — stumbling only slightly — with her sheep and the sheep burst into song:

> *Shall we gather by the River,*
> *Where bright angel feet have trod;*
> *With its crystal tide forever*
> *Flowing by the Throne of God . . .*

Still nothing.

In fact, there was even the faintest indication Yaweh found the singing sheep displeasing. He wrinkled His nose and seemed about to sneeze.

Hannah held up a napkin.

The sneeze passed.

Even seeing his Friend's distress, Noah was unable to cut the song off mid-flight because he knew that sheep, once started, could not be stopped until they recognized the end of a number. They were so stupid! In something of a panic, Noah approached the dais, even as the song continued.

What was clearly required was a frontal attack on Yaweh's depression and Noah stepped all the way forward, setting one of his smaller magic tables directly in line with Yaweh's knees.

Hannah shifted along her step to one side.

The song continued.

> *Ere we reach the shining river*
> *Lay we every burden down;*
> *Grace our spirits will deliver,*
> *And provide a robe and crown . . .*

Noah drew forth a tall bottle of the purest glass.

He also drew forth a large, beaten copper penny and placed both the bottle and the penny on the little table.

> *Yes, we'll gather by the river,*
> *The beautiful, the beautiful river . . .*

Noah drew Yaweh's attention, first to the penny — *thus* — and then to the bottle — *thus* — placing the penny on the table and the bottle sitting over it.

"My Lord still quite clearly sees the penny through the glass of this bottle? . . ."

Yaweh nodded; yes.

"Then — behold, my Lord, the utterly remarkable and magical results as I pour this liquid slowly into the mouth of the bottle. May I draw my Lord's attention to the penny? Keep Your Majesty's eye upon that — and only upon that. . . ."

Noah then reached round and brought forward a silver jug of pure, unadulterated water and poured it into the bottle as he had said he would.

> *Soon we'll reach the silver river,*
> *Soon our pilgrimage will cease . . .*

Yaweh gasped.

> *Soon our happy hearts will quiver*
> *With the melody of peace.*

Yaweh leaned forward, the better to see what he could not see.

The penny had disappeared.
"Do it again," Yaweh cried. "Do it again!"
Success at last.

Yes, we'll gather by the river,
The beautiful, the beautiful river;
Gather with the saints by the river
That flows by the Throne of God!

Noah repeated the trick — not once, but three times again —
and each time Yaweh was more and more intrigued.
"By the sheer application of water . . ." He said.
"Yes, my lord. Yes . . ."
And Noah repeated the trick one last time.
"Like a miracle . . ." Yaweh almost whispered now, as the
final flow of liquid spilled from the mouth of the silver jug into
the mouth of the tall glass bottle — pouring, pouring down the
insides . . . filling the bottle and, to all intents and purposes,
obliterating the image of the penny, still in its place beneath
the bottle. "By the sheer application — of water . . ." Yaweh
said; ". . . it *disappears*. . . ."

Gather with the saints by the river
That flows by the Throne of God . . .

∞ Later, when the sheep had retired and Mrs Noyes —
more tipsy than ever — had returned to her place in the Pavilion, Noah caused the great blue sides of the tent to be raised.
There he put on such a show of magic as a climax to his entertainments that even his wife was mightily impressed with the
wonder and beauty of what her husband could create, if he put
his mind to it.
And what he showed — out under the sky beyond the Pavilion — was nothing less than The Masque of Creation — beginning with a gust of wind that guttered and extinguished all the
candles — so that everyone cried; "oh!" in one voice.
Next, there was a looming figure outlined in phosphores-
cence, moving on its side, as if swimming, and this was the
spirit of God moving upon the waters.

And when God created light, there was such a grand Chinese explosion — not just of luminescence but of gradual, growing, rising and climaxing glory — that it drew loud cries as well as webbed applause, and even the stamping of approving feet.

Heaven and earth were banners of velvet and satin — trees and grass and vines made of painted cloth rose up and even burst into flower and, after the flowering, fruit appeared: glass plums and cherries, brass pears and copper peaches, candied grapes and frosted berries . . .

Then the planets, moon and sun, some competing with their counterparts in the sky — but this did not matter. Each appearance drew its sigh of pleasure from the watchers and each ascendancy, its proper cry of approbation.

Canvas birds flew into the air and circled the painted trees, and then disappeared in the direction of a dazzling ribbon of many colours, arching across the sky. Wooden deer were chased across the velvet earth by mechanical bears and lumbering dragons. (The dragons, as all villains will, drew laughter and cries of *boo!*). At last, a great blue paper whale rose out of the sea and this was such a popular appearance, it completely stopped the show.

The acolytes, especially, wanted to see the whale again — and while it was being shown for the third or fourth time, the Faeries suddenly appeared, drawn from the wood by the lights, perhaps — and everyone but Mrs Noyes accepted their appearance as preordained with the aid of the magic lantern — so that it was only she who recognized the Faeries as themselves.

At last, it was time for man's appearance, and this time it was Mrs Noyes's turn to not quite believe her eyes: for Ham stepped up from the pit of the shadow box set in the dark by Noah — and he was painted a dreadful pink from head to toe and wore an enormous cardboard fig leaf that reached almost to his knees.

This much had been planned in advance of the event — and Noah was about to draw whatever strings or threads — or throw whatever lever he must use to produce his Eve — but when that paper cut-out meant to rise from Ham-Adam's side was given its cue — nothing happened.

Instead, it was Lucy who made her appearance — clothed in a long,transparent gown and wearing a crown of golden hair that fell to the ground all around her, gracefully hiding every bit of sexual evidence.

The final tableau, of Adam, Eve and the whole of Creation — including the great blue paper whale spread out behind them — drew a roar of approval from all and sundry, while even Yaweh raised His hands and slapped His knees with His palms — since He dared not bring His hands together, lest He break His fingers.

Only Michael Archangelis, by this time returned with Abraham, had any misgivings about the figure of Eve. And he kept these misgivings to himself. It mattered too greatly that Yaweh had finally smiled — and he could not bring himself to produce the circumstantial evidence of the long bronze feather in his pocket, nor to reveal the identity of the angel playing Eve.

∞ Yaweh was now so relaxed, He had talked for more than an hour — and a circle of spellbound listeners sat beneath the candlelit Pavilion, listening to him intently — angels and mortals alike, caught up in the wisdom and glory of His words.

Long after midnight, Yaweh addressed the following story directly to Noah, though His hand was on Hannah's shoulder.

"It is known to all the Elders and Rabbis and priests that powers such as you have exercised here tonight have been held since time began by the Few. What dangers these powers conceal can be guessed at, if One only thinks of the evils that now surround Us as We sit here so secure in One Another's company, high on this hill. The Cities reek of that evil danger. And yet, there can be glory in it, too: in the power.

"Think now, and conjure an orchard. That place which, since time began, as you showed its beginnings to Us here tonight, has been the most Sacred Sanctuary of all that is Holy. That Orchard where only the truly prepared and the truly wise may walk in safety. Think of this Orchard — in all its wonder and all its mystery. . . ."

Yaweh's brittle fingers dabbled, as He spoke, in Hannah's hair — while His other hand caressed the heads of His restored and now purring cats.

"Make in your minds the images of four men — sages all and the wisest of the wise. Let Us even give them names: for names are everything in the creation of legend. . . . Let us stand them together at the gate to the Orchard — the Sacred Orchard of Wisdom — and witness Rabbi Akiva, Simeon Ben Zoma, Simeon Ben Azai and Elisha Ben Abuya — four great sages, it so happens, who were once known to Me. . . ."

(He said *"Me"*; Mrs Noyes almost said aloud. He said *"Me"*. . .)

"They will be led into the Orchard by the wisest of them all: Rabbi Akiva — a gentle and a careful man, whose love We treasured almost as deeply as We treasure that of Noah Noyes. And Rabbi Akiva — being the wisest of the wise, laid all the traditional cautions out before his brothers — as one would lay carpets to protect the feet of one's beloved from the nettles. He told of all the dangers — and he told of all the pitfalls. Above all, he cautioned his fellow wise men of the dangers that lie in *words* . . . in the injudicious and incautious use of words . . . in the prideful use of words; those words that even We do not utter, lest We bring Creation to a halt — or cause it to veer down some darkened channel from which it might not be retrieved. All said; 'we hear you.' all said; 'we shall not fail to heed you.' And so — they entered the Orchard. . . ."

Here, Mrs Noyes leaned forward and in the agitation of the moment, she locked her fingers together in that sign which had not yet been explained to her: that sign which the Faeries had delivered to her above the roofs and chimneys of her house but a few nights before.

And Sarah, catching sight of this sign and knowing the sign to be among the Holy of Holies, began to leave Yaweh's lap surreptitiously and to make her way in Mrs Noyes's direction. None of this was known to Yaweh, who was so caught up in His story that a tiger could have left His lap and He would not have noticed.

"Men are men and only men," said Yaweh. "And even the wisest of men must fail. Pride, foolishness and daring are traps into which even Adam fell — to Our horror — to Our sorrow. And so, as they walked in the Sacred Orchard, where all that may be lies in hiding — Simeon Ben Zoma — Simeon Ben Azai — Elisha Ben Abuya — the wisest of the wise — were tempted, even as Eve was tempted — though, being men, they had more powers of resistance. Here, make the picture if you will: Ben Azai put his hand to the creation of man — and died. Ben Zoma turned no more than his mind to the forbidden word — and lost his reason. Elisha Ben Abuya fell to the ground and, lost in the wonder of the plants and herbs beneath his fingers, he began to tear them from their place in that sacred earth and to eat them — and in doing so, disrupted the temper of his system and was crippled and useless all the rest of his days. Only Rabbi Akiva emerged intact from that journey beneath the trees. Only he, who knew not to reach out with his hands; who knew not to dwell upon the word; who knew not to fall upon the ground and eat — only he — only he . . ."

Yaweh's voice trailed off into silence.

Sarah was making for the symbol of infinity, claws unsheathed.

∞ When order was restored, Mrs Noyes had to be led away and her bleeding fingers thrust into a jar of vinegar and later bandaged.

Sarah was reprimanded — but gently — by Yaweh and after she and Abraham had been settled in the depths of Yaweh's great chair, Yaweh turned to Noah and said to him; "show me once more this trick of yours with the bottle and the penny."

∞ After the Masque of Creation and after Yaweh had told the parable of Rabbi Akiva and the Orchard, Michael Archangelis slipped away into the darkness again.

He was greatly disturbed — for, though Doctor Noyes and his family had succeeded to some degree in bringing The Lord God Yaweh out of His depression, there was still a sinister underlay to all that had taken place in the Blue Pavilion. Michael could not shake it. His intuition kept informing him that something was deeply wrong. Abraham's wandering and reappearance were only a part of it. Even the feather — of major importance — was not the whole of it. And Lucy's taking on the role of Eve, while appalling in its implications and audacity, was nothing more than proof that Michael's suspicions had been well founded.

No — it was more than this. More even than the sum of these things. It was the questions raised and the dreaded answers implied by Yaweh's growing horror of mankind, coupled with Lucy's presence here.

Michael's deputies had remained behind with Yaweh. The Guard must always be maintained, even in the Pavilions of Yaweh's closest and most trusted friends. Michael Archangelis stood alone in the dark — his sword on his hip, his hunting spear in his hands.

The stars and the moon (real stars, real moon) were reflected softly — diffused in the golden gleam of his breastplate, with its hammered images of past battles and inevitable victories. Michael had never lost, but once, in battle. His war with Lucifer — though proclaimed a victory in Heaven — was no such thing in Michael's eyes. In Michael's eyes, his brother had not been vanquished; he had escaped.

The Hill was full of noises — some from the Blue Pavilion, others from the dark. Birds that could not or would not sleep made sudden songs. Crickets and frogs were singing, too, though their songs kept shifting, quite impossible to track — first there, then over there, then further down the Hill towards the wood. The Vixen barked on his left — and the Fox replied from behind him, high in the cedar grove. Something gave a death cry from the wood and the Owl flew up to feast in the trees. Far, far away — perhaps beyond the river, there was another cry — affirmative: *"I am here — where are you?"* from a beast of some size. Michael stood and listened to it all and he saw the stars and he saw the moon — and he could smell the great groves of trees, the fields half-mown, the earth itself, the flowers in Mrs. Noyes's garden, the dust and cinders of the dooryard and the rank enigma of the pond and he thought: of all God's dwelling places, this is the most mysterious. Heaven, with all its suns and all its shadowless white, was perfect and predictable — known; the Garden was an overgrown wonder — but empty; and the road to Nod, with its cocaine dust, and Nod itself, with its dark green hiding places and red poppied fields, was a haven — yes — but there was no challenger in Nod; it was a place for sleepers only. And Michael was awake. He never slept; and never wanted to.

He began to move down the Hill, with the feather burning his thigh through his pocket. But he didn't mind the fire. It was a reminder of other times — some better and some worse — when he'd marched against his brother's armies and won: when he had moved on his brother and lost.

Even Yaweh could not be convinced the battle was a loss. "He's gone, hasn't he? Pushed and fallen?"

"Yes, Father."

(No, Father: fallen only because he leapt.)

"We saw his star go down Ourselves."

"Yes, Father."

"And where did it land?"

(Over there.)

"In hell."

The Lord God Father of Us All must never know the truth; Michael decided. The Ancient of Ancients was now so enfeebled and distraught, so distracted with the sins of mankind, that to tell Him, force Him to acknowledge that Lucifer had joined the human race — would push Yaweh over the edge into — what?

Madness?

Edges.

Yaweh on the edge.

Unbalanced.

And no strength to leap (if He chose) but only the tendency of age to fall.

Still, Michael Archangelis could save Him.

∞ The hillside was thriving with night life: mice, ferrets, beetles, owls. Down by the fences, the Faeries were in a state of excitement. There was something lurching out of the wood and the Faeries were apparently the cause of its being driven into the open. But it could not get over or through the fence and, being caught, was in something of a panic.

Michael could see a great, swatting tail thrashing in and out of the Faeries' lights — and, at once, he recognized an old, old enemy: the Dragon.

"Hah!" he said aloud — and all his juices began to flow. Here was the prospect of battle: the best of all possible pursuits.

Michael lifted the spear in his hand, finding its balance even as he began to run down the Hill. With his other hand he loosened his sword in its scabbard, ready for the beheading already making its image in the air before him as he ran.

If the Faeries would co-operate, they might drive the Dragon straight onto his spear — though half of the pleasure of the kill would be lost if there was no pursuit; no final cornering; no submissive cry of the defeated. Still, a dragon was a dragon — and every dragon's death was one more blow at Lucifer. And who was to know? *This* dragon might be the traitor himself.

But the Faeries did not co-operate. When they saw the Angel, looming up out of the Hill itself — spear poised and sword half-drawn — they paused, astonished.

A human running down the Hill might only be Ham or Shem. At the worst, it might be Japeth. But an Angel of these proportions — gleaming in the star-and-moonlight, flying towards them, armed, was quite another proposition. There was already, in the wood, one rogue angel — the dog killer — and here came another.

The Faeries — though no more willing to admit defeat than Michael Archangelis — were, however, shy by nature and cautious. Their officiousness, their insistence on a certain kind of order — their sense of duty — were far more likely to get them into straits than any sense of daring or recklessness. Attacking dragons was not delightful to them — it was something more in the line of duty. It took great courage to attack a dragon — but it was one of those things that a creature had to do.

This particular dragon — the centre of so much attention — was extremely large and, in fact, obese. It had been feeding for weeks on forest folk and had come across the river to pick off a few of the smaller, sweeter, fruit-and-bark-eating animals — a finish to its meal before retiring. In the course of making its way to the wallows, the Dragon in question had paused to take a young lemur to whom, it so happened, the Faeries were about to bring a gift of honeyed gnats.

Seeing the young lemur threatened by the Dragon, the Faeries had abandoned the gnats and attacked. Their strategy with dragons was based on the fact that dragons were prone to seizures and became disoriented and confused if they were exposed to certain patterns of light. Alarmed and dazzled by the Faeries' sudden appearance, the Dragon had been turned from its intended prey and driven towards the fence. Almost at once, in the throes of its confusion and fearful of what it thought must surely be the first signs of an oncoming seizure, the Dragon had become completely entangled in the fence rails.

When Michael Archangelis appeared, the Dragon must assuredly have known it was having, if not a seizure, an experience that boded ill. It began to throw fence rails in every direction — some even landing in the trees. Fire and noise being its greatest weapons, it set about trying to manufacture both, but either because it was overfed or because it was so violently disoriented, it failed to produce much of either. A few dry sparks — a few mild roars were all it could manage.

The Faeries, meanwhile, retired to a nearby cottonwood where, along with Bip and Ringer and a few others, they watched the scene unfold.

Michael Archangelis was certain, now, that he had never seen a dragon so large, so sleek, so beautiful. His whole imagination was turned to justifying why this particular dragon should be — must be — *was* his brother Lucifer.

Lucifer's pride would have demanded this dragon's size, to begin with. Its beautiful, scaly skin, its wonderful and awesome countenance made a remarkable hiding place. In Paradise, there were no dragons. But in childhood, Lucifer had always claimed their part in games, while Michael had chosen the role of Slayer.

Now, here they were in earnest: Lucifer in scales—Michael in armour. All the white suns of paradise had never shone so brightly as the earth's moon shone in Michael's eyes at this moment—poised above his brother, trapped and flailing in the fence row. One strike — just between the shoulder blades — the spearhead driven deep through the spinal cord and down through the heart — all the way to the soft, rummaged earth where the Dragon had scrabbled in his desperate struggle — and the beast was dead. Only a faint, last gust of fire remained — a mere and harmless token — and the Dragon toppled sideways at Michael's feet.

It smelled of pine trees and riverweed and scorched moss and its great blue eyes appeared—though it could not be—to be overwhelmed with tears.

Michael Archangelis was shaking with the wonder and horror of what he had done. He was shaking so greatly he could not withdraw the spear — nor could he even raise his leg to place his foot upon the beast in that fine, traditional pose: *The Slayer in His Triumph* — hand on scabbard, foot on neck.

He breathed against the pounding in his chest until, at last, he was able to move.

Up went his foot upon the shoulder — up went his hand to the sword at his waist. His toes crawled over the oozing back until they found the depression they sought, where the spear had entered, caving the bones, and he stood there, perfect in the star-and-moonlight, golden over his brother, whose head he would lay before Yaweh.

"Done," he said; *"and done forever."*

"Did you speak?" said a voice.

Michael Archangelis froze in his place.

Was it the Dragon?

"I thought I heard a voice," the voice said. But where was it coming from?

"Is that you?" Michael said, at last, to the Dragon. "Did you speak?"

"No, *I* spoke. Up here, overhead."

Michael looked up, almost losing his balance.

There, in the branches directly above him, was Lucy — wearing something pale, and staring down from a whitened face with a great, wide grin.

"*Wonderful* scene," she said. "Very nice try, ducky. I suppose you thought that Dragon was me. But it wasn't and it ain't."

Michael stepped back from the Dragon still looking up — and said; "yes. I did think I had you. But I'm not a complete fool. Something in me knew it couldn't be you. It wasn't proud enough for you. It didn't put up any fight. You, at least, would have made better use of the fire. . . ."

"Damn right I would."

Michael prepared to withdraw the spear.

"Are you sure you want to do that?" said Lucy. "I mean, find out who you've really killed?"

Withdrawing the spear would release the captive form in the Dragon — if there was one — and the victim would become briefly visible as it escaped. Not all dragons embodied captive forms — but it was thought the larger ones did, in particular.

"Well?" Lucy taunted him.

"Knowing I have missed you yet again," said Michael; "I don't care two figs who this is." And so saying, he withdrew the spear.

Lucy leaned forward, staring down at the beast in the grass, whose tail was still entangled in the fence rails. Bip and Ringer and the Faeries all leaned forward, too, hoping for the release of some friendly captive — or at least, for the thrill of seeing a slain devil. But there was nothing. No change at all.

The Dragon just lay there — steaming and very much a dragon. Dead.

"How very disappointing," said Lucy. "A sort of double disappointment for you, Michael, my love. Not me and not *any*body. Too bad. Better luck next time."

Michael wiped the spear on the grass and then stood looking up at his brother in the tree.

"You seem to be enjoying yourself," he said.

"Greatly," said Lucy, and she slipped down out of the tree to the ground.

"What do you hope to accomplish by all this?" Michael asked.

"All what?" Lucy shook out her frail skirts and lifted her hand to her hair.

"Well — dressing as a woman to begin with. *And* a foreigner."

"Nothing wrong with dressing as a woman. Might as well be a woman as anything else. And what, may one ask, do you mean by 'a foreigner'?"

"Someone not of these parts," said Michael, as if he was quoting from a book of rules for border guards.

"The slanted eyes, et cetera? The black, black hair — the white, white face? You don't like it? I *love*." Lucy took a few steps across the grass, showing off the dress — which was loose, though bound very tight around the waist with a wide, dark sash. Almost at once, she stumbled, though she did not fall. "Forgive," she said. "I haven't quite got the hang of this one yet. But I will. . . ."

Michael watched her passing in and out of the moonlight and the shadows of the trees — and he said; "the rumour goes you're getting married."

"That's right."

"But — he's — he's a . . ."

"A man. Yes. So what?" Lucy pulled at her gloves, in order to make her fingers even longer.

"But you're a . . . *you're* a . . ."

"Don't say *man*."

"I wasn't going to. But you *are* male."

Lucy shrugged. "I like dressing up," she said. "I always have. You know that. Me as the Pope — me as the King. Why not? It's harmless enough."

"It won't be harmless if he beds you. Human beings do that, you know."

Lucy smiled. "Yes," she said. "I know."

"Well — what are you going to do about it?"

"I don't think that's any of your business but, if you must know, I'll make it up as I go along." Lucy looked up the Hill towards the Blue Pavilion — shining, translucent, in the dark. Her mood swung wide of the banter she and Michael had been trading. "Tell me how He is," she said. "He looked so old . . . so ill . . ."

"He's dying," said Michael.

Lucy stared at him and then, very slowly, back at the Pavilion.

"He can't die," she said, almost whispering.

"Why not?"

"He isn't able to die. . . ."

"I thought that, too. But He *is* God. And if God wants to die . . ."

"Then God is able."

"Yes."

There was near silence then. Only insects; only frogs. In the trees, the Faeries and the lemurs slept.

"Wouldn't it be wonderful," Lucy said, presently; "if you and I could weep?"

"If you and I could weep," said Michael; "I doubt you'd weep for Him. For yourself, perhaps, with your damned and damnable pride — thinking you were His equal . . ."

"I never thought that. Not ever. All I ever thought and all I ever said was . . ."

"*Why?* All you ever said was *why?* Why this and why that and why everything. How dare you. How *dare* you."

"Michael. *Don't.* I can't be bothered. You're a bore . . . and this is boring."

Up Noah's Hill, there was a cock crowing — even in spite of the dark — and, for the first time, the brothers realized how very late it was. And early.

"I should have known," said Lucy. "I still get a twinge, just before dawn. But since my star has fallen — I forget what time it is."

They looked at each other.

"Go away," said Lucy.

Michael turned and started to march — but he could not resist turning back. "I have sworn not to tell Him you are here," he said. "It would ruin the end of His days if He knew you were here and not in hell."

"What a pity," said Lucy. "I was just going to send Him my love."

"That is a message I would never deliver," said Michael. "*Never.*"

"Yes. Well . . ." said Lucy. "I presume we shall meet again — you and I. And I trust you will miss me, yet again."

Michael turned without a word and started up the Hill. Lucy watched him with a mixture of relief and regret. Human company was not the same as angel company. Only an angel knew that. Lucy would miss Michael above all her brothers. Like enemies everywhere and always, in their hatred there was devotion. Even love.

"Goodbye!" she called.

Michael went on marching. He did not turn.

"Goodbye!" Lucy called again. "Remember — always remember — only Michael Archangelis can kill me! No one else! No one! Ever!"

The cock crowed again.

The first pale light slipped out of the east. It was silver.

Michael raised his spear — a kind of farewell — but he still did not turn. He still went on marching. Up the Hill.

The grass stirred. A bird sang. The first beast made its entrance into the field. Lucy drew her image around her very tight. It would be lonely here — but wonderful. After all — she had joined the human race for a reason.

Something young was sitting on the fence: a bird of some sort. One of those large, gangling baby birds — all great spots and staring eyes and stubby wings. No tail as yet. A Raven child, perhaps — with a naked, yellow beak that never ceased to open, screaming: *Food! Food! Feed me! Food!* While its mother rummaged in the Dragon corpse for liver bits and heart. *Feed me! Feed me! Food! Food! Food!*

It was the great cry of life: of all that lived.

Feed me.

That was why Lucy had joined the human race. Survival. In order to survive the holocaust in heaven. In order to prevent the holocaust on earth.

∞ None had been allowed to sleep.

Yaweh was seated upon the steps of His dais with Hannah resting on the floor at His feet and Noah sitting on the lowest step.

The tall glass bottle, the round copper penny and the jug of pure water sat on another step on their table top — like the pieces in a game of men and gods.

Yaweh had wept through much of what remained of the night — and now He was feverish with words.

Had Noah understood the story of the Orchard? Was it not monstrous that even the wisest of the wise should attempt to usurp their God? That they should ask of God: *why and how?* Had Noah *truly* understood?. . .

He had.

Yaweh then reiterated yet again the horrors of His journey — the jeerings — the assassinations — the blood-letting — the hideous scenes of depravity and evil. And all this while, He toyed with the penny—toyed with the tall glass bottle—toyed with the water jug — pouring, pouring, pouring . . .

Finally, He rose.

Noah rose with Him.

Hannah was summoned to her feet from somewhere dangerously close to sleep.

All three stood together.

And Yaweh said to Noah; "in Our tale of the Orchard, We did not speak of the moral. And the moral — as it stands between Us: you and Ourself — you and your God. And that moral is: that only the single chosen of the Lord may hear the Word. . . ."

Noah felt a dreadful chill pass through him — which was the chill of recognition.

He was being chosen.

∞ "Let us walk together now, alone, in your orchard,"
said Yaweh, placing His arm around Hannah's shoulders for
support. *"You,"* He said to her; "may come with us and stand
at the gate — though you may not enter."

As they moved away, the sun gave every indication of rising,
in spite of the absence of the morning star — and Yaweh was
saying to Noah; "that trick of yours . . . the bottle . . . the
penny . . . by the sheer application of the water . . ."

It disappears.

∞ They gathered where the lane turned down the Hill:
Yaweh and Doctor Noyes at the centre — Hannah and Shem,
Japeth and Emma in a cluster to one side; Ham in the shadow
of the Pavilion — waiting.

Michael Archangelis was overseeing the placement of the
outriders — each one ten paces apart from the other, ready to
precede the carriage and its entourage of angels and acolytes.
Some of these would walk, while others would ride in wagons
drawn by mules. All the great animals in all their great cages
were being left behind in Noah's care. No explanation was given
for this, in the sense of a public announcement, though it was
apparent that Doctor Noyes himself was aware of the reason
and, for all that anyone could tell, content that so many beasts
of such great variety should suddenly be his to house and his
to nurture.

The sun had risen, though not beyond noon, while Yaweh
and Noah had walked in the orchard. Hannah, by the gate, had
overheard nothing but had certainly borne witness to the intensity with which they spoke. Again, Yaweh wept: again, He
was forced to pause for long moments to regain His composure.
But that was all that Hannah could tell. When they emerged
from their conference, Yaweh was smiling — Noah very white
and drained, with much perspiration — but no words.

As the moment for Yaweh's departure approached, Mrs
Noyes came down from the house with Mottyl in her arms.
She had made a jar of chamomile tea, with pieces of ice to
keep it cold — and she presented this to Yaweh.

Yaweh then made a gift to Noah of His two cats — Abraham

and Sarah. He parted from them sadly with kisses and good-byes and turned to His carriage.

Mrs Noyes was finally accorded the privilege of her rightful place and she stood, with Mottyl, one pace behind and one to the left of Noah.

Yaweh was through, now, with speech. His movements were grand and sweeping: final. Perhaps it was His intention to leave behind an impression of His Person that would last — who could tell — forever. He was very tired.

Michael Archangelis himself held the door of the carriage — and just as Yaweh held up His arms to reach for the straps with which He would haul Himself inside, there was a sound that no one at first could identify.

It came from within the darkened carriage; as one might hear the sound of voices down an unlit hall whose distance could not be reckoned. Mottyl was the first to grasp the source.

It was flies. A thousand of them: waiting.

On hearing them Yaweh paused, but then, without turning, He hoisted Himself and was heaved by Michael, and He disappeared.

The carriage door was shut with a hollow bang.

A great deal of dust went up. Outriders, winged horses, the carriage itself and all the walking angels and all the wagons began to move away down the Hill, with Noah and all his family following, waving — and all the sheep sending up a shout: *Hosanna!*

Mottyl wondered; did no one else know? Was it only she — and Yaweh — who could tell the meaning of the crown of flies?

It was so. By entering the carriage, by seating Himself in their presence and by closing the door, the Lord God Father of All Creation had consented to His own death.

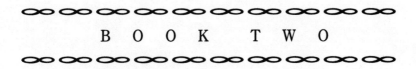

B O O K   T W O

*Of clean beasts, and of beasts
that are not clean, and of fowls,
and of everything that creepeth
upon the earth, there went in two
and two unto Noah into the ark,
the male and the female, as God
had commanded Noah.*

Genesis 7:8

∞ ∞ ∞ ∞ ∞ ∞ ∞ ∞ ∞ ∞

 THERE WERE MANY good reasons for building the ark at the top of the Hill — both strategical and practical. For one thing, at its crest, the Hill was barren. Nothing there but the Noyes's family altar and the pine tree. Just below the altar and the pine tree — on the far side — there was a circular, open meadow which, prior to the building of the ark, had been filled with pale blue flowers and waist-high crackling-grass. But before the construction began, Shem had the fore-sight to harvest this field, and consequently, when the drivers arrived with the ox-carts, bringing the wood up from the forest beyond the river, the oxen could be fed with the flowers and the grass. This way, in the days before the rains began, the meadow had taken on the look of a dusty, thriving lumber yard — and this way, too, it caused no concern to the common people walking to and fro on the road. "Oh, look," they would say; "someone is going to make his fortune in the lumber business."

∞ Gopher wood was the chosen medium, a strong, light-textured wood with some of the qualities of cork. Beams and planks were hewn from gigantic trees whose bark was a bilious green and whose flesh was yellow. None of these trees was to be found except at the greatest distance — over the river and into the forest. Crews of tall, blond men who hardly ever spoke were hired from the fringes of the forest — a place that seemed almost exclusively to be peopled with blond giants and dwarfish foreigners whose language was unintelligible. The giants and the dwarfs had not always lived there — but no one could say when they had not. The forest had once been a place exclusively for dragons — though no one living could remember such a time.

Some of the tall blond men were Emma's brothers, although Doctor Noyes forbade her to speak with them. The combination of the forest folk's natural reticence and Doctor Noyes's dictum produced a curious human silence at the work place. Shem gave the orders — but, being oxlike, he was almost as quiet as the labourers. The result was like a gathering of mutes.

Noah was pleased with this. It meant no questions were asked — questions about the ark which he could not possibly have answered. Certainly, there had to be speculation: *why are we doing this?* But the speculation was never voiced. On a few occasions, Noah would discover he was being stared at — heads would be scratched and expressions would reflect the general bewilderment regarding the whole project. They plainly thought; "the old man is crazy," but they had always been of this opinion. So the ark was just another manifestation of the craziness. So be it. Noah did not care. In time, these men would all go home — and Noah would never see them again. They would drown — and with them, their opinions.

It was harder on Emma, who loved her brothers and missed them dreadfully. She and Mrs Noyes — who was also very fond of Emma's family — would climb the Hill in the early morning and secretly watch the men arriving. Once the day's work had commenced, there was too much dust and confusion to pick out the individual faces they were looking for. Everyone, to begin with, was tall and blond — and very soon their faces were masks of sweat and grime, obscuring the last vestiges of individuality and character.

One day, Mrs Noyes was certain she had seen Emma's father who, years before, had delivered firewood. She saw him driving one of the lumber wagons — such a good-looking man with a kindly face you could never forget. He had been so distraught when his daughter had been brought across the river to marry Japeth Noyes — and Mrs Noyes had grieved for him. There had only been the two girls — Emma and her sister Lotte — and all the rest of his children — hundreds of them, so it seemed! — had been boys.

When she saw him, she told Emma and, together, they hung about the road above the orchard, where there were trees to obscure them from Noah's view. Two whole hours they waited — risking the Doctor's wrath — and, finally, coming on to dusk, the last of the wagons came down the cart track with a horde of young men bouncing in the back with their legs hanging over the sides — and the driver could be no other than Emma's father — or her "Pa," as she called him.

Mrs Noyes stepped out before the oxen, who were moving slowly, and she flung up her apron to stop them.

Once the wagon had been halted and the great cloud of dust had begun to settle, Mrs Noyes emerged with Emma in tow and she went straight up to the driver and said; "let us ride down the Hill with you. We don't mind walking back."

Emma's father pulled his forelock at Mrs Noyes and grinned — though he didn't say a word. He put down his hand and pulled her up — easy as a rag doll — onto the seat beside him, while Emma's brothers lifted her into the wagon box where she, too, stuck her legs over the edge and was in heaven all the way down the Hill.

Mrs Noyes asked about Emma's mother and Lotte and about conditions on the far side of the river.

Emma's mother was fine and kept herself busy feeding the horde in the back of the wagon. Emma's father said this with amusement and affection. He was devoted to his wife and he knew she was no chattel. Life on the other side of the river was "dreadful hard" as he put it; "dreadful hard and wonderful, if you put your mind to it. She wouldn't live anywheres else and nor would I. . . ."

Lotte was another story. She missed her sister Emma "something pitiful" but her health was fine. "Just the usual. . . ." he said, enigmatically. Lotte would never be married. She was a stay-at-home child. The reason for this, though known to Mrs Noyes, was never discussed.

"Oh, I do wish," said Mrs Noyes; "that Emma was allowed to come and see you. And it's crazy that I have to bring her to you this way — so secretive and brief. But he simply won't allow it and we have to be obedient. . . ."

"So I noticed," said Emma's father — and he looked at Mrs Noyes and gave her a wonderful smile.

Mrs Noyes blushed. She was being about as disobedient as a wife could be — riding this way with another man on a lumber wagon. Still — she burst out laughing — it was worth every minute. Just to hear that Lotte and Emma's mother were still there and thriving — just to hear Emma's rare, rare laughter in the rear of the wagon — just to have sat these few brief moments beside this tall, sane, loving man — yes, it was worth every minute of jeopardy and danger.

They had reached the bottom of the Hill.

Mrs Noyes got down and discreetly walked to the rear of the wagon to greet Emma's brothers, while Emma and her father said hello and goodbye.

She only glanced at them once — and it nearly broke her heart to see them. The blond, dusty giant was holding his daughter — small and dark as her mother — just as he must have held her as a child, high against his shoulder while she clung to him and wept.

At last, it was Emma's father who had the sense to realize they had stretched the time to its absolute limit — and he told Mrs Noyes she must take Emma home.

Suddenly, "home" was not the top of the Hill, but across the river — and this made their parting unhappy.

Mrs Noyes stood holding Emma's hand as they watched the great lumber wagon disappearing into the growing dark and the dust and they both called out; "goodbye!" And Emma said; "give my love to Ma and Lotte!" And all the pale hands were raised from the back of the wagon and then there was a turning in the track and they were gone.

Walking back up the Hill, the only thing that Emma said was *"thank you."*

And Mrs Noyes squeezed the child's hand and said; "you're welcome, dear. But let us both be thankful."

Emma did not know that her father and mother, her brothers and Lotte were to be drowned. Mrs Noyes, who did know, could not bear to think it was true, and she dreaded the day — which she knew was coming — when Doctor Noyes would say the words aloud.

∞ There were no more meetings with Emma's father or her brothers. Japeth had become suspicious when he found his wife sitting beside the cart track with a basket of fruit one evening — and, knowing that her father and brothers were in the work force, he forbade her ever to go near the cart track again. This time, the ban was effective. Emma was kept in the watchful eye of Hannah and, at nightfall, she was locked in her room.

∞ The building of the ark was a monstrous undertaking — and once the keel frame had been laid and the ribs of the ark itself set in place, it was obvious how vast its size would be: the largest structure ever built in the whole district. The workmen were now in awe of it, as though they were building a temple, and this produced a thoroughly satisfying atmosphere of *"no more questions asked — no more questions needed."* Noah was able, now, to stare each workman squarely in the eye and dare him with a look to challenge the grandeur of the project. As if the grandeur of the ark was its whole justification.

∞ In the meantime, during all this hectic and furious activity, Ham and Lucy were married. Doctor Noyes rebelled against it — Hannah would not speak of it and Japeth was furiously jealous. He surmised, quite correctly, that in his brother's union, there would be no pause between the joy of marriage and the joys of the marriage bed. And why should Ham, who had never so much as looked at a woman or even mentioned a woman's name, have such good luck? It wasn't fair. Japeth would hate Ham and Lucy — secretly at first, then openly — for the rest of time. Everything Japeth wanted, someone else either had at birth or acquired with a snap of the fingers. Only *his* life was fraught with difficulties — only *his* life was hell.

As for Doctor Noyes and Hannah, although they neither approved of nor enjoyed the prospect of Sister Lucy (as she must now be called) being a member of their family — there was nothing to be done about it short of canvassing the neighbourhood for another candidate. To do this would have taken weeks — and might, for all that anyone could tell, have produced nothing better than another Emma. Yaweh's Edict had clearly stated: "Noah, his wife, his three sons *and his sons' wives.*" Such must be the family Noyes as it entered the ark — and now that Ham had been married to Lucy, so it was.

∞ Hannah had had problems of her own. Some time in the second month of ark-building — which was around the time of Ham's marriage — Hannah had finally admitted to herself she was pregnant. Three months pregnant — or was it four? Could she be mistaken . . . ? Every month, as she missed another period, she tried with all her wit to deny it had begun four months ago. The first month had been a fluke; she'd been under stress; she'd lost track — miscounted . . . At any rate, *three* was the figure she quoted to Shem. If time proved her wrong, then — of course — she would not be the first among women to give birth prematurely and, by then, the excitement of the child's presence would dampen anyone's enthusiasm for figures.

Nonetheless, every night Hannah prayed; "please let me be wrong."

∞ The ark was completed on a day of dust storms.

Nothing had ever been so ugly. As it sat deserted on its hillside, its poop deck and its castle were shapeless and its colour was a horror, made worse by the great running streams of pitch, oozing down its sides like so much inedible frosting on a poison cake.

Noah made Hannah walk him up the Hill — both of them swathed in dust sheets — just so he could bless the monstrosity and walk away from it.

Staring at it, Noah wished, in a moment of weakness, that he could renegotiate his contract with Yaweh. If this appalling creation—swept about by clouds of dust—was to be his home for the next hundred years, there was nothing to recommend it but the hope that it would float.

Standing down in the yards, also wrapped in flapping dust sheets, Mrs Noyes and Emma, Ham and the elegant Lucy watched in silence as the last of the lumber wagons rolled down the Hill with their silent crews of workmen. No one waved and no one called goodbye. The last that was seen of all these men was their dangling legs and their bowed heads — and the last that was seen of the wagons and the oxen was the ghostly image of a fleet of wooden flat boats — whirled away, slow motion, down a river of sand.

∞ The wind continued to blow for two or three days — a low, hot constant wind that came down the Hill as if its source was at the peak. In the night it made noises of its own — and by day it was alive with the cries of lost birds, blown up high above the trees where the sky was shockingly clear and blue. Below them, the earth was obscured with scudding topsoil and eddies of grit and twigs.

It was difficult enough to see — but a person could manage by turning away from the wind and walking backwards. Thus, going up the Hill was awkward and walking down was a cinch.

Noah had consulted the Edict—part of it a timetable, part of it a book of rules — and he decided there was nothing for it — despite the dust and wind — but to commence the loading of the animals.

This created instant chaos.

To begin with, there were only the family members to help. All the woodsmen and all the itinerant workers had been dismissed and were miles away, unwittingly living out their few remaining days.

Visibility was an obvious problem — and establishing the route to the ark and maintaining it was another. It was decided that if ropes and chains could be tied between the trees, it would be simplest to use the existing track. At least it had stretches already fenced on one side or both—and it went all the way from the foot to the crest.

The worst and the greatest problem was the animals themselves.

It was all very well to have written into the Edict "two by
two" — but animals do not come in pairs, and choosing this
mare and that stallion was easier said than done.

The sheep were a nightmare. Mrs Noyes had taught them
all how to sing. She had favourites — as it turned out, *all* of
them were favourites — but there could be only seven. One
ram, six ewes — no lambs. Finally, Mrs Noyes had to be physi-
cally removed from their presence and the job of choosing them
was given to Shem.

All the great beasts had to be released from the cages in the
meadow: elephants and lions; giraffes and camels; hippos and
water buffalo . . . seventy pairs of beasts in all and over half of
them vicious and all of them terrified.

Japeth had the good sense to think of his hunting techniques
— and he put his brothers and Lucy onto horses and provided
them with spears as prods. Mrs Noyes and Emma were assigned to the fowl and to the smaller animals in cages — rabbits,
guinea pigs, rats, et cetera. The et cetera here went on for
pages — and every animal, every kind and every sex, had to
be checked against Hannah's list as they were pushed or carried or herded on board.

Some were trampled on the hillside. Some were attacked
by panic-stricken others and left to die. Some ran away beneath the ropes, while others leapt beyond the fences, losing
themselves in miles of distance. Others wandered into the yards
and even into the house. Mrs Noyes got the peacock aboard,
but could not find the peahen. By the time she had found the
peahen, the peacock had escaped and she had to round him up
again.

Out in the meadow, Whistler and the Vixen cringed in their
burrows, thinking the earth itself had sprung to life. Mice were
buried alive and demons ran riot in terror.

Indeed, the sound of the great parade and round-up was heard
on the other side of the forest and it went on for one night and
two days.

At one moment, Emma and Mrs Noyes had clambered onto the roof of the house to bring down a pair of storks, and had paused to look out over the Hill and up towards the ark and down towards the river. What they saw was an endless rolling mass of backs and shoulders and heads, pushing upward against the wind and through the dust, some of the heads held high, with horns or antlers, others butting low with massive brows and sand-blinded eyes. All of them were crying out in confusion and fear and many were calling to their abandoned young or to others of their kind who were penned or corralled or stabled—doomed. Above them, the great sky filled with birds and there was not a trace of cloud but only the merciless sun which seemed determined not to set.

It was then that Mrs Noyes turned to Emma and held her with an arm around her shoulder and said to her; ''dear one, never forget what you have seen down there — for this is the beginning of a new world.''

Emma stared and Mrs Noyes went over to the further side of the roof, where she sat down and wept in the shadow of the chimney.

In the kitchen, Mottyl hid throughout the whole episode — beneath the stove. Even her blind eye never closed.

∞ Mrs Noyes went running — headlong down the darkening halls — her skirts and aprons yanked above her thighs — running with the blank-eyed terror of someone who cannot find her children while she hears their cries for help. Smoke was pouring through the house from one open end to the other — and at first Mrs Noyes was certain the fire must be inside, but when she reached the door and saw the blazing pyre, she knew it was not the house but something else — alive — that was in flames.

She paused only a second — long enough to throw up her arms against the heat and to wrap an apron round her head because the air was full of sparks the size of birds and her hair was dry as tinder-grass — and then she was running again — racing through the streaming smoke and she was desperately trying to find out what it was that was making the high-pitched wailing sound that was — and wasn't — a cry she recognized. And she also tried to count the shapes that were moving with her through the furnace (for it seemed a furnace now) — and to see whether they were human shapes — her sons — her husband — her daughters-in-law. . . .

Nothing she saw that moved had feet or legs — but only arms and necks and heads — and everything was floating — heaving up through the waves of smoke like beasts who broke the surface of a drowning-pool, then sank and broke again. And again — and then were gone.

It was useless to call out names. She hadn't the voice to call, and every time she opened her mouth it was filled with ashes. And the wind — whether fanning the flames or created by the flames — made a noise of its own that was hollowed out of the fire and it seemed to be tangible.

Mrs Noyes fell down — all at once — no warning. Suddenly she was on the ground beneath the smoke and the palms of her hands had been scorched — and what had scorched them was a burning piece of flesh and, looking up, she recognized at last the shapes of what it was that was moving all around her. It was sheep and cattle and goats and dogs. . . .

Mrs Noyes pushed herself to her knees and then to her feet and then she stood there — rooted — but staring from side to side with her hand against her mouth. And as she watched and as she listened she began to be overwhelmed with a dreadful certainty. She fathomed what it was that was happening here — and the panic this caused turned her legs to stone and her mind to paste and she was frozen before a single piece of knowledge: *all that is happening here is deliberate and the meaning of this fire is the sacrifice of hundreds.*

Noah . . .

If only her voice would come. If she could even summon a remnant. . . .

Noah . . .!

Stop!

But there was nothing. Nothing came of the words — and the only sound was the sound around her of all her cattle — all her sheep — all her horses — all the dogs and all their cries being driven towards cremation in the name of God.

Mrs Noyes — at last — could move: and she put out her hands towards the nearest beast, not even knowing what it was, and a voice said; *"mother — your skirts are on fire"* as calmly as a voice that might have said; "your laces are undone. . . ."

The face before her was a face that — yes — she recognized, though its features were streaked with soot and spotted with blisters. It was Ham and he was saying that her clothes were on fire and he was falling to his knees in order to put out the flames with his hands — but before he fell, he pushed something living into her arms and she automatically pressed it to her breast, not knowing what it was, and held it there while Ham wrung out the flames around her feet.

When he rose again, he put his arm around her shoulders and drew the apron further over her hair and he led her away from the centre and towards the edge of the yard on the windward side of the smoke and it was only then that she heard the creature at her breast and looked and saw that it was Mottyl, blind and pregnant, and she said; "was he going to kill her too? For Yaweh?"

Ham looked away — ashamed.

Mrs Noyes gave a cry. "I will kill him," she said "I will. Kill him."

Ham looked down at the ground, pretending he had not heard.

Mrs Noyes held Mottyl very gently now and soothed her with a piece of cloth — wiping the milky, blinded eyes and heaving the pregnant weight so the cat lay flat against her. Safe.

"Does he really mean to kill them all — these animals? . . ." she said to Ham — looking around to see if she could find some sign of Doctor Noyes or of her other sons. "Every last one of them?"

"He says it's the final sacrifice before we embark," Ham told her. "This is his gift to Yaweh for having . . ." and though he tried, he simply could not resist a smile; ". . . for having spared us."

Mrs Noyes grunted and pressed her chin against Mottyl's head.

"I won't go," she said. "To hell with him. To hell with '*being spared*.' It's as simple as that. I will *not* go."

Mrs Noyes walked a few paces off and then turned back to look at Ham.

"Will you come with me?"

Ham did not move.

He was young, after all, and had just been married. He wanted to board the ark — to be spared. Mrs Noyes was quite prepared to understand — and she did appreciate the way he leaned towards her; as if a part of him would follow, if only his circumstance was different.

"Very well," she said — and she smiled. Still smiling, she narrowed her eyes and looked at Ham briefly — memorizing his expression and the way he stood. And then she said; "goodbye," and turned to march away down the Hill with Mottyl in her arms, when — suddenly — she was seized by a hand and someone was standing in her way.

It was Shem, and all he said was; "he wants to see you." Then he turned her by the shoulder and led her away.

∞ They climbed all the way to the top of the Hill where Noah had raised himself as far as possible above the holocaust below. He was standing on the family altar — almost as if he might sacrifice himself, though Mrs Noyes knew this was hardly likely. The sacrificial bell was ringing.

Noah's arms were raised above his head, and his face was turned to heaven — so that all Mrs Noyes could see of him was his soiled white robe and his tangled beard and his mane of white hair, thrown back.

Shem still held her by the shoulder, the fingers of his great horny hand biting into her bones — and she could smell the fire on his arm and everywhere else there was the smell of burning flesh and of grass fires and animal fear and terror. Mrs Noyes held Mottyl closer to her breast and tried to draw the tatty bit of cloth up under her chin, in order to hide her.

When whatever prayer he was saying had been said, and Mrs Noyes had listened to it open-eyed and unbowed, Noah let down his arms and looked at his wife.

"You disappeared," he said.

"I was busy."

"I see."

(That she had been busy preparing the larder for a sea voyage of some months' duration was not even mentioned. . . .)

"You wanted me?"

"Yes. I had rather hoped you might witness the sacrifice: take part."

"I had no wish to take part — and I was a witness. Thank you."

"You seem short-tempered, madam."

"I am."

Noah was helped from the altar by Hannah. Mrs Noyes was quick to see she was dressed in spotless white.

"Doubtless, you are overtired. . . ." said Noah, referring to his wife's short temper.

"No," said Mrs Noyes. "In fact, I'm rather exhilarated, thank you."

"You were uplifted by the sacrifice?"

"Hardly."

Doctor Noyes paid no attention to her remark — but simply ploughed on with his explanation of the afternoon's events, while he sat upon the altar.

"Should you care to know what this — the greatest sacrifice we have ever offered to our Lord — is about, I can tell you in a sentence. . . ."

"I'd rather you didn't."

"No, madam. We can't have that. You are, after all, my wife, and therefore I am responsible for your education."

At this point, Hannah stepped forward, carrying water with which the old man washed his hands — after which, Hannah knelt and washed his feet as he continued his conversation with Mrs Noyes.

"It was our duty, madam, not to waste these animals — which, after all, were prime sacrificial specimens raised for that purpose. Something in the nature of a hundred sheep and fifty head of cattle. Various fowl, not to mention goats . . . they should all have been drowned, madam. A great waste.

Unforgiveable. And—as a parting gesture—and, as I say, as a gesture of gratitude to our Lord . . ."

"You haven't mentioned the horses."

"What?"

"The horses. You haven't mentioned the horses. The non-sacrificial animals. The pigs. Or the oxen. Or the mules. Or the turkeys. Or the dogs. Or the peacocks and peahens. Or . . ."

"Stop that . . ."

"*Or my cat!*" Mrs Noyes bellowed — and even though her voice failed halfway through the words, she had said them and he would know that she knew what he had done — and what it meant to her.

"Your cat, madam?"

"*Yes.*"

Mrs Noyes drew back the bit of cloth and showed a bit of Mottyl, cowering against her breast — terrified of the presence of Doctor Noyes.

Doctor Noyes drew his breath in through his wooden teeth and made that hissing noise that was always a sign of great displeasure. Then he waved his hand—dismissing Mottyl entirely and said; "we have two cats already, madam. Two very special cats, I might add . . . and the Edict very plainly states *two — and two only.*"

"You could make an exception."

"Oh? But why should I?"

"BECAUSE SHE IS MINE!"

Hannah faltered — and half the water in the basin was lost. No one moved — not even Noah.

Finally, seeing that nothing had been changed by what she had said — nor by the manner in which she had said it — Mrs Noyes finished in a whisper.

"I shall not come with you, Noah. If my cat—if Mottyl may not come, then I shall not come."

Hannah cringed. She thought the earth might open.

Noah kicked aside the basin and rose to his full height as if he had never been old but was still a youth and a giant and he drew back his arm and struck Mrs Noyes with the back of his hand.

She fell — of course — and Mottyl, being afraid, ran out of her arms and was gone.

Mrs Noyes lay absolutely still where she was. All she could think was; *she is blind — and I will never see her again.*

∞ Doctor Noyes sat down. And the truth was, he had to. The effort of striking his wife had nearly crippled him, and — all at once — he was old again.

Still, he summoned his wits about him and — as Hannah completed the washing of his feet (having poured fresh water from the pitcher) — he attempted to reason with Mrs Noyes, though she barely heard him.

"There are other cats . . . very beautiful cats, Abraham and Sarah—and your cat is pregnant; old—and a wildwood cat — to say nothing of blind, madam. She'd only have fallen overboard. . . ." He almost chuckled kindly. "And think how badly *that* would have made you feel: *swallowed up by the sea . . .*"

"She's already swallowed by the sea — being left behind. . . ."

"Well—be that as it may, *you* are better off without her and *she* is better off where she is. She will die with her own kind— in her own place."

Mrs Noyes was silent — and Doctor Noyes smiled — and this appeared to be the end of the matter. She got to her feet and he got to his and they stood — though not side by side — looking down the Hill, with the great ark rising behind them and the sacrificial fires below them. And he said; "it is right. It is proper. We are obeying God. And when we go aboard the ark together, we shall have fulfilled our mandate here — and have a future mandate to fulfill and we shall be glad we have done our duty. Yes?"

No.

She would not be glad.

And she would not forgive him.

Ever.
Very slowly, it began to rain.

∞ Because there had been so many weeks of drought, the first rain brought on a wave of relief. Ham and Lucy and Emma came up onto the deck of the ark and Emma danced and sang all the rain songs: *"rain, rain, go away and come again some other day"* and *"rain on my window, rain on my door, please don't rain on my roof anymore!"* In fact, there was so much singing and so much laughter and so much running around and splashing in puddles that none of them seemed to notice, at first, the oddness of the rain. And then Emma — pointing at Lucy, who wore a long white gown — said; "look! It's coloured rain! . . ."
And it was. It was mauve.

∞ On the third day of rain, the rain clouds lowered, almost touching the highest branches of the pine tree and the roof of the ark. The deep seams of mauve-dyed clay down which the rain was carving streams and waterfalls began — very slowly at first — to run with less colour and with more force. Thunder was everywhere — but distant, still — surrounding the Hill with echoes. It was now that the rain — having lost its translucence and it mauveness — began to take on an opaque and milky look, and Noah said that what had been an "evil" rain was now a "passionate" rain being poured from the sky — spent and wasted on the dying earth and this he called "the rain of Onan."

∞ Mrs Noyes had disappeared.
No one could find her.
Doctor Noyes was frantic.
Not, it must be admitted, because he feared for the loss of someone he loved — but because he feared for the loss of someone he needed. Without Mrs Noyes, the ark could not depart, and its voyage would be doomed. This was Yaweh's Edict:

"you and your sons and your wife and the wives of your sons . . ." These eight — or none would be saved.

Hannah came and stood with Doctor Noyes beneath his umbrella, both of them staring down through the rain from the deck above the gangplank.

"She will kill us all," said Doctor Noyes.

Hannah drew her shawl across her belly.

"She will kill us all!" Doctor Noyes shouted at the sky. "SHE WILL KILL US ALL! STOP HER!"

∞ At first, Mrs Noyes hung about the bottom of the Hill while the rain continued to fall and the wood began to fill with renegade dogs and turkeys, driven from abandoned homesteads far down the road. Other animals had also begun to appear along the swollen riverbank and in the wood — and soon there were so many, the resident lemurs took to climbing up to the tops of the trees and shouting; *"no more room! No more room!"*

In the back of Mrs Noyes's mind had been the vague, but now despairing hope that Mottyl might somehow make an appearance from the midst of this welter of stray and homeless animals; that the magic of chance might help them to find one another.

But the long grass — beaten to the ground — and the edges of the wood and the rapidly diminishing stretches of road she could reach in her growing exhaustion — all yielded nothing of Mottyl. Mrs Noyes's clothes were now soaked through and the smell of wet wool, burnt apron and singed hair made her feel like a dampened fire. She should have been cold, but she wasn't. The rain was surprisingly warm and — at times — it seemed almost hot — and the valley was filled with drifting mists that had the wispy look of the steam that used to billow from the simmering pots on her stove.

Every time the grass moved or a twig snapped or a branch fell, Mrs Noyes would stop in her tracks and whisper; *"Motty? Mottyl?"* It was pointless to raise her voice and especially pointless against the shouts of the lemurs. The world was a wilderness now — and if she was to find her cat, she would find her entirely by chance.

∞ In the dark — for it was always dark — Mottyl ran and ran from the sound of Noah's voice and the smell of fire and the stench of burning flesh. Fire was everyone's enemy — but Doctor Noyes had always been her special enemy: creator of her blindness and the killer of her children. And now, he had tried to kill her, too.

The darkness she moved in was not completely dark. There were edges to it — pale, thin watery edges over which the shape of static things and sometimes moving things encroached: a flight of birds, a running dog or the leaping, jerky motion of a lemur. Trees and rocks and walls were the worst of her enemies — never seen whole and rising up suddenly — flat and undimensional — threatening collision and all too often, causing it.

She made off down the Hill — conjuring all the memory she could of walls and trees and gates and where they were — and where the openings were, the little bits of light that let her through — but she had to make a great and unfamiliar detour around the circle of cremation in the yard and almost at once she became entangled in the corpses smouldering on its perimeter.

Mottyl very rarely cried aloud. She had always been a stoic cat and mostly, when afraid, was silent — and when in pain, she went into hiding. But here, in the yard, with her nostrils overwhelmed by the violent stink of smouldering fur and the sound of burning innards singing in her ears and the oozing paste of marrow pulling at her paws and the terror of the smoke and the fear of the fire she could not quite see; she was overcome and she stood — immobilized — and threw back her head and wailed.

No one heard her.

There was no one near but the dead and — overhead — the silent wheels of buzzards, waiting.

When, finally, Mottyl was able to move, it had begun to rain and she had lost all sense of place and direction.

∞ Mrs Noyes had to forage for her food, since all the edibles had been removed from the gardens and the larders and the root cellars. Every egg from the hen-house—every bag of flour from the storehouse—every bit of meat from the smoke-house and every herb that had hung from the rafters of her summer kitchens—all of it was gone. And every seed from the granary. Nothing had been left; it had either been burned or was deep in the hold of the ark. And to think she had taken part in this operation—and taken part willingly . . .

Well.

There was soggy grass and there were bitter roots in the ground and sour yellow berries hanging from vines and there must be apples . . .

What a fool she was!

Surely there would still be apples in the orchard. . . . After all, apples were forbidden to so many that very few got eaten. Women were absolutely forbidden to eat them, as were children and domestic animals. Only the elders like Noah—men who had been inducted into the mysteries—could feed from the orchard. Yet the orchard had been filled with apple trees. Dozens of them—all with their blossoms in the spring and the smell of their skins in the autumn rain. Why hadn't she thought of it?

Now she went running even in spite of the mud and the slippery grass and the tangled mess of flowers that covered the hillside. She cut across the fields—moving upward—angling over towards the cart-track and the low stone walls with the jagged glass on top and the gate that had always been locked, but which now she was already breaking open in her mind.

All those apples will be mine; she thought.

When she reached the track, she was desperately out of breath and had to pause, collapsing to her knees and then to her hip—just for a moment . . . *"Just for a moment's rest,"* she whispered. And then—all at once—she sat bolt upright.

Ben Azai had died . . . Ben Zoma had lost his mind . . . Ben Abuya had pulled the plants of reason from their place . . .

So Yaweh had told—*because they had entered the orchard.*

Mrs Noyes sagged down again—with her hip against a large round stone—and perhaps it was the pain of the stone pressing into her bones that prompted her to think; *but they did not enter the orchard for apples . . . they went in there for knowl-edge and all I want is food!* (She stood up.) *And — besides: wasn't there one of them who lived? Who came out whole from the orchard?*

Yes.

Mrs Noyes turned and looked up the track towards the gate with its chain and its lock.

Rabbi Akiva went into the orchard whole and came out whole.

And so would she.

∞ Mrs Noyes tore one of her petticoats into long, thick strips and a few of these she draped around her neck against some future usefulness she could not yet predict. She had been a wife and mother long enough to know that absolutely noth-ing was without some use. The rest of the petticoat she wound into several layers of bandage round her hands, leaving only her thumbs exposed. The effect was not unlike a pair of cot-ton mittens — somewhat misshapen, but they would do the job.

It had occurred to her that the breaking open of the gate might spring the effects of some magical curse that Yaweh or Noah had uttered over the lock. St Elmo's Fire or the Great Snake of Eden might be conjured — and she didn't relish the thought of that. Better to take her chances with the wall and its jagged glass.

∞ The blind can will a kind of sight. Though nothing is ever clearly seen, a shadow can be given shape and a source of light identified.

Mottyl had found the orchard, too — though earlier than Mrs Noyes. It was not a place she had much frequented in the past — due largely to the fact that Doctor Noyes and Hannah had left their scent on all the paths and the gate posts reeked of their handprints. A very long while ago, she had tried the wall and cut her pads — but this had been in her kitten-days and the memory of it was dim. Approaching it, early on the morning after the burning of the animals, her *whispers* told her to be wary of the wall — but nothing more.

It was still pre-dawn and only the faintest light had touched the sky. Mottyl's overall impression of the world was grey — everything drifting, double misted — everything rained upon and steaming — everything seen through the shifting globes of her cataracts. She'd spent the night — the darkest part of it — locked to the branch of an evergreen tree, never completely sleeping — her ears pricked forward and her claws, unsheathed, sunk deep in the bark — so deep that a stream of resin had flavoured her dreams. Her coat, with its patches of rust and red and black and white, still smelled of fire and smoke, though less and less of this was evident the longer she'd crouched on her branch in the rain. And now — as she made her way towards the orchard wall, the fire scent was hardly evident at all. If the dragons she feared had come, they'd have caught the gist of her at once, since all her own scent was exaggerated by the wetness of her hair and the warmth of her body rising to overcome the morning chill. This could present a problem and she wondered where she might find some dung to roll in or some herb, perhaps, which would have the double advantage of soothing her flea bites — and of perking up her spirits.

The smell of apples beyond the wall was absolutely overpowering, though its attraction hadn't the same connotation for Mottyl as it had for Mrs Noyes. For Mottyl, the attraction had nothing to do with food and everything to do with identifying where she was. It provided a centre around which she could draw a circle, defining distance and direction in much the same fashion as before, when there was safety in houses and at least in some of the people she lived with — when she could gauge her whereabouts by the smell of Mrs Noyes and kitchen smells and the smell of her beloved porch — its beloved edges where she had lain in the sun — and the rocking chair with its carpet seat and its arms that were oiled with centuries of sweat from the palms of Mrs Noyes's hands. . . . And so, as she approached the orchard, Mottyl rejoiced in the smell of its apples.

So evidently, did a flock of birds. Not very large birds — but very noisy. If only they would make up their minds what sort of noise they wanted to make. They were sounding, in the treetops, every kind of birdcall and even some other calls — a barking dog — a lemur's cry — a female human being. And whirring things — like clocks and Doctor Noyes's mechanical devices . . .

Starlings

Mottyl ran closer, down the slope towards the wall. The light was increasing, now, though the sun itself made no appearance.

If only her *whispers* weren't so loud, she could try the wall with impunity. But they would not be quiet. They became, in fact, so very loud they began to irritate.

> Why don't you tell me what it is? Instead of all this buzzing *"be careful! Be careful!"* why not tell me *why* I should be careful — what I should be careful *of*? Is there someone there? The angel? Is the angel there?

> *No. Only birds. Not dangerous.*

> What, then?

> *Wall. Wall.*

> Wall. As if *that* helped! Tell me *why* the wall.

> *We can't. We don't remember. Only . . . the wall; the wall; be careful.*

Mottyl was now on the downward slope about six leaps or seven from the wall, which she could "see" as a low, dark shape that made a ribbon through the grey. The smell of apples rose towards her and the noise of the starlings.

Starlings were stringy — wiry little things — hardly any meat at all and what there was, was not pleasant. It was bitter flesh and vaguely metallic — not unlike the rust one encountered in certain springs and pools. There was even the vaguest hint of aloes — as if they fed on poison berries and holly leaves. Still . . .

Mottyl sat upright — rabbitlike — and faced the singing trees. "Bird!" she called. "Bird?"

The starlings — instantly — fell silent.

Mottyl lowered herself — ran sideways along the slope — and stopped.

"Bird . . ." she called again — softer. "Bird?" with a twisted inflection. The technique was much like mouse-calling — though necessarily somewhat harsher because the voice was projected upward instead of low, along the earth and through the grass.

"Bird!" Very sharp, this time. "Bird!"

In their trees, the starlings muttered — wondering . . .

Knowing now that she had their attention, Mottyl began to chatter.

Chatter could be so wonderfully fatal — if the tone was right. Not every bird was tempted. You could never tempt a robin, for instance — but starlings, cowbirds and finches could not resist — and practically crawled into a person's mouth when chattered to.

One of the starlings gave in.

It flew from the apple tree and lighted on the wall, looking down into the mess of soggy grass and undergrowth below, muttering as it did so.

Mottyl was cursing her blindness. She knew the bird was there, because of its voice — but its shape was too much like the shapes of the jutting stones surrounding it. If only it would move. Mottyl was also cursing the weight of her kittens, sufficient now to throw her off balance when she leapt — though, if she'd had her sight, her balance would not be affected.

Speak again. Speak, she prayed to the bird. *Speak!*

As if the bird had heard her prayer, it called back something to the others in the tree.

Mottyl crept forward towards the voice, using the overhanging branches of a myrtle grove as cover — letting the branches press against her back in order to be ready for their weight to lift as they lightened towards their tips. . . . *Go on talking. Speak again. Speak.* . . .

The starling was leaning down — staring at the earth below the wall — incautiously looking for insects.

Mottyl was now a single leap from her prey — and was certain that she had its shape defined and singled out from the other shapes of the stones.

Suddenly the bird gave a cry.

It had seen her.

Mottyl leapt.

The starling flew away — and Mottyl, inches from the stones, all at once heard a shout from her *whispers*. . . .

GLASS!

∞ All the starlings whirled up — screaming with indignation at Mottyl's shape as it hurtled high — clearing the embedded glass — and fell to earth on the orchard side of the wall. The birds flew further off down the rows of trees, where they lighted again — dispersed amongst the apples and leaves like shrieking harpies; *"cat! Cat! Cat!"*

Mottyl, who had landed on her feet, was shaken — and crouched against the wall with her heart pounding and her tongue pouring salivation and her ears laid back. She could barely summon breath — and the misted air was filled with small white dots that made her dizzy. Deep inside her belly she could feel her babies shifting — pushing one another — tumbled and alarmed. Quickly, she lay on her side and stretched her flanks as wide as she could, in order to lengthen their cavern. She closed her eyes — not wanting light — and concentrated on breathing longer draughts, pulling the breaths down harder into her lungs — slowly curling her paws — *in — out — in — out —* until all the tics and jumps and shivers had subsided and she could listen for the heartbeats that were not her own.

One.

Two. Three.

Four. Five . . .

Nothing.

Six; there should have been six.

Where are you, six? Where are you?

Nothing.

Mottyl turned on her other side.

Six? Six?

Six?

She pulled her head deliberately down across her belly, lying now on the curve of her back — nipping at her skin in order to force the babies to move again. *Move! Move!*

They shifted — gently now — falling through the liquids in which they were couched — one — two — three . . .

Four.

Five.

∞ Six.

Mottyl lay against the wall and slept for five whole minutes. All six heart beats and her own came into harmony under the rain.

∞ The orchard looked so peaceful, with its ordered rows of trees and its grassy paths and it seemed extremely strange for Mrs Noyes to be standing there afraid of such a place. But she was afraid. All her life it had been dinned into her female conscience that only women with the highest dispensations were allowed to walk beneath those trees and on that grass: women such as Hannah — who was, in fact, the only woman Mrs Noyes had ever known for whom the necessary concessions had been made.

She approached the wall.

All this while, she was acutely aware that someone might be spying on her from the ark and — consequently — every move she made was slung towards the ground. Crouching and dragging her cotton mittens through the dirt, she made her way across the last open patch of track and threw herself against the wall where some currant bushes grew in sufficient profusion to hide her.

She waited.

Not a sound above the rain — and no indication at all that anyone had seen.

The wall, above her now, was slightly less than her own standing height. The stones themselves were pointed — and the profusion of glass was greater than she had remembered.

Well; the sooner begun, the sooner over.

She stood up — all the way to her full height — and pulled at

the ends of her mittens, tightening them around her wrists.
And then she placed her hands, very gingerly — but firmly —
on a place where the shards seemed the least offensive and
heaved herself from her feet. . . .

Oh God.

She was caught.

Her hip, dragged down by her skirts, had landed full on the
top of the wall and she could feel the glass very slowly entering her flesh like so many dragon's teeth.

She lay quite still, afraid to move for fear of tearing herself,
and then—as someone else might perform a one-armed push-up
— Mrs Noyes lifted her weight and rolled to the ground on the
other side. She would bleed—but if she did not look, she would
not faint.

∞ After Mottyl had slept her five minutes — relieved and
contented that all six babies were alive — she awoke still
hungry.

Sitting up, she nosed the air and very quickly realized she
was not alone in the orchard.

The Vixen was in there with her.

Mottyl stood — and bristled. This reaction was automatic.
When you smelled the Vixen, you prepared at once to defend
yourself—though the best defense was to run as far away as
possible. The trouble was — it was not quite clear precisely
where the Vixen was walking. More than likely she was looking—as Mottyl was—for something to eat. The Vixen often
poked about in the orchard and along the edges of fields in
search of young rabbits. But the air was so damp and there
was not a breath of wind, which meant that the Vixen's odour
was everywhere — spread evenly through the mist.

Given her blindness, Mottyl was more or less defenseless.
Certainly she presented all too easy a target for any beast who
perceived she was blind—and if the beast were large enough,
then Mottyl and her babies would be doomed. Not that she
wouldn't fight. But some fights you don't win. . . .

Mottyl listened with intense scrutiny. But there was not a
sound. Certainly nothing she would associate with a fox.

Mottyl moved away from the wall and — avoiding the looming shapes of the trees — she wandered out beneath their
branches, thinking, if the worst came to the worst, she could
climb a tree.

All at once, the Vixen was upon her — appearing, apparently,
from the long grass.

Mottyl shot up the nearest tree as far as she dared trust
the branches to hold her.

At the foot of the tree, the Vixen went mad with barking.
Furious with Mottyl for having escaped, she flung every epithet she could muster up through the leaves while Mottyl —
safe — settled in for a long siege. But then a very strange thing
happened.

Loud and vicious as her tirade against the cat had been, the
Vixen stopped mid-yelp and sank to her side in the grass.
Mottyl could hear her panting — and then, very slowly, she began to make out another sound: the Vixen was exhausted. She
was muttering and complaining. She was on the verge of
howling. There was nothing to eat. There was nowhere safe
to hide. She was starving and her kits were already dead. . . .

Mottyl, it so happened, had just discovered a full clutch of
eggs in a blue jay's nest.

"Vixen?"

The fox looked up.

Mottyl pushed two eggs from the nest — leaving three for
herself.

"Eat."

∞ The orchard in all its ordered splendour spread itself
before Mrs Noyes.

She ran — or rather, she hobbled quickly to the nearest tree
where the apples were a pale, sweet yellow and she took down
one — two — three in rapid succession and ate them, using
both of her mittened hands to hold them up to her mouth. As
she ate, she also drank — and the juices ran from the corners
of her lips, down her chin and down her neck and into the cleav-
age between her breasts. It was a virtual bath in nectar and
she revelled in it — wishing she could squeeze the cores out

through her hair. And the flesh of the apples was better than any food she had ever tasted before — though almost any food might have had the same effect, since half the pleasure was in quenching her thirst and her hunger with anything but water.

Looking around her, she saw how many of the trees still bore their fruit and she thought; *I must make a store of this beyond the wall — then every time I'm hungry, I won't have to wear these silly mitts and slash my legs.*

Red apples, green apples, purple apples, yellow apples, even white apples — hanging from the boughs — fell into her apron as she shook the branches and stooped to gather what had already fallen under the weight of the rain. And the grass was sweet with them, sweet with its own wet smell and Mrs Noyes thought that, of the earth, there could be no better memory than this — than of the shapely branches of its trees and the taste of its fruit and the smell of its grass and the warmth of its rain.

∞ Two aprons full of apples would feed her for a month, though she could not believe that by then she would be alive to eat them. Mrs Noyes sat down on the ground and ate a dozen apples in a row. She was sitting with her skirts pulled up, so the rain would wash her legs, and every time she finished an apple, she rubbed its core very gently over her wounds. The acid stung her, but she knew it would help to heal the cuts.

The proliferation of the rains was unpredictable — but Mrs Noyes's awareness of Noah's trickiness and her memory of Yaweh's rage had prepared her not to hold out hope for moderation. It might very well continue to rain like this for days — with the soft, warm pall of what, in later times, would come to be known as "Scotch mist." But it wouldn't last. Surely the holy thunder must come and the jagged fury of Yaweh's lightning-bolts, with which He so often tried to bamboozle His people into being afraid. And the cataracts. And the blinding sheets of freezing sleet. And the raging torrents, blown about with noisy storms and whirlwinds. And finally . . . what? The pools undoing their edges — all the rivers overflowing their banks — and all the ponds cascading down the hills — and the waterfalls gone silent, swallowed whole by the rising lakes and the falling mountains. And then . . .

Mrs Noyes stood up.

And then . . .

She threw away the final apple core and drew the back of her hand across her mouth and belched. *I am like a cow*, she thought. *Standing in the rain and staring at space. Any minute, I will began to chew my cud!*

And then . . .

Mrs Noyes could not imagine more, though she knew very well that more could be imagined. And had been, already, by Yaweh and Noah. But that was not her business. For her, whatever rain there was, was all the rain she'd ever need — its intentions having been clear from the moment it began to fall.

Turning briefly, she looked back at the orchard, breathing in a final draught of its sweetness. But there was something else on the air besides apples. "I smell an animal," she said. Large? Small? Dangerous? Benign? How could she tell? It was just — an animal.

"Mottyl?"

But no — the smell was wilder than that.

Mrs Noyes shook down her skirts and, slinging the aprons filled with apples over her shoulders, she moved off down the Hill. There was — for some strange reason — an odd sort of comfort, she decided, in the smell of apples mingled with the animal smell. Perhaps it was just the signal that something else, besides herself, was alive and wandering over the Hill. If only it had been her cat.

∞ Mottyl was trotting down to the edge of the wood. It was coming on to evening now, and the lemurs were screaming for the sun. Mottyl was thinking of Bip and Ringer — wishing they were safe aboard the ark.

The steady fall of rain and the sodden grass had soaked her through to the skin, so before she entered the wood, Mottyl sat on the broken fence where Michael Archangelis had slain the Dragon, and she began to dry herself — using her paw to press the water from her coat.

Looking down at her from their cottonwood tree, Bip and Ringer were not too certain it really was Mottyl. She seemed so ridiculously small.

"Is it you, Mottyl?" Bip came sliding down one of the reedier branches — showering everything below with a rain of soaking leaves.

"Bip?"

"Why aren't you at home?"

Mottyl did not explain about her flight from Doctor Noyes. Her whole concern was to get her friends to board the ark.

She told Bip and Ringer about the animals being taken on two-by-two and that she was certain there were no ring-tailed lemurs yet and that Bip and Ringer must save themselves by going to the ark as quickly as possible.

Bip was dubious. "It's only a rainfall. Admittedly, the worst we've ever seen. But that drought was also the worst we'd ever seen so you'd expect it to rain like this."

"No." Mottyl was adamant. "You won't survive this, believe me. Something dreadful is happening."

Ringer swung down to join them. "What? What's dreadful?"

Mottyl debated telling them about the imminent death of Yaweh — and the pact that had been made between Him and Doctor Noyes to destroy the world. But the pact was only suspected — a rumour — and the ark was real — and the rain was real and tangible — and these could be understood.

Finally, she told Bip and Ringer that if they got on board the ark and she was wrong — then all they had to do was get off. But, if she was right, they'd already be on board and safe when the disaster struck.

"What about you?" Bip wanted to know.

"I'm waiting," Mottyl lied. "I'll be up in time. I have to do one or two other things first."

"Give birth to your kittens?"

"Maybe. Maybe not."

Bip looked at Ringer. He did not like the sound of *maybe not*.

"Are you all right?" Ringer, too, was concerned for Mottyl. "Are you in trouble?"

"No. Not in trouble. Yes. I'm all right. But you two won't be if you don't go — *now* — to the ark."

Finally, though against their will ("we'd rather wait for you") — Bip and Ringer agreed to go up the Hill.

∞ The wood had become the focus of almost everyone's wandering: a haven for every kind of animal refugee in every kind of condition — a roosting place for the birds — a hiding place for the injured and a marketplace for the predatory. Marsh animals — field animals — river animals — domestic animals — every one of them out of place — moved in. Hunters and prey; hosts and parasites; a whole variety of birds and beasts and insects — all in competition for the same food — prowled through the twilight. Every berry, every succulent leaf, every frog and every mouse was being destroyed. Squirrels, rabbits, monkeys, moles and a dozen kinds of birds could find no place to hide — and their cries were everywhere — and the stench of blood and offal.

Yet — even potential victims could not bring themselves to abandon the wood. It was as if the trees — and the trees alone — were salvation.

Mottyl, having said farewell to Bip and Ringer, entered the wood, though cautiously, without alarm. Her experience of blindness gave her a kind of doggedness when it came to surviving in the wood. She had had much practice here — and she made for her objective with her head down and her shoulders pushed forward. Her destination was the tree not far from the furthest edge, near the road — where Crowe had her nest. If anyone could help her, Crowe could. And Crowe would. They had not been friends for nothing all these years. There had been so many favours and exchanges of food and warnings. And what Mottyl needed now, above all, were Crowe's eyes and Crowe's nest.

And she was so hungry. Not being very large, the eggs had only whetted her appetite.

Stepping forward, claws retracted, her babies swaying in her belly, Mottyl set out — determined that if all she could find on the way was insects, she would eat them.

Faeries scattered before her — squealing. Their wood had been invaded by so many strangers they did not know where to hide. Some had already perished — while others were so weakened they could barely lift themselves from the ground. All their traditional food — the honeys and the resins normally so plentiful — had been depleted and the wood had become, in that sense, a wasteland for them. Mottyl encountered at least three groups who were so exhausted and enfeebled by hunger she had to walk around them. They could no longer move.

∞ It was such a curious time for Mrs Noyes — what with her being so utterly alone, losing track of the days, feeding entirely on apples and sleeping in the trees. But she did have moments — wandering through the fields or walking along some trackless path — when she felt that civilization was falling away from her shoulders, and she was gratified. What a burden it had been! "You bet it was!" (She spoke aloud to the birds). Carrying all that *behaviour* — all those strictures: "sir" and "madam" — bowing and scraping and kissing hands — falling down and rising up on cue. Using knives and spoons and plates in the proper order — putting up one's hair and wearing caps and scarves and veils to cover this and that and the other so the gentlemen wouldn't be corrupted — and having it all torn away whenever your husband felt like taking his pleasure. The oppression of time — the daily ritual of violence — all that prayer and blood and wine — and the dreariness of protocol: having to ask permission to speak and touch and move. And the lies . . . and the empty smiles . . . and the hidden jars of gin. . . .

One morning, Mrs Noyes lifted up her skirts and — squatting in full view of the windows of an abandoned carriage — she peed.

How wonderful that was!

Just to squat there, knees apart, thighs and pudenda exposed to the rain — and the sweet relief of watering the
grass . . .

. . . as if the grass needed watering . . .

Then — suddenly — Mrs Noyes scurried to her feet and threw
down the hems of her skirts. She even felt her hand — unbid-
den — rising to touch her hair and adjust the closing at her
neck.

There was someone there.

Walking . . .

Mrs Noyes laid her arm against her forehead, attempting to
prevent the rain from sliding into her eyes.

A figure, stooping — standing — was moving beyond the river
on the farther side.

Mrs Noyes almost called out. She almost waved. She almost ran down the Hill. But she didn't. She stopped just in
time and stood stock-still.

Maybe what was there was dangerous.

What could it be? . . . Or who?

Did it seem so small because it was so far away — or was it
an animal . . . a dwarf . . . a child?

An illusion? Someone's ghost? Her mother? . . .

"Oh! My mother . . ."

Mrs Noyes rubbed her eyes.

But no. It was not her mother's ghost and not an illusion.
There was really someone there. A person.

∞ The river was greatly swollen and the current had become so swift that even the largest objects were being swept
downstream — whole trees and farm carts and signposts and
public notices from the distant Cities: MARKET STREET and
PROCLAMATION: BE IT KNOWN THAT . . .

The person — whoever it was — was obviously trying to cross
and could find no way. The shallows that had once been there
at the widest part of the bend were now a deep-running cataract.
Up and down the bank the person went — wading out from
time to time and then hurrying back, afraid. Mrs Noyes remained on her hillside, watching — though she took a few

involuntary steps towards the flats and dragged her aprons of apples with her.

From what she could tell — though the mists made it very hard to see or to be certain — the figure must be that of a dwarf. Its legs were extremely short. It could also be a child, Mrs Noyes decided, taking a few more involuntary steps. Now, without being at all aware of it, Mrs Noyes had come to the lower reaches of the hillside and with every new perception of the figure by the river's edge, she moved towards it as if drawn by a magnet. It certainly wore what appeared to be a child's dress: slightly torn and made of pale cotton. The dress had little puff sleeves and a flounce around the bottom — and a soft, white collar. Quite a pretty dress, in fact, and it had a wide blue sash with a bow at the back.

A disturbing memory had begun to take shape in Mrs Noyes's mind as she watched the figure and the slow, patient process of the journeys it was making back and forth from the river's edge . . . the way it stared at the water . . . the way it bent down—ungainly—to touch it, as if to verify it was really there . . . and then the moving backward — the slow, almost sad deliberation as it scanned the stones and reckoned what way the stones might help her . . .

Her.

Lotte.

It was Lotte. Emma's sister.

Mrs Noyes ran, dropping both the apple aprons, lifting her skirts in order to speed more quickly over the grass and over the road and over the stones.

Dear God — it was Lotte. Alone.

∞ Lotte was Emma's older sister — though none of the Noyes had ever known how old that was. All they knew was that Emma had been eleven when she was married to Japeth — and that had been, roughly speaking, a year ago. But Lotte's age was not important. Not her physical age, at any rate. It was her mental age that mattered—and that had been gauged as *"anywhere between two and nil"* when Noah had described her, although her own parents never spoke of her that way.

Lotte's parents loved her — for all that it was dangerous to love such a child. Her existence had to be kept a secret and they had made a life for her apart from the lives of their other children — apart from everyone. Mrs Noyes knew all about such things since, many years before, she too had had such a child as Lotte — and had done what most people did in that event.

She had killed it.

∞ Sometimes, if you did not kill it yourself, other people came and killed it for you. This was the rule — though not the law. The law said nothing about such matters — perhaps because the law assumed that anyone civilized knew the rules. Mrs Noyes had briefly disobeyed the rules and had allowed her forbidden child to live, as Lotte was allowed to live, and the results had been tragic. She had come to love the child in its short, short life — and that was her downfall. Mrs Noyes had never forgotten her unwelcome baby — her pariah — nor how it was she had lost it. As a consequence, she had both applauded Lotte's parents for their bravery in keeping her and had worried for them (mourned would be more apt) because there was no avoiding the destiny of such a child.

∞ Mrs Noyes could recall the very first time she had been aware of Lotte.

One evening — months before Japeth and Emma's wedding — months before they were betrothed — Mrs Noyes had gone to the river searching for crayfish in the twilight. Mottyl had been with her. This had been in the springtime, perhaps, or very early summer. All the trees beyond the river at the forest's edge had been lit with pale young leaves and the smell of them — and the smell of their sweet, oozing resin had filled the air. The evening, along with its bird song and lemur chatter, its mist and its pale orange light, had seemed enchanted. Mrs Noyes had carried a lantern as well as her pail — though the lantern need not be lit till later. She could not, she supposed, be seen too clearly, with her skirts hoisted high and her sandals thrown far back behind her on the stones, because the light was all on the farther shore and she was stooping down at the water's edge. She was lifting pebbles, trying not to scare the crayfish, and her fingers were in the river, when a shadow — or a reflection — caught her attention . . . people walking upside down in the water . . . and the sound of laughter.

Looking up, Mrs Noyes had seen her then for the very first time. Lotte — with the woodsman and his wife — and she thought they were walking a pet. Until she saw the "pet" was wearing a dress.

The three of them were strolling — ambling — dawdling in the evening light — much as Mrs Noyes liked to do — each of the parents holding one of Lotte's hands — and Mrs Noyes had stood transfixed, because she saw in this image the kind of wonder and happiness that she had put behind her — denied herself, and her child, by consenting to its murder.

∞ Mrs Noyes pressed forward through the mist — the child in her eye, moving between the past and the present. *Shout, why don't you? Maybe she'll hear you. . . .*

No. It would frighten her.

Mrs Noyes stumbled for the hundredth time and fell to her knees on the grass where it verged on the flooding river. It occurred to her, kneeling back and sitting on her heels, that her body was getting sick of pain and bruises.

"Damn it all — it hurts to fall down," she said out loud.

Someone heard her — and there was a sheet of noise, moving off through the grass.

Faeries? By the river? It was unheard of. They never went to the river. They could be caught in the slightest current and swept away.

Were they climbing on her?

Mrs Noyes touched the wetted folds on her skirts and her aprons very carefully with her aching fingers — and felt inside her pockets. But all she found was her bits of soiled rag and the usual collection of torn lace caps and bits of string. . . . She also brushed her shoulders — but she found no Faeries.

None.

Nevertheless, she was certain they were near her and she

spoke to them. "You shouldn't be here," she said—not quite sure where to say it. "It's dangerous. . . ."

There was another sheet of noise — moving to her left and coming parallel with her squatting figure, about eight paces distant. Mrs Noyes addressed them directly, using her "mother-tone" and glad, for a change, that she had almost lost her voice. Human voices of certain kinds — and every voice, if raised — could blast the Faeries like a hurricane and lift them into the trees. Mrs Noyes remembered the last time she had shouted at the Faeries—when they flew up over the house and made the forbidden sign for *infinity*, which—later—Lucy had told her was a warning: *time is not what you think it is. Beware.* Now, it was Mrs Noyes's turn to warn the Faeries.

"You should go back across the road and into the woods where you belong and where you'll be safe," she said. "The river is deadly."

She could see them now—which is to say, she could see the impression where they stood and it was clearly a very large congregation—maybe even a whole community: hundreds of them, covering at least a square yard of sodden grass. The noise approached her—trickling forward: not very much of it. Perhaps they were sending a delegation. The sound they made was like crystals forming—glass noises "very like wind chimes" as Mrs Noyes had once said to Hannah, who had never seen or heard the Faeries. "Wind chimes—but not . . ." Mrs Noyes had such a difficult time describing it. The sound was unique.

"Yes?" Mrs Noyes addressed the ground and sat very straight on her heels and drew her shawl around her shoulders. "You mustn't climb on me," she said. "I'm about to be dangerous. I'm going across the river to get that child over there — and you'd drown."

There was a conference somewhere down by her hip.

Mrs Noyes — waiting — peered through the mists at Lotte, who was still walking up and down the opposite shore. Her dress was soaking wet. Perhaps she had made an attempt to cross the river while Mrs Noyes was being distracted by the Faeries.

"Tell me quickly what you want of me," she said.

There was a murmur in the grass and then Mrs Noyes felt a shiver passing over her skin. She was being boarded — like the ark — and the delegation was climbing up her thigh and onto her arm. . . .

"But—I'm going through the river," she protested, frightened for them. "Don't you understand — you will *die*. . . ." Then she thought; why aren't they flying? What can be the matter with them? Maybe they were sick. . . . "I'm going to have to swim," she said. "Don't you understand?" But all of her protestations were to no avail. The delegation was moving up past her elbow and crossing the folds of her shawl towards her shoulders. She could feel them pausing there — and she waited, motionless.

There was a signal given then — a sort of glassy shouting — and Mrs Noyes saw that the grass was rippling — and she heard a surge of Faerie noise. They were pouring towards her — all of them — running to join the others on her shoulder.

"Hurry, then —" she said. "If you insist on crossing over, you must hurry. That child won't wait — and neither will I."

She could feel them — hundreds of them — pressing forward onto her thigh and up her side and onto her arm and over the shawl, just as the others had done and she cautioned them not to hide in her pockets, however comfortable and safe they might appear. "Those are going underwater," she said.

When it seemed that all the Faeries were "aboard," she said; "I'm going to get up now. Hold on. . . ." And she staggered to her feet. The weight of them was not very great, but it did throw her slightly off balance. She could feel them moving over her shoulder towards her neck and some were already clinging to her hair.

"I'm moving forward now," she said. "I'm stepping forward. . . ."

And she did — and as she moved, the Faeries clambered into her hair and tied themselves down.

∞ The river was warm — as the rain was warm — but the shallows that had once been there were now as deep as Mrs

Noyes's knees and then, very quickly, deep as her thighs, her waist, her breast. . . . Midstream — or not quite midstream — she realized she had made a terrible mistake in not having called to Lotte earlier, since now — because of the Faeries in her hair — she could not call at all. The loudness of her voice would tumble them. She could only . . .

Pray she almost thought, that Lotte will not be afraid when she sees me coming.

But I will not pray: not to You, gone mad up there with Your vengeance. I will never pray to You again. I will pray to anyone — to anything — I will pray . . .

To the river.

Yes.

Dear River — please — allow me through to the other side. I crave your mercy and I beg your pardon — that I should trespass here. But there is a child — and the child is frightened of you — and she wants — she needs to be taken to the other side. And only I can take her — please — allow me to pass. . . . Amen.

And — oh, yes — I beg your mercy, too, on these frightened creatures who travel with me.

There was a singing noise in her hair as if the Faeries had heard her prayer and she felt them holding faster, pressing into her scalp as she reached the very centre of the river — and the very worst of its current.

For a dreadful moment, Mrs Noyes could feel her feet being swept away from beneath her and she turned upstream and pressed against the current, moving — crablike — sideways.

∞ Lotte was watching now, from the shore — having climbed to the top of the bank. She was staring through the rain, with her hands on top of her head, and it seemed that — perhaps — she had recognized Mrs Noyes because she was waiting and hadn't turned to run away.

"Dear River, please . . ." Mrs Noyes prayed aloud.

And the Faeries whispered, praying too, perhaps. And if not praying — then they had best learn quickly.

Mrs Noyes's clothes were swollen with water — billowing now in the current — dragging at her — pulling her downstream.

And she turned again, with her arms above the river, but only just — reaching out for the other side — while Lotte watched. *"Oh, please — don't let a child see me drown. . . ."*

Mrs Noyes leaned against the river's weight and pushed with all her remaining strength until, by slow degrees, she felt the depths receding. Her armpits and breastbone had broken through the surface and then her breasts emerged and the weight began to shift, until it was all around her waist and she was thinking she was safe — that she had arrived on the other side and was alive — when, all at once, she sank and was submerged.

The Faeries will be drowned! Oh, Yaweh — you bastard!

She beat her way to the surface — flailing against the dragging weight of the depths below her — some sort of pit. Desperately, she tried to find the bottom with her toes, but it evaded her.

At last, with her strength departing through her arms and legs and her lungs about to fill with water — coughing and spluttering and dying for certain, Mrs Noyes felt her heels go down on solid rock. The pit was behind her.

∞ She had to drag herself ashore, using the branches of river shrubs as handles — praying to the shrubs; *"please hold!"* And, with a final heave, she was lying on the clay above the water mark, with her arms outstretched and her hands in the flattened weeds.

Lotte put her fingers in her mouth and stared.

Mrs Noyes looked up and saw her — and a great, wide smile showed all of Lotte's teeth as, very slowly, she began to bob up and down with pleasure.

Mrs Noyes crawled forward over the clay and weeds and rocks until she felt she had the strength to stand. Once standing, she cautioned Lotte to be silent and she raised her fingers to her hair.

"Are you there? Are you there?" she whispered to the Faeries.

At first, it seemed there would be no reply, but then — very slowly — there was a stirring, which tickled, and a ripple of sound: very faint.

Mrs Noyes moved further up the bank and went as close as she dared to the trees, the sight of which caused great excitement on her scalp.

"Do you want me to let you down on the ground?" said Mrs Noyes. "The trees could be dangerous, you know. This is the forest, not the wood."

The answer was a tug at nearly every hair on her head.

"Very well — I shall kneel right here and let you off."

Mrs Noyes knelt down and lowered her head, as if in prayer, until it touched the earth. All the Faeries rushed forward, crying and singing, until they stood before her on the grass. Mrs Noyes raised her head and looked at them. Lotte came and stood beside her — putting out her hand to have it held. She seemed to understand the Faeries were there because she, too, was staring at the ground in front of Mrs Noyes, where the weeds were depressed — and extra wet.

"Goodbye," said Mrs Noyes. "Goodbye — and I wish you well. . . ."

There was a swelling sound of chiming: very glasslike — very definite: a cheer!

Thank you.

Mrs Noyes nodded and rose, still holding Lotte's hand. The earth before them was swept with a wide departing sheet of Faerie noise — and they were gone.

But they were not gone far. As if their ordeal in the river had magically restored their powers, the Faeries made for the giant trees, whose oozings of amber resin were apparently the staff of life. Some of the Faeries even managed to fly — though their flights were brief and barely carried them off the ground.

They were climbing now — flittering, struggling up towards the sticky flows of resin, and once they had reached them, there was such excitement and feasting it was tantamount to a riot — almost to an orgy. Somehow, the resin would save them — that was obvious: the same way the apples had saved Mrs

Noyes. And Mrs Noyes wondered how it was she had paid so little attention to the trees in her life.

∞ Lotte began to chatter and cry. She had been so long alone by the river that she had despaired of anyone coming to save her.

"Where are your parents?" said Mrs Noyes.

Lotte fell silent.

"Have they gone away to the City?"

Lotte shook her head and looked at her feet.

"Are they at home?"

Lotte again shook her head and did not look at Mrs Noyes.

"Did you run away?" (No.) "Does anyone know where you are?" (Maybe.) "Are you meant to wait here for someone?" (Not really. No.) "Lotte. Tell me the absolute truth. . . ." Mrs Noyes bit her lip before posing the final question. She was afraid she already knew the answer—and didn't want the answer confirmed. Nonetheless—the question had to be asked. "Did they leave you here? . . ."

Lotte put her arms behind her back and scuffed the ground with her feet while she pursed her lips and thought of the answer.

"Lotte . . . ? Tell me."

Lotte looked up. Her eyes were full of tears.

"Did they leave you?"

Yes.

Mrs Noyes ran across the space between them and threw herself on her knees before the child and embraced her. "Never mind. Never mind," she said. "I'm going to take you through the river. I'm going to take you through the river and up that Hill . . . do you see where I mean?" She pointed and Lotte looked. "We'll go up the Hill together and we'll be safe. I promise you. I promise you. All right?"

Lotte nodded and put her arms around Mrs Noyes's neck. Mrs Noyes kissed her and stood up, still holding her. She looked at the river — wider already and deeper than when she had crossed only minutes before. "I'm really quite good at crossing rivers and saving people's lives. . . ." She tried to laugh for Lotte's sake. "I just saved all those Faeries. Did you see them? Hundreds of them."

Lotte nodded. She was fiddling—playing with Mrs Noyes's dress — lifting the drawstrings up from the neck and sucking on them.

"What I want you to do," said Mrs Noyes; "is climb up onto my shoulders and hang on tight. All right?"

Lotte nodded.

"Up you go, then."

Mrs Noyes hoisted Lotte onto her back and started down the bank.

"Don't be afraid. . . ."

∞ The first thing they saw when they went down the bank was a large group of sheep, all dead, being swept downstream.

Further out, there was a great, flat corpse that could not be identified — slowly turning in the heavy current — a corpse so large that it pushed a whole collection of debris before it — broken chairs and a china cabinet; someone's shoes and a sunhat.

Mrs Noyes stepped back. Something — perhaps a human hand — had touched her ankle very lightly beneath the surface. She could not risk taking Lotte out in that; the child would be terrified beyond reason. She was already screaming and pounding Mrs Noyes's shoulder in protest.

No.

There would have to be another way to cross.

The nearest bridge was leagues away. They could never hope to reach it by nightfall.

Mrs Noyes set Lotte down on the ground and kept a firm grip on her hand.

"Don't be afraid. . . ." she muttered. "I won't make you go through the water. What I'm looking for is some way to make a bridge. . . ."

Lotte at once looked knowingly at the trees. Her father and her brothers, after all, had been woodsmen. Many trees must have been felled in Lotte's presence. Perhaps many bridges made. But how was Mrs Noyes, without an axe, to accomplish such a feat? It was impossible. Push?

Nevertheless, she went to inspect the trees to see if any of them were "pushable" — and while she was doing this, her back was to the river. Lotte's back, however, was not to the river — and after a moment she began to tug very hard at Mrs Noyes's sleeve.

Finally, Mrs Noyes turned and looked and there on the river there was a miracle: a man in a rowboat.

"Hello!" she called.

The man did not hear her.

Mrs Noyes, clutched at by Lotte, ran to the river's edge and called again; *"hallo!"*

Still, the man did not respond.

Perhaps he was deaf. Perhaps, on the river itself, the sound of the rushing waters was louder than it was on shore.

Mrs Noyes waved.

Nothing.

The man was alone in the rowboat — and seated right at the centre with the oars in his hands. He seemed to be bending to his task, though there was mighty little strength in his efforts. The rowboat in fact had begun to turn round and round in the eddies and was slowly making its way closer to the shore.

Mrs Noyes took a longer, closer look at the man in the boat — leaning far out to do so. . . .

Then she made a decision.

"You must wait here, Lotte. Promise not to budge an inch. I'm going out to help the nice man get his boat to shore. Then, we can row to the other side. Won't that be wonderful? . . ."

Mrs Noyes was already slipping and sliding down the embankment and submerging herself waist high in the horrors of the water. Something kept touching her — pulling at her — slapping at her beneath the surface, but she grimly kicked whatever it was away and ignored it.

Reaching the boat was relatively simple. It had drifted very close and all she had to do was grasp it by the stern and give it a yank.

As soon as she did this, the man fell all the way forward over his oars. *I'll say that he's asleep*, Mrs Noyes was already deciding. *I'll simply move him to the bow and tell her the poor man wore himself out rowing down from the Cities.*

He was obviously a City man, with very fine clothes and manicured fingernails. He could not have been dead very long — because his body was still quite pliant as Mrs Noyes shifted him up to the bows and arranged him — head down — in a decent, curled up position — with his arms folded.

Heart attack, she decided. *Lucky.*

"Come along, Lotte. Here we go!"

∞ Lotte sat cringing in the stern while Mrs Noyes, facing her, rowed. Luckily, Mrs Noyes's bulk effectively hid the boat's owner from the child's view. Lotte seemed to have accepted utterly the tale of over-exertion and tiredness.

Mrs Noyes tried not to look at the water, but only at the opposite shore as she turned, from time to time, to peer over her shoulder.

There were no more sheep — and that was a blessing. There were, however, many objects — the most startling of which was someone's washline, replete with a family's clothing still attached and waving from the muddy waters: mother, father, children, babes . . .

∞ When they reached the other side Mrs Noyes explained to Lotte that the dozing gentleman ("doesn't he look the picture of comfort?") would probably prefer to continue his journey, even though he slept. Surely, he would waken by the time he reached his destination — and to let him go on was the only proper thing to do.

"Goodbye," she said. "Go in peace." And she gently pushed the rowboat back towards the centre of the torrent. In moments it was gone, and with it, their unwitting saviour.

∞ After they had eaten some apples, Mrs Noyes and Lotte — hand in hand — went up the Hill.

"Don't be afraid."

∞ Emma was trotted out and made to stand with Doctor Noyes and Hannah beneath the black umbrella, looking down from the deck of the ark.

Seeing Lotte, Emma gasped. She was afraid. Lotte was a secret and, long ago, Emma had been made to swear she would never tell of Lotte's existence. Now — here she was in full view of everyone. In spite of her joy at seeing her sister, Emma wanted to hide. But Hannah pushed her back into place and Doctor Noyes restrained her with his hand on the back of her neck.

"Are you sure," said Mrs Noyes—addressing her husband — "that what I have to say is something Hannah should hear?"

Noah was thrown by this. He had guessed there would be a trick to Mrs Noyes's gambit, but he hadn't thought it would be a trick below the belt. He considered for a moment what sort of damage might be done if Hannah were to stay. There had been such a firm understanding between himself and his wife that nothing should ever be said about the subject of Lotte and . . . other Lotte-like children. He could not believe Mrs Noyes truly meant to betray their secret. And yet— she was fighting for her life, and Lotte's — and that could only mean she was fighting with no holds barred.

He nodded and turned to Hannah.

"Go in," he said. "I will call you when this is over."

It took a good deal of self-control for Hannah to overcome her curiosity and to force a civil "*yes, sir*" in reply. She handed the black umbrella grudgingly to Emma and said to her; "just remember how much there is to do. When this is over, I'll expect you in the galley."

Emma got out her handkerchief (a rag) and blew her nose as she took the umbrella in her other hand. Doctor Noyes let go of her neck and she stood beside him meekly, hoping that whatever was about to happen might end happily.

After Hannah was safely out of earshot, Doctor Noyes looked down at his wife and at Lotte and said; "very well. Let me hear what you have to say. But remember . . . Emma is here to say goodbye to her sister—not to listen to a song and dance." He adjusted his robes and heaved a great sigh and then said; "I assume you hope to strike a bargain. Well . . ."

"There will be no bargain," said Mrs Noyes. "I intend to come on board — and Lotte is coming with me."

"Dream away," said Doctor Noyes. "It isn't going to happen."

"Oh yes, it is. Because if it doesn't, I shall tell Emma why she was really chosen as Japeth's wife. . . ."

"Go right ahead and tell her," said Noah.

Mrs Noyes was taken aback by this, but she tried not to show it. Instead, she gave a sort of laugh and waved the suggestion aside. "You can't be serious," she said. "You can't really want it known."

"I said; 'go ahead and tell her,' didn't I?"

"Yes. But . . ."

"Go ahead and tell her."

Mrs Noyes — perturbed — gripped Lotte's hand a little harder and then coughed before she spoke again. When she did speak — it was to Emma.

"I'm sorry to have to tell you this," she began. "It doesn't seem fair. You and I have had our own differences — but I love you, Em — and I have to say that before I begin."

The effect of this was instantaneous silence. Even Doctor Noyes was impressed. Emma was listening with sober interest and, obviously, a respect for his wife he had not known existed.

Mrs Noyes continued — having to raise her voice only to be heard above the rain.

"You've always been taught to believe," she said to Emma; "that yours was the only family to have a Lotte-child. Well, that simply isn't true. Other people have them, too — including (she looked at him almost tenderly) . . . Doctor Noyes and me. We had a Lotte-child. Eighteen years ago."

Emma was alarmed — but silent. It was true: she had always been told that Lotte was unique — and never to be spoken of. Other people would not understand. . . . She stared at Mrs Noyes and then at Lotte, whom she adored — and then at Doctor Noyes, who turned away.

"Something you may or may not know," said Mrs Noyes;

"is that, years ago, the Doctor and I had a whole other family. Lots and lots of children — ten of them, in fact. But all of them died. There was a plague, you see — and that killed six of them. Six wonderful children — dead, like that.''

Doctor Noyes shot her an irritated look and said; "get on with it.''

Mrs Noyes said; "the other four children died for other reasons: accidents, fevers, animals. It took a very long while for Doctor Noyes and me to recover from all those deaths. We loved our children very much. . . .''

"Get *on* with it, madam!''

Mrs Noyes coughed. And then she said; "in time, we began again. Other children. More. A whole new family. Shem was the first of these children — and, for a while, the only one to live. We had — I don't remember — two or three more who died. Then Ham. And then . . .''

Doctor Noyes himself gave a cough; very sharp and sudden.

"You don't want me to tell?" said Mrs Noyes.

Doctor Noyes waved her on — and looked askance at space.

"When Japeth was born . . .'' Mrs Noyes began — but she got no further.

Emma — who had been looking concentrated, with a furrowed brow, and whose fingers had been moving over the handle of the umbrella, counting — suddenly shouted; *"eighteen!"*

Mrs Noyes waited.

"Japeth is eighteen,'' said Emma.

Mrs Noyes nodded. Lotte was fidgetting and she picked her up and held her under the shawl, with her head exposed beneath her chin.

A wild, crazy look of incomprehension came into Emma's eyes. "But you said this other Lotte-child was born eighteen years ago. . . .''

Mrs Noyes didn't even bother to nod this time. She let Emma have her say.

"Are . . . are you telling me that . . . ?'' But — no. It was impossible. Japeth was not like Lotte. "I don't understand,'' Emma finally said, completely flummoxed.

"Japeth had a twin,'' said Mrs Noyes.

Silence.

"Oh, dear," said Emma, hushed. "You mean he had a twin like Lotte?"

"That's right."

More silence — and then; "Oh, dear," again.

Mrs Noyes addressed her husband. "You still want me to go on?"

Noah grunted. "Finish," he said. "Get it over with."

"Well," said Mrs Noyes to Emma; "this is where you come into the picture. You and Lotte."

Emma narrowed her gaze. She was deeply suspicious, now, and wondering what on earth could be coming next.

"It was me, I'm afraid, who saw Lotte first," said Mrs Noyes. "And — like a fool — I could not contain myself. It was just so wonderful to see another child — after all that time — who was just like Japeth's brother . . ."

"Where *is* Japeth's brother?" said Emma, looking over her shoulder as if he might be there.

"I'll tell you that in a moment. But first I have to explain about you and Lotte. Otherwise you won't understand what happened to Japeth's brother — and, God knows, perhaps you shouldn't understand."

Noah winced at God's name. It was automatic.

"The thing is," said Mrs Noyes; "when I saw her — Lotte — I ran up the Hill — I was so excited — I ran up the Hill and all the way home and blurted it out to Noah; 'there's *another!*' I said. 'Another . . .'"

Noah cut her off, furious; "that baby didn't have a name!"

"Yes — he did," said Mrs Noyes. "You know damn well he did. His name was Adam."

"Stop that!"

"His name was Adam," said Mrs Noyes. "And — seeing Lotte, I had seen my Adam again and I told you! I told you . . ." She waited a second to regain her composure. "Well . . . I should not have told him. I should have kept it a secret, the way your mother and father wanted it kept a secret. But I'd seen them by the river — walking — with Lotte in between. And they looked so happy . . . No. Not happy. Sad.

Sad. And my heart went out — and my heart was broken and
I thought how wonderful it was that someone else had the courage and the pride . . . the love, that allowed them to keep
such a child. And I thought: Noah deserves to know there is
another. He deserves to know that other people let such children live. That we are wrong. *WRONG!"* she shouted at
Noah. "Wrong!"

He turned away — mute.

Emma waited — guessing, perhaps, what had happened to
Adam — but still not knowing what it had to do with her and
her marriage to Japeth.

Mrs Noyes told her.

"I should not have told Doctor Noyes," she said. "I'll never
forgive myself — and I'm sorry. I had forgotten who he was.
And . . ." She paused. "I'm sorry — because Lotte is why
you were chosen for Japeth's wife. When Noah heard about
Lotte — at first he was afraid. The appearance of other children
like our own might mean that someone would remember —
even though he knew there was no one who *could* remember.
No one but me — and, of course, himself . . . But he thought
about Lotte all one night: all one night — he thought about Lotte.
And the next morning came — and I knew very well he hadn't
slept — and he came into the kitchen and he said to me; 'you
know these people with this child?' And I said; 'of course, I
do. He brings my wood. She tats my lace.' And I asked him
why he wanted to know. And he said; 'never you mind . . .'
Never you mind. Dear God — I should never forgive you," she
said to Noah. Then, to Emma; "we went down then — and he
asked to see your father's daughters — knowing, of course,
that Lotte would not be produced. But that didn't matter. What
he wanted to know was . . . did there happen to be, by any
chance, a daughter of marriageable age for Japeth — our son?
And there you were."

"Why?" said Emma. "Why?"

"It's all too simple, really," said Mrs Noyes. "Going down
the Hill and crossing the river, he told me all about it: this great
scheme of his — this *plot*. If Japeth — whose twin had been like
Lotte — could be married to a girl whose parents had produced a

child like our Adam — then the blame for future Lottes and Adams could not be laid on us: on Noah Noyes and his wife — on the confidant of Yaweh — on the true inheritor of Old Adam's name. And, since Japeth would be the most likely to produce a Lotte-child — an Adam-child — then Lotte's sister, Emma, must be courted and caught at all costs. So — when a child is born — it will be *yours* — not Japeth's. Your blood, not his: your ancestry . . . your blame . . . your fault . . . your responsibility. And yours to do what must be done.''

Emma shook. She could not contain the tears, though she did contain the cries that wanted to emerge — both of fear and of confusion. ''What? . . . What do you mean — 'what must be done'?'' she said.

''What we did to Adam . . . what your parents refused to do to Lotte.''

Emma stared.

Mrs Noyes closed her eyes and held Lotte close. The child was almost asleep, and she rocked her back and forth a little before she spoke again. ''We killed him,'' she said. ''I did. . . .'' She looked at Noah. ''We did.''

Rain.

And the unposed question: how?

Mrs Noyes looked down at Lotte and placed her hand across her ears. ''We drowned him,'' she said. ''Not down there in the river. It wasn't deep enough then. We drowned him in the pond. None of the others knew. . . . Japeth was just a baby; one day old. And Shem and Ham . . . were sent away. So they never saw him. And none of them know to this day.'' Mrs Noyes was looking, now, at Noah . . . ''unless, of course, Emma tells.''

Doctor Noyes's posture was noticeably affected. He slumped.

''She only has to blurt it out once . . . and all your well laid plans go down the drain. Though, I'm sure — if Lotte was aboard, there'd be nothing for Emma to say. And when such a child arrives, as it may — or may not — then the cause will be self-evident. That's my bargain, Noah. And I trust that Emma will enter into the bargain, too, for Lotte's sake. . . .''

''Yes,'' said Emma. ''Yes. I will.'' (She didn't quite grasp it, yet. But she knew enough to know that whatever she was saying yes to would save Lotte's life and that was all that mattered.) "Oh, yes," she said. "I will. . . ."

Doctor Noyes had still not spoken.

Now he looked down at his wife — and finally he said; "very well. You win, madam. You may bring the child aboard."

Mrs Noyes could not believe her ears. She had not expected victory.

"Aboard?" she said.

"That's right," said Noah. "Bring her aboard — but not below, for the moment. You must give me time to go and tell our sons. I must find some excuse to have waived the Edict." He looked almost tenderly at Lotte, fully asleep now in his wife's arms. "I will say there has been a death. They will understand. I will say there has been a death and . . . that this *child* (he gave the word a twist of distaste — almost of abhorrence) . . . is being allowed on board as a . . ."

"Surrogate," said Mrs Noyes, helpfully.

"Yes, yes. A surrogate. They will understand. They will *have* to understand."

Having had his say, Doctor Noyes became brisk — and his posture straightened, perhaps in anticipation of his confrontation with his sons — and he took the black umbrella out of Emma's hands and retreated with it to the portal beneath the awning. "I shall only be a moment," he said. "In the meantime, you may bring her aboard."

He disappeared into the dark beyond the portal and Emma burst into tears of joy.

"Shhh . . . shhh . . . shhh," said Mrs Noyes. "We mustn't wake her now. Let her sleep — and when she wakens — she will be safe inside."

Emma beamed with pleasure and blew her nose and wiped her eyes and went across the deck to the opening where the gangplank was.

Mrs Noyes — who felt like a whole parade of triumph — marched through the mud and puddles and, holding Lotte firmly to her breast, she started up the gangplank. If only Mottyl was there, there'd be nothing left to win — and even the horrors of the impending flood would be acceptable.

As she crossed the threshold and stood — at last where she had thought she would never stand — aboard the ark, with its deck beneath her feet — she kissed the top of Lotte's head and whispered to her; "safe, at last. You're safe, at last — as I promised."

She should have known better.

∞ When Noah returned to the deck, his wife and his daughter-in-law were huddled together beneath the awning and the child was still asleep in Mrs Noyes's arms. But it was not his sons who came with him. It was the seemingly ubiquitous Hannah, who was carrying a woollen blanket and smiling.

"The poor little creature will be soaking wet," she said to Mrs Noyes, as she crossed the deck. "Let me take her from you and warm her in this blanket."

"No," said Mrs Noyes. "I prefer to hold her myself."

Hannah turned to Doctor Noyes for support. But he seemed unperturbed. Perhaps he had expected as much.

"Where are Shem and Ham and Japeth?" said Mrs Noyes. "And Lucy? Where are they?"

"Below," said Doctor Noyes, dismissing even the thought of them. "I had thought you would be glad of the blanket, madam. A very thoughtful gesture on Hannah's part — and not to be rejected. I would have thought — under the circumstances . . ."

He was looking at his wife in such a way as to tell her their ploy would not work if she did not hand over the child.

"Do let her take the little thing," he said, with cloying sweetness. "Sister Hannah is, after all, about to be a mother. The practice will do her good. . . ." He smiled at his senior daughter-in-law.

Hannah smiled back.

Mrs Noyes, who was never quite certain of Hannah's motives — especially when she smiled — nonetheless felt compelled to do as she was asked.

Very tenderly and carefully, she released the child's arms from her neck and kissed her and held her out towards Hannah and the blanket.

Hannah's mouth fell open.

"But — she's wearing a dress!" she said.

Her surprise at this discovery seemed to be quite genuine. But Mrs Noyes was too involved in her attempt not to wake the child to do more than say; "be quiet. We must let her sleep. . . ."

"Of course," said Hannah — and accepted Lotte into the blanket, folding it over the still sleeping child with what, to Mrs Noyes, was an even more curious statement than the others she had made since laying eyes on Lotte. "I never thought they could be so lovable," Hannah said. Surely a strange thing for a pregnant woman to say of a child.

Hannah stepped towards the portal and Mrs Noyes and Emma made to follow. But Doctor Noyes now stepped between them — with his arm out.

"What are you doing?" said Mrs Noyes.

"You must wait," said Noah.

Mrs Noyes — at once — was in full panic.

"Let me past," she said. "Let me *past!*"

She was striking at her husband's arm and even at his face with her fists — and calling out to Emma; "don't let Hannah take her! Stop her! Stop her!"

Doctor Noyes tripped Emma up with his foot as she passed and swung his wife behind him with a blow that sent her against the wall. There had not been so much violence since the killing of the animals — and with just cause. . . . "Oh, God!" Mrs Noyes was screaming at the top of her lungs. "Oh, God! Oh, Lotte! . . ." tearing her vocal cords . . . "Oh, GOD!!!"

∞ It was Japeth who killed her.

And though Mrs Noyes would never forgive her — Hannah hadn't been party to what happened. She had merely done what she was told and had carried Lotte through the portal, wrapped in the blanket.

Japeth had waited — just as his father had instructed — hiding out of sight of his mother and of Emma, and once Hannah was inside, he had taken Lotte from her and slit her throat while she slept. Hannah went into shock — since the child was killed before her eyes — and it was feared she would lose her baby. She locked herself in her cabin and did not speak for two days.

Since Mrs Noyes and Emma had been prevented from following, they were still on deck when Japeth appeared with Lotte's body.

Noah said; "give her to your mother. Let her mourn. You — go away and scourge yourself. There's blood on your face and arms."

Japeth thrust the body at Mrs Noyes.

Mrs Noyes was standing with her back against the wall, where Noah had thrown her. She accepted Lotte without a word — without a sound — and sank to her knees, the child and its blood in her lap on her aprons. The cotton dress was torn — and the soft white collar was scarlet. Mrs Noyes arranged the child so its head lay up against her heart — and she held her there without any further movement — staring at the rain.

Emma — for once — was quite unable to cry. She went away and stood at the prow of the ark and the only sound she made was a kind of song.

Doctor Noyes went away entirely — retiring to his cabin.

After maybe half an hour there was a noise on the stairs inside and Ham came running onto the deck.

"Mother? . . ."

He stood before her — knelt before her — tried to take her hands.

Mrs Noyes could only whisper to him; "please," she said; "know better than to comfort me while the dead are laid in my arms."

Ham sat back on his heels and hunkered in the rain. He would watch and wait as long as need be.

Lucy came — with her torn paper parasol — and stood beside him, watching Mrs Noyes and Lotte with her strange green stare. Her long feathered gown was not even wet—in spite of all the holes in the parasol—though her bony face was streaked with blacking from her lashes.

At last, Mrs Noyes stood up (and Ham stood with her) and she lifted the child towards the rain.

"There is no God," she said. "There is no God worthy of this child. And so I will give her back to the world where she belongs."

After saying this, she held Lotte close again and — with a look at Ham and Lucy that thanked them for their vigil—she went to the gangplank and descended.

"Goodbye," said Ham. But whether this was said to his mother or to Lotte, could not be told. Strangely, he did not even raise his voice.

∞ Japeth scourged himself with brushes and pumice and finally with ashes. It was very painful—even though his skin had become somewhat immune to pain because of all the scrubbing done in his attempts to rid himself of the blue dye.

He was thoughtlessly obedient and always had been. Therefore, when his father had said he must scourge himself, he had done it without protest. But he did think it strange that so much fuss was being made. After all—he'd only killed an ape. And an ape was only an animal. Nothing human.

∞ Mrs Noyes carried Lotte down the Hill towards the compound—talking to her all the way—holding her head against her breast, with the heel of her hand against the wound and her fingers laid on Lotte's cheek—and she said; "it's raining now, much worse than it was. Coming down in buckets and pails. No matter. Not when you've been through the river, eh? You and me—veterans of the river wars . . . Who gives a damn if it rains? I don't; you don't. Anyway—it's gone all hot —not like the nice rain we had, you and me and the Faeries— all that soft, warm rain. Wasn't it lovely?" She began to quicken her pace. "We're going down the Hill, now. You feel that? Bumpity-bump! Lickety-split! Higgledy-piggledy, here we go!"

Mrs Noyes slid down a part of the path that had turned to

grease—regained her balance and went on walking, using her heels to make steps in the muck where the stones had come loose and been washed away. Soon she was walking under the trees again, her favourite part of the path between the altar and the compound—the great, tall cedars where Ham used to disappear to watch the stars—coming down in the morning—spreading all his findings out on the kitchen table; ''this one's the wolf-star, mother—red in the morning, red in the evening . . .'' All the stars were gone, now.

''What do we care? Eh, Lotte? Why should we care—all the stars can go to hell!''

She peered up through the pouring trees. ''Why not drown them, too—you Son-of-a-bitch! Drown the stars! Who cares? *And* the god damn moon! Who needs it? I don't—we don't . . .''

The path was full, now, of frogs and toads, moving up towards the ark.

''Turn back,'' said Mrs Noyes. ''You won't be welcome up there. Go sit under your mushrooms. Do what I'm going to do: bury the dead and celebrate. Free at last, eh Lotte? No more rivers to cross. No more being taken out and left in the rain.''

There was the house.

She could see its roof—its mosses and its vines—its tiles, its chimneys, its nests and even its storks.

''Don't you know any better?'' she screamed at them, the *scream* a mere whisper. ''Don't you know any better than to go on sitting there? Stupid, stupid storks! The world is ending!''

She wept with rage at the sight of her house. It was meant to be a haven. What else were houses for? Why else put up four walls and set a roof on top? Even the storks knew the answer to that—and the mice and the rats who had lived in the walls and the spiders in the corners and the weevils in the floorboards. Even a *termite* knew that!

''Never mind,'' she said, patting Lotte on the back. ''We know what houses are for. I shouldn't have yelled at the storks. What a fool I am. The roof is all they have left.''

She had reached the terrace where she once grew sunflowers

— the last plateau before the steps that led to the bath house
and the latrine. She could see the yard from here — the cre-
matory, strewn with the blackened corpses of the cattle, sheep
and goats — the dogs, the oxen and the horses. Ravens and
bandicoots and buzzards were doing their work — even in the
rain.

"Oh God . . ." she said.

Lotte.

"I can't leave you here. I can't leave you here for them. . . ."

Mrs Noyes turned back and started to run up the path towards the cedar trees. But she stopped before she had gone
ten paces.

"I can't leave you anywhere."

Can I.

Subdued and defeated, Mrs Noyes turned once again towards the terrace and the steps. And the charnel house that
had once been her home.

∞ "Where is your mother?" said Noah to Ham, on the
deck of the ark.

"Gone," said Ham.

"That's quite obvious. But gone *where?*"

"I don't know, sir. I didn't go with her. . . ."

Lucy, under the slowly dissolving parasol, giggled.

Noah, whose black umbrella was standing up to the downpour without a single rip or tear, shot a look at Lucy — but
made no comment.

"I fail to see," he said to Ham; "that this is a situation for
levity. . . ."

"On the contrary, father, I should have thought *levity* would
be the subject of all our prayers."

More giggles — Lucy turning away coyly — standing on one
foot.

Noah reddened, realizing Ham was gaining the upper hand
and must not be allowed to do so — especially in front of this
giggling geisha in white-face. "And what, precisely, did you
mean by that remark?"

"I mean, sir, only that if the ark won't float, it might be wise to address ourselves to God."

Noah shot another look at Lucy, waiting to see if she would giggle and thus inform him if the remark was funny.

Apparently it was not; Lucy remained silent.

"I remind you," he said to Ham; "that unless your mother is brought aboard this vessel — and brought aboard *today* — it could not matter less whether it floats or not."

"I know, sir."

"So what are you going to do about it?"

"I suppose I could go and look for her, father. If that were something you would allow."

"Yes. Yes. I would allow that."

"Thank you, sir." Ham made a move towards the gangplank.

"And take your wife with you. . . ."

"Yes, sir."

∞ Mrs Noyes set Lotte in her rocking chair, curled up as if asleep. Her ape's body was so like that of a human child, it startled Mrs Noyes into speaking aloud; "but this *is* a human child! Lotte, like my Adam, was born of human flesh and doesn't that make her human?" All she got for an answer was the collective cry of feeding birds.

Mrs Noyes did not know what to do. Where in the world could she leave Lotte — safely leave her? Digging a grave would be next to impossible, given the increasing downpour. Certainly, there was nowhere she could leave her outside — where all the scavengers had gathered over the bodies of the sacrificial victims and yet — she could not just abandon her. She had loved her too much for that.

If only there were just one jar of gin.

And there must be.

Must be. She had hidden so many out here, over the years.

She inspected the lattice work and the trumpet vine — but they yielded nothing.

The box she had rested her foot on?

Nothing.

The floor boards . . .

Yes! That was it. Oh—*surely* (she was already on her knees and breaking her fingernails, prying at the cedar planks)—surely there would be something here. *I must have put two hundred jars beneath these boards in the last twenty years. Three hundred.*

She managed, at last, to lift first one and then another of the planks and she lay down flat on the floor to look underneath.

It was cool down there — and it smelled so wonderfully full of earth and dead leaves and old cobwebs. She reached in, far as she could force her short arms — first one and then the other.

Ah!

Yes! Yes!

One — two — three jars of gin.

But would they be full — half-full — or empty?

She drew them forth like crystal vases, terrified of breaking them. *Please. Please. Please.*

Pray, Lotte. Pray!

∞ Mrs Noyes had not tasted gin since before the rains began — when Noah had smashed or, rather when he had enlisted Japeth to do the smashing of, every last jar she had owned. At least — every last jar they could find.

But not these three.

Hallelujah!

And if Mrs Noyes had not tasted gin since the rains began, she had not been tipsy or drunk since Yaweh's visit.

"Oh, Lotte . . ." she keened aloud, almost singing. "If only you had seen all this when all this was living and divinely beautiful. The porch — the view — my cat . . . the yard without its dead . . . the view across these lawns . . . the hill — the wonder of the floating trees! All the lemurs crying at the sun and the birds going up — oh — Lotte! If only you had seen that world. It looked so — it smelled so — it *was* so cool. Half an hour — an hour, every day — you didn't have to sleep to dream. It was all out there — as real as you and me. *Wonderful!* I used to sing, out here. Me and Mottyl. We sang every evening, sang every night. . . . and sometimes, I used to go in there —

back in there in the parlour — and I would play and play. And sing. Oh — I used to drive them all crazy!''

She laughed.

"Stop! Stop! Stop! They used to cry. *Stop that caterwauling! Have you no mercy? STOP!* But I wouldn't stop. Never, never. I just got quieter — and went on singing. Go on singing — that's what matters.'' Mrs Noyes took a long, hard pull at the jar and rejoiced in the long, hard burn it produced — in her mouth — her throat — her chest — her stomach . . . *More. More.*

She looked at the child, asleep in her rocking chair.

''I bet you've never even heard a piano. Maybe you never even heard a person singing. Did you? Did you? Listen . . . I know what I'll do. I'll play you the first and the last of all the songs you'll ever hear. Wait, now. Wait . . .''

Mrs Noyes — very tipsy now — pushed through the doorway into the parlour, where she lighted a lamp. She sat — with her jars of gin in a row — on the bench where Mottyl used to sit beside her — and she took a great haul of liquor that set her spluttering and coughing. And then she began to play.

She played *"The Riddle"* and she played *"The Foggy, Foggy Dew."* She played *"On Top of Old Smokey," "Scarborough Fair"* and *"Bendemeer Stream."* She played *"Careless Love"* and *"Home, Sweet Home"; "The Bluebells of Scotland," "Clementine," "Au Clair de la Lune," "Drink to Me Only With Thine Eyes," "Auld Lang Syne," "I Dreamt I Dwelt In Marble Halls," "The Three Ravens"* and *"John Peel."* On and on she played . . . nipping at her gin . . . bursting into song, though there was hardly any voice to ''burst'' with, but only the cracked remains of what had once been a cross between a sailing soprano and a wavering alto. *"Carry Me Back to Old Virginny," "Barbara Allen," "Green Grow the Rushes-Oh!" "Shenandoah"* and *"When Irish Eyes Are Smiling."*

At the end, as always, she played what Ham had once called her ''favourite favourites'' — the trio of songs that never failed to lift her head — her voice — her back — the piano and the piano bench, gin-jars, Mottyl and all — until the whole house shook with the reverberations and the echoes. And these were:

"I'll Take You Home Again, Kathleen," "My Lord, What a Morning" and the rousing, thumping shout of *"The Holy City."*

Jerusalem.

∞ She was done. It was over.

She lifted her foot from the pedal — and even so, the final chord went on sounding — as if the piano would go on singing by itself.

Then gin and silence and a roll of thunder.

No more music: forever.

Mrs Noyes stood up — dizzy with the roar of the songs in her mind — more than faint with hunger — and reeling with the gin. She waltzed, half falling out through the parlour and onto the porch, where she slumped against the doorjamb and whispered to Lotte.

"There. That's all the songs there are. . . ."

But Lotte had not heard them.

Dead or alive, she was gone.

The rocking chair was empty.

∞ For one truly crazy moment, Mrs Noyes started calling her.

"Lotte? Lotte? . . ."

Not on the porch and not in the parlour. Not in the kitchen — not in the larder. Not in the drawing-room. Where — where — where?

Oh, Lotte — what have I done?

Mrs Noyes went back to the porch. *She was here. She was right here, right there. On the chair.*

Be calm.

More gin.

Mrs Noyes threw back her head and drank until the gin was pouring from the corners of her lips and down her chin and — as she was tilting forward to catch the spill — she caught, as well, the sky in her eye.

Ravens.

Jehovah!

Mrs Noyes went running—gin jar and all—tearing her shawls and skirts and aprons on every nail and protrusion the porch and the intervening trees and fences and raspberry canes had to offer. The rain was pelting, now, so hot it hissed when it hit the ground and all the buzzards — all the ravens — all the bandicoots were steaming as they ripped and tore at the charred remains of the cattle, sheep and goats.

"Scat! Scram! Scat!"

Mrs Noyes ran amongst the scavengers, flapping her arms and spilling her gin and whirling her shawls above her head.

"Get off! Get off! Get OFF!"

She was frantic, and even though she had not seen Lotte, she was afraid — with a dreadful, sickening certainty — that she would find her there, amongst the other corpses.

The buzzards were easier to scatter than the ravens, who simply hopped to one side — and the bandicoots kept scurrying out of her reach—running on all fours, then pausing beside some half-burned, half-eaten carcass — cramming their pouches full of meat and their mouths full of offal. The sight of this so enraged Mrs Noyes that she stooped down and gathered stones, pebbles, rocks — whatever came to hand — and heaved them at the ravens and the bandicoots. She even went so far as to spit at them — and once she got near enough, to kick them.

"Get away!"

At one point she stumbled over the carcass of a cow and, reaching down, she tore a rib from its backbone and began to flail the air with that.

Then she saw her.

Or rather, she saw her dress, with its sash.

Lotte was lying face down amongst the sheep, with her long, furry arms flung out on either side and her dress a mass of holes where the ravens had been trying to get at her flesh.

Mrs Noyes knelt down in the mud and ashes and covered Lotte's body with her own.

She didn't speak. There was nothing to be said.

She hardly dared look at what she had found, but she knew that she would have to look. So, when she turned the body in

order to lift it into her arms, she saw that Lotte had no eyes.
Mrs Noyes went numb.

She stood up and carried Lotte — under her shawl — away.
And when the birds flew down to get her, she just kept walking — kicking at the bandicoots and stepping over the cattle
without emotion. She walked all the way to the porch and all
the way through the parlour, passing the silent piano, and all
the way to the kitchen — where, at last, she laid Lotte out on
the harvest table and sat down beside her and wept.

∞ Mrs Noyes went upstairs and dragged her trousseau
chest — bumpity-bump — down the steps and along the rasp-
ing slates of the hall. In the kitchen, she flung out all the lengths
of Dutch brocade and all the Chinese silks and all the Egyptian
cotton. Mrs Noyes had never used them. In the long run, they
had been set aside for the daughters who had died — and then
for the daughters-in-law — the grandchildren — the great-
grandchildren. Well. None of this had happened. Noah, during
one of his fundamentalist purges, had decreed that anything
not white or black, brown or grey was sinful and all the bro-
cades and all the silk and linens had been put away.

There were jars, too, of buttons — boxes of buckles — long
silk envelopes of ribbon — precious paper packets of needles
— spindles of thread and cards of metal hooks for the backs of
dresses.

Mrs Noyes fingered all these things — sipped a little gin —
and wondered why it was that all these things had gone to
waste. Not that it mattered, except in terms of all the dreams
that had been dreamt for nothing — ten thousand years ago
when she was a child — a girl — a bride. All those visions of
curtained windows and long soft gowns and hats with ribbons
down her back and chairs with brocade seats and velvet cushions . . .

Hah! She laughed out loud.

You didn't decorate an ark with Dutch brocade.

So. She lumped it all on the floor and ignored it.

Except the needles. Except the thread. Except the buttons.

∞ Mrs Noyes wrapped Lotte tight, her ape arms folded over her heart, in the long thin strips of petticoat left from Mrs Noyes's orchard mittens. The head, she left unbound, with its underslung jaw and its wondrous, irrepressible grin. Even in her death — Lotte smiled. And the smile was almost a kind of revenge. If only Doctor Noyes could have seen her now. *I am an ape — but I had a human mother and I had a human father*; said the smile. *I was loved — I was cherished — I was held by human arms.*

Mrs Noyes cursed herself silently for having been weaker than Lotte's parents. Well. She would answer to that weakness now. Lotte would have a human burial.

Closing the lids of the eyeless sockets, she set brass buttons where the deep-set eyes had been in the black face, and then, having kissed the child on the lips as a kind of reassurance that what she was about to do would not involve pain, she sewed up the wound on her throat and in place of the blood-stained collar she tied a bright blue ribbon.

Having done all this, she made a deep-folded cushion of brocade and, placing that in the bottom of the trousseau chest, she picked up Lotte and laid her inside and surrounded her with all the Chinese silk and all the Egyptian linen and — saying goodbye — she closed the lid.

"No one can get you now," she said. "They wouldn't stand a hope in hell."

After that, Mrs Noyes dragged the trousseau chest along the hall again and out through the great oak doorway and left it, like a sign against the impending flood, blocking the entrance.

"Now I deserve a good stiff drink," she said — and sat on top of the chest and opened her final jar of gin.

∞ "So, your father's a magician?" said Lucy.

"Yes. Of sorts," said Ham.

"Can he make gold?"

"He's tried."

"And?"

"Failed."

Lucy smiled. They were seated on a rock beneath the thickest of the cedars, hardly being rained on at all. Lucy was stripping away the last of the paper from her parasol—exposing its bamboo frame.

"Most people do," she said. "Fail."

"Most?" said Ham. "That's not what I've been told."

"Oh?"

"*Everyone* fails," said Ham. "There's no such thing as alchemy. It doesn't make scientific sense."

"Does everything have to make scientific sense before you'll believe it?"

"Pretty well. Oh—I realize there are exceptions . . . music, for instance. Yes, you can make a science of music—but in my opinion, once you've made a science of it, it ceases to *be* music. And becomes . . ."

"What?"

"Discreet, I guess. Calculated and careful. Unadventurous."

Ham put his hand on Lucy's knee. "I don't know how I got so lucky," he said. "Finding you. The perfect lover and the perfect companion. I've always had to have all these conversations alone, before — me and my notebook."

"Didn't you ever discuss these things with your father?"

"You don't *have* 'discussions' with my father, Lucy. What you have is arguments and edicts. His problem is — even when you've provided him with the scientific evidence — he finds some way of refuting it. '*No such thing as a waterwheel, boy!*' he'd shout. Even when I showed it to him."

Lucy laughed.

"But when volcanic ash fell from an August sky, it was '*snow!*' A miracle! *That* he'll believe. Miracles *and* alchemy. Even though he's failed at both."

"Well," said Lucy, raising her parasol over their heads; "one day I'll give him lessons."

Ham sat up and his mouth fell open.

Lucy got to her feet and dusted the cedar droppings from her feather gown. "Come along, now," she said. "We're supposed to be looking for your mother."

Ham stood up — away from her — backing off. "But . . ."
He was staring at the parasol.

"What *is* the matter?" said Lucy.

"It's . . ." Ham was pointing at what, only moments before, had been a bamboo skeleton. "It's covered with *gold.*"

"That's right."

"But . . ."

"I told you, ducky, didn't I?" She reached out and tickled him under the chin with her gloved, gifted fingers. "Some day, I'll give your father lessons. In the meantime — *mother* calls. Come along."

∞ Mrs Noyes was sitting very still and straight and drunk on the trousseau chest in the dooryard.

In her mind she was *"barring the way,"* as the angel had at Eden. This was a whole new world, where some people boarded ships and sailed away, while others stayed behind and slept in the trees — buried their children in trousseau chests — sat in the rain and inherited all the apples.

Hah!

Had anyone thought of *that?* she wondered. Leaving me here with the orchard — handing me the keys to wisdom and saying . . .

Drown.

This gave her pause — and she slumped a bit.

Well: I'm not drowned yet. Still here alive. Still me — and, in fact, a little more me than I was before all this began.

"You hear that?" she said, looking up at the ark. "I'm finally me, *all over.* Like it or lump it."

Eh, Lotte.

Mrs Noyes slumped completely, hands pressing down on the lid beneath her.

There were ribbons round her neck and an apple in her hand — the apple half-eaten, the ribbons — of every colour — slowly melting into the patchwork of her shawls and aprons. In appearance, Mrs Noyes had become a kind of walking flea-market: all her strips of petticoat and ribbon, rag and rope and sashes hanging down in front and behind; and all her pockets, plackets and dangling purses bulging with bits of string and jars of buttons, lace caps and clothes pins, needles, scissors, bags of medicinal herbs and books of pins. Rose petal *sachets* salvaged from the trousseau chest. *ANY OLD ANYTHING!* might have been her sign.

Mrs Noyes belched and took another swig of gin.

What now, old lady?

One last look at everything — and down the Hill to die.

I DON'T WANT TO DIE.

But — I'm going to.

∞ Mrs Noyes stood up and flung the ends of her "neckwear" over her shoulder with a dramatic gesture. In fact, she did this so forcefully, she almost fell down — not having been aware, as usual, of how very drunk she was.

She looked around at all the animal wreckage in the yard — rainblown and scavenged — and spoke to it as if it were her congregation; "who the hell do you pray to, I wonder, when you want to live and there isn't any God?"

She was trying to bring them into focus under the downpour, but she couldn't — and all she saw was the lake that was forming around them and all of them lying so still and so silent — and none of them with any answers.

"Maybe we should pray to each other," said Mrs Noyes — walking closer to them, not even trying to lift her feet from the water — simply walking into the centre of the lake, ankle deep. "Pray to each other — is that it? The way I prayed to the river, when I was drowning. . . ." She stood still, the gin jar hanging down from her fingers. "Maybe — if I prayed to Mottyl, we might even find one another. Do you think that's possible? I wouldn't mind finding her. I mean — if I found her — we wouldn't be alone."

The rain had begun, now, to pelt — the size of pine cones.

Mrs Noyes went up the Hill and sat in the bath house.

∞ In the bath house, the sound of the rain was muffled. Tubs and buckets and abandoned flannels sat on the shelves or lay on the floor. The great white sheets that Noah had wrapped himself in on the nights when he had come here to purge himself and commune with Yaweh over the steaming rocks, hung down from their pegs like so many flags of surrender. The bath house, now, was the driest building in the compound and Mrs Noyes sat and revelled in the smells of old cleanliness and cedar tubs.

Something scurried out of sight.

Rats.

But Mrs Noyes didn't even bother to move. She wasn't afraid of rats any more. Now, she was one with them.

"Maybe she's gone in there. . . ."

It was Lucy — right outside the door.

Mrs Noyes leapt.

Ham entered first and Lucy followed.

"No. Not here . . ." said Ham.

"Well, she has to be *some*where. You go and check the latrines and I'll take a closer look in here."

Ham departed, saying; "don't be long. Father is getting anxious."

For a moment after Ham had left, Mrs Noyes attempted to hold her breath. But it was impossible. Behind her winding sheet, she gave a sigh. It could not be helped.

Lucy sniffed the air and counted over: soap and clean sheets and cedar. . . .

And gin.

Mrs Noyes could see her through an opening in her sheet and for one appalling moment, Lucy turned and looked right at her.

Mrs Noyes looked right back.

Then Lucy marched to the door and opened it — and Mrs Noyes was certain she was about to be betrayed.

But instead, Lucy stepped outside and just as she reached to close the door she leaned back into the room and said; "have you found your cat?"

Mrs Noyes said; "no."

Lucy said; "keep trying. Good luck."

And then she was gone.

Mrs Noyes said; "thank you."

∞ Mrs Noyes's last hiding place was the barn.

Above the horses' stalls were all their names: Lily, Betsy, Tom and the others. Mary Mae and Alice, Jasper and Blackie. And there were the lambing pens, where all her lambs had been born — her children's choir. And the ewes' corral and the rams' box — altos, sopranos, basses and tenors.

Oh, the winter nights she had spent out here — and the summer nights in the fields, teaching them all how to sing! Those were her favourite times of all. Her *favourite* favourite times. And now . . .

"In Paradisum deductant te Angeli," she muttered, looking down at where the sheep and lambs had been in other times. "Into Paradise may the angels lead thee; at thy coming, may the Martyrs receive thee — and bring thee into the Holy City."

"Amen."

Mrs Noyes almost fainted.

"Who said that," she whispered. *Am I going crazy? Voices?*

"I did," announced a dark voice — somewhere above her.

Mrs Noyes looked up.

"Who's there?"

"Just me," — and there was a *whooshing* sound as Crowe flew down and landed beside Mrs Noyes on the railing of the lambing pen. "I've been looking for you everywhere. I've come to take you to Mottyl."

∞ Mauve rain had given way to Onan's rain and Onan's rain to the rain that had been like steam and the steaming rain to the hot and the hot to the present rain: the pine-cone rain. The sound of it, alone, was frightening—not so much because of its loudness, though it was loud enough—but more because of its strangeness. Each of the cone-sized globules was a *package* and, as each *package* hit whatever surface it first encountered, it burst — letting forth a stream of liquid more like oil than water: golden and lucent. The effect of this was that all the trees and buildings — all the grass and the earth — took on a coated, shining appearance that was eerie as well as treacherous.

Peering out from the barn, Mrs Noyes beheld a world that might have been anointed with Balm of Gilead. It even smelled of resin and rich herbal juices. What would Yaweh think of next? It seemed that with every new kind of rain there was a new kind of sinister beauty.

∞ Mrs Noyes went out into the barnyard and, pulling her shawls and aprons over her head, she went through the gate and down the Hill beneath the golden rain. Crowe, with some difficulty, flew above her calling out directions; "this way — that way — over here!" Mrs Noyes could barely keep pace.

"Where are you taking me?"

"Down through the wood. Hurry! Hurry!"

Hurrying was the last thing Mrs Noyes had to be told to do. She was "hurried" in spite of herself. The grass had an oil patina on it and — though she could not keep up with Crowe — she felt as if she was skating down the Hill. *Pray God I don't hit any groundhog holes!*

For Crowe's part, the journey had another kind of worry. Her feathers were slowly being coated with the oil, though it might have been more appropriate to say she was being *gilded*.

"I'm being pulled down by the rain," she cried to Mrs Noyes. "Hurry! Hurry!"

At last they reached the entrance to the wood where Mottyl had gone in the day before. But now there were no Faeries and perhaps no animals, either. Certainly none was evident.

Looking through towards the other side, Mrs Noyes saw the whole wood was golden. Every tree and every twig and branch had been coated with the gleaming balm and all the leaves, grown heavy, were falling as she entered. Given the twilight, the spectacle of this was breathtaking — and Mrs Noyes was silenced.

Where can everyone be? she wondered. Where can all the animals have gone? And then, as her eyes adjusted to the light, she understood.

On the ground — on the branches — on every fallen tree, there was a golden menagerie: stilled and mute and slowly drowning in Yaweh's alchemy.

∞ At last they arrived at a tree on the farthest side of the wood — and Crowe, who could not have flown another feather-length, settled in the upper branches. Her voice was very weak.

"Here we are," she called down to Mrs Noyes.

"Where?" Mrs Noyes asked — breathless and voiceless, herself. "It's just an old tree and I don't see Mottyl anywhere."

"Look up," cried Crowe. "Look up here!"

Mrs Noyes looked up.

Nothing.

Not even Crowe.

"I can't see you, let alone my cat," said Mrs Noyes. "Stop playing games. Where is she?"

"You'll have to climb up to find her. And if I were you I'd be quick about it."

The tree in question was luckily a redwood, which meant there were many branches to climb on and when there weren't branches, there were owls' nests and gilly-pits and other holes and hollows in which to set her toes as Mrs Noyes obediently followed Crowe's instructions: "turn left — turn right — keep on climbing."

Finally, Mrs Noyes could see where Crowe was sitting, five or six yards from the top of the tree and — just underneath her, two or three branches lower down, there was a sight that Mrs Noyes had thought she would never see again.

Mottyl's tail.

Like everything else, it was covered with a golden gloss — and it was hanging down towards Mrs Noyes, suspended over the edge of what appeared to be a very large sun hat made of faggots.

Mrs Noyes, with her last remaining strength, pulled herself up until she could look inside this inverted "sun hat" and there, very wet — but also very alive — was Mottyl.

All of her.

Mrs Noyes was too tired to scold and too tired to weep and too tired even to rejoice. All she had strength for was a single word.

"Hello."

∞ When Mrs Noyes appeared on the field before the ark for the final time, it was the seventh day after the rains had begun. From gold they had turned to silver — and from silver to grey and from grey to black. And so it was that in this inky rain, she stood before Noah with her aprons full of apples and her hair falling down and her shoes dissolving and her skin a welter of spots and bruises.

Noah stood in his usual place on the deck, sheltered beneath the black umbrella — the umbrella held in place by the ever-hovering Hannah.

"So. You have come to your senses at last."

"Yes . . ."

"I didn't hear you."

"Yes, sir," said Mrs Noyes.

"Your wanderings are over?"

"Yes, sir."

"And are you satisfied?"

"I don't understand what you mean. . . ."

"Are you satisfied that the Edict must be obeyed?"

Mrs Noyes licked her lips, which were oddly dry. Her mouth was dry, too, and the saying of words was extremely difficult. Noah, however, was patient. He would wait.

"Yes. I am . . . satisfied. Yes."

"Tell me what is in those aprons," said Noah. "Do you intend to bring all that on board? What is it? Souvenirs? Candlesticks? Heirlooms? There isn't any room for all that kind of junk, you know. What is it?"

Mrs Noyes summoned enough saliva to ask; "which question do you want me to answer?"

"Don't play the coy one with me, madam. Those days are gone forever."

"Yes, sir."

"What's in the aprons?"

"Apples."

"Apples?" The question was neither angry nor accusative. If anything, there was an edge of amusement. "So — you finally trespassed beyond the gate. . . ."

"No, sir. I went over the wall. The gate was locked."

"So it was. Well — did you enjoy yourself?"

"Not much. I cut my thigh on the glass."

"Yes. Well — that's what the glass was there for. And now you want to bring the fruits of your trespass aboard with you — is that it?"

"Yes. If I may . . ."

Doctor Noyes looked down at the aprons — bulging in the mud before his wife's feet.

"Are you sure there's nothing there but apples?" he said.

"Yes, sir. Nothing but apples. . . ."

"Maybe you had better untie those apron strings and let me have a look. . . ."

Mrs Noyes gave a cough and tried to adjust her hair, but it only fell down again and she had to keep pulling it away from her mouth.

"You seem extremely nervous, madam."

"No. No — I'm not. I'm . . . I'm *tired*, Noah. For pity's sake — I've been walking for days. I had to bury Lotte. I wanted to find my cat . . . there wasn't anything to eat. I'm tired, that's all."

Noah said; "Ham and Lucy looked everywhere for you. When they came back without you, I was certain you were dead."

"Well — I'm not dead. I'm here."

"Did you find your cat?"

"No." Mrs Noyes was weeping with exhaustion. "*Yes*."

Doctor Noyes leaned forward.

Hannah leaned forward with him, tilting the umbrella to cover his back. This put her in the rain and — very slowly — she began to turn black.

"Oh?" said Doctor Noyes. "You found her after all."

"Yes. Dead. She was dead."

"Unh-hunh . . ." Doctor Noyes leaned back again, Hannah and the umbrella leaning with him. "Well then, undo the aprons, show me the apples, and then you can come on board."

"I . . . the apples will be ruined," said Mrs Noyes. "Do you want to eat *black* apples?"

Noah thought about this — but only briefly — and then said; "come aboard."

Mrs Noyes said "thank you" and reached down to pick up the aprons by their strings. *"Be quiet,"* she said.

"Did you speak?" said Doctor Noyes.

Mrs Noyes was struggling with the aprons — hoisting them to her shoulders and over her back. "Speak?" she said. "Yes. I said *'thank you.'*"

Doctor Noyes nodded at her. "You are welcome, madam." He began to turn away. "I shall wait for you inside."

Thunder.

"There, you see? Yaweh is pleased at your surrender to reality. And — if I were you, madam — I should be grateful that He put up with so much delay."

Mrs Noyes did not answer this.

"Come along, then. Come in out of the rain."

Doctor Noyes departed and Hannah with him.

"Yes, sir," said Mrs Noyes. And she went on board — with her apples.

∞ And the rain — that had been black — lost all its colour and began to fall in waves. And all those who would survive the flood were now on board the ark. And Yaweh — with His final gesture — shut them in.

∞ Much as light will draw the lost towards it through the dark, the ark became a kind of magnet pulling a stream of would-be survivors up the Hill. As the rains increased, long strings of mice and hordes of ants and beetles — and a mass of all those other creatures that live in the ground — whose ground was being flooded and washed away — came up first. They were seeking the safety of earth and nothing more, since nothing more seemed possible. But the prospect of the upper reaches — of anywhere not yet drowned — soon led them to the wonder of the great yellow barn that Noah — (whose Hill they knew this was) — had built on the strangely angled stilts in the middle of the field.

Small clouds of mice spread over the meadow — wind-rushed from side to side — sometimes merging into larger clouds — until whole storms of chattering mice had congregated in a mass of callings to lost children and cries of *"families — stay together!"* Finally, having gained a vantage point from which they could all stare down onto the ark, they stopped — a thousand strong — to study it; poring over its possibilities; perusing the spectacle of its hugeness — bigger by far than any barn that anyone had ever seen.

Yet — how did a person get inside?

∞ Whistler — looking out very cautiously from underground — debated joining the hordes of refugees streaming up the Hill.

His earth was deeply flooded and even his sleeping chamber was being invaded by the waters. All his store of food had been ruined and in a few hours, his caverns and tunnels would be useless to him, as well.

But there were so many on the Hill, including other groundhogs from fields other than his, that he could not imagine finding a place for himself in their grand pilgrimage.

There was flesh, it seemed, everywhere — a whole hill of backs and scurrying feet. Not that Whistler didn't know what their hopes were. He also knew their hopes were doomed. It had something to do with Yaweh and Noah and the swath of death being cut as wide and deep as a person could imagine. He had heard the sounds and seen the fires of the sacrifice in the yard — and he knew these animals moving up towards the altar — unaware, for the most part, of what an altar was — all had the same hope of being saved. Well — he had no right to dash their hopes.

Go right ahead — keep marching.

He looked along the field and up towards the further reaches, below the stone wall — and he thought; this is where I belong. Better to face the great death here, than to join the doomed horde and be trampled and pushed to one side. His age — his weakened sight — his bones already sore — Whistler knew he could not survive the crush of all those others.

No. He would wait. In time, the mass would thin — and the panic lessen — and he would cross his field, moving upwards through the rain, and over to the east — and he would sit in his favourite burrow and watch the world's last days from there.

∞ By evening the flood had reached the tops of the cedar grove and by dark it had reached the lower edges of the upper meadow.

The meadow now was massed with creatures of every size, covering every blade of fallen grass and every branch and twig of the pine tree and every stone of the sacred altar. Birds and insects and beasts of every kind had gathered there and the tolling of the altar bell, whose rope had come undone, was mingled with a siege of voices crying out towards the silent ark.

The immense congregation had gone beyond panic. It had returned through stupor to a bleak kind of reason that was now approaching shock. Its members had waited out all the days of rain and all the days of running, all the days of hunger and all the days of endless climbing as each plateau was washed away beneath them. For as long as it was possible, they had moved in and out of one another's presence, avoiding with whatever grace they could summon those confrontations that were hardest to bear: the panther turning away from the antelope and the vixen from the hare. Thrown into every kind of river, hoisted onto every kind of shore and beaten under every kind of rain and waterfall, they had come to understand — though slowly — that death was herding them all towards annihilation in one incomprehensible gesture — and the chase was over. Now, on the Hill — in the dark — beneath the rain and beneath the sound of the bell, they were numb to every sense but the faintest sense of hope that formed itself in the shape of a yellow ark, with walls and floors and a roof; and a door beyond which every one of them imagined there was a pass to safety.

They waited.

The door did not open.

The rain did not stop.

The darkness made a tent and covered them completely.

∞ Around the time when the stars go out — if there are stars — a light appeared.

It floated over the water — whole, then broken — one light, then many — and whether in fragments or bonded, it moved so close to the beaten surface that its reflection could be seen. And even in spite of the tolling bell there was a sound that came with the lights and it fell on the waiting ears like a familiar shout, though, in fact, it was little more than a whispered sound: like bits of glass that are blown in the wind.

Every creature assembled on Noah's Hill had known the Faeries from the day of birth. They had watched their lights and their ripples in the grass and they had listened to their voices deep in the wood or skeetering up and down the animal paths and through the underbrush. One time or another — young and old — almost everyone had been rescued by the Faeries — as the lemur had been saved from the dragon slain by Michael Archangelis — and this because the Faeries were the only creatures not afraid of dragons or of caves with voices in them and a dozen other universal terrors.

Now, all the animals leaned further forward to watch as the Faeries veered towards the ark, made an initial pass from top to bottom, and then moved behind it, passing slowly out of sight.

"Do you think anyone will hear them? Do you think anyone will see?" wondered someone, barely audible.

These were questions no one dared answer. There was no reply.

As they waited, hopes were raised. Perhaps there was an entrance on the farther side . . . and perhaps Mrs Noyes, who was kind — or Ham or the Angel Lucy would look out through the cracks and see or hear the Faeries. And — if the Faeries were admitted — would the doors not open then to everyone?

If only the bell would stop its noise. If only the rain would cease just long enough to let a person *see* . . .

"Have they returned? Where are they? . . ."

All leaned forward again and every eye was pressed upon the dark and every ear upon the air, while every pulse seemed stilled and not a breath was taken.

Minutes passed and there was nothing.

Nothing.

And then . . .

The lights returned. One and then another and then the mass. The Hill breathed out — and the bell, at last, had meaning.

One or two bits of light broke away from the whole and flew up over the ark, as if in search of an entrance there — but all too soon they returned — beaten back by the rain.

The whole Hill was watching. Waiting.

The Faeries crowded then, and pressed their lights against the walls of the ark — and even from the distance of the hilltop, the crystal sound of their crying could be heard. And the lights went on beating at the walls so long that some of them went out and the mass, diminished, regrouped and flew up over the top of the ark and beat against the roof, in spite of the rain.

But with every new manoeuvre, the light was growing dimmer — fading by numbers as well as strength — and the sound could no longer be heard, but only the pulse of it — seen going out in the darkness — losing its edges — caving in at its centre — webbing, now, as if a spider was spinning against the rain — until the last few strands of brightness fell — and were extinguished — silenced and removed from life and from all that lives forever.

And the bell tolled — but the ark, as ever, was adamant. Its shape had taken on a voice. And the voice said: *no.*

∞ ∞ ∞ ∞ ∞ ∞ ∞ ∞ ∞ ∞ ∞ ∞

B O O K   T H R E E

∞ ∞ ∞ ∞ ∞ ∞ ∞ ∞ ∞ ∞ ∞ ∞

*. . . and the waters increased,
and bare up the ark, and it
was lifted up above the earth.*

Genesis 7:17

∞ ∞ ∞ ∞ ∞ ∞ ∞ ∞ ∞ ∞

INSIDE THE ARK there was a Well of darkness and a multitude of voices — and the air was already fetid with the stench of animals confined without windows. There were also the heavy smells of rancid pitch and the fresh-cut planks of gopher wood, which gave off a perfume of almost sickening sweetness. The only mitigating smells were those that came from the lofts of straw and sweetgrass and the warm, familiar smell of cooking oil from the galley.

The Well of darkness itself was right at the centre of the ark and its depth was the depth of the lower three decks. Above it, the upper and only open deck (where Noah had his quarters in the Castle and his Chapel with its Pagoda) formed a roof from which there hung a number of unlit lamps. Each of the other decks was open to the Well — and each was a labyrinth of corridors and passageways that ran behind and in between the various cages, pens and stalls where the animals were housed.

On the second deck there were birds and reptiles and insects caged and confined with bars and wire. Some of these cages were hung from the rafters. All the smaller mammals, too, were housed on this deck: the rabbits and squirrels and foxes — monkeys, rats and mice — the raccoons and porcupines — the ferrets — the tamarins and the unicorns. There were also, here, four cabins for human passengers and one of them contained a rough-hewn cradle which awaited the birth of Hannah's child.

On the third deck, the beasts of medium size were housed in pens and box stalls. Gutters ran beside the passageways here and emptied into spillways that, in turn, were emptied through spouts into the waters outside. And the animals here were the horses and zebras and deer — antelope, oxen and lions — emus and ostriches, dodos and all the other flightless birds and creatures who needed room in which to run — if only from side to side of an open stall.

On the fourth and lowest level were all the beasts whose size it had been feared would sink the ark: and here the darkness was absolute.

∞ Outside, the waters not only fell, but had begun to rise from the earth itself. Fissures opened in the rocks and let out all the underground rivers. Wells exploded and great, tall spouts of water shot into the air until even these were drowned as the hillsides began to crumble and the earth to give way.

The ark on its keel frame began to shake and shudder and to heave towards one side. In the darkness, all the animals cried as they lost their footing and were thrown against walls and bars. Mrs Noyes and Lucy clung to the aprons filled with apples and to each other as they were flung to the deck amidst a horrendous creaking and cracking that sounded as if the ark were going to be torn apart before it could be launched.

Birds took flight in their cages, but because of the darkness they lost their way and fell like stones.

Noah lay prostrate on the floor of his cabin and prayed in a loud and furious voice, begging that Yaweh should "right the ark at once!" And when these cries for mercy appeared to be ignored, Noah cried out again—but this time for Sister Hannah.

∞ At last the sky descended utterly — and the waters rose to meet it and a great resounding *bang* sent a shiver throughout the whole of Creation and the ark — with a universal sigh of relief from its riders — was righted and floated free from its frame and from its hillside and from — in every sense — the whole earth itself, which sank with a hiss beneath the waves that had risen to claim it.

Slowly, the people and the animals began to rise to their knees and — even more slowly — to their feet. Each one and every one tested the flooring below to see that it was still there — and the walls — and the bars and the wiring of the cages. And each one and every one muttered some kind of thanks — if only to acknowledge the fact they were still alive. And each and every one stood waiting — wondering what might happen next.

But the only sound they could hear was the sound of breathing and of their own hearts beating beneath the rain.

∞ When Mrs Noyes had hoisted the apples onto the deck — so exhausted she almost had to crawl up the gangplank on her hands and knees — a muffled duet of voices could be heard: first from the depths of one apron — then from the depths of the other — blending in a mutual cry of complaint.

From the first apron, Mottyl's voice; "hurry! Hurry! I've started!"

And from the folds of the second apron, Crowe's distinctive voice; "do you think you would be good enough to let me out? I'm afraid I simply cannot breathe in here."

And Mottyl had whispered; "hurry! Hurry . . ."

And Crowe had added; "if you please . . ."

Mrs Noyes had looked up and down the rain-washed deck and — seeing there was no one there to witness the stowaways' release — she had knelt before Crowe's apron and — having had to fight with the knots until every fingernail that had not been previously broken was split and torn in the effort — she had set Crowe free.

"What will you do?" she had said. 'I beg you to be careful. I'm so afraid of Japeth."

Crowe, who was still — though only partially — gilded, had assured her; "you must give up being afraid for me, Mrs Noyes. Your first concern is Mottyl. . . ."

"Yes!" Mottyl had moaned; "*please!*"

"You don't have to worry," Crowe had added; "I will find some way of staying with the ark."

Mrs Noyes had pointed out the sheltered chimney rising from the chapel roof over Noah's sacrificial altar and she had said; "so long as there's no burnt offering, you should be safe in there."

Crowe had given thanks and had tried to raise herself from the deck — but the gilding and the suffocation of the last few hours had held her down. "I'll have to walk," she had muttered. And had done so, waddling from side to side and more than slightly dragging her gold-black wings along the deck.

"Hurry!" Mottyl's voice was urgent. "Hurry! I've already had one. . . ."

Mrs Noyes had thrown the folds of Crowe's apron back in place and had been just tying the knot when Ham had appeared with Lucy close behind.

Lucy had spotted Crowe at once.

"You mustn't — oh, please don't harm her," said Mrs Noyes — still uncertain of Lucy's loyalties. "*Please.*"

But far from harming Crowe, Lucy had minced across the deck and had said to her; "where are you walking to, Crowe?"

Having explained what Mrs Noyes had told her about the safety of the pagoda-roofed chimney above the altar, Crowe had been lifted ("*my wings! My wings! Don't press so hard on my wings!*") — and carried like a ceremonial icon over to the chapel roof and set where, with a grateful look at Lucy, she easily waddled up the shingles and out of the rain.

In the meantime, Ham had knelt before Mottyl's apron and untied the knots, while Mrs Noyes had cautioned him to be careful. When the knots had finally been undone and the apron flung open, Mottyl had been revealed lying on her side in the process of labour — with one of the kittens, meanwhile, crawling across her belly in search of milk — small, blind, hairless and blunt-ended as a slug.

"You've had one," he had said.

"And I'm about to have number two . . . oh . . . I'm sorry, I can't hold it back. . . ."

Even as Ham and Mrs Noyes had watched, the second kitten had been born, and Mottyl had begun to free its face from its cowl.

"Where can we hide her?" Mrs Noyes had asked Ham. "If your father finds out — he'll kill her."

Ham at once had had the answer — and though he had cautioned Mrs Noyes it could only be a temporary hiding place, he had also told her it might have been made for the occasion.

∞ The door at the top of the stairs blew open and a great, cold shroud of rain was flung down the steps and over the figures waiting at the bottom.

Japeth — wearing his leather breastplate and greaves — stood on the landing, holding a lantern above his head and carrying his sword, unsheathed.

"What is it? What's the matter?" said Mrs Noyes — looking up at her son. "Has one of the beasts got loose?"

Japeth did not reply to this, but only gestured with the lantern — stepping aside and throwing its light further down the steps.

"He wants you up, now," he said.

"I assume you mean your father," said Mrs Noyes. "And — if you do — then please call him by name."

Japeth wiped his mouth with the back of his hand, embarrassed and confused. He was trying very hard to copy the manner of the ruffians who had captured him on the road and who had wanted to turn him into chowder. He had been so afraid of these men that he now took it for granted all he had to do was make a passable imitation and everyone would fall down before him, quivering with fear.

"Uhm . . ." he said. "Father wants to see you."

"Much, much better," said Mrs Noyes. "Now — how about *'please'*?"

Japeth turned mauve and mumbled something that might have passed for "*please*," but he refused to amplify or repeat it. Some things, like "please" and "thank you," were beneath a soldier's dignity. Or so he had gathered from what Michael Archangelis had said.

"Are we all to come up?" said Mrs Noyes.

"Yes. The lot of you."

Mrs Noyes had her foot on the lower step when Japeth added; "and be quick about it."

"I beg your pardon?"

Mrs Noyes stepped all the way back into the corridor.

Lucy said; "I think he said" (and here she lowered her voice at least an octave below the tentative tenor of Japeth) ". . . *'be quick about it!'* "

"Don't you make fun of me!" said Japeth, swinging the lamp instead of brandishing the sword, but realizing his mistake too late to correct it. "I'm not in any mood to be tampered with."

He scowled.

Lucy said; "I hadn't really thought of 'tampering' with you, ducks. Is it something you want me to consider?"

"I mean it," said Japeth — this time using the sword. "Don't fool around."

Lucy made a moue and was going to say more when Ham stepped forward.

"Why the hell are you waving that sword at us, Jape?" he said. "It's only *us*, for heaven's sake."

"You and the animals," said Japeth. "I'm not taking any chances."

"But for God's sake, Jape: they're in cages and I'm your brother. *That's* your wife and this is your *mother!* Are you crazy or something?"

Mrs Noyes said; "don't start an argument, Ham. It sounds quite reasonable to me. Japeth always was afraid of cows. . . ."

"I was not!" said Japeth, mortified and outraged — almost in tears. "I was never afraid of cows. . . ."

"Do we have to go on standing here like this?" said Emma. "I want to go to the latrine. And there's only the one up there — "she pointed past Japeth; "or the one way back there in the dark. So couldn't we go up, please? *Please?*"

Mrs Noyes gave the nod and went up, still unsure of her balance — not having gained her sea legs yet — and consequently being thrown from side to side of the stairwell, banging her elbows — one and then the other — on the railings.

As she passed her youngest son, she said to him; "aren't the others going to have the pleasure of your company below decks, Japeth? Don't you want to be with your wife? There's a sweet little cabin, right next to hers. . . ."

"Father wants me with him," said Japeth. "I'm to live up here."

Mrs Noyes smiled.

"Well then," she said; "at least you and I shall see something of one another."

Japeth did not reply. He was busy herding his brother and his wife Lucy past him through the door — clamping his jaws together and moving them from side to side, imitating yet another remembered image from his encounter on the road: the image of the raw-boned leader of his captors, grinding his teeth in anticipation of the chowder.

∞ The deck had a rope strung along it, leading from the entrance to the Well to the entrance beneath the canopy, beyond which the lights of Noah's cabin could be seen.

One by one, the family passed along the rope, hand over hand — being pelted and blinded with rain and almost swept away with the wind. Nonetheless, as they approached the Castle — where Noah's quarters and the Chapel were housed — Mrs Noyes looked up to see if there was any sign of Crowe in her chimney hideaway.

Perhaps — though maybe it was just the rain making shapes out of wishes — there was something up there, pressed in beneath the angled roof of the Pagoda — and Mrs Noyes even imagined she saw the movement of a wing.

Japeth stooped and went under the canopy, opening the door.

At once there was a burst of warmth and light — and the smell of something cooking with cheese in it.

Hannah was waiting for them, and — surely — had made their dinner. Surely, too, they would all sit down together and maybe even drink some mead.

But it was not to be.

The food (whatever it had been) had already been eaten and the smell of it was only the leftovers, sitting on a sideboard — the dish uncovered and the wooden spoon with which it had been served resting on one of Mrs Noyes's favourite blue and

white plates. Half a loaf of bread and a milk jug sat nearby —
the milk jug covered with a linen napkin.

Noah was seated at a great wide table that Mrs Noyes had
never seen before. His beard had been washed and combed
and the gown that had been stained with mauve and golden
rain had been exchanged for another gown — much richer: pure
wool, and blue — worn over a white cotton shirt Mrs Noyes
remembered turning the hem on not a month before. He was
holding Yaweh's cats in his lap: Abraham and Sarah.

"Excuse me, please," said Emma — from somewhere in
the rear of the clustered bodies in the doorway. "But I . . ."

Noah cut through her words as if they had not been spoken.

"Have the animals been fed?" he said.

"They were fed this morning, father," said Ham.

"And this evening?"

"Well — everything is rather a wreck, I'm afraid," said Ham.
"What with the ark capsizing . . ."

"Did we capsize?" said Noah.

"Well . . . whatever," said Ham. "It certainly felt as if we'd
capsized. . . ."

Noah turned to Hannah and smiled at her. "Were you aware
of this, daughter? Our *capsizing?*"

Hannah looked down at her folded hands and Mrs Noyes
could not help noticing how clean they were. Such lovely, un-
broken nails and all the cuticles as white as doves' eggs.

"There was some . . . commotion," said Hannah, who
seemed embarrassed — and Mrs Noyes wondered why. "But
— really hardly any trouble . . ." Hannah finished.

"There, then." Noah turned back to Ham. "That puts an
end to tales of '*capsizing.*' Next thing you know, you'll be calling this squall a storm and using *that* as an excuse." He waved
his hand, dismissing the subject. "Well — you always did
exaggerate, boy. Can things be righted by morning?"

"I dare say they could be, father — if Shem and Japeth were
to help."

Noah sat back in his chair and used his napkin to smooth his
moustaches, which Mrs Noyes now noticed had been trimmed,
so that they blended very nicely into his whiskers.

"Shem and Japeth may help you this once," he said. "Shem can supervise. It will give him an opportunity to check the stores. There will have to be rationing, of course. Perhaps we should devise some system of locks and keys. . . ." He waved at Hannah, who drew a four-legged stool in near the table, seated herself and commenced to write with a pencil in a hand-made book: *divisions of ye lockes and keyes. . . .*

"Don't be ridiculous, father," said Ham. "No one is going to walk away with the hay. . . ." He laughed.

Noah did not laugh.

"I was thinking of your mother," he said. "And her innate susceptibility to acts of *kindness.*" He moved his fingers around on the table top, picking up crumbs and caraway seeds and putting them into his mouth. *"Kindness"* (he gave the word a kind of twist, with his lips extended — as if he were lapsing into a foreign language) ". . . *kindness* is wasteful at the best of times, but in times like these — it is criminal."

"Excuse me," said Emma; "but I really do have to . . ."

"Were you spoken to?" said Noah.

"No, sir," said Emma. "Not that I heard. But . . ."

"Were you spoken to?"

Emma locked one leg around the other and hung her head— mouth hanging open . . .

"She needs the latrine," said Mrs Noyes.

"She needs a good keelhauling," said Noah. "That's what she needs. Look at her! Filthy from head to toe. And she smells . . ."

Mrs Noyes gave a loud sigh in order to cut off what sounded like the beginning of the all too familiar litany of poor Emma's faults.

"What is a 'keelhauling,' dear?" she said, quite brightly. She had not called Noah "dear" for over sixty years.

Noah ignored the epithet (he would have considered it an epithet) — and prepared to answer the question. He had been studying various books and pamphlets on the subjects of sea-faring, naval warfare and nautical terminology — and was really quite proud of his grasp of it all. "Keelhauling," he began, "is . . ."

At that moment, Emma launched one of her more spectacu-
lar wails upon the air and everyone was driven back towards
the walls.

"I don't want to be keelhauled!" she screamed. "I don't
care what it is! I can't help it if I have to go! I CAN'T HELP
IT!!!"

No one else spoke. There wasn't room enough in the air for
another voice.

And then — as it must — as it had to, because the wail had
been so mighty it had released all her tension — Emma's bowel
began to flood her drawers.

Still — no one spoke. What, after all, could be said? They
simply stood there and watched — some in horror — some in
disgust — as Emma completely lost control of her sphincter
and made a grab at her drawers with both hands and ran from
the room.

In the silence that followed, Shem made his entrance.

"What's going on?" he said.

No one answered.

And then Shem must have caught a taste of the air — for he
shrugged and said; "oh." And then he said; "Emma?"

"Yes," said Noah. "But what can you expect from someone whose sister was an ape?"

∞ Mottyl had given birth to all six kittens — two in the
apron and the rest in Hannah's cradle. They were healthy —
or certainly seemed so, judging by what she could feel and
smell. There were no deformities, no extra limbs, no two-
headed monsters, no club-feet and none of the kittens appeared
to be underweight or undersized. Two males — four females:
that was easy enough to tell. But Mottyl longed to know what
colour they were and if any of the females was, like herself, a
calico. "*The rarest of the rare,*" Mrs Noyes had informed her,
long ago when Mottyl was young and had wondered why it
was there were never any males to mate with who looked like
her. "There can't be calico males," Mrs Noyes had said.
"Don't ask me why; it simply isn't possible. Doctor Noyes

says his experiments have proved it — and furthermore, he says, if there *were* to be a calico male, it would be a miracle. And we all know how many 'miracles' there are. *Real* ones, at any rate.''

Mottyl had grieved over this. It made her feel very lonely. She had rather not be unique than endure the consequences of it. Doctor Noyes was too intrigued by uniqueness — and every time that Mottyl had kittens, the calico babies had disappeared first.

The memory of Doctor Noyes and his experiments put her in something of a panic. Somewhere above her, she could hear his voice — rising and falling with the rhythm of the storm. As the ark was lifted — the voice of Doctor Noyes was lifted with it, loud and clear — and, as it fell, his voice fell, too — and was drowned in the shuddering crash as the ark struck the water and everything shook and shivered and all the other animals cried out; *''help us!''*

What a time and what a place to be born, Mottyl thought, as she fed and washed her babies. Lying on her side — dry and warm for the first time in days — she wondered what sort of hiding places the ark might offer. She knew nothing of its geography — nothing of the great Well — nothing of the various gangways and corridors — nothing of the hay lofts and feed bins — nothing of the different levels. All she knew of the ark was its vastness and its smells: its crushing weight as it fell upon the waters and the sound of its squealing timbers and wailing beasts.

The storm was quite evidently getting worse — if that was possible — and the sound it was making now was like the sound of ten thousand Mrs Noyes — all making bread together — thumping and kneading their dough on the deck overhead. Once, long ago, it had been a comforting sound — the making of bread — and a sound that Mottyl could sleep by — safe beneath the table at home in the warmth of the kitchen. Mrs Noyes had always crooned to herself as she'd pummelled and pounded the dough — but there wasn't any crooning now and these ladies of the storm — ten thousand strong — were a different story altogether.

What a time and what a place to be born . . .

Mottyl could feel the kittens pushing at her belly — kneading her milk lines and pulling at her nipples — and she was overcome with a flood of tiredness. She began to purr. If only she could sleep. If only she dared. The smells of milk and birth and straw were like opiates and the sound of her own deep singing carried her close along the edges of a trance — where the rain did not exist and her nest in the cradle was a close, sure place — as close and sure as the arms of Mrs Noyes. Slowly, Mottyl sank towards a dangerous dream of safety, oblivious to everything but absolute fatigue.

∞ They sat at the table, ranged down either side like factions at a treaty conference: Noah, Shem and Hannah on one side — with Japeth standing behind them — and Mrs Noyes, Lucy and Ham on the other side — Emma crouching in the doorway, still in disgrace and almost lost in the shadows. Overhead, a lamp swung to-and-fro with the motion of the ark, which was not from side to side but from end to end — the prow rising high above the waves and crashing down without achieving any forward movement. The ark, in fact, was basically stationary — caught by the pull of the enormous depths that had once been all the valleys lying in the lee of Noah's Hill. It was only the storm that moved.

"Well," said Noah — narrowing his eyes and gazing at the others sitting opposite; "four and four make eight."

Lucy almost laughed — and Mrs Noyes was about to say *yes — and two and two make four*, when both were brought up short by the realization Noah was stating more than a mathematical fact. He was drawing a line between them — right down the centre of the table: *we and thee*, he was saying, *us and them . . . four and four make eight*.

Shem had brought with him a chart which Noah now called for and spread upon the table.

"Now," he said. "Draw closer."

Oddly — or so it seemed to Mrs Noyes — it was only those on her side of the table who did "draw closer." The others — Shem and Hannah and Japeth — remained as they were, poised and silent — and powerful (that was the word that occurred to her) — almost ignoring the chart, as Noah leaned towards it and placed his fingers on its centre.

Clearly, the chart was a diagram of the ark, showing it open along the side, revealing all four decks and the animal pens and enclosures, the hay lofts, the storerooms, the cabins, latrines and galleys — and, above, a cutaway of Noah's Castle, where they presently were seated, and the Chapel with its sacrificial altar and chimney. Beneath the hump of the poop deck, there was a storeroom designated as "the Armoury."

"Armoury, Noah?" said Mrs Noyes.

"Yes. In case of Pirates."

"Pirates? What are Pirates?"

"Barbarians, madam. Vandals of the seven seas."

"Are you saying you expect we shall be attacked?"

Noah shrugged. "There is always the chance," he said.

"But — in Yaweh's Edict," said Mrs Noyes; "'only *we* were to survive.'"

Noah waved the suggestion aside. "Clearly, in the long run, it is true that we alone shall prevail. But not without trial, madam. Not without tribulation . . ."

"And not without Pirates?"

"Just so."

The subject was abruptly changed, though Mrs Noyes was not at all satisfied that she had fully grasped the full implications of the Pirates. From where would they appear? And when might they be expected? And who had informed her husband of their existence? It was all beyond her — quite, quite mystifying and alarming.

Noah was clearly somewhat nervous of the item he now brought forward and placed on the agenda. In fact, he was so nervous — or was it embarrassment? — that he sat far back in his chair and flicked his fingers at Hannah, indicating that she should articulate what followed. Abraham was purring loudly. Sarah's blue stare was on Mrs Noyes.

The straightness of Hannah's back, despite her pregnancy and despite the motion of the ark, was awesome to behold. The same could be said of the expression on her face, which was absolutely blank and immobilized. She drew her handmade

book from its place in her lap—opened it—turned a few pages
and read, with every eye upon her from the opposite camp.

"The dispensation of the living quarters shall be as fol-
lows. . . ." and here she interrupted herself, though nothing
in her expression changed — and she said; "it will be useful, now, to refer to the chart, if you please." And then she
went on reading from her book; "the Most Reverend Doctor
Noyes . . ."

Here, it was Mrs Noyes's turn to straighten her back — in
wonder and indignation. "The most *what?*" she said.

" 'Reverend,' " said Hannah — not looking up.

Mrs Noyes looked at her husband, unbelieving and astonished. She could not even bring herself to stammer or to
stutter her objection, but only made a guttural noise. . . .

Noah regarded the ends of his beard and settled his wooden
teeth against his lips, clamped shut.

Lucy—who might have been expected to say or to do something gay and disrespectful — also said nothing. Beneath her
powder and her rouge, her expression was unreadable as un-
cut stone.

Only Ham, it seemed, was not surprised by the change in
his father's titles. "Most Reverend Doctor," it seemed to
him, was only proper for one who was on his way to becoming
a god.

Hannah continued; "the Most Reverend Doctor Noyes shall
be quartered in the Castle on the main deck. He shall have at
his disposal the offices adjoining—the retiring room for medi-
tation—the Chapel and its vestry—the latrine and bath house
on the starboard side of said Castle and the saloon in which we
presently sit. . . ."

Throughout this recitation, Noah had nodded in response to
each item—and now he waved his hand for Hannah to continue.

"The Reverend Doctor's eldest son, Shem, shall be in charge
of the maintenance of the ark and of its stores and he shall also
apportion and assign those labours and duties necessary for
the upkeep of said ark—and for the comfort and well-being of
its inhabitants and the safety of its cargo. . . ."

"Cargo? What *cargo?*" said Mrs Noyes. This was the first she had ever heard of any "cargo."

"Why — the animals," said Hannah — breaking with tradition long enough to force a condescending smile.

"Oh, I see," said Mrs Noyes. "The 'cargo.' Of course."

Hannah looked at Noah for permission to continue. He nodded.

The reading of the lists went on, setting forth the news that "Brother Shem" and "Sister Hannah" were to have the quarters across the corridor from Noah and that Japeth would be in a cabin next the Armoury.

This left only those on the other side of the table, where Mrs Noyes was already in partial shock at the open shame of having not been assigned the quarters she was due across the corridor from Noah, who was — after all — her husband, lord and (apparently) Reverend Master. Why Sister Hannah had been offered the privilege of being quartered there was not explained — and what was worse — far worse — was the definite impression that no explanation was thought to be necessary. Hannah had been elevated and Mrs Noyes demoted. Period. And not a word of comfort or of why. Though guessing produced the easy answer that it did not pay to rebel — no matter who you were or what your station — this did not accommodate the elevation of Hannah. That remained a secret.

Noah's hand was already crabbing forward onto the chart — and his fingers were tapping out the designated places as Hannah concluded her reading.

"Mother Noyes shall be on the second deck and her quarters in the starboard cabin adjoining that of Sister Emma. Sister Lucy and Brother Ham shall be quartered also on the second deck, port side. The latrines for these quarters are on the third deck. . . ."

Tap-tap-tap — the finger moved down steps and ladders and proceeded along the darkened corridors to the stern of the ark's third deck to locate the latrines. And then, as Hannah finished, it moved along that deck to the prow, where the galleys and saloon for these quarters were located.

Hannah gave a discreet little cough and closed her book, still unmoved and still with her maddening, non-partisan *"I've-only-done-my-duty"* expression.

Mrs Noyes was the first to speak.

"Are you saying that we are not to eat together?"

"Yes — but only for the most practical of reasons," Noah said. "Your duties, madam, will predicate a regimen out of kilter with the regimen here on the upper deck. It would be ridiculous to require that you dine at eight, when you will much prefer to dine at six — or even five."

"But we have never dined at eight," said Mrs Noyes. "In all our life together — five hundred years! — we have *never* dined at eight."

"Till now," said Noah — and shrugged.

Mrs Noyes stared, unbelieving. *"We* shall keep farmers' hours — and you shall keep those of the Most Reverend Doctor, is that it?"

"If you want to put it that way — yes. And why not?"

"And when, then, shall we meet? When shall we sit down with one another? When shall we . . . speak with one another?"

"In Chapel," said Noah.

"Chapel? But who can talk in Chapel?" said Mrs Noyes. "All we do there is listen to you pray and watch you wield the knife."

Again, the offhand shrug: the noncommittal wave of the hand. "I have my duties, madam. I must commune with God and you must listen and obey. Since Yaweh has charged *me* with the safety of this ark and all who sail on her, it would seem to be elementary that my dialogue should be with Him."

"I see. And this means you will no longer *commune* with us?"

"Your sarcasm bores me, madam. I will brook no opposition. You have your place and you will either accept it with grace — or go on making a fool of yourself: a facility, I might add, for which you appear to have an alarmingly active talent." Noah rose to his feet, and the cats, not content to be dumped, walked out and sat on the table. "I must also add that I will no longer tolerate your continued attempts to make a fool of me. Need I repeat this? *I* am in charge here. You, madam, are not. You are nothing, now, but a fellow passenger, without station and without rank. And I would suggest that, on that note, we terminate this meeting."

Mrs Noyes was also on her feet — and furious.

"Meeting!" she shouted. "*Meeting?* What is this *meeting?* Have we become, in my absence, an institution?"

Noah blinked.

"And if we have, madam — what is your objection to it?"

"WE ARE A *FAMILY!!!*" Mrs Noyes bellowed. "NOT A TOWN COUNCIL!"

Emma wailed.

Even Hannah went as white-faced as Lucy.

Japeth put his hand on his sword.

Noah said; "it is true. We are a family. And *I* am head of that family."

Mrs Noyes sneered; "and I'm the foot? Is that it?"

"You may be whatever part you choose, madam. I merely state the facts. God has put you in my charge — and I must act accordingly. Good night to you."

Noah immediately left the saloon and went into the Chapel, where he fell to his knees and prayed for patience.

Mrs Noyes looked from Shem to Japeth and back to Shem.

"How can you have let this happen?"

Shem merely shrugged.

Mrs Noyes bit her lip and shook her head. She turned on her heel and departed — tripping, as she went, over Emma — who was still crouching in the doorway.

"Damn!"

Ham and Lucy also departed — saying nothing — only lifting Emma to her feet and taking her with them into the dark and back into the rain.

When they had gone, Japeth said; "shall I chase them?"

Shem said; "no. They don't need chasing. They're beaten."

But Hannah thought; *are they?*

∞ When Mottyl awakened she had a need to make scat. The sleep, however short, had refreshed her and she was keenly and pleasantly alert to all the sounds and smells around her. For a moment, she even felt unthreatened.

The kittens, piled against her belly, were still asleep — mollified by the sound of her heartbeat. The nest of hay in the cradle was scented with their milky breath and the deeply comforting warmth of their bodies against her own gave off a smell that Mottyl could only describe as *safety*. The universal darkness was also a comfort, since it provided a hiding place in which few creatures, if any, could find her. At least, for now.

The kittens would probably have remained asleep till hunger woke them, but Mottyl could not afford to indulge them in this. The need to make scat could not be put off — though it presented problems. She could not simply leave it unburied in a corner of the cabin, nor even in the corridor beyond. Its smell would invite every prowler on board the ark to discover her presence — and thus, her nest and the kittens. Rats might arrive or, worse, Doctor Noyes.

The memory of his voice caused her to scan the ceiling with her ears — but the voice above her had ceased and all she could hear was the storm and the creaking ark.

Is it safe to leave?

Yes — there's nobody nearby. But hide your babies.

Before leaping down from the cradle, Mottyl buried the kittens deep in the hay — pushing it against them with her nose and drawing it over them with her paws. Not one of them awoke and she blessed the motion of the cradle: it would deepen their sleep in her absence.

Mottyl stood in the centre of the floor, squinting against the dark and trying to conjure even the least bit of light with her one good eye — which, for all it was not completely blind as the other, was less and less able to deliver any sense of a break in the darkness. Light would soon be nothing more than a memory: but not quite yet . . .

I can't find the doorway.

There — ahead of you.

There was an oblong, vertical shape that hovered in the air — and Mottyl guessed it might be the crack of an open door. She sniffed for signs of a draught — but all she could smell was apples. Mrs Noyes had left the apple aprons underneath the bunk, and their sweetness flooded across the floor and blanked out every other smell.

For a moment, Mottyl considered burying her scat amongst the apples, thinking their aroma was strong enough to cover anything. But her *whispers* argued against it.

Dangerous. Too close to your nest.

Hurry, then — help me get out of here.

Doorway.

But *is* it a door??

Move.

Mottyl went over through the dark towards the oblong shape, moving against the violent motion of the floor beneath her, and found it was, indeed, a door. It was easy enough to open once she had put her whiskers through, and pressed quite hard with her shoulders.

What is this?

A hallway.

Where does it lead?

Turn left.

Mottyl used her shoulder to find the wall and, driven by the contractions of her bowel, she moved along the corridor towards the Well — not knowing, of course, that she was moving towards a pit four storeys deep. Nor could her *whispers* tell how deep it was. All they knew of it was the draught it created, carrying the smells of hay and of other animals.

Hundreds of them!

There must be a manure pile.

The thought of this — that she would soon find somewhere safe to lay and to bury her scat, made Mottyl careless — and she began to hurry forward, drawn by the growing strength of the draught and the overpowering need to relieve herself.

Don't hurry so! Careful!

But Mottyl paid no heed.

All at once she came to the edge of the Well and, though it was protected by a railing that went round all four sides, there was no protection at all for a creature the size of a cat.

Of course, Mottyl knew from the updraught that she was standing at the edge of some kind of hole or pit. But nothing helped her to gauge its depth. Having climbed many trees in her time — including the impossible heights of Crowe's redwood — she knew that if heights could only be judged by climbing, depths could only be told by descent.

I'm going to jump.

Find a stairs.

There isn't time for that. And there may not even be a stairs.

But . . .

Mottyl leapt.

Halfway down, realizing what she had done, she gave a terrible cry.

"Oh, my babies!"

Then — silence.

∞ Mrs Noyes came bursting through the doorway — pushed beyond endurance by her anger.

"What does it mean?" she cried. "What does it *MEAN?*" she shouted — all but falling down the steps in her rage. "What does it mean that we are all to be separated? I simply *DO NOT UNDERSTAND!*"

Ham pulled the door behind them and shut out the storm.

Mrs Noyes was sitting on the bottom step, refusing to move. This left Lucy and Emma stuck on the stairs, with Ham at the top.

"Could someone light a lantern, please?" said Emma. "I really am afraid of the dark."

Ham struck a match.

"Thank you," said Emma.

The match went out.

"Does anyone remember where there's a lamp?" Ham asked, feeling around in the dark.

"Yes," said Lucy. "There's one right here."

Ham felt a metal lantern being placed in his hands.

"That's funny," he said. "I don't recall there being . . ."

"I brought it with me," said Lucy — cutting off further speculation. "I liked it — so I stole it."

The lantern was made of what Lucy called *"classy brass"* instead of the mundane wrought iron of which the lamps in the hold were made. It burned very bright and as it turned out, Lucy had to confess she had also stolen some of Noah's better class candles, too. "Wicks made of tungsten," she explained. "Burns everlasting. Brighter than any old *string . . .*"

"That's funny," said Ham — having to shade his eyes in order to examine the candle in question. "I don't recall tungsten."

"Of course not," said Lucy. "You don't know everything, you know."

"Yes," said Ham. "But I would have known about *this*. I mean . . ."

"Why don't you shut up?" said Lucy, sweetly. "Why not just accept the nice, bright light — and shut your mouth about it."

Ham started down the stairs, giving Lucy a look, but saying nothing.

Mrs Noyes, however, was not so easily silenced.

"What does it mean?" she said. "What does it mean?"

"It means we're alone down here," said Lucy. "That's what it means. Us and the animals. And if you want my opinion, frankly I don't give a damn. Better alone down here than 'together' up there with Highfalutin' Hannah. Besides . . ." she stepped around the still-seated Mrs Noyes and started down the corridor after Ham, "I always did prefer the depths."

"Why?" said Emma, following after.

"It's warmer," said Lucy. "Can't you feel it? Cozy as a fireplace . . ."

Emma stopped in her tracks and threw back her shawl.

"Why — you're right!" she said. "It is. Much warmer."

"It's only because of the animals," said Ham. "They give off heat. . . ."

"Like burning coals," said Lucy.

"Or tungsten wicks," said Ham. "This lamp is hot!"

Lucy, Ham and Emma went on towards the cabins — but Mrs Noyes still sat on her step.

"What does it mean?" she said. "I don't understand. We were a family. . . ."

∞ It was Ham who first noticed that Mottyl wasn't in the cradle.

But Mrs Noyes — who by then had joined them — said that more than likely Mottyl had only gone somewhere to make scat.

"Well—" said Ham; "I guess we had best get started feeding the animals their supper. And Mama . . ." Ham turned to Mrs Noyes. "Maybe you could feed *us.*"

"Yes," said Mrs Noyes, distracted. "Yes. I'll get started right away."

Lucy gave each of them a tungsten candle and after a moment the lower decks were lit with bobbing aureoles of light as each of them went a different way in the dark.

In the cradle, the kittens stirred and were almost ready to wake. They, too, were hungry — and wanting to be fed.

∞ Japeth came, yet again, and stood at the top of the stairs, swinging his lantern and carrying his sword. "Mother!" he bellowed, his voice cracking. "*Mother!*"

Mrs Noyes — who was obedient to all her children's voices, especially when there was an edge of panic or of pain to the cry — came flying along the corridor with a wooden spoon in her hand and said; "what's the matter? You hurt or something?"

Japeth said; "of course not. I've just come to get you, that's all. He wants you again. . . ."

"Who?" said Mrs Noyes — as rudely as she could manage.

"Papa. He wants to ask you something."

Mrs Noyes said; "tell him I'm making dinner. I'll come when we've eaten." And she turned back towards her galley, where she had just put several potato cakes in a frying pan and was about to put the Brussels sprouts into boiling water.

"I think he wants to see you right away," said Japeth.

Mrs Noyes kept walking.

"I said . . ." he said.

Mrs Noyes turned. "And *I* said," she said; "*after we've eaten.*"

She kept on walking.

"HE WANTS TO SEE YOU RIGHT NOW, MAMA!"

Mrs Noyes stopped in her tracks.

"All right," she said. "I'll go and see your father, if you go and turn the potato cakes." She held out the wooden spoon — standing provocatively at the foot of the steps.

Japeth looked at the spoon and lifted his chin.

"Men don't go in kitchens," he said. "It isn't done."

"Fine," said Mrs Noyes — turning once again on her heel and heading back along the corridor; "then you tell him I'll be there when we've eaten."

Japeth summoned all his breath and almost choked on it.

The image of his father rose before him. Enraged.

"All right," he said. "I'll go and turn the potato cakes."

"That's better," said Mrs Noyes. "And you can put the sprouts on while you're at it. . . ."

Passing him, she thrust the wooden spoon into his hand and stepped out into the gale, which slammed the door behind her, almost taking off her fingers in the process.

Japeth studied the corridor below him and saw that it was empty. Going down the stairs, he began to sniffle, and by the time he had reached the bottom, he had to use the back of his hand on his cheeks.

Going further along the halls, turning and twisting back towards the galley in the prow, he hit all the walls with the spoon

which, by the time he got to the stove, was broken. "Serves
you right," he said to the spoon. And threw it into the fire.

∞ "All right," said Mrs Noyes. "What is it?"

Noah was standing beyond the table, reading from a book
called *Famous Battles of the Seven Seas*.

"Madam, I warn you: I will not be spoken to in that manner,"
he told her. "And where is our son?"

"He's turning the potato cakes," said Mrs Noyes. "And if
you want him back, then tell me what you want and let me
go."

Noah gazed at his wife with a mixture of irritation and ad-
miration. She was not without courage — and that was useful.
But he would have to find some way of breaking her contempt
for him. However, that would come later. In the meantime, it
was his painful duty to flatter her.

"Madam," he said. "Perhaps you were aware on your previous visit to these quarters that I had been given something
made of cheese for my dinner. . . ."

Mrs Noyes bit her tongue and said that, yes, she had noticed.

"Then you may also have noticed that it went unfinished."

"I most certainly did," she said. "And I wondered why, its
not being finished, you didn't offer it to us."

"You should not have cared for it, madam. That was my
reason."

Mrs Noyes looked at her husband and almost wept. She had
to work very hard to control herself — so that neither her relief at what she had heard nor her anticipation of what might
next be said would show.

"Are you saying," she said; "that the only reason you did
not offer us food is that . . . the food was not good enough to
offer?"

Noah managed something like a *yes* that was not quite the
word itself — but only a kind of noise into his fist.

Mrs Noyes beamed. "Does that mean you will ask us, then,
to sit with you when the food is more to your liking?"

This time the noise behind the fist sounded something like

"perhaps" and *"maybe"* but also — *"no — not really."* Mrs Noyes could not make it out.

She waited — wiping her hands on her apron.

Noah said; "the thing about the cheese dish was . . . I'm afraid Sister Hannah did not quite have the ingredients right."

"I see," said Mrs Noyes. "Oh."

"Yes. Well . . . and, you see . . ."

She watched him coldly as he fumbled for a way to say it — and then, when he couldn't, she said it for him.

"So — you want me to give her my recipe."

At least he had the decency to be embarrassed.

"Well — damn it, madam!" he said. "It has always been my favourite dish — and one that you manage supremely well."

Mrs Noyes bobbed automatically, as if she were a child receiving a compliment. But she said nothing. Her hair was hanging down, very wet, into her eyes and she brushed it away.

Noah turned to the door behind him and called out to Hannah and — while they waited for her — Mrs Noyes asked if she might sit down.

Noah said; "yes," and gestured to the chair in which she had sat during her previous "visit." When Hannah came in and seated herself — pencil poised above her handmade notebook across the table — Mrs Noyes let all her hair down: placed all her pins on the polished wood and, while she gave the recipe, wound her hair into plaits and set them — very tight — on top of her head.

"You can either bake the pastry beforehand, or cook it with the filling," she said. "I prefer the latter, since then the pastry is not so crisp that it flakes on the dish."

The pencil wrote — then paused.

"Shall I tell you how to make the pastry, too?" A new page was turned — quite eagerly, it seemed to Mrs Noyes, and the pencil hovered expectantly.

Noah sat down in the lamplight and watched his wife as she spoke. The voice she used was so gentle — reflective — and the play of light on her face . . . Four hundred years fell away, or so it seemed, as he listened to her . . . and the smells of the kitchen as it used to be came back into his mind. He could even see her hands, as she worked the dough . . . four hundred, five hundred years . . . Amazing. And sad. They had lived in houses, then, and the trees gave shade and the world was with them. Now . . .

". . . it is essential that the fat and flour be of equal weight. . . ."

We are old. But then . . .

". . . always use unsalted butter . . ."

. . . we were children. Or the next best thing. Children in a garden — near an orchard — eating quiche. And I loved her, then. I did, you know. I . . .

". . . a quarter gill of cold water and a pinch of salt. The salt to taste . . ." Mrs Noyes looked at Noah. "He likes a largish pinch," she said. "Like *that* . . ." and she showed her thumb and forefinger — just so.

The pencil was lifted from the page. It did not know how to write this down.

"Just look — and memorize," said Mrs Noyes. "Like *that* . . ."

After a moment, the pencil went back to the paper.

Noah stood up and went away, and when he came back, he had blown his nose and was folding his handkerchief into his pocket. Taking it out again, he began refolding it, dabbing at his moustaches — folding the handkerchief over and over until, in the end, Mrs Noyes gave such a sigh and shot him such a look that he put it abruptly behind his back, where it hung down out of his hand like a tail.

"Now — about the filling," said Mrs Noyes.

Five hundred years.

". . . a hard cheese, from full cream, is best. And it must be finely . . . *finely* grated. None of this cutting it up with knives and hoping for the best . . ."

Mrs Noyes was quite enjoying herself. She hadn't taught another soul how to cook since all her daughters had died.

". . . a well-beaten egg . . . a half-pint of evaporated and a half-gill of *whole* milk . . . your cheese and a dash of paprika."

"Ahhh!" said Noah.

"Yes," said Mrs Noyes. " 'Ahhh!' indeed. No doubt you left out the paprika and one more essential ingredient. . . ."

She looked at Noah — quite unable to contain herself. "Do you remember," she said; "what it is?"

Noah shook his head.

"Then I shall tell you," said Mrs Noyes. "Are you sure you don't remember?'

"No, I don't remember," said Noah — leaning forward. "Please . . ."

Mrs Noyes turned to the pencil and whispered; "*nutmeg.*"

"Ahhhhhh . . ." said Noah.

"Yes," said Mrs Noyes; "and only *that* much." She made a noise in her throat — a grating cough — and then smiled. "Do you understand? *That* much — and not a flicker more."

Hannah made the noise in her own throat — while Noah watched and Mrs Noyes squinted at her.

"Good — just so."

It was over.

"May I go now?" she said.

Noah stared at her and blinked.

"I really must," said Mrs Noyes. "My potato cakes will be ruined."

She stood up and swept a few remaining pins into the pocket of her apron. And then she made for the door.

"Goodbye," she said. And went away.

Noah did not know how to stop her.

"Goodbye," he said. "And . . ."

Hannah closed the book.

"It's late," she said. "May I go to bed now?"

"Yes," said Noah. "Please."

Hannah went to the other door, holding the handmade notebook close against her breast. "I will memorize all of this," she said. "Including the nutmeg . . ." and she gave the grating cough. "Good night."

"Good night," said Noah.

After she had gone, he took the handkerchief and folded it again and put it deep in his pocket.

"Well," he said — aloud; "that's that, I guess."

And — a second later — "yes," he said — and turned to find his book.

Famous Battles of the Seven Seas.

∞ When Mottyl landed in the dark at the bottom of the Well, she landed — as any cat would — on her feet. But the shock that might have been absorbed if the fall had been slighter wrenched her shoulder and cracked a rib. She was also bruised over much of her back and cut on the underside of her chin. A tooth had pierced her cheek and her insides were badly twisted.

Her *whispers* were silent.

Mottyl's first impressions, however, were not of herself but of where she was; of how complete the darkness was; of a peculiar animal scent she could not identify; of a fetid dampness whose stench was separate from the animal smell and which seemed to be as much a taste as an odour. But above all, she was aware of a sound that was totally new to her: a sound that was menacing and meaningless at the same time.

This — the sound — was Mottyl's first concern, because she was helpless and it threatened her.

She was lying on her side, onto which she had collapsed after the initial impact of her fall, and it became very quickly obvious that — for whatever reason — she was unable to move. Feeling was the last of her senses to return (aside from her *whispers*) — and as it made its slow progress through her body, she could at least sense where the pains were — though nothing informed her of why she was paralysed.

Into this paralytic state came the reverberations of this noise that was absolutely terrifying to her, because it was so alarmingly close. Something was moving the floor beneath her, simply by standing on it — first on one foot and then on another. She could feel this weight shifting from side to side, and its power was so great that Mottyl could not connect it to any beast or being she had ever seen. It was as if a building the size of the bath house were able to rock from side to side. . . . And the noise this created was like disintegrating, splintering wood.

Still Mottyl could not move, no matter how much effort she applied to the attempt, and she was overwhelmed with panic because it seemed this shifting weight might descend on her at any moment.

It was now that she gave up trying to rise and attempted, instead, another means of escape. What she wanted to accomplish was a kind of swimming motion: a drawing in of her legs towards her centre. She wanted, by doing this, both to make herself as small as possible and also to gather all her power so that she could push away from whatever it was that threatened her. Her legs, at least, appeared to be obeying her — though she could not yet manage to rise from her side. And as her hips and back were thrown into motion, she realized how appallingly hard the surface was on which she lay — and how wet it was.

What if the wetness was her own blood?

This thought galvanized all that remained of her energy, and she began to struggle — much as a dying fish will struggle on the shore — to move herself simply by the force of her contortions. This proved so painful to her side and to her cracked rib that she almost cried out, as much in surprise as in pain.

It then occurred to her that, since whatever threatened her must be an animal (she could feel its breath — she could hear its gigantic stomach) — she might attempt to speak to it. One new factor prompted her to take a chance on words — and this was the odour of the beast. Whatever it was, it did not eat flesh.

Neither its breath nor its skin nor its traces — of which it now gave off a veritable cataract — had even the slightest smell of telltale blood or bone.

"Is someone there?" she asked. And immediately realized what a silly question it was — but it was the first one to occur to her.

Silly or not, it brought all motion to a halt — and Mottyl imagined that she heard an intake of breath.

"*Is* someone there?" she repeated.

"*Where?*" It was a very large voice that seemed to be

contained within a very small mouth. "I haven't seen anyone. . . ."

Mottyl's reply was quiet. "I am lying, I think, quite near you. I am a cat."

"A *what?*"

"A cat. I am somewhere down by your feet — and I cannot move."

Silence — due perhaps to a contemplation of what a cat might be.

"May I ask you," Mottyl continued; "not to move your feet around quite so much? . . ."

At last the great voice above her was heard again. But it did not address Mottyl in quite the way she might have expected so large a creature to speak to one so small. Its tone was rather plaintive. "Is a cat — by any chance — anything like a rat?"

"Not at all."

This brought a sigh of relief so great that Mottyl could smell it. Hay — mingled with stale, almost rancid stomach juices.

"Have you an ulcer?" Mottyl asked.

"I'm afraid so, yes," the beast replied. "It's become much worse these last few days since we came aboard the ark. I cannot abide the dark. A little dark, perhaps, but not this endless dark. It makes one so afraid."

"Who are you?" Mottyl queried.

"My name is One Tusk." The voice came from the dark. "I am an elephant."

"I must be as much in the dark about elephants as you are about cats, One Tusk. All I can tell is that you're very large."

Now, Mottyl felt a strange sensation that at first alarmed her. A soft, not unpleasant and very gentle probe was being made of her body. But what alarmed her — for all the gentleness of the probe — was that it might have been a snake who was conducting the inspection.

"You don't *smell* dangerous to me," One Tusk sniffed. "But you have been injured."

"I know that. I just don't know how badly."

"And you are currently nursing young. . . ."

"Yes—and they want me. Can you—by any chance—help me to get out of here?"

"That depends where you want to go. Where have you come from? How did you get here?"

"She *fell.*" Another voice spoke—somewhere off in a corner. A gruff, bad-tempered voice.

"Who's *that?*" Mottyl asked.

"Only Hippo," was One Tusk's reply.

"Oh, yes." Mottyl nodded in the dark. "I've heard of Hippo. She was described to me. Always complaining."

"You'd be complaining too, Cat, if they took all your water away. I want a bath. I want to submerge — and all I get is a pailful of water every morning. Would that keep *you* alive?"

Mottyl did not answer this.

"Where did you fall *from?*" One Tusk sounded concerned.

"I don't really know how far I fell—but I fell from the top— wherever the top may be."

"Then you've fallen three whole decks."

Hippo seemed impressed. "It's a wonder she's alive. If I fell even *one* deck, I'd be flattened."

"Yes," rumbled One Tusk. "And so would the rest of us. But this creature here is nothing like you and me and Rhino. She is extremely small — and covered with fur, not skin — or scales."

Mottyl was puzzled. "Who is Rhino?"

"Rhino is lying down asleep. He is very depressed. His situation is just the opposite of Hippo's. For him, the ark is much too damp. He needs a dust wallow—and of course we have no wallow here, only bilge and wet manure."

"Oh, please," cried Mottyl. "Can you get me away from here. My children . . ."

One Tusk thought about it at length and, in fact, he thought about it so long that Mottyl was afraid he might have fallen asleep, like Rhino.

Finally, Hippo had a suggestion. "Why not lift her up with your trunk? You could at least raise her as far as the next deck."

"That's true." One Tusk waggled his huge head. "But she's
so small . . ." And then peered down at Mottyl. "Do you trust
me, Cat?"

"I suppose I have to."

"Very well then. I am going to pick you up. And the only
thing I can tell you is that you must not struggle."

Mottyl again felt the soft explorations of the elephant's probe
— felt herself being taken very gently and held, just as she
might have been held in the crook of a large elbow — the way
Mrs Noyes sometimes held her. And then she was *lifted.* . . .

What's happening?

So, there you are.

Yes — but where?

There's no time to explain. We're in the middle of the
air somewhere.

Rising!

One Tusk lifted Mottyl up very high and swung her back
towards the floor of the next deck above them.

"Can you feel anything there?" One Tusk asked — still holding on to Mottyl.

"Yes. There are planks."

"I will push you onto those planks and then I will let go. Do
you understand?"

"Yes."

"Are you ready?"

"Yes."

Mottyl felt the floor slide into place beneath her — after which
One Tusk withdrew his probe.

When this was done, Mottyl found herself — still lying on
her side — in a dimly lit corridor not unlike the one from which
she had fallen. She could see no detail — but she could see the
barest trace of light.

"Thank you," she called down into the dark. "You have
been very kind, One Tusk. You have saved my life — and my
children's lives."

"Don't even mention it." One Tusk's voice was now muffled and seemingly a long way off. "We are all in this together — and we must do what we can do."

The amazing thing was that, for all the lifting and all that time being held, Mottyl had never been held so gently. And not a single wound had been irritated. Not even her cracked rib.

One Tusk called up from below.

"If you have any influence up there, Cat, could we have some light down here?"

"Yes," Hippo added. "And some water."

"I'll do what I can," Mottyl assured them. "I'm certain someone will help."

∞ In half an hour, Mottyl had managed to crawl around the inside of the Well — hugging the corridor wall, until — exhausted — she could go no further.

She was worried about her babies.

They would want her now — it was feeding time — past feeding time, in fact. But she knew that her strength could carry her no further.

"If only I could send a message . . ." she murmured, unaware she had made any sound at all.

"You can," assured a familiar voice. "You can, if you tell me where the message is to go."

It was the Unicorn — somewhere above her in his cage — and Mottyl almost fainted in gratitude for the sound of his voice.

∞ When it dawned on Mrs Noyes that Mottyl had been too long away simply to be making scat, she began to ask the others if by any chance they had seen her. She tried very hard not to panic, and not to let the other animals know how afraid she was. Afraid — and also beginning to shake quite violently. What she wanted most in the whole world — aside from Mottyl's safe return — was a drink.

But there was no drink.

Just a little taste of gin would have tided her over the tensions crowding around her: the horror of the ark itself — the loss of her cat — the loss of her place in the scheme of things.

Oh, please — oh, no; she said to herself, already having to use her apron as a handkerchief; *please, no crying; please, no tears* . . . She licked her lips and fervently wished that every tear was a drop of gin. *"Salty gin,"* she said aloud. And that made her laugh.

When she got to the sheep, Mrs Noyes was in very bad shape. There was still no sign of Mottyl — still no hope that a magic jar would appear from beneath the bales of straw and hay. *Oh — if only I had thought,* she thought. *If only I had imagined I would be here, I would have filled whole bins with gin jars.* . . .

The sheep looked so forlorn and sad. And the lambs were all so listless. The cattle were having a problem learning how to stay on their feet with the violent motion of the ark — and the horses were thirsty — but had already had their ration of water and would have to be denied — and the goats wanted shoes to eat or flowers — and the oxen were so crowded in their pen they could not lie down — and the hens were . . . and the geese were . . . and the pigs were . . . and . . .

"Oh — *everyone!*" Mrs Noyes suddenly said aloud — standing in the midst of the hay, with a pitchfork in her hands and tears pouring down her cheeks. "Why must we be so helpless here, and so unhappy? . . ."

All the animals turned to stare at her, alarmed. And she saw them watching her — and she felt so sorry that they had seen her breaking down. It was the one thing she had sworn they would not witness — because they needed her — they needed someone — anyone — to be strong.

For a moment — looking back at them almost defiantly — Mrs Noyes found herself thinking: I don't want to be strong. Why can't I rest? Why can't somebody else be strong? Why is it always me that has to do this — come up first to the surface when all I want to do is *sink*. When all I want to do is *stop*. When all I want is my *gin*. And, damn it! (She looked at the sheep.) I want someone to bring *my* hay!

Then she forced herself to smile.

"Why don't we sing?" she said. "Yes? We can all sing a nice — happy — song. . . ."

There was then a pause while Mrs Noyes tried — and failed — to think of a happy song.

"We must sing for Mottyl," she said. "Especially for Mottyl — because she is lost and we don't know where she can possibly be. And if we sing loud enough, maybe she'll hear us. . . ."

Just at this moment, the ark gave a dreadful lurch as the storm began to worsen. The lantern swung so violently that Mrs Noyes was afraid it would fall and start a fire. Dropping her pitchfork, she took the lantern down from its hook — and held it tight so it could not fall.

Very slowly, very tentatively, as if the old hymn was creating itself in the moment — Mrs Noyes began to sing:

Eternal Father, strong to save,
Whose arm doth bind the restless wave,
Who bidd'st the mighty ocean deep
Its own appointed limits keep:
Oh hear us when we cry to Thee
For those in peril on the sea . . .

The sheep were the first to join her — ewes and then rams and finally the lambs. Even the goats began to sing — and the oxen — who had never been singers in the past — began to hum — but only to hum because they did not know the words.

Oh Sacred Spirit, who didst brood
Upon the chaos dark and rude,
Who bad'st its angry tumult cease,
And gavest light, and life and peace:
Oh hear us when we cry to Thee
For those in peril on the sea!

By the time that everyone was singing, the message, passed from the Unicorn to the Porcupine and from the Porcupine to the Weasel and from the Weasel to the Vixen, had begun to make its way from the lower levels to the upper, and as though in return for this message — *that Mottyl had been found and*

was safe — the song and the singing of it made its way in the
opposite direction, until all the animals were whispering and
roaring:

> *. . . our brethren shield in danger's hour;*
> *From rock and tempest, fire and foe,*
> *Protect them wheresoe'er they go;*
> *And ever let these rise to Thee:*
> *Glad hymns of praise from land and sea!*

And a safe place for Mottyl;
And a wallow for Rhino;
And water for Hippo;
And light for One Tusk;
And a jar of gin for me . . .
Amen

∞ The days passed — becoming weeks and the weeks
left their marks of depletion on everyone's patience and stamina. The routine above decks was fastidious and sparse. Events
were as hard to come by as sunny days. Hannah's child became so large, by all accounts its birth might happen tomorrow.
Shem found less and less to occupy his time and soon gave
over to sitting alone in amongst the Reverend Doctor's private
stock of delicacies — where he gorged on dates and avocados,
bread and butter and bananas. Soon, he was keeping pace with
his wife in growth.

Japeth, boiling with youth, could think of nothing but sex.
Every day, he put on and took off his swords and knives, his
greaves, his breastplate and his helmet — and every day, as he
caught his armoured image in his shield, he would stop — amazed
at the beauty of his reflected blue limbs and, before he could
stop himself, his organ would rise into his hand and demand
attention.

Every morning Noah cloistered himself in the Chapel and
read from the Holy Books and scrolls. In the afternoons, he
read from his naval books. In the evenings, he sat with Hannah and the two cats and either she would read aloud to him
from the works of various Gnostic magicians — or he would

dictate his theories on *The Art of True Alchemy* or *The Anatomy of Quadrupeds*, in which he further explored the uses of zinc on the one hand, and the possibility of crossing a sheep with a goat on the other. Twice a day, he walked upon the deck and stared at the sky.

Although Noah was quite unaware of it, Hannah was gradually gaining more control over his daily routine — the kind of control a nurse will exert when dealing with an elderly, confused patient. Sometimes they simply sat together for hours — silent and still.

Below decks, there was a good deal more activity — though most of it was simple labour. Emma fed the birds, Ham the larger animals and Lucy the animals in between. Mrs Noyes took care of her sheep and fed the people. Mottyl was ensconced in a secret nest above the Unicorn's cage and her kittens flourished and, after the allotted time, they opened their ears and eyes to the world of the ark.

Mrs Noyes took many days to fully recover from her need for drink — and on occasion, had to be helped to recover from her dreams. Sometimes, she walked in her sleep, and this did lead to one extraordinary experience.

Four weeks after setting forth on its journey, the ark encountered a dreadful storm in which a good deal of lightning flashed and thunder roared. In spite of all the banging and crashing, Mrs Noyes went unknowingly — if dangerously — off on one of her midnight walks. This brought her, in time, to a cage in which two bears were somewhat the worse for wear on account of the storm. Mrs Noyes had always been appalled by bears. They both terrified and infuriated her. More than likely, the anger stemmed from her fury at not being able to overcome her fear. At any rate — in her sleep, she came upon the bears and one of them was weeping. Mrs Noyes dreamt of Lotte and — even in her sleep — her heart was broken by her remembrance of the lost child. Coming awake in the midst of a gigantic crack of thunder — Mrs Noyes heard the bear and, still with Lotte in her mind, opened the gate of the bear cage and stepped inside.

"Poor, poor Lotte," she said, and put out her arms to the weeping bear. "Don't be afraid — it's just a storm. . . ."

The bear stepped into the proffered embrace and hung its head on Mrs Noyes's shoulder.

"There, there, there," said Mrs Noyes, and only realized what was in her arms when she patted it soothingly across the back. Fear and fury battled for possession of her, but in the end, it was practicality that won out.

Well — she thought — *what do I do now?*

The answer was relatively simple.

She sat on the floor of the bear cage and held the terrified bear until it fell asleep with its head in her lap. . . .

In the morning, that was how Ham found them—his mother in her nightdress—snoring in the straw, with a bear on either side, asleep.

∞ One morning the rains had been so great all through the night that the waters were utterly flattened and stilled. A fog had come down, yet it did not reach the surface of the great sea, but moved above it — swirling here and there, obliterated by gentle squalls — lifting a little higher — opening vistas — closing them — but never obscuring the waters themselves — or the rain that fell upon them, light as a gentle massage.

The great swells came and went and the ark rose up and fell with its Castle roofs and the Pagoda shifting in and out of sight until it became unnerving to watch them.

Japeth — who had observed all this from the doorway of the Armoury — was about to retire to his bunk for another wasted day, when he spied something out beyond the ark which sent a chill through his bones.

Oh, God — oh, God! he thought — *we are not alone out here. . . . we are not alone!*

He started for the centre Castle, but turned immediately back to arm himself. When he re-emerged — already running — he was carrying sword and shield and breastplate — net and trident — three knives — two axes — his bow and arrows and his hunting spear. Slipping and sliding, falling and rising, Japeth raced for the Castle and burst in, shouting; "war! War!"

"What?" said Noah, who had been eating his breakfast — feeding Abraham and Sarah in his lap, as Yaweh had done.

"War!" Japeth said again. "*War!*" He pointed out towards the water with his spear. "*WAR!*" Otherwise, he was totally incapable of words. His mouth was full of knives, his hands full of buckles and swords and the floor around him heaped with fallen weaponry.

Noah, attempting a calm he could not possibly maintain, rose from his chair and dumped the cats in the process. Reaching for his umbrella, he strode to the door—turned back and said; "go find Shem and Sister Hannah at once."

Then he was gone.

Twenty seconds later, he was back in the Castle crying out a single word — as Japeth had done.

But Noah's word was not *war.*

Noah's word was: "*PIRATES!*"

∞ The scene on the deck was one of veritable chaos. Even Sister Hannah — bulging with child — was brandishing a sword. Shem and Japeth were dashing from one end of the ark to the other, hacking at the rails in order to prevent the Pirates from climbing over.

Noah — in full glory — stood on the poop deck beneath the black umbrella, his robes flapping and his beard flowing out around him, shouting at the others; "no boarding parties! No boarding parties!" and, many times over, the utterly meaningless word; "*avast!*"

Hearing the commotion, Mrs Noyes, Ham, Lucy and Emma rushed to the doors of their dungeon — certain that the ark was sinking.

Noah, seeing them emerge, called down from the poop; "all hands on deck to repel the boarding parties!"

Shem stared at his mother, wild-eyed (unheard of, for Shem) and said the single word; "Pirates!"

Crowding forward, with Emma literally holding onto her apron strings — and Ham and Lucy following in close order — Mrs Noyes led her people into the centre of the deck where they could get a view of what was happening.

The ark—becalmed and heaving beneath the fog—was surrounded on all sides by hundreds of playful and frolicking creatures — leaping out of the water, waving their flippers at the ark and its occupants and calling out; *"hallo! Hallo!"* before they fell back beneath the surface.

Further off, there was what appeared to be a flotilla of Noah's blue paper whales from his Masque of Creation — except that these whales were real and of other colours than blue. (Paper would have disintegrated — sunk — Mrs Noyes decided, very quickly.)

One look informed her — as it also informed both Ham and Lucy — that the Pirates were friends. (Emma did not benefit from this single glance — or from any other. She kept her eyes shut tight throughout the whole incident.)

"Stop!" cried Mrs Noyes — searching wildly for Noah. "Stop! Can't you see they want to be *friends?"*

Japeth, at this very moment, rushed past his mother, waving his sword and pushing at her so violently that both she and Emma were felled and rolled across the deck.

Rising without thought of injury (she was bleeding) Mrs Noyes — with Emma ever-after — ran to the foot of the poop deck and called to her husband — who stood, still raging — begging him to stop the slaughter.

"Friends!" she called to him. "Friends! They want to be our *friends!"*

But Noah refused to hear her.

Were these creatures not on every side?

Had they not, already, in numbers so great they might overwhelm the masters of the ark, come hurtling over the sides and onto the deck? And it was only thanks to the glorious arm of his warrior son that they were being dispatched as quickly as they came.

"Madam—" he called down through the smoke of his beard — as he raised his arm and the black umbrella at heaven — "these are the creatures of hell! Pirates from the pit! Spewed from Satan's mouth! Do your duty, woman. Kill them!"

Mrs Noyes turned away. Sick.

A great, grey pearly shape — all gleaming and straining against the air — leapt up before Mrs Noyes — and fell at her feet.

Rolling on its back like a cat at play, it raised its head and looked at her with eyes she would never forget.

The whole visage was a message of joy and of greeting.

But in that moment of recognition, as Mrs Noyes and the creature looked at one another and smiled — Japeth's sword descended — swiftly and fatally.

∞ Mrs Noyes gave a great shout of rage and shook herself free from the encumbrance of her daughter-in-law — and threw herself, whole, upon her son. She battled with his arms — she battled with his eyes — she battled with his legs and with his sword. But she could not stop him. Shem would not let her.

The Ox strode up behind her and kicked her on both arms — forcing her grip from his brother's legs.

The Ox strode up behind her and kicked her on both arms — forcing her grip from his brother's legs.

Emma had already fallen down against the wall of the Armoury, wailing at the top of her lungs. Ham and Lucy, having seen that the only way to save the marauders was to cast them bodily back into the sea, were doing this when Japeth ran for his trident and net and snared them like birds, securing the net to the deck by piercing both it and Lucy's ki-mono with the trident.

At last, with the waters all about the ark not only stained with their blood, but crowded with the corpses of their brothers and sisters, the raiders retreated in confusion. Still lying on the deck, unable to rise because of the violence of Shem's kicks, Mrs Noyes looked out beneath the blanket of fog and watched the creatures regrouping between the ark and the brooding shapes of the whales. She wanted to shout at them — *go back* — but, knowing her husband's vehemence in moments such as these, she remained silent.

But in her heart she said; *go back. Go back. They will kill you all.*

Surveying the wondrous carnage below him, Noah proclaimed a great victory in Yaweh's name. The sanctity of the ark had been preserved and the Pirates repelled.

∞ Waste-not-want-not Shem was not one to settle for victory alone.

The Pirate corpses, he told his father, would do very nicely for the lions.

∞ Having identified the Pirates and having established a place for them in the order of things, Noah returned to the problem of the growing discontent amongst his own faction. Locks and keys and hard labour would keep the others in their place, but what of Shem and Hannah? And Japeth?

It was already a well-established fact, long before Noah's time, that life for the leaders of men was far from easy. Any thinking person had only to imagine the political problems inherent in separating the bloodlines of Seth and Cain to have a good deal of sympathy for Adam. The Father of Men had also, perforce, been the father of diplomacy. Yet, for all his efforts, everything had failed.

During Noah's darkest days aboard the ark he thought much and often about his illustrious forebear. After all—historically, they shared the same responsibilities: the survival of the human race; the subjugation of nature; the establishment of law and order. All to say nothing of the warring in their own families. Three times over, Adam had begun the experiment and three times over he had begun with nothing but his own determination, his ingenuity and his relationship with God. Once, after Yaweh had scratched him from the dust of Eden—yet again, beyond the gates of Paradise and—lastly—after the death of Abel.

In the Garden: the naming of animals—the appalling loneliness—the birth of Eve and trial by temptation. *Failure*. After Eden: the breaking of stony ground—the rejection of Lilith—the creation of a family—and the stones of Cain. *Failure*. Yet, there was hope when, after the murder of Abel, came the birth of Seth—after the sin of Eve, the subordination of women—and after the sons of Adam had mated with mankind, the Sons of God had been born. But then the giants of corruption had appeared and the worship of Baal and Mammon—foreshadowing the end of everything.

Failure.

It seemed no matter what decisions had been made, no matter what course of action had been followed, that — despite successes — failure was inevitable. And no matter how many times Noah walked around the deck beneath his umbrella — calling out for new and different answers — the answers were always the same: every birth foretells a death: in every new beginning lie the seeds of ruin. Eve and apples — Cain and murder — giants and corruption. Humankind and rain.

And of this present new beginning — whose symbol was the ark — Noah had been appointed steward. And, as such, he had already seen the seeds of ruin sprouting: in his wife; in Ham and Lucy. These three were already at work in the bowels of the ark — spreading opposition to the Edict — drawing the lines between the will of Yaweh and the mere will of men.

But they would not be allowed to prevail. Noah had sworn it. All he need do was maintain his power amongst the others.

This time, success. This time, mastery by whatever means. This time, the will of God would triumph, no matter what the cost.

∞ One day, walking on the deck during his deep depression, Noah said many prayers. Why did the children of the mighty always turn out so badly? There was not a son in his possession he could love. Ham — the worst of all — was a rebel and a malcontent who had married beneath him — some kind of *courtesan* whose powdered face and white-gloved hands were the hiding place of vicious deceit — and even treachery. Japeth — blue and dangerous — was useful with his arms, but nothing more. His whole mind had turned to sex and sensuality — his whole demeanour was that of an animal and his whole life was given up to petulance and sloth. And there was worse: the one dread thought that Noah could not prevent whenever he came to Japeth in his mind: *you cannot be an ape and be of God!* And he is *mine.* . . .

Noah fell with all the weight of his despair against the rail and wept with fury. Shem — the Ox — whose whole existence was just an excuse for strength and brute force. Who barely had any words at all . . . whose duty to his father was so *dutiful* that Noah almost wished it would break and let out even a single word of opposition — one little *no* that would indicate there was someone in there, *thinking!*

Thinking. Thinking. Must I do all the thinking.

Yes. It was all too plain. And, were it not for Hannah, he would go mad with loneliness. If only Yaweh would return. If only He would speak — if only He would . . .

Help.

Noah went up through the downpour and stood at the prow of the ark.

The wind had dropped, but the saturated air was cold enough without it. A fog was looming over the sea and the forward movement of the ark was barely apparent. Looking down, he could see the swelling waters beneath him, calm and pitted with rain, and the heaving bulk upon which he stood made hardly any noise, but only the sound of its weight as it rose and fell. Noah wiped his eyes with his handkerchief and peered — the world's first Admiral of All the Oceans — into the fog bank ahead.

Below him he could hear the shouts of elephants and the cries of lemurs, the bleating of goats and the gargle of hens laying eggs. And above him and all around him — riding out on the waters — the sea birds mewing and the great Pirate beasts, who appeared to be singing. But there were no human voices — none. And never, never, never the voice of Yaweh . . .

Tell me; he prayed — almost shutting his eyes in the hopes of opening them to see a miracle — *will You walk upon the water? Will You float upon the air? Where will You reappear? Where may I look for You next? Where are You now?*

Noah looked up — tilting the black umbrella over his shoulder — letting the rain fall onto his face and through his beard. But there was nothing there. And no one. He turned and gazed at the deck behind him — searching out the outlines of the Castle, the Pagoda and the Armoury beyond and the curving lip of the poop deck's railing. Everything was shrouded in fog and every surface was crowded with the shapes of birds — but nothing, no one else.

The air was larded with the most unholy smell of fish and of animal manure and human wastes, and the sea itself had a putrid stink about it, perhaps of rotting corpses.

Noah turned back to face the prow and resolved not to look at the waters below him again, lest he see what was there. Instead he drew his sights on the fog bank — rolling towards him.

His earlier suspicions that Yaweh was tired and had gone to Nod were turning to the disturbing thought that more could be wrong than mere exhaustion. What if Yaweh were ill? Truly ill. Could Yaweh die?

It was inconceivable.

Yet, the flood itself had been inconceivable — nothing more than a penny and a bottle, nothing more than a childish trick. But here it was: entire.

The fog began to hide the ark, and the stink of dead things became almost palpable. The oppressive silence of the universe itself began to blossom beyond the mere cries of birds and the bawling of the beasts — and it pressed against Noah's ears until he thought his ears must surely pop. And the eerie lights that pervaded the fog made him yearn to see and to feel the sun, which had not been seen nor felt since . . . He could not tell how long it had been. Forever — or so it seemed.

He was lonely. For the sun. For everything that had been and was no more. His body ached in its great and terrible age. All his bones were as brittle as candy now. His feet were stones and pebbles inside his slippers and his robe was impossibly heavy, weighted down with all its many layers and its damp. He wanted two young men — as Methuselah had had — to hold him up by the elbows: women to carry his sleeves and to hold his umbrella: other women to fondle and to comfort him — to prepare his table and fold down his bed — to draw his bath and make his toilette — someone to hold his hands and to rub his legs and bring them back to life. He wanted someone to carry the spoon and place it against his lips. . . .

He wanted wives and daughters — but all he had was Shem and Ham and Japeth. And her. That woman!

And a silent God who refused to materialize.

Noah forced his growing panic down to the pit of his stomach and said aloud; *"I will not speak."* His mind was swept with fearful images of space and of endless fog through which the ark might drift forever — and the dark foreboding of a death by drowning.

"I need You here," he whispered; "if not as a God — then, at least, as a friend. . . ."

Surely I will not be alone forever; he thought. Surely that is not what will be.

He stood at the prow beneath the black umbrella and he waited. He waited for an hour. For two hours. For three. He waited all that afternoon.

From her secret place in the Pagoda, Crowe was watching Noah. It seemed the old man was watching for land as keenly as she was. But she knew it was not there. If it had been — she would have smelled it. And if the old man had not been Noah, she would have flown down and told him so. As it was, she was not inclined, and she fluffed out her feathers and settled deeper into the comforting shape of the chimney pot that was her nest. If that old man had any sense, she thought; he would give up the vigil. There was nothing in the waters there (she had been so often to look) — but the lumbering shapes of the whales who were learning to swim and the corpses of some children and the pages of some books.

∞ *Yaweh?*
No.

∞ At table that evening, Noah ate very close to his dish. He held his spoon as a child will hold its spoon — full-fisted — and he drew the soup in through the sieve of his beard as if unaware that he had a beard. His eyes were very busy, playing over the table and his sons, Shem and Japeth. And Hannah.

"What is this dreadful gruel?" he asked.

"Fish chowder," said Hannah, who — in fact — had become rather proud of what she could achieve with nothing but what the sea provided and the little that remained in Noah's larder that was special to his needs: his herbs and teas and cheeses.

"Pagh!" Noah pushed his dish away and fell against the back of his chair. "When will there be food that is food?" he said.

"When there is land," said Shem.

Noah paid no attention. The answer was too straightforward and gave no room for an argument: and he wanted — desperately — an argument: a fight: a debate: a conversation . . . anything with minds behind it. Anything with some imagination. "You have had the benefit of practice now for *weeks*," he said, still addressing Hannah. "Yet all we are given is garbage. I will eat no more of it. Bring me an egg or an apple. Anything but this."

Hannah said nothing and rose from her place and began to make for the galley.

Noah rapped the table.

"My dish!" he said.

Hannah returned and took up the dish in both hands. She was shaking with contained anger. Sullen and bitterly tired of her pregnancy, she bit back every word that might have told how she felt these days and merely mumbled yes and no. When the urge was on him, she took down the old man's dictation and patiently read it back to him. Never arguing — never saying "this is right" and "this is wrong" or "I agree with this" and "disagree with that." Nothing. Never a word. but she was full of words. Sentences and paragraphs. Whispers and shouts. Hundreds of them. *Thousands.* But she was a woman and she could not speak. Aloud. But only think in silence and go mad. And now, when she might have legitimately spoken in her own behalf — she maintained her dreadful silence and took up the dish and went with it through the little door that led to the galley, letting it bang shut behind her.

Noah flashed a look at his sons: Shem on his right — Japeth on his left — both opposite, where he could keep an eye on them. (Hannah, when seated, sat at the end of the table nearest her duties.)

Shem was calmly feeding — lifting and lowering his spoon — never pausing between the mouthfuls. Not a word. He came to the table to be fed and nothing more. His enormous shoulders were rounding down towards his belly — and his belly had

begun to bloat and to push him back from the table's edge and
Noah thought; if he doesn't stop eating, he will go entirely to
flesh, like his mother. . . .

Japeth was like an animal just let out of its cage. His eyes
had followed Hannah's retreat to the galley with such open
longing that it turned Noah's stomach. And Japeth held his
spoon like a knife — turned down — and picked the little bits of
fish from his dish with his fingers, licking his fingers crudely
and — somehow — lasciviously, till Noah had to say to him;
"stop!"

Japeth's breast was gleaming with perspiration and he smelled
of stale sweat. Noah could not imagine how this could be, since
he himself must use two gowns to keep his body warm and —
tonight — the extra warmth of a shawl around his shoulders.
But Japeth sat nearly naked — bare legs and bare arms and
open tunic, with his curly hair in matted strands, all damp across
his forehead. Just like a man in the midst of a heatwave . . .

"Take your eyes off that woman," Noah said.

Japeth had not been aware that his father was staring at him
and he sat bolt upright — his soup spilling down into his lap and
bits of fish laid out along his lower lip.

He drew his hand across his mouth: confused. "Sir?" he
said.

"Keep your eyes where they belong. In your head."

"I don't understand you, father."

"You were feeding on that woman's shape. I saw you."

Japeth swallowed hard and started to choke.

Noah ignored this — and turned to Shem.

"Haven't you noticed your brother's attentions to your wife?
What sort of husband are you?"

Shem looked at Japeth and shrugged.

"He's a child, father." (*Noah's* attentions to Hannah had by
no means gone unnoticed — but Shem could not mention these.)

Noah sneered. "A child? He is a married man."

Japeth's choking had become so violent, he rose from his
place — knocking over his chair.

Hannah came and stood in the doorway to the galley, with a

pear in one hand and a tea-towel in the other. She was drying the pear and staring at Japeth.

Noah stood up and walked around the table.

Japeth was purple and near death.

Noah walked behind his son and picked up Japeth's sword from where it lay on the table.

Hannah stepped forward, the tea-towel falling to the floor.

Noah stood back and struck his son on the shoulders with the flat of the sword's blade.

Nonetheless, the blow drew blood and Shem leapt to his feet.

Japeth fell across the table — his hands full of spoons and dishes and his face wet with chowder, exposing his behind to the air.

Noah could not resist, and struck once again.

Then he put the sword on the table and went around to the other side and sat.

"Go and stand in the rain," he said to Japeth — who had stopped choking, but who could still not speak. "Stay there till you're frozen."

Hannah had retrieved the towel from the floor and was about to wipe Japeth's face and shoulders, but Noah said; "that pear will want a dish beneath it — and a knife to cut it and a piece of cheese beside it."

Hannah gave the towel to Japeth and retired.

Noah said; "the rain. Go and stand in the rain."

Japeth blew his nose in the towel and absent-mindedly wiped his face with it and went out through the door to the deck without looking back.

When he had gone, Noah looked at Shem.

"In spite of the fact that your wife is carrying a child," he said; "it would be wisdom not to leave her alone with him."

Shem was still incredulous. "I cannot believe that . . ."

"Is she not attractive to you?"

The question only confused Shem, who could not quite follow where Noah was leading him. Hannah was his wife. She didn't have to be attractive to him.

"What are you driving at, father?"

Noah glanced across his shoulder at the galley door. It was closed. Then he leaned across at Shem — using his napkin to brush aside the mess that Japeth had made.

"Are you having relations with your wife?"

Shem sat back and almost stood up. Such a question had never been asked of him before, and he was, in fact, so shocked that he could not answer — except to say; "what?"

Noah smiled.

"I could tell you how, if you were interested. A pregnant woman *can* be taken, you know."

Shem was appalled.

"Your wife has never carried a child before. You have not had to deal with this situation. But your desire for her must be alive . . . eh? Tell me. Isn't it?"

Shem looked down at his lap and shut his mouth hard.

"I always suspected you had a woman tucked away in the cottages. A big man like you . . . you can't have made do with your wife alone. Am I right?"

Shem shook his head.

"No other woman, eh? Well. You've even less imagination than I thought."

Noah thought of Japeth again. The vision of his dead twin rose up before him, standing in the doorway — with its long arms dangling down and its little eyes staring and its mouth hanging open. And a dreadful thought came into his mind.

"This child is yours, is it not?" he said to Shem.

Shem looked up from his lap and stared at his father.

"What child?"

"This child — Hannah's child — it's yours, for certain?"

"Of course it is, father."

Noah looked at the door to the deck again and said; "you can't really mean it when you say you haven't seen the way he watches her. His eyes are never anywhere else. And what about her? Eh? Tell me. Has she ever looked at him?"

"Never."

"You say that so quickly, I wonder if it's true." Noah squinted at the Ox. "Tell me you know beyond a single doubt that child is yours."

"It is mine, father."

Noah wiped his fingers with his beard.

"Nevertheless," he said, "I think the time has come to force a certain issue."

Shem waited.

Noah said; "I think the time has come to bring that young man and his own wife together."

Shem bit his lip.

"When we have finished dining," Noah said; "I want you to go down into the hold and bring her up. Say nothing. Merely bring her here. To me."

∞ Japeth had delivered Pirates for the leopards and the lions that morning and all that Mrs Noyes could say was that she was profoundly glad they were delivered dead. The cleaning and the gutting were reminiscent enough of the slaughter-house at home — thank you very much — where the cattle and the pigs had been hung by their feet while their throats had been cut and their eyes had watched.

Ham, with his almost disturbing sense of practicality, had said that nothing must go to waste. And nothing did. Not even guts. In fact, the guts were fed to the bears, who found in them fish and other creatures eaten by the Pirates. And in the fish and other creatures — other creatures still — and in those creatures, more — till Mrs Noyes could not begin to count the numbers. But Ham could — and found them wonderful.

Emma's tears had been shed profusely over the slaughtered young whose lives had been sacrificed to feed the leopards and the lions before the advent of the Pirates, but now she became stoic and silent. Her job was to feed the flesh-eating birds and though she was completely in awe of birds, it did not seem to faze her when she was asked to carry up trays of hearts and liver for the eagles and the hawks, the buzzards and the owls. Mrs Noyes only understood why this was so when she happened to overhear the child in the bird gallery, chanting in a singsong voice as she pushed the bits of delicacy through the bars. Moving from cage to cage in time to her words, Emma was chirping in her small bird's voice; "one-less-mouse-for-you . . . one-less-rabbit-for-you . . . one-less-toad-for-you . . . one-less-sparrow-for-you! . . ."

Mrs Noyes had gone away smiling — and, when she had next fed a Pirate to the lion, she had curtsied to him, saying; "one-less-pony-for-you!"

Still, she could not get over the tragedy — or what certainly seemed to her to be a tragedy — of all these dead Pirates, whose merry eyes and enchanting laughter had been so magical as they played beside the ark and called to Japeth, thinking that his bow was a harp. Her rebellion against their slaughter had cost her dearly — and the others, too. Now Japeth locked them in and none of them could take the air between their bouts of servitude. And her arms were unbearably sore where Shem had kicked her in order to break her hold on Japeth's legs. The bruises were yellow, now, and she feared she would lose the use of her fingers, since every pull on her forearms when she exercised her grip was agony. Cutting up the meat, she had to hold it in place with the palm of one hand while she sawed at the flesh with a knife that Ham had tied to her other hand and wrist, held fast in a splint of sticks.

Lucy was strangely withdrawn these days, as if the Pirate episode had also affected her. But while withdrawn (which meant that she told no more jokes and never laughed), she had also become less slovenly. Her posture regained its earlier poise and she stood erect and walked with the wonderful silence that Mrs Noyes remembered as having been so alarming when Lucy first appeared. Her powdered face was whiter — if that was possible — and her painted brows more firmly drawn and her black-red lips more firmly set. Her hair had regained its glossy sheen — as an animal's coat will do when an illness has passed. Its blackness and its sable richness were more beautiful than ever. And as she watched her moving through the passageways and going about her work, Mrs Noyes recalled what Lucy had said when, however long ago it had been since they had left the earth, Mrs Noyes had asked her

how tall she was. "Seven-foot-five: and every inch a queen."
It was true. And her gowns, which she called ki-monos, were
made of silks that a queen might have owned. Mrs Noyes could
not help but question how a single trousseau chest could hold
so many of these ki-monos and still have room for all the other
wonders that Lucy kept producing for their comfort and en-
tertainment: the musical instruments, the porcelain dishes from
which they ate and the pearl-handled knives with which they
cut their food. And the magic lanterns — never mind the lie
that she had stolen them from Noah. What a strange, enchanting
creature Lucy was — and Mrs Noyes was increasingly satisfied that her son, whom everyone had said would never marry
at all, had married a woman of such taste and wealth and
fortitude. And such a great actress, too; "with all them funny
voices!" which Mrs Noyes — from time to time — would try to
imitate.

Now, as the night drew in and all the animals had been fed,
Mrs Noyes made her way along the passage and down the
steps to the hidden shelf above the Unicorn where Mottyl and
her kittens were lying in the dark.

"Hello, my dear one," she said as she drew the curtain of
straw aside and lifted her lamp to the hook above her head.

Mottyl was drowsing and lying on her side, with the kittens
in a feeding row, though sound asleep. They were making the
warm, deep noise that, for Mottyl, was like a sedative.

"I've brought you a piece of liver and a little bit of kidney,"
said Mrs Noyes as she settled herself at the top of the secret
steps drawn down to bring her up to Mottyl's height.

"Oh — must she feed you kidneys and liver!" the Unicorn
lamented, in its whispering voice. "Why can't a cat eat sensible things like flowers?"

"A cat," replied Mottyl, sitting up and stretching; "does
eat sensible things like flowers. But only in sensible seasons
like spring and summer."

"Do you?" the Unicorn asked. "What sort of flowers?"

"Herbs. Catnip," and Mottyl bent down to the liver and
kidney; "for which I would almost sell my unborn at this
moment." She laid her head on one side, throwing the kidney

back onto her molars in order to extract as much juice as possible.

"Tell me what else you like by way of flowers." To the Unicorn, anything — even the *name* of a flower — would be better than the smell of all that meat.

"Eucalyptus leaves." Mottyl was nosing around the plate for more kidney. "Asparagus, lavender. Leeks." She hunkered close to the meat. "Mimosa."

"Mimosa. Oh — I wish you hadn't mentioned that." The Unicorn sighed. "Mimosa was one of my favourite things of all. There were so many things I loved. . . ."

Mrs Noyes, on her step, was leaning back against the joist and only vaguely listening. She stroked the kittens, one and then another, with her aching fingers, wishing she could curl them enough to pick the kittens up. The silvery one was especially nice. . . . Yaweh's cat had done it, all right, though four of the kittens were more like Mottyl than like him. Only the silver one was the spitting image. And the white one was slightly less like Mottyl than like Abraham. Six kittens. *Six.* Four females and two males. And every one had lived. So far.

Though the ark was absolute hell in so many ways and though all their lives were so appalling — caged and underfed, left without air and daylight, separated from all their kind but one — there was nonetheless some comfort here in the lamplight, all of them warm together, nesting and being rocked together in this great, fat cradle on the waters — a comfort that was not like any other. No house, no barn, no burrow had ever been like this. No single place had ever held so many lives in its embrace, and none had ever been so peaceful at its heart as this could be, in this hour before sleep and after feeding. So many shapes and sizes lying down in so many different positions, filling so many different kinds of space and breathing so many different kinds of sighs: it was a mystery to Mrs Noyes. It was as if in the old days on earth, she could walk into the middle of the wood, not caring whether she stumbled into a dragon wallow or stepped on a snake. Nothing mattered here, of that. The wood — though half the animals gathered on the ark had made their living there — had no such potential for danger as this place had. And yet—Mrs Noyes felt safer here. Though sadder than she might have in the wood. Safer and sadder: what a strangeness, she thought.

Nearby, the foxes and raccoons lay side by side with nothing but chicken wire between them, and up above them, Bip and Ringer were staring into space—wondering still where all the trees had gone. There was a dreadful sadness over them all—and in some, an almost elegiac lassitude, as they sat with lowered heads and counted their toes. They felt as she did. If they raised their eyes, their expressions were quite unbearable to see: mourning the loss of space and air and sky. The monkeys and the other animals who ran in packs were none of them able to understand—no matter how many times it was explained — why one or twenty or a hundred more of their kind could not be saved. Nothing of this place and nothing of their circumstance could ever be made quite real for them. Many of the animals thought that this—and not what had been left behind—was death. Or certainly something very close to death.

Mrs Noyes was all at once acutely aware of the darkness and the walls around her and the roof above her and the floor below. Her arms ached—and part of the ache was the memory of why they were in pain. We are truly captives here, she thought; every one of us—and yet they have called this: *being saved*.

Maybe that was what she had meant by safety and sadness: that she and all these creatures with her shared their captivity in a way they could never have shared the wood. That when you are caught together in the same trap, you share the same fear of darkness and of walls and you also have the same enemy. You fear the same jailer. You share the same dream of freedom — waiting, all together, for the same door to open. You also learn to survive together in ways the uncaged would never think of. Could she ever have imagined, for instance, that — being in the wood and hearing a bear in pain—she would walk amongst other bears to comfort it? Yet, on the ark, she not only walked amongst bears — she *sat* amongst them and was unafraid. Just as the Unicorn was unafraid of her. And that, too, had once been impossible to imagine. Yet here they were. Together. Safe with one another — but . . .

What is this cruelty, then, she wondered; that battens those doors up there and locks us in, as if we were dragons — and fearsome?

The thought of Noah's rages and of Japeth armed gave her the answer.

Cruelty was fear in disguise and nothing more. And hadn't one of Japeth's holy strangers said that fear itself was nothing more than a failure of the imagination?

That was why Mrs Noyes had been afraid of bears.

She had not been able to imagine consoling them.

∞ "Mother!"

Mrs Noyes almost tumbled from the steps.

"MOTHER!"

It was Shem, the Ox.

"MOTHER!"

He was alarmingly close, and Mrs Noyes had to work so fast at hiding Mottyl and the kittens and at retrieving her lamp that she inadvertently used her fingers and cried out in pain.

Shem came around the corner and almost collided with her.

"What are you yelling about?" he said — ignoring the fact that he had been yelling, too.

"I banged my arm," said Mrs Noyes. Just as she spoke she heard, to her alarm, the sound of Mottyl's kittens. Shem, though dense, was not so dense that he could not tell the sound of kittens and Mrs Noyes leapt to their defense by suddenly bursting into song.

"*O Rock of ages, cleft for me!*" she bellowed. "*Let me hide myself in thee!*"

"Mother . . ."

"Why don't we step down the hall?" said Mrs Noyes. "We don't want to wake the animals . . ." and then she went on singing at the top of her voice; "*let the water and the blood . . .*"

Mrs Noyes gave Shem a push with her elbow and urged him back along the gangway towards the stairs.

"Now, tell me what it is," she said—once they were on the steps, and the kittens safely out of hearing. "Why have you come down to bother us this time?"

"I want Emma," said Shem.

"Well — you can't have her," said Mrs Noyes. "She belongs to Japeth."

She pushed him in the ribs and made him walk up in front of her.

"All you and father ever think about is sex," said Shem.

Mrs Noyes stopped in her tracks. "I beg your pardon?" she said.

"All you and father ever think about is sex," said Shem again.

"Never mind about me," said Mrs Noyes. "Why do you say that about your father?"

"I don't mean his own sex," said Shem. "I mean other people's. Seems to me it's all he talks about these days."

"Oh, really . . ." Mrs Noyes tried to remain calm. "And now you want Emma? . . ."

"Yes."

They got to the top of the steps and turned towards the galley, where Emma — more than likely — would be found.

"*Why* do you want her?"

"Not allowed to tell," said Shem. "Only meant to come down here and get her."

Mrs Noyes was about to throw up another defense when all was lost through the sudden appearance of Emma herself.

"Did someone call?" she said. "I heard my name."

Indeed you did, thought Mrs Noyes. *Alas.*

"You're to go with Shem," she said aloud. And then, to Shem; "isn't there time to let her change her dress, at least?"

"Meant to take her straight up," said Shem.

"Won't you even let her brush her hair?"

"Straight up," Shem said — unfolding his Oxen arms and giving Emma his tight little smile that was meant to be a pleasant greeting.

Mrs Noyes saw how clean her son was. The hairs on his arm were shining in the lamplight and the back of his neck was clean and his toenails were clean. It made her feel quite odd, when she realized she hadn't been clean herself for days and possibly weeks. The civilized parting in the centre of Shem's sandy hair and the smell of his tunic almost made her weep.

"Well," she said to Emma. "You'd best go with him. Don't be afraid."

She passed Emma on towards the stairs to the upper deck and kissed the top of her head as she let her go. And then she said; "here. Wait . . ." and took a few quick steps in Emma's direction. "Take this," she said — and handed Emma her handkerchief. "Wipe your face as you cross the deck. And do up the bow at the back of your dress."

"Yes'm."

Emma took the handkerchief and smiled. It was wrong. Whenever she should have been in tears, she never was.

"I'll take a good deep breath of fresh air for you, Mother Noyes," she said. "Goodbye."

Mrs Noyes gave a wave — and instantly regretted it. A pain shot through her arm.

"Goodbye," she whispered.

And smiled, for Emma's sake.

∞ When the door above her opened, Mrs Noyes thought she saw a star — but it was only a lantern, hanging from the portico.

The sound of the bolts being shut was worse than any sound she could imagine.

Turning back, she saw that Lucy was standing in the gloom below her. Her eyes were strangely luminous.

"What's the matter?" she asked.

"I don't really know," said Mrs Noyes. "I only know I wish I believed in prayer."

∞ "So there you are," said Noah, as if the child Emma had wilfully absented herself. "Let me see you — let me see."

Emma had managed to make a circle of cleanliness right in the centre of her face, so that her eyes shone brightly out of a moon. Her hair was restrained with several ratty bits of cloth that were tied here and there and no two pieces of one colour.

Her dress was severely torn and her aprons covered with grease and soap stains. Bird droppings and straw dust were matted on her shoulders. Her arms, with the sleeves of her dress rolled up in order to save them from the dish pan, were brightly and inappropriately pale and unspotted.

Noah stood up and gave the nod to Shem, who retired against his will. He was leery of his father now, and dreaded what might be going to happen — though not for Emma's sake. Shem's dread had all to do with the mood his father would be in if events unfolded against his will.

"Send Sister Hannah," Noah said — just as Shem had made it to the door. "Tell her I want her."

Once Shem had gone, Noah smiled — though his smiles were difficult to find in all that beard. And his wooden teeth were troubling him: locking shut when he wanted them open — and remaining open when he wanted them shut. He put his hand to his mouth and pushed the rows of teeth together, almost biting his finger as he did so.

"Well, well, then. Say hello," he said.

Emma bobbed.

Noah coughed.

"We have been concerned," he said.

Emma waited.

Noah had nothing more to say about "concern," apparently. Or at least as far as Emma understood the word.

"You are looking fat and sassy," the old man said, with his eyes very bright and his fingers in his beard. "How old are you now. Tell me the truth."

It did not occur to Emma to lie about her age. "I don't know," she said. "I think I'm twelve."

"You cannot be twelve," said Noah. "You were twelve a year ago, at least. I was rather hoping you'd tell me you were fourteen."

"I might be. I don't know."

"Well — whatever age you are," said Noah; "you are not a child any more."

Emma knew that.

Hannah appeared — dressed entirely in white and wearing a

heavy cardigan over her long and voluminous gown. The child inside her might be twins, Emma thought. She's huge.

"Yes, yes. And good," said Noah. "Here's your young friend, Sister Hannah." Noah coughed and waved Hannah forward in Emma's direction. "She — ah — she perhaps — ah — she . . ."

Hannah said; "perhaps she could do with a bath, Father Noyes."

"Precisely," said Noah. "Yes. A bath. A good, hot bath. Yes."

Emma sniffled and drew Mrs Noyes's handkerchief beneath her nose. A bath, she thought, would be lovely, but . . . why?

"Come along, Em," said Hannah — putting out her hand and smiling.

They were being so friendly.

What did it mean?

"I'll be waiting," said Noah. "Right here."

Hannah led Emma towards the galley.

Not more pots and pans, thought Emma — already drawing back.

Recognizing Emma's reluctance from long practice, Hannah said to her; "the bath house is through here."

Oh.

"Sister Hannah . . ." said Noah.

Hannah turned back and Noah leaned in towards her ear.

"You might consider a little of that almond oil you use."

Hannah nodded.

Emma wondered what all the whispering might be about. But it did not concern her greatly. She could see that all the pots and pans and all the dishes in the galley had been cleaned and put away — and she could also see the bath towels warming by the oven.

A bath, she thought; a bath . . . I hope it's nice and deep, so I can soak.

∞ The bath house was already full of steam, the sponges set out in their bucket and the birch switches hanging down from their pegs on the wall above the bench. Hannah was well prepared for Emma's arrival and could have bathed an army. If there had been an army. (No more armies, she thought, pouring another bucket of scalding water into the tub. All our terms of reference have been changed forever. Now, everything will be *"before the flood"* and *"after the flood."* And *"she could have bathed an arkful. . . ."*)

Hannah went away, locking Emma in. She had forgotten the almond oil.

Emma went and stood by the tub and stuck her finger into the water. Hot. Too hot to climb into yet. She took off her shawl and stood there — mesmerized — with her shawl in one hand and the buttons of her blouse, one by one, in the other.

The birches looked like animal tails, hung up the way that Shem used to hang them in the slaughterhouse on earth — the long ones like cows' and the short ones like calves'. Emma put her buttoning hand out to touch them: dead as tails, with their withered leaves curled in tufts.

The smell of the soap and the warmth of the steam were so comforting they made Emma drowsy. Everything here reminded her of her parents and her brothers and the bath house at home, where everyone sat together once a week while her father told stories. Steam and stories were forever linked in her mind — and the feel of her mother's fingers massaging the back of her neck. Her brothers, like her father, had all been giants with pale hair and woodsman's arms and they spoke, like her father, with the low, gentle voices of animals. Some of them had moustaches that curled towards their chins — and the steam would gather at the ends of these moustaches in big, pearly drops that Emma was allowed to gather on her finger and fling against the stones, where they sizzled like insects. Her mother had been quite the opposite of all these quiet, blond men — being small and dark and excitable. She had been a gay and playful woman, whom all her children had adored. Her eyes had been a shade of brown that only Lotte's had imitated — and her hand was always out to touch you.

Lotte had been everybody's favourite — spoiled by all the brothers, carried by her father in his arms and on his back and her arms were so strong, he could swing her up to his shoul-

der while she did a somersault. Lotte had hardly ever been
out of her mother's sight and the only time she had ever been
unhappy was when she got left behind if the family went on a
shopping excursion — everyone piling into the democrat except Lotte and one person (always someone different) who
was chosen to stay behind with her. The hiding was different.
Every time a stranger came to the door, Lotte had to be hidden from sight and the bath house was where she was hidden.
It had been chosen as the hiding place especially because the
bath house was a place where everyone was always happy.
Sometimes, it was Emma's turn to hide with her and they would
play at being woodsmen like their brothers — cutting down
birch-switch trees and piling them all in the centre of the floor,
criss-crossed in stacks of miniature lumber and firewood.

What Emma remembered most of Lotte, though, was how
soft she had been and how lovely it had been, in their big straw
bed in the loft, to lie up close to her and stroke the long, thin
downy arms and, in the wintertime when they were cold, to
creep down into the centre of the bed and curl up together
underneath the covers while the wind had howled around them
and the owls on the rafters had flown down to sit at the foot of
the bed. . . .

"What are you doing? You're not even undressed."

It was Hannah, returning with the almond oil. She filled the
open doorway briefly with her great height and bulk — and all
the steam rushed out towards her and made a great cloud
around her head.

"I was thinking," said Emma.

How unusual, Hannah thought — and closed the door. At
once, all the steam fell away from her and she was revealed in
a high flush of colour that made Emma think of Hannah sitting
in the sun, her face pressed eagerly towards the light.

"Oh, my," Hannah said as she crossed the floor to the stove
and began to shake out the towels she had previously brought
from the galley. "I'm out of breath. I tire so easily, these
days. . . ."

Emma said; "you're carrying such a big child in there. No
wonder. Do you think it will be twins?"

"I hope not," said Hannah.

"Oh," said Emma. "If I was going to have a baby, I'd want it to be twins."

"Yes—*you* would. Hurry up now. We haven't got all night."

Hannah had already removed her cardigan and was rolling up her sleeves. White — white — white: every bit of her clothing was white.

Emma stared at Hannah's belly.

"May I touch the baby?"

"No," said Hannah. "Take off your clothes."

∞ The tub was so deep a person had to climb up over the top and drop down through the water, reaching for the bottom with her toes. Emma was so round and tiny, she almost filled the tub and the water rose around her neck and spilled out over the rim and onto the floor.

The first thing Hannah did was cut away the bits of cloth that served as ribbons in Emma's hair and then she pushed her all the way under so that her hair would be soaked.

Spluttering and squawking, Emma resurfaced and clung to the edge of the tub with every ounce of strength she could muster. Being drowned was everything she had feared it would be, with everything turning black and making a great ringing noise in her ears.

"Don't," she said. "Don't!"

Hannah applied a thick bar of soap — of the strength that Japeth had used in his desperate bid to remove the blue from his skin. It was the strongest soap that Mrs Noyes could manufacture and it smelled so heavily of lye that Emma was driven further into a state of stupor.

Hannah's fingers were very strong and as they worked the soap through Emma's hair, they sent deep messages of pleasure all across the top and back of Emma's head and down her neck.

The fingers worked their way down the skull and paused at the nape of the neck to massage the muscles there, spreading the message further down the spine and across the shoulders. . . .

Emma gave up her grip on the edge of the tub and simply stood there, breastbone high in the water, head bowed and mouth open.

Hannah was working her way — vertebra by vertebra — down the child bride's back, pressing with her thumbs at the centre and spreading her fingers out across the flesh on either side. Emma had never felt so relaxed or warm or confused.

"Turn around," said Hannah.

Emma managed an almost balletic turn, rising up on her toes and spinning slowly in the water until she was facing Hannah.

Hannah said; "dunk."

Emma, her mouth still open, bent her knees and sank.

Hannah stood up and went across the room to the stove, where she removed the lid and began to throw in Emma's clothes: her stockings full of holes and tears, her half-melted cardboard shoes, her skirts and her bloomers, her underblouse and her overblouse and her shawl.

It was just at this moment that Emma rose from the water and wiped her eyes and saw what Hannah was up to.

"What are you doing? . . ." she said — only half aware of what she was seeing.

"I'm burning your clothes. What does it look like?"

"But — you can't! You mustn't! Not my shawl! My mother made that for me. . . ."

A wail began to rise.

"*Emma.*"

Emma bit her lip — and the shawl fell into the fire.

Next — and finally — Hannah, using a stick, picked up the filthiest of all of Emma's clothes — her apron — and held it out to the flames.

"Not my apron! NO!"

But the apron was already gone. And with it, all of Emma's feathers.

Emma had half-clambered out of the tub and one of her fat little legs was hanging over the edge. "My feathers . . ." she said. All the feathers so patiently collected during her bird feeding duties — the feathers with which, in daydreams, Emma manufactured wings. Wings for Mrs Noyes. Wings for Ham

and Lucy. Wings for Mottyl and wings for the Unicorn — so
that one day they could all take off and fly away with Crowe
and leave the ark forever.

Emma sank back — her leg flopping helplessly over the edge.

∞ After the bath, Emma stood quite silent — thinking of
her apron and her shawl — while Hannah dried her all over.

Finally, Hannah sat down on a three-legged milking stool
and drew the almond oil from her placket.

"Come and stand here," she said.

Emma went and stood before her sister-in-law.

"Put your hands up on top of your head," said Hannah.

Emma — assuming she was about to be inspected for any
surviving lice, in the way that her Mother had always inspected
her children after a bath — did as she was told and locked her
hands in place on top of her head, gathering fistfuls of hair to
hang onto. She also closed her eyes.

"What's that?" she said.

"You just be quiet and don't move," said Hannah, whose
voice sounded oddly excited.

The smell of almonds floated up to Emma's nostrils and she
felt Hannah's fingers touch the sides of her breasts.

"Oh my," she said. "Oh my . . ."

Hannah's fingers were capable of much more gentleness than
Emma would have suspected. Round and round they flowed
— spreading the oil up over her breasts and down between
them and underneath them, caressing them with oil and working — very slowly — towards the nipples.

"Oh my, oh my . . ."

Emma pressed forward.

Hannah stopped.

Emma opened her eyes — but Hannah was only spilling more
of the almond oil in the palms of her hands and rubbing her
hands together, preparing for another assault.

"Be still."

"I can't be still. I don't know what you're doing. . . ."

"Never mind what I'm doing. Be still."

Emma re-locked her hands on top of her head and waited. Where would the fingers touch her next? This was not at all like Japeth, whose hands were all fingernails and fists and thumbs.

The fingers landed — light as butterflies — and began moving down across her belly and up across her thighs.

"Just be still. Just be still. . . ." Hannah whispered.

But that was impossible.

∞ When Emma was returned to Noah, she was wearing one of Hannah's white shifts and she was almost in a trance. Her hair had been dried and brushed and pulled back loosely — tied with a single ribbon on her neck.

"Well, well," said Noah. "What have we here?"

"Clean from stem to gudgeon," said Hannah.

"Everything?"

"Everything."

Noah sat forward in the great chair and his eyes were glittering. His voice, when he spoke, was not like any voice that Emma remembered his having used before: thick and wet with a quaver in it.

"Come and stand here, in front of me, child."

(He had gone back to calling her a *child* again. Why did he keep on changing what he called her? *"You're not a child any more"* and then, "come here, child. . . .")

As Emma shuffled forward, afraid of tripping on the shift, Hannah went and sat on the far side of the table — one arm resting over her belly. Her hair was damp from having been in the bath house so long and she looked very beautiful sitting there in the lamplight, apparently at rest.

"Now," said Noah — giving the shift a twitch with his fingers. "I want you to raise this above your hips."

Emma just stared.

"Up, up," said Noah — as if he was doing no more than asking her to raise a window blind. "Come along."

Emma looked at Hannah for help — but Hannah was not even watching and, perhaps, not even listening. She was simply sitting there across the table — staring into space.

Emma reached down and took the folds of cloth in her hands and drew them to her thighs — but could go no further.

"Up," said Noah. *"All the way."*

Emma closed her eyes and lifted the shift all the way to her waist, where she held it tightly, like a girdle.

Noah muttered; "yes, yes . . ." and she could feel his breath on her legs.

The ark heaved up and down and the rain could be heard on the roof of the Castle — but nothing more.

Noah reached out with his fingers.

Emma shivered.

"You cold, girl?"

"No, sir."

The fingers rode up her thighs towards her centre, soft as tongues in the oil. Emma pulled away.

"Stand still!"

The fingers of one hand reached the mark and the fingers of the other — seeking entrance — gently pulled to one side.

Emma wept. "That hurts," she said. "That hurts."

But one of Noah's fingers was already inside her — exploring.

"That HURTS!" Emma screamed — and pulled away so violently that she fell against the wall behind her.

But neither Noah nor Hannah seemed to be concerned with her hurt. All that Noah said was; "no wonder the poor boy can't get in. She's so tick and tight, a pin could hardly enter."

Hannah said nothing.

Emma sank down to the floor and pulled her knees to her chin.

And Noah just went on talking — not as if she was being harmed, but as if she was being helped. As if they were being kindly.

"I want to go back now," she said. 'I want to go back."

But she might as well not have uttered. Noah, with his back to her, was bending forward — leaning across the table to Hannah.

Emma heard: ". . . something sufficiently firm . . . something sharp . . . I should hate to use . . ."

Emma moaned and put her hands across her ears.

∞ What they brought (it was Hannah who brought it) —
was the Unicorn.

∞ Emma's screaming lasted for an hour.

In the bowels of the ark, Mrs Noyes could hear it, but she
could not guess what it meant. Emma's whole life, it seemed,
had been spent, since she had been married to Japeth, either
wailing or sobbing or screaming. And all that went through
Mrs Noyes's mind was; "good for her! Resisting him to the
end."

On the other hand . . .

If Japeth succeeded . . .

But, no. She must not allow herself to think of that.

∞ Just as Noah was withdrawing the Unicorn's horn,
Japeth — who had also heard the screaming as far away as the
Armoury — came bursting through the door to the saloon. He
was armed to the teeth, quite literally, since he carried a knife
between his lips and his lips were bleeding.

The scene before him was meaningless at first. His father
holding the dog-sized beast with the horn — Emma held in an
angular embrace by his brother, Shem — while Sister Hannah
crouched at Emma's feet, with a small red towel, and dabbed
at something there that seemed to be a wound. Emma was
screaming, still, and stamping the floor with her feet like someone trying to kill a snake.

It took a whole minute for all these images to come together
and deliver a single meaning which — even then — Japeth could
not believe.

But the Unicorn's horn was covered with blood and that
said everything left unsaid by the rest of what he saw.

"We were just . . ." said Noah.

Japeth drew his sword.

Noah stood his ground — a gesture he knew from long experience would intimidate his son. A single step back — and all
might be lost. But Japeth could not bear a man who did not
move. It confused him. Especially if that man was unarmed.

Noah's hand was on the Unicorn's back — and the Unicorn

had collapsed to its knees, already very nearly unconscious. The only voice it could manage could not be heard by human ears. There was blood all over its face, as well as its horn, and its horn had been almost torn from its brow. Some of the blood was its own — and it was bleeding to death on the table. But no one paid it the slightest attention — and the weight of Noah's hand was so heavy that the Unicorn could not breathe.

Hannah stood up and went away with the dark red towel.

Shem let go of Emma's arms and — at once — she ran to the darkest corner of the room and turned her face to the wall and was completely silent and completely still.

Noah spoke to Japeth in a monotone — his voice the very sound of reason — and he pacified his son by saying; "we have solved all your problems: the ones you could not solve. She is able to take you, now. It was not your fault, before — but hers. This was necessary . . ." he gestured at the Unicorn. "Nothing more than a midwife would have done: nothing more than the apothecary would have advised her mother to do, if her mother had taken half the responsibility that any decent mother takes and had gone to the apothecary for advice in the first place. Your *own* mother should have seen to this. . . ." Here, Noah took that always wild and unpredictable turn that was meant to save him from any kind of blame: that turning which even convinced himself that he was blameless and — more than blameless — that he and he alone was saving the entire situation by salvaging everyone and everything from certain ruin: that wrenching that began with his arm extended and his finger reaching out through the air to find the true and absolute culprit: the inevitable cause of all that was threatening, all that was dangerous; all that was foolish; all that was madness. That finger of reason that always found someone *else* — and most usually, his wife.

"Blame your mother — but don't come at me with that sword drawn. I have only done my duty as a father. Nothing more."

Japeth slowly lowered the sword and withdrew the knife from his mouth and — for a moment — it looked to Noah and to Shem that he was going to leave them without a word, since he half turned away and took one step that seemed to be leading to the door. But all at once he turned again so quickly that neither Shem nor Noah could truly see what he was doing.

The sword went up through the lamplight — and came down hard, two-handed, on the table, where it severed the Unicorn's horn from its head.

∞ To Noah, this was no more than a reasonable reaction.

Every man must exact his vengeance how and where he sees fit. The objects of vengeance have no importance. It is only the act of vengeance itself that matters, since it delineates the man. Later, Japeth would come to understand he had acted as the arm of God. Noah would explain this for him.

∞ They seemed to have waited forever — and the longer they waited, the closer they drew together.

Mrs Noyes had gone to sit with Mottyl — partly out of fear for her — as soon as Hannah had departed with the Unicorn.

∞ "What do you want with him?" Mrs Noyes asked, as Hannah lifted the Unicorn from its nest. "He's very delicate, you know. He's been ill."

"It's not me that wants him." (Hannah was folding the Unicorn into the crook of her arm — drawing the end of her pale blue rain shawl up over her shoulder to protect him from the storm.) "Doctor Noyes has asked for him."

"Oh — so it's 'Doctor Noyes' again, is it? And what does *this* mean — experiments or divinity? Is it the Reverend Doctor who wants him, or just the plain old doctor?"

Hannah drew the peak of the shawl up over her head and prepared to climb the steps.

"I cannot answer that question, Mother Noyes. I only know he wants the Unicorn."

"And where is Emma? What has become of Emma?"

"Emma is fine, Mother Noyes."

Hannah was climbing the steps, taking them very slowly, and by the time she had reached the top of the first flight, she was quite out of breath.

Mrs Noyes was close behind her and saw the way her

daughter-in-law had to pause, with her hand on the railing and her shoulders falling forward. Quickly, Mrs Noyes moved up beside her.

"What's the matter?"

"Nothing. I'm tired."

Mrs Noyes walked around and looked into Hannah's face, with its waning colour and its tightly drawn mouth.

"Don't lie," she said. "There's something wrong."

∞ Hannah was obviously in a quandary. Aside from Emma — with whom you simply could not have a serious conversation or to whom you could not express a serious concern — she had not seen another woman for weeks — except in the throes of a crisis. She desperately needed — and wanted — someone to talk to, especially a woman; but she could not bring herself to do it. All her pride was shuttered in her silence: all her ambition was locked in the choice she had made to sit on the right hand of power. Of all the people on the ark — aside, perhaps, from Doctor Noyes himself — Hannah was the only passenger who had thought about survival clinically: who had reasoned through the whole long process of staying alive at any cost: whose perseverance was calculated from moment to moment. And this was one of those moments.

Looking into Mrs Noyes's face — and seeing there the almost embarrassing frankness of her mother-in-law's concern — Hannah wanted to renege on all the holds and checks she had maintained with such care for so long. She wanted to admit she was afraid: she wanted to tell about her loneliness: she wanted to say out loud; *I am in pain.* She wanted to tell about the child she was afraid had died inside her. And about the blood she was passing.

And the hundred-and-ninetieth answer was the same as Hannah's. Silence.

∞ Ham came and leaned against the railing, staring down into the Well. Lucy went walking with her lantern, passing along the cloister on the far side, pausing at every cage to put her gloved fingers through the bars of the wire. No one spoke. If there had been a clock, the clock might have ticked so loudly that everyone would have heard it on every level — including the faraway bears and the elephants and rhinos on the lowest level of all. But the unspoken question was universal: *when will Emma be returned — and the Unicorn?*

Way off, beyond the sides of the ark and deep in the pitch and roll of the sea that was now an ocean, the whales were singing and the Pirates gathering for the next assault. The whales were in Ham's mind, also — and the Pirates in Mrs Noyes's. And Ham was thinking; one day, I'll understand what it is they're singing. And Mrs Noyes was thinking; if only the Pirates understood we are not a game. . . .

∞ While there was still this blood and before there could be absolution, there must be prayer.

Noah said of himself and of Shem and Sister Hannah; "we three may pray as we are. But Japeth and his bride must share the blood of this beast, since this beast is now the very symbol of their consecration before Yaweh."

While Noah and Shem went away to prepare the Chapel, Hannah brought Emma to her feet. The oversized shift still rode above her hips and her thighs were streaked with smears of dried blood. Emma, whose whole demeanour was governed now by shock, looked down at her mutilated parts and said to Hannah; "I don't want to live."

Hannah said; "this is over, now. It will soon be forgotten — and it *must* be forgotten. The thing you feared is in the past."

Emma's gaze lifted beyond Hannah's shoulder.

"There's still Japeth," she said. He was standing with his back to her, cleaning his sword.

"Yes. But remember — Japeth, as much as you, has been changed by what happened here."

"How?" said Emma, looking down at her thighs and the bloody folds of the shift. "Nobody's sliced *him* up. . . ."

"You don't seem to have grasped that what has been done to you has been done for Japeth's sake. You were not like other girls and women. You were difficult. Japeth could not gain entry. And . . ."

"He couldn't gain entry 'cause I wouldn't let him!"

"No." Hannah's voice was calm and deliberate. "He could not gain entry because of the way you were made. Now, because of what has been done to you, he can."

Some of this got said — against Hannah's will and even without her awareness of its being said — in her expression, which Mrs Noyes could read, if only partly. Six hundred years' experience of carrying children and of being alone and of being afraid went far towards opening the doors of another woman's face. But all Mrs Noyes could see was the scope of the problem and that Hannah was very close to being overwhelmed by whatever it was. She could know of the pain, but not the blood. She could know of the fear, but not the child that might be dead. She could know of the trap that Hannah had created for herself — but not how to find the door to let her out. Those things must be spoken. And Hannah would not speak.

"Won't you sit down for a moment, at least, and let me get you a cup of broth or a lump of sugar?"

"No," said Hannah. "No."

"Tell me what it is," said Mrs Noyes. "For heaven's sake . . ."

"No," Hannah said. "No. There is nothing to tell. I must get back."

And back she had gone. And the Unicorn with her.

∞ Now, Mrs Noyes was sitting on the secret step, with the straw drawn back and Mottyl blind in the lamplight, purring.

Below her, the Unicorn's cage was empty and his nest, without him in it, seemed alarmingly small. The female, as always, was hidden so far back in the shadows that only her horn was visible and Mrs Noyes could not prevent herself from putting the question yet again — for perhaps the hundred-and-ninetieth time — "why don't you speak?"

Emma said; "I want to wash. I want you to wash me. I want it to be you, not him."

"No," said Hannah. "That can never be again. That can only be when you are a child. Now you are a woman."

"But I don't want Japeth!"

Seeing the wail about to break free, Hannah put her hand —

though gently — over Emma's lips. The folds of the bloody shift fell down between them and Emma's hands went up to Hannah's wrists. But Hannah's wrists were stronger than Emma's fingers.

"Wait," said Hannah. "Wait and listen to me."

Emma considered biting Hannah's hand—but resisted. She was afraid there would be more blood.

Hannah said; "from now on, what you want no longer matters. . . ." (Had it ever mattered? Emma wanted to shout. Did I want to be a Noyes? Did I want all those pots and pans? Did I ask for a blue husband?) "All that matters is that Japeth has claimed you and you are his wife. We are governed by an Edict. We are the last of the human race. We are *all* in service here, to that fact. And your service is owed to Japeth Noyes. It's the way things are, Emma—and the way they will always be. Make up your mind to it. *Now.*"

The word "now" was a command—and Emma knew it as such. It had been said as Mrs Noyes would have said it—it was even said as her own dark, loving mother would have said it. She could not refuse because refusal to obey a parent was sacrilege. Unholy. *Holy* meant: *no way out.*

"*Now,*" said Hannah. "*Now,* Emma."

Emma subsided.

Hannah removed her hand from Emma's mouth—and she placed both hands on the girl's shoulders. "Good," she said. "You have taken the first step to wisdom."

Emma asked; "was this done to you, what was done to me?"

Hannah hesitated just a fraction of a second before she answered. "No," she said. "No. It was not."

Emma's eyes filled with anger — but her voice was calm, and for the very first time, Hannah thought; there will be ice in the girl, after all.

"Why wasn't it done to you?" Emma said. "You were just another bride, like me."

Hannah shook her head. Her hands were resting on her child — the child she would not let Emma touch.

"The difference is not in me and you," she said; "but in the men who claim us."

"But you said the difference was in *me*."

"No," said Hannah. "I said the *difficulty* was in you."

And then she turned away and sat down. The pain was returning and it was like the beating of small hands against her heart.

Emma could see that Hannah was suddenly very pale. "What's the matter?" she asked.

"Everything," said Hannah. "Everything. Don't ask."

∞ The Chapel was small, since it had been constructed with Noah's needs in mind rather than the family's. Its declared purpose had been to serve as a place where the Reverend Doctor could seek communion with his God. But it had become (though only the Reverend Doctor was aware of this) — a place where Noah had sought and failed to find communion with his Friend. Yaweh had not once been present within its icon-plastered walls; nor had His voice yet spoken from the depths of its curtained Sanctum. Never.

The sacrificial altar, which stood beneath the Pagoda from which the smoke of its fires was meant to escape, had never yet been used, since it had originally been Noah's purpose not to make sacrifice until the rains had ceased and the great storms abated. But the killing of the Unicorn had presented an occasion for sacrifice that could not be ignored. To ignore it was to court disaster. The Unicorn had been one of Yaweh's favourite beasts. Therefore, Noah had transformed the killing into what he — rather too quickly — insisted on calling a *ritual death*. Yaweh must be placated: wherever He might be.

The *ritual sacrifice* must also serve to placate Noah's decidedly uneasy conscience on the matter of the Unicorn. And perhaps on one or two other matters, not to be thought on now . . . (Be quiet.) Had he not called for the Unicorn in aid of Emma's mutilation, the beast might still be alive. Therefore, a holy purpose must be manufactured for its death.

But the body of the Unicorn was unclean: its cloven hoofs forbade that it should be placed on the altar. Its horn, of course — the sacred Phallus — was acceptable and even now Shem was rendering its amber to dust with a hammer.

Noah turned his mind to ritual.

This holy dust . . . (Very good! *Holy dust* was good) . . .

This holy dust will be mixed with mead (*holy* mead) and with the blood from Emma's wound (holy wound?) and it will be drunk by the two young people in remembrance of the Holy Beast whose horn facilitates the consummation of their marriage. And whose Holy life has been sacrificed so that . . . In order that . . .

Noah faltered.

In order that . . . apes . . .

Noah looked behind him. Was someone watching him? Was someone there?

No.

Whose life had . . . whose *Holy* life had been sacrificed to the greater understanding of . . . apes . . .

STOP THAT!

All the icons — many with the face of Yaweh — were watching him.

So that . . .

Silence. All the gilded eyes and all the ruby eyes of Yaweh were on him: implacable.

Noah stood in the very centre of the Chapel, utterly panic-stricken.

How should he pray?

The icons glittered.

Should he invoke the eighteen benedictions — from praising the faith of the fathers all the way through to the request for peace in the world?

But there were no fathers.

There was no world.

And all that was left of the faith was all too fast going the way of peace.

Noah dared, at last, to stare the icons in the face.

"*Tell me,*" he said out loud. "How shall I pray?"

The ruby eyes — the gilded eyes — did not and would not answer. All the mouths of Yaweh — every one — were shut against words.

Noah turned and faced the altar, where he laid three squares of incense. He would pray the formal prayer of mourning for the Unicorn itself — for the Unicorn as the last of its kind — deploring its irrevocable loss at the hands of the untamed beast. . . .

Japeth, the ape.

And Emma.

Noah stood stock-still before the altar with the smell of incense on his fingers.

If I can find a prayer at all; whatever else I pray, I must pray for one more death.

He brought his hands together — closed his eyes and fell to his knees, and it was in this position that Shem and Hannah, Japeth and Emma found him when they arrived to take part in the *Ritual Ceremony of the Holy Phallus, in Remembrance of Yaweh's Holy Beast, the Sacred Unicorn.*

Even Emma — who would hate her father-in-law forever — found it wonderful that he should pray so fervently.

∞ Crowe was seated, numb, in her chimney-pot within the Pagoda. Her forays into the rain were increasingly less adventurous. She was tired: tired of sitting (if only I had an egg to sit on; that, at least, would make this worthwhile) — tired of being rained on — tired of being cold. And the great, wide waters over which she ranged as she dared, had presented so many images recently of carnage and of horror that her flights were now confined to mere circlings of the ark.

It is one thing to lose an enemy in combat; to see her fall and to feast on her entrails. But when all your enemies have fallen to the sea, it is sad. With whom would one enter the joyous battles — as of old — for food? Not even with one's mate — since she had no mate and the only other crows were deep inside the ark. And flying down in the dark to feed on a steady diet of dead fish was boring. Where was the battle in that, that made being alive worthwhile?

And though she knew that Mrs Noyes and Mottyl were nearby — and though she even saw Mrs Noyes from time to time — there was nothing like a person's presence to buck up the spirits. The jokes, the deals, the bargaining, she missed it dreadfully. It dulled the wits not to have to gull your friends out of their treasured bits of liver and brain. . . .

And the Pirates were no fun. They didn't want to play with birds. All they wanted was to join the human race. The fools. Not even all the deaths they had suffered at Japeth's hands had convinced them to stay away. She could hear them talking about it — and firmly convinced, they were, that "if only we have patience, we will make them understand we are their friends." Well—so much for the native intelligence of Pirates. At least the whales had the good sense to keep their distance.

"Now, what's that?" she wondered. "All of a sudden, it's got very warm. . . ."

And there was a smell.

Burnt feathers?

No. Not burnt feathers. The smell of churches, remembered from a very brief week she had spent in a belfry, before being driven off by the sudden, unexpected Sabbath.

Doctor Noyes had lighted the fires beneath her and was making sacrifice.

Crowe lifted off from her nest and went and sat on the railing, where she could watch the incense and the smoke emerging from her chimney. She wondered how long it would last.

My rump smells of sandalwood, she thought.

Well — at least it would fumigate the lice.

∞ Mrs Noyes was seated on the secret step, with her arm inside Mottyl's nest and Mottyl asleep in the crook of her elbow. The kittens, pushed into a corner, were wriggling with dreams. And the silver male was obviously dreaming of violence, lying on his back and fighting off enemies with all four paws. Mrs Noyes tried to quiet him by offering her finger. Slowly, sucking on her nails, he subsided. He was a sweet, dear kitten — very trusting and much too adventurous. Perhaps his dreams of violence made some sense, though. He lived in this appalling confinement, surrounded by storms and roaring beasts.

Right now, however, several of those roaring beasts were

snoring, while others had gone into their midnight trance —
eyes open — with their gaze on ghosts and ancestors, not on
dreams or Mrs Noyes.

Ham still leaned against the railing, staring down at the great
beasts below and redesigning the world according to their various shapes and sizes. The elephants, for instance, would require a place of wallows and of water and of trees that grew in
profusion, but not too densely: a wood or a forest where there
was room to pass between the eucalyptus and the beeches:
grasslands where they could graze. . . . And what would be
compatible there: the zebra, who grazed, and Long Neck, who
would want the plains to run on and the plain trees to feed
from. . . .

Lucy had paused by the Gryphon's cage and actually had
her fingers through the bars! Ham wondered if anything dangerous fazed her. Always, Lucy's greatest fascination seemed
to be with the outcasts and the pariahs, the strangely formed
and excessively delicate: the Gryphons and the Glassmice,
the Demons and the Unicorns; the Cobras and the Platypi.
Her favourite birds were the immensely ugly Dodos and the
immensely unpopular Cuckoos, whose eggs were found everywhere, including in Lucy's wigs and Emma's bed.

"Did you know," said Lucy — calling across the Well-space
between them — "that Gryphon is a linguist? Knows every
language there is, including mine. . . ."

"What do you mean, 'including yours'?" Ham asked.

"Nothing," said Lucy. "Just a turn of phrase. Don't you
have a language of your own?"

At this moment — before Ham could answer — the great
door opened from the deck, one storey above them.

Mrs Noyes was wide awake at once and stood down, withdrawing her arm from Mottyl and her fingers from the silver
male.

"Excuse me," she said. "This may be Emma, returning."

Quickly, she thrust the steps into their hiding place and drew
down the straw curtain.

In the meantime, Ham had already begun to move along the
corridor towards the steps, and Lucy's lantern had turned from

the Gryphon's cage and was bobbing along the opposite side
of the Well.

"Hurry, hurry," Mrs Noyes was saying to herself; "hurry,
hurry . . ." because she had discovered, to her chagrin, that
her legs had fallen asleep.

∞ At first, there was nothing but the noisy draught to tell
that anyone was there. Mrs Noyes, Ham and Lucy started up
towards the upper level—thinking at any moment they would
hear Emma's voice. And even if it wailed, the voice would be
welcome. But there was only the wind and the creaking of the
door.

When they got to the second stairs, they saw—all too clearly
—that it was Japeth who was standing there, though he carried no lantern and could only be seen in the light from Lucy's
lamp. Japeth was holding his sword in one hand and something
else, not identifiable, in the other.

Finally Mrs Noyes cleared her throat and said; "where is
Emma?"

Japeth said; "Emma is up here, to stay. She is one of us,
now."

Ham said; "that's impossible." He almost laughed out loud.

Japeth said; "no. It is not impossible. Father has performed
a ritual and Emma is finally and truly my wife." He was even
standing straighter, as if to prove it.

Ham was still dubious. "Emma's always been your wife,
Jape. You just had a bad time trying . . ."

"Don't you start that!" said Japeth. "Don't you start that
again!"

So, thought Mrs Noyes; it is finally done. Well—damn him.

Japeth stepped further into the light and held out the thing in
his hand that was not his sword. But its shape was meaningless.
Only its condition told a story — dead and bloodied. And the
whole of Japeth's arm was also covered with blood. "Here,"
he said. "Here's your other friend. . . ." And he threw down
the body of a small and mutilated beast whose wounds were
so bloody, no one could recognize or guess who it was.

∞ When Japeth went away, he made a great show of bolting and battening the door, while a great gust of wind blew in around him. The noise of this was like the hammering of nails and the pounding of spikes. It left all those below caught rigid in the circle of Lucy's guttering lamp light — motionless and staring at what was at their feet. The Unicorn. Dead.

Mrs Noyes could not fall down, though she wanted to. Her knees would not give.

Lucy — silent — handed her lamp to Ham and knelt without bending her back. She lifted the Unicorn in towards her breast and held him there with one gloved hand, closing her other hand over his eyes.

"Never mind," she said. "Never mind." And then she stood up.

Mrs Noyes put out her fingers to touch the body of her friend; but she could not do it. Her hand withdrew before it reached its destination. How very small it was. The Unicorn. Her hand.

Lucy began to walk — almost aimlessly — making her way along the corridor — passing the Bird Gallery — winding on through the maze of insect cages and reptile tanks until she came to what they called the Stable, where the cattle, sheep and goats were kept. These were the animals whom the Edict had decreed should be brought on board the ark not "two-by-two" but "seven-by-seven" — all the expendable animals, whose young had provided so much food for the carnivores before the advent of the Pirates. One day — after landfall — they, too, would be the stuff of sacrifice.

The smell of straw and of hay and of oats and barley filled the Stable with indelible reminders of the earth and of the barns that had been on the earth and of all the lost others who had filled those barns: of Lily and Hannibal, the horses; Panic-the-cat; the Sheep Choir; the hens; the owls and all the cattle, goats and pigs whose lives had passed beneath the family's hands being milked and fed and cajoled into giving away the hiding places of mint beds and of truffle mines. In the Stable, Mrs Noyes inevitably thought of all the days and nights; of all the sicknesses that ever were and all the births and all the deaths that had taken place in those barns with herself in attendance: midwife to the world — and loving it. And for all those reasons, the Stable, of all the places on the ark, was most like home.

Lucy sat down on a mound of hay beside the cattle and laid the Unicorn, curled, on her lap.

Mrs Noyes had disappeared, but Lucy said; "she has only gone to bring Mottyl."

And she was right. Three minutes later, Mrs Noyes appeared in the Stable, carrying Mottyl against her shoulder and accompanied by a surprise visitor.

"I flew in over Japeth's head when he was trying to close the door," Crowe explained. "He was blinded by the rain and he didn't see me."

Mottyl, in spite of the Unicorn's death, could not help purring at the sound of her old friend's voice. Mrs Noyes set her down in the straw on the floor, and Crowe hunched down beside her.

"You smell of something," Mottyl whispered.

"Churches," whispered Crowe.

"Good to hear you."

"Good to see you."

Everyone fell silent.

The lantern swayed where Ham had hung it near the sheep pen and the faraway noise of the rain was less like rain than children's fingers drumming on the roof and the only other sound was the sound of the ark itself, as it lifted and fell and lifted again in the deepening waters.

∞ Slowly — so quietly that the sound of her voice was almost imperceptible at first — Lucy began to speak.

It seemed that she was addressing the Unicorn, since she spoke with her head still bowed above the creature lying in her lap. The Unicorn's back was to the others, with his bloodied head curving inward like the head of a sleeping child. One of Lucy's gloved hands was resting on his side, her fingers caught in the goatish hair.

"Believe me," she said; "you need not fear. There will be

some vengeance here. His sword is not equal to my fire.''

Mrs Noyes looked over at Ham, confused, and Ham mouthed; "*Japeth.*"

Mrs Noyes nodded.

"If I could only take you home," said Lucy, "you would live. It would be so easy there — just to set you down on the ground and to say to you; '*rise up and walk.*' And I would touch your forehead with my fingers (which she did) . . . and say to you; '*be whole.*' At home. But I cannot say that to you here; rise up and walk — because the ground is not holy here. And I cannot say; be whole — because my fingers have lost their power."

Mrs Noyes and Ham leaned forward.

Where did Lucy mean by "*home*"?

But Mottyl did not lean forward. Not that she didn't care — but only that she already knew, and had known from the first, where Lucy had come from — though she did not necessarily know who she was. Bip had wanted to know if Mottyl had ever known a rogue angel and Mottyl had said; "*no.*" She might still have said no. Nothing she knew of Lucy made her think of violence or contentiousness. And Lucy's only fear was of wolves and dogs and foxes — and they were just as afraid of her — a stand-off. Surely, above all, it was wonderful that Lucy was one of them, in the bowels of the ark — that she was opposed to Doctor Noyes — opposed to his experiments — opposed to his Edict — opposed to his methods and his tactics and his . . .

Mottyl had almost thought; *evil ways.*

Why had she stopped herself, when she was so obviously right?

They *were* evil ways.

Hadn't Doctor Noyes set himself above everyone? Hadn't he blinded her ? Hadn't he killed her children? Hadn't he condemned her to the great fire? Hadn't he sentenced his wife to the life of a prisoner? Hadn't he turned away the Faeries and all those countless animals?

Well.

What could a person truly know, when the whole world had

been reduced to this: to four storeys of earth and heaven, rounded by the stinking yellow walls and sticky pitch of a leaking gopher wood ark?

∞ Lucy said; "believe me; we could sit here forever — and all that would die would be our memory of this moment. But not this moment. I know this from where I have been and from what I have seen. Believe it. All the moments of this creature's life can be with us in an instant. All we have to do is remember it alive. If we can forget its death — it will live. Not forever: not beyond the moment of its death — but before its death, where its life is constant. Look . . ."

Lucy slowly withdrew one hand from its glove and then the other.

Mrs Noyes drew away at the sight of the webbed fingers but she did not speak for fear of distracting Lucy. Only angels had webbed fingers. . . . everyone knew that. Mrs Noyes had seen them, in Yaweh's service: Michael Archangelis — the angel in the orchard — the tall, blond angels who had supported Yaweh as He had walked to the Pavilion.

Lucy seemed to be pulling her self up through herself and out through her fingers, as her fingers hovered over the Unicorn. She began to perspire — and her make-up ran — the finely drawn brows, the deeply kohled eyes began to lose their shape and to course down her whitened face like the black rain of Yaweh and the tears of clowns.

But from within the Unicorn — still lying in her lap — a light began to shine and his body stirred. His legs began to quiver and his neck to stretch, until at last — he lifted his head and stared at Lucy, watching her intensely — wondering where he was.

Lucy put her fingers down towards the Unicorn's forehead and she moved her lips — though no words were audible.

The Unicorn rose to his feet and stumbled — guided by Lucy — down from her lap until he stood, unsteady — but definitely standing — in the straw before her — facing the others, switching his tail and trying to walk. And all this while, the light from within him grew stronger—until all their faces were lit with it. And all of them were smiling.

From the Unicorn's brow, even as they watched — an amber horn was growing. All that Mrs Noyes could think was: after all these years of living with Noah Noyes, at last I have seen a miracle.

∞ But all too soon, the miracle was over.

The Unicorn became increasingly unsteady on his feet and he turned to Lucy as if for help.

Lucy put out her hand towards him and she said; *"Hoda'ah tam."* And then she said; "goodbye."

Mrs Noyes looked up — alarmed. *Goodbye?*

But before she could ask her question aloud, the Unicorn sank to his knees and from his knees to his side in the straw, where he gave a great sigh—though not, Mrs Noyes surmised, an unhappy sigh — and expired.

Everyone — angel, animals and humans alike — leaned towards the tiny body as its light went out and the Stable slowly darkened.

The Unicorn was truly dead. He had lived and died and lived again. And died. And as Lucy would say he would spend eternity living and dying. Just as people either did or didn't—could or couldn't — would or wouldn't return to the memory of the moment when the Unicorn was flesh and blood and lived in the wood at the bottom of Noah's Hill.

∞ "If you could make him live," said Mrs Noyes; "why couldn't you keep him alive?"

"I could ask the same of you, Mother Noyes," Lucy said; "of all your dead children."

∞ Lucy sat on her hip in the straw, resting her weight on one hand, with the Unicorn's head still lying in her lap. Mrs Noyes, whose body wanted to drop from sheer exhaustion, did not move. She stood—one moment just inside the circle of light from Lucy's lamp, where it was hung near the sheep pen — and the next moment in darkness, as the ark rolled forward, swinging the lantern to and fro.

Mottyl—uneasy, now, at being so long away from her kittens
—was trying to make an image of the scene around her, based
on what she could smell and what she could hear. The deep,
sweet aroma of the hay, the gentle, occasional coughing of the
sheep, the alfalfa breath of the nearby cows and the muffled
shifting of their weight as they moved from side to side, the
vaguely disturbing smell of the incense on Crowe's tail and
the ever present sound of the rain and the nearness — somewhere — of Mrs Noyes made a circular picture in Mottyl's
mind, surrounded by endless darkness. At the centre of this
picture was the figure of Lucy — made up of sulphur and of
rustling silk, and the memory of a high, white face that rode
so far away it might have been the moon.

Slowly, almost imperceptibly at first, this figure simulta-
neously floating in a blind cat's mind and sitting in the middle
of a stable began to speak. And its voice was not a voice that
any of those who were present had ever heard before. It was
a darkened voice — with a harshness to it that was foreign to
the woman they had known.

"A long time ago," she said; "in a place I have almost forgotten—I heard a rumour of another world. With all my heart
— because I could not abide the place I was in — I wanted to
see that world. I wanted to go there and to be there and to live
there. Where I was born—the trees were always in the sun. I
do remember that. The merciless light. It never rained—though
we never lacked for water. *Always fair weather!* Dull. I wanted
storms. I wanted difference. And I had heard this rumour . . .
about another world. And I wondered — does it rain there?
Are there clouds, perhaps, and is there shade in that other
world? I wanted somewhere to stand, you see, that would give
me a view of deserts and of snow. I wanted *that* desperately. I
wanted, too, someone I could argue with. Someone—just once
— with whom I could disagree. And I had heard this rumour:
about another world. And I wondered . . . might there be people there, in this other world, who would tell me the sky was
green? Who would say that dry is wet — and black is white?
And if I were to say; '*I am not I — but whoever I wish to be,*'
would I be believed — in this other world? . . .'"

Here, Lucy withdrew a piece of cotton from her pocket and began to remove her make-up. All her white powder — all her dark rouge — her finely drawn eyebrows and the kohl that coloured her lids.

Even Mottyl, blind as she was, could sense that something was happening to Lucy. She could feel the other Lucy being erased: departing.

"Just now when the Unicorn died and I knew I could not save it — I was angry," said Lucy. "Why should it be that a life can only be restored to those who are laid out in a place where it never rains? And where there is no shade, but only the sun? Why should there not be life for *everyone*, in the midst of storms — or hiding, as we are here, in this dark? Why not?"

Lucy removed her rich, sable wig and set it aside. The face beneath the face that had been was sallow in colour — almost grey. Its mouth was wider and its lips fuller than the mouth and the lips that had been. Its nose was longer — sharper — stronger — more divisive. The face it halved was angular and harsh: a face without room for laughter, or even smiles. Above it, there was a short-cropped crown of copper hair — and right down the centre of this hair — a strand of white.

She stood up, now, and laid the Unicorn aside — very gently — carefully.

Undoing the ribbons that had held her ki-mono about her and releasing the great wide sash at its waist, she stepped from this garment — already clothed in another — her gown of long bronze feathers.

Her great height seemed even greater now and her ungloved hands even larger.

"We have come upon this voyage together. And before this voyage, I heard another rumour — didn't you — of another promised land. Well — *this* is that promised land, right here, my friends. *This* is all we have and it may well be the only promised land we shall ever know. The Unicorn has already perished here. And look — the lantern flickers. Any moment now it, too, may die." She paused and then she said; "this is a place without magic. All that was magical and wonderful has been left behind us — drowned — in my world that was before your world — and in your world that was before this. . . ."

The candle — once guaranteed to burn forever — sputtered and went out.

In the dark that followed — Lucy said; "where I was born, the trees were always in the sun. And I left that place because it was intolerant of rain. Now, we are here in a place where there are no trees and there is only rain. And I intend to leave this place — because it is intolerant of light. Somewhere — there must be somewhere where darkness and light are reconciled. So I am starting a rumour, here and now, of yet another world. I don't know when it will present itself — I don't know where it will be. But — as with all those other worlds now past — when it is ready, I intend to go there."

And, just as though she was going to go there in the instant, Lucy stood up and walked away.

Some — including Mottyl — could feel the draught of her passing towards the corridor.

"Don't!" said Mrs Noyes.

Lucy stopped.

"Wait one moment. Please . . ."

Lucy waited.

Mrs Noyes was fumbling with her pockets and the multitude of useful objects there: the string, the rubber bands, the bits of cloth, the hair nets and the apple seeds and the candle ends . . .

Everyone could hear the match being struck — and failing.

They waited: breathless.

A second match was struck.

And failed.

And then a third — with a wide, bright aureole that gave off, of all things, the smell of sulphur.

The candle ends were lit and passed from hand to hand.

"Even if it takes a thousand years — we want to come with you," said Mrs Noyes to Lucy. "Wherever you may be going."

"Now," said Lucy — and she smiled; "you have begun to understand the meaning of your sign. . . ."

Infinity.

∞∞ ∞∞ ∞∞ ∞∞ ∞∞ ∞∞ ∞∞ ∞∞ ∞∞ ∞∞

B O O K   F O U R

∞∞ ∞∞ ∞∞ ∞∞ ∞∞ ∞∞ ∞∞ ∞∞ ∞∞ ∞∞

*. . .and the fear of you and
the dread of you shall be
upon every beast of the earth,
and upon every fowl of the
air, upon all that moveth . . .
into your hand are they
delivered.*

Genesis 9:2

∞∞ ∞∞ ∞∞ ∞∞ ∞∞

∞ ∞ ∞ ∞ ∞ ∞ ∞ ∞ ∞ ∞

E GGS, MILK AND butter were at a premium and the supply of cheese was also depleted. All of these things were essentials in the preferred diet of Doctor Noyes. Sister Hannah — being pregnant — required a supplement of fruits and vegetables — as well as an extra quota of milk.

At first it was Sister Hannah — sent below with a shopping list — who came to requisition these goods. With her willow shopping basket on her arm and her shawl drawn over her hair, she would arrive precisely as one might pay a visit to the local grocery store with the singular exception that she carried no pouch of coins: nothing to tip out over the counter, saying; *and how much does all that come to, Mrs Noyes?*

Mrs Noyes would say; "but you've only just *had* two dozen eggs yesterday. . . ." and " . . . *we're* on a milk ration, too, you know. And — as for butter — I haven't had time to do any churning. Don't forget — we're short-handed now, since you took Emma. Every single thing she did down here has fallen to me. And just by the way — while I'm at it — have you any notion how hard we work down here? The feeding of all these animals? Every day and twice a day! And you have the gall to come down here and ask for butter! Shame on you! *Shame!*"

To Hannah's credit, shame was still something she could feel, though she called it modesty. Its root was mostly in the fear that haunted her — an uneasy awareness that she had traded too much of her self in return for what she had thought

287

would be security and esteem. This uneasiness was like a second child in her belly and it shifted with her every time she moved; hovered beside her every time she paused; lay with her every time she slept. And yet, there was nothing of what she had gained that Hannah's ambitions would allow her to abandon, though she had begun to wish—and fervently—that what she had gained had been got in different company.

Consequently, in a few days' time, Hannah ceased to be the one who came below to requisition in behalf of Noah's wants and even in behalf of her own needs. She began to pretend that her condition forbade the perilous journey across the open deck and down the long, steep stair that led to the hold. She also began, at this time, to retire for longer hours of contemplation and reading in her cabin—locking its door against Shem's entry and, not incidentally, Japeth's and Noah's as well. It was during these days that she copied out in twenty separate margins of her handmade book the following quotation from the volume of tales with whose exclusive company she was cloistered: *By god,* she wrote; *if women had writen stories, they would have writen of men more wikkednesse than all the sex of Adam may redresse.*

She also wept, who had not wept since before memory.

∞ It was Shem who descended next, though he brought no willow basket.

Mrs Noyes greeted him with a shocked expression, since— in all truth — she barely recognized her eldest son. "What have you done to yourself?" she said. "Is that *you*, in there?" And she gave him a poke with her finger — just about where his belly button floated on the surface of several layers of newly acquired fat. "You look sick, if you don't mind my saying so . . . a healthy boy like you, and not an ounce of muscle! And where did all your colour go? And your hair is falling out! That's a sign of an unbalanced diet. . . ." Here, Mrs Noyes bit her tongue. The subject of balanced diets was, of course, an open door through which the Ox could launch his first request; "green vegetables, mother. We know you have them — cabbages and Brussels sprouts—and I've come to collect them.''

Mrs Noyes became indignant; ''cabbages? Brussels sprouts? I don't know what you're talking about. . . .what makes you think we have such delicacies as that? Cabbages indeed! Brussels sprouts, my foot!''

''We can smell them cooking,'' said Shem. ''In fact, I can smell them cooking right now.''

Mrs Noyes went scarlet.

''Oh, well. . . .'' she blustered. ''Just a little one and the last.'' And then, inspired, she came back at him with a taunt as old as Shem's childhood. ''And imagine you, of all people, asking for a cabbage! Oh, the weeping and the screaming and the teeth clamped shut when I tried to make you eat one leaf! One leaf of cabbage — and you'd throw it across the room! Now, you come down here pretending cabbages are the food of kings and you're going to die if you don't get your hands on one. Well — I'm here to tell you, Shemmy,'' (a name he could not abide, of which she was well aware) ''you won't get any cabbages out of me! Why, *they're all we have!* Are you here to steal the last morsel from your own mother's lips? Shame on you! *Shame!*''

Shem could not find an answer to this that he dared speak aloud, since the unspeakable answer was *yes* — that, when all was said and done, he had come down to steal the last morsel from *anyone's* mouth, if that morsel happened to be cabbage.

Finally, he hit upon a way of winning at least something for his efforts. ''But—it's not for me, Mama. It's for Hannah and the baby.''

Oh dear; thought Mrs Noyes. The baby. Yes, yes—the baby. Above all, the baby. In the hierarchy of need, the unborn came first, the newborn second. And nothing must stand between them and life.

''Very well,'' she said. ''You may have one cabbage and twelve Brussels sprouts — but only on the express condition that they pass directly into Hannah's hands.''

''Yes, Mama.''

Mrs Noyes went away and fished around in the depths of the sawdust in which the cabbage and sprouts were stored—

alarmed at how very few of either she could find — and came back with the promised goods.

"There you are," she said tersely. "One cabbage, twelve sprouts."

The Ox turned them over in his enormous hands.

"They're not very big," he said.

"Tough," said Mrs Noyes.

"And there's a *worm* . . . !" Shem almost dropped the cabbage on the floor in horror. (It had been the threat of worms that had long ago caused his cabbage phobia.)

"Good," said Mrs Noyes. "A guarantee that cabbage will end up where it belongs — on Sister Hannah's plate, not yours."

∞ Thereafter, Shem the Ox did not return to market. Since he, himself, had no desire for cabbage and since there was still some store of what he did desire — namely dried fruit and sweetmeats — he was content to go on gorging in Noah's larder and otherwise feeding on the noodles and fish chowder of which Hannah's cooking almost entirely consisted. In his off hours — which is to say, those hours that were not devoted to eating — Shem took up the occupation of cleanliness. He began to change his undergarment twice a day and to insist that his tunics have starch in their collars and that all his whites should be bleached. These were jobs for Emma. For himself, there was the labour of personal cleanliness: the growing and trimming of a moustache; the washing and endless combing of his thinning and receding hair; the polishing and whitening of his long-neglected teeth and the trimming and buffing of his nails. At the end of these labours, spotless and gleaming and starched, he would squeeze his bulk into the softest chair he could find and stare into the spaces around him, dreaming of hot summer afternoons on the hillside and listening, in vain, for the sound of twenty, thirty, a hundred scythes and the songs of as many peasants. But neither these nor the smell of new-mown hay could be conjured. His memory of them had faded beyond recall beneath the overlay of his flesh.

∞Japeth arrived with sweat in his eyes and a sword in his hand.

Mrs Noyes stood her ground and said; "yes? And what do *you* want?"

Japeth barged past her, making for the Stable.

Mrs Noyes ran after.

"What? What is it?" she cried out, panic-stricken by the direction in which he was marching. "Why are you going in there?"

At the entrance to the Stable, Japeth turned on his mother and said; "go back."

"I will not go back! How dare you? What are you doing down here with that sword?"

Japeth marched across the floor where the Unicorn had died and made for the sheep pens.

"No!" said Mrs Noyes. "Stop!"

Japeth made a one-handed leap over the barrier and landed amongst the sheep.

Mrs Noyes watched in dread as she heard the first cry — and then she turned and ran back into the corridor, calling for Ham and Lucy.

But Ham was in the pit of the Well with One Tusk and Hippo and Lucy was far away, feeding the Gryphon.

"Help!" Mrs Noyes cried. "Help! Help! Help!"

Everyone heard her, including Mottyl and Crowe — but since both were in hiding, they did not know whether to emerge or not. As for the others — aside from Ham and Lucy — they were all in their pens and cages and could not have come to her assistance until their doors were opened.

Lucy, being closest, did at least reach Mrs Noyes before she was harmed.

Having thought that no one was coming to her aid, Mrs Noyes had rushed at Japeth as he re-emerged from the Stable — her intention being to trip him up with a pitchfork. But Japeth was no longer the gauche and awkward warrior-boy who, months before, had mistaken his lantern for a sword. Since his battles with the Pirates and his slaying of the Unicorn, he had become an efficient warlord and accomplished butcher. Consequently, rounding the corner from the Stable, all his reflexes were in perfect order — and when the pitchfork came at him — aimed between his knees — he simply gave it a backhanded blow with his sword and sliced its handle in half.

The effect of this was to send Mrs Noyes reeling back against the wall, where she struck her shoulder very hard and fell to the floor. Japeth was standing over her with his sword when Lucy appeared.

"Who are you?" he said, never having seen Lucy in her present incarnation.

"That," said Lucy; "is for me to know and for you to guess."

They stared at one another — Japeth with narrowed eyes, Lucy with her eyes wide open.

One of them had to back down and off — and it wasn't going to be Lucy.

Japeth said; "I'm leaving now. Do not attempt to follow me."

"I wouldn't dream of it," said Lucy.

Japeth pointed his sword at his mother. "Don't ever come at me again like that, or I will kill you."

Mrs Noyes did not speak. *Her own son . . .*

Japeth turned then and walked away down the dimly lit corridor, with his bounty hanging down his back.

When Mrs Noyes saw what was there, she was so over-whelmed by the horror of it that she began — at last — to scream and she went on screaming until she had lost her voice.

Lucy knelt down on the boards before her and, holding Mrs Noyes, she rocked her back and forth until the voice gave out and all that was left was a silent sobbing and a clutching of hands.

Japeth's trophies had been the heads of four calves, whose blood was pouring down the backs of his legs and whose mouths, when he had killed them, had still been full of milk.

∞ That night, Noah fed on glazed tongue and calves' brains, and as he dabbled his fingers in the dish and lowered them into his lap for the waiting mouths to suckle, he was thinking; *if the altar stone were bigger, I could sacrifice that bullock I've been saving. Still, there is that ram — and if he's grown too big to manage, then we shall make another offering of lambs. . . .*

The suckling mouths pulled harder.

"Oh—you like the thought of that, do you. Well, my babies, there is every chance that Yaweh will like it, too. And when He smells the sweet savour of our sacrifice, it may well be that we can tempt Him with our prayers to smile on us again. And to return to us . . .'*

. . . from His great sleep, Noah thought. *Or from His great journey . . . or from his great sojourn in the land of Nod.*

Noah hung above his plate, with his fingers still descending, and his mouth hanging open. And his brain went up against the wall it could not pass — which was the tomb of Yaweh — and it pressed against the stones and it stammered; *no — no — no — not dead. Do not be . . . dead.*

∞ Later that same night, Mottyl was in her nest preparing to feed her kittens, when she realized the silver male was missing.

She chattered for him — and chirruped — but there was no reply.

"You must wait," she told the others. "Your brother has wandered off and I must find him before Japeth does. . . ."

Japeth's name was now synonymous with violent death and all the kittens understood this and they went into the furthest corner and hid, as Mottyl had taught them to do, beneath the straw.

Pushing aside the curtain of camouflage devised by Mrs Noyes and Lucy, Mottyl started clambering down the wire enclosure of the Unicorns' cage below her.

Inadvertently and against her will — since any animal who is ill or in grieving is considered to be in sanctuary — Mottyl glanced inside the cage. But she could not tell if The Lady was there or not. Ever since the Unicorn's death, The Lady had fallen under what appeared to be a spell and would neither speak nor eat nor drink.

Mottyl sniffed the air, and though the faintest scent of the Unicorn himself could be had from the wire where he had rubbed his horn, there was not a trace of the Lady's scent, nor of Unicorn scat nor of any other sign or signal that she was present there at all. What Mottyl did catch, however, was the definite scent of her son.

"Are you in there?"

"Yes, Mam."

"Well, come out. Come out at once. The Lady is not to be disturbed. I've told you that. Come out."

"Yes, Mam."

"Aren't you aware it's suppertime?"

"Yes, Mam."

"Out, then. Out — out — out . . . I've told you not to wander."

"Yes, Mam."

The silver kitten struggled forward on his wobbly legs towards the image of his mother, hanging before him against the wire.

"How did you get in there?"

"Through the corner."

"Can you get out on your own?"

"Yes, Mam."

"Did you see The Lady?" Mottyl whispered, as the kitten reached the corner of the cage and started to push his way through towards her. "Did she speak to you?"

"No, Mam."

"I suppose she is still very sad. . . ."

"Maybe so, Mam. But I don't think there's very much of her there to *be* sad. Or *Anything*."

"Oh? Just how do you mean that? *Not much of her there . . .*"

The kitten was pushing at the corner and Mottyl was making her way down the wire in order to be closer to him as he came through.

"That's all," he explained. "There's hardly any of her left."

Mottyl went cold.

"All right. I'll put you up with the others and then I think I had better go and get Mrs Noyes."

She picked the kitten up in her mouth and carried him back to her nest and told him to hide in the corner. As soon as he was safe, she clambered back down and hung again against the wire.

"Lady? . . ."

There was no immediate answer. But there was a sound. Flies.

Had they been there all along? Why had she not heard them? "Speak, Lady. Speak. Are you there?"

Mottyl wished that she was small enough to crawl through the wire as her son had done. If The Lady died . . .

Mottyl dropped to the floor and hurried along the corridor, using the draughts to guide her, until she came to the foot of the stairs where she stopped and threw back her head and yelled as loud as she could.

Mrs Noyes came running from one direction, Lucy from another and Ham from another. All three crowded onto the stairs and Mrs Noyes started down, almost falling.

"What? What is it?"

"Hurry! Hurry!" Mottyl cried. "Hurry! Hurry!" And she sped back down the corridor towards the Unicorns' cage and her own nest.

Mrs Noyes, Ham and Lucy followed and watched as Mottyl clambered back up the wire and hung before the Lady, gasping; "*there* . . ."

Mrs Noyes picked Mottyl up and held her aside as Lucy and Ham undid the cage door and opened it.

Lucy reached inside as far as she could and muttered; "flies. . . ."

"Yes, I know," Mottyl told her. "It means . . ."

"Shhh, shhhh," said Mrs Noyes, holding Mottyl tight and rocking her from side to side. "It's all right now. Lucy's got her."

Lucy brought The Lady forward as far as she dared—lifting her gently as a piece of glass. But, at once, it was all too clear what had happened. The Lady had starved herself to death and there was nothing there but skin and bones—a breeding place for flies.

Lucy withdrew her hands and she and Ham and Mrs Noyes stepped back.

"Is she dead?" Mottyl asked.

"Yes," said Mrs Noyes. "Now they have both gone back to the wood."

∞ Across the way, the Vixen and the raccoon, Bip and Ringer and the others were watching as the crown of flies descended and the Lady disappeared.

Suddenly, everyone was aware of how small the cages were and how low the ceiling was and how little air there was to breathe and the Gryphon asked; "are we all going to die like that?"

For a moment, no one spoke. And then Lucy said, very quietly; "yes. We are all going to die like that. But not here."

∞ "Where are we going?" said Mrs Noyes, hurrying after Lucy down into the depths.

It was well past midnight and Mrs Noyes wanted to be in her bed, but Lucy had said that no one would sleep this night. Now, while Ham was preparing an arsenal of weapons made up of pitchforks, broomsticks and paring knives, Lucy and Mrs Noyes were descending to the pit, each with a burlap sack and Lucy with a candle lantern. Her burnished hair was all that Mrs Noyes could see below her on the steps.

"We are going to capture a pair of useful allies," said Lucy.

"If they are allies," said the ever practical Mrs Noyes; "then why do we have to capture them?"

"Because they don't know they're allies," said Lucy. "Yet."

Mrs Noyes had not been so often as the others in the pit, though it was here that she visited her Bears. On those occasions, however, she made a bee-line for the Bear cage, waving over her shoulder at One Tusk and Hippo — of whom she was only moderately afraid — and ignoring all else about her: the Dragons, the Ohnos, the Crocodiles and the Rhinos.

Right now, almost treading on Lucy's feathers — she was walking so close behind her — Mrs Noyes was silently praying they had not come down to make allies of the Ohnos or the

Crocodiles. Certainly, they could not be going to make allies of the Rhinos or the Dragons, since neither of these would fit in a burlap sack.

"Oh—please do tell me what it is we are doing here. . . ." she said.

"I don't need to tell you," said Lucy. "All you have to do is look."

Mrs Noyes looked.

There, in the corner of their cage, were two of the ark's passengers she had completely forgotten (more than likely because she had not been delighted to have them on board in the first place). Four demons, two of the one-headed kind and two of the other, were staring out at her from glowing eyes; twenty-six eyes, in all—and all of a rich burnt orange colour.

The smell near their cage was of singed hair and forest fires, and as soon as it was apparent that Lucy was going to open their cage, they crowded up close to the bars and started to reach out for the Pirate meat which Lucy had brought in her burlap sack.

"Now," said Lucy—having emptied the sack and handed it to Mrs Noyes—"take this and your own and soak them thoroughly in the water barrel."

Mrs Noyes—very carefully—did as she was told, which meant that she had to stand for two whole minutes, holding the sacks underwater, right beside the Crocodiles.

In the meantime, Lucy was cajoling the demons, placating them, petting them, scratching them under the chin and talking to them in one of her foreign languages, which the demons seemed to understand.

"Why do we want *them* as allies?" Mrs Noyes asked.

"You'll see," said Lucy.

"I have a whole roomful of furniture at home absolutely ruined by demons," said Mrs Noyes—more than slightly exaggerating, since what she had had was precisely one chair in which the demon brought home by Japeth had been seated while Mrs Noyes had given it lunch. Admittedly, Mrs Noyes had later found the chair a very useful conversation piece. "Guess what made these marks . . ." she would say. But no one could even begin to guess, since it had never been the custom to invite demons in to sit on your chairs or to share your lunch.

When the burlap sacks had been soaked and only partially wrung out — according to Lucy's instructions — Mrs Noyes tiptoed past the yawning and vaguely inquisitive Crocodiles and said; ''now what?''

''Now you hold the bags open and I will put in the demons.''

''You mean you can actually pick them up?''

''Yes,'' said Lucy. ''I'm protected. Hurry. We don't want to miss the hours of darkness.''

Mrs Noyes, accordingly, opened one and then the other sack as wide as she could and held them out to Lucy at arm's length.

''We may have to douse them again before we're through,'' said Lucy — popping the single-headed demons into the first bag, docile as rabbits. At once, there was the smell of an extinguished fire, as the demons settled in against the dampened sacking.

The second pair was less co-operative — complaining (apparently) that there was very little room inside the sack for all their heads and other appendages. Mrs Noyes, not understanding what all the squealing was about, almost dropped the sack and ran — but Lucy persuaded her that the crisis was a minor one and that she mustn't pay attention.

''You may carry the one-heads, if that will make you feel any easier,'' said Lucy — exchanging sacks with Mrs Noyes.

''Thank you,'' said Mrs Noyes. ''And just how do you carry a sack of demons?''

''Simple,'' said Lucy. ''You sling them over your back, just like a sack of anything else. You'll see . . . they rather love it.''

Lucy swung the others over her shoulder and there was a chorus of delighted squeals.

''Heavens!'' said Mrs Noyes. ''You're quite right. They do like it. . . .'' And she hefted her own sack onto her back, swinging it through the air as she did.

''*Wheee!*'' said the one-heads to Lucy, from deep within their bag. ''Tell her to do that again!''

"There isn't time," said Lucy. "When you've done your job, you can have lots and lots of being slung over shoulders. Now, we have work to do."

∞ Carrying demons was an odd sensation, to say the least, for Mrs Noyes. Their heat was not unpleasant — and since the sack was wet, they caused no fires. "These would be very useful for the bed at night," she told Lucy. "Or for when you have an arthritis attack."

They hurried out of the pit and along the corridors and up the next flight of stairs and only had to stop once to douse the demons. When they got to Ham and his arsenal, Mrs Noyes was flushed with the excitement of it all.

"I'm carrying demons!" she said. "I'm carrying demons!" — not unlike a child who has managed for the first time to pick up a cobra.

Ham was not impressed. His mind was on what lay ahead.

∞ The plan was relatively simple and straightforward. With the aid of the demons, Lucy meant to burn through the wooden door at the top of the stairs that led to the upper decks — and once they had got there — to overpower Japeth in the Armoury.

"If we can dispense with him, the others will be helpless. Sister Hannah is not very likely to fight and Doctor Noyes is too old to fight and Shem has become so lazy he won't be *able* to fight. Emma, of course, will be on our side and can help us. But the main thing is — to achieve surprise. That is why the demons will be doubly helpful: they will get us through the door — and they will get us through the door *quietly*. No hammers; no chisels; no hack-saws — just a nice clean burn."

Ham had assembled a meagre store of arms — but sufficient to give them each a paring knife and a pitchfork. With the brooms, he had made a set of spears — six in all — which he would carry with him. Each of the spears was tipped with yet another of the kitchen knives, though he had not been able to bring himself to use the larger, butcher's knives because their sharpness and their size were so intimidating he could not imagine using them in battle. The wounds they might inflict were too grisly to contemplate.

Lucy said this was cowardice of the worst kind — "intellectual cowardice," as she called it. "A knife wound is a knife wound," she said. "Your brother's blood is no less your brother's blood just because you happen to have drawn it with a smaller blade, Ham. What nonsense you people talk sometimes."

"Yes — but I don't want to *kill* them," said Ham.

"Well, my dear one," said Lucy; "I'm sorry to have to say this to you — but the fact is, if you aren't willing to kill them — we aren't going to win."

"But — I can't kill my own brother!" said Ham.

"All right. Then tell me this: can you imagine Japeth saying that?"

As Ham fell silent, Mrs Noyes received a vivid picture in her mind of Japeth in the corridor, brandishing his sword and saying; *if you do that again, I will kill you. . . .*

"No," she said. "I can't imagine Japeth saying that."

"That's all right for you to say," said Ham; "but it's *me* that has to kill him."

"Why not cross that bridge when you come to it?" said Lucy.

Ham subsided. He wished the subject had never come up, and secretly he was still determined that no one should be killed. Nevertheless, to argue the point with Lucy was useless. She had a streak in her of ruthlessness that he would never understand and perhaps not ever be able to cope with. But he did recognize this much: without that streak of ruthlessness, there would be no revolt aboard the ark — because the ruthlessness would all remain on the other side of the door they were now about to broach.

Lucy went up the stairs to the top and cautioned Mrs Noyes to be quiet and to follow her. Ham also followed, but he stood to one side. When they had burned away the wood around the locks and bolts, he would be the first to go through and he was already sweating, in spite of the freezing draught that was blowing under the door and guttering the candles.

"Bring your demons here," said Lucy to Mrs Noyes.

Lucy crouched by the door frame, with Mrs Noyes beside

her and the sacks of demons in between.

"I'm afraid you'd better bring a pail of water," said Lucy. "The sacks are beginning to burn. Hurry."

Mrs Noyes rushed off down the stairs to the Stable, where she knew there would be a pail and a barrel. In the meantime, Lucy reached inside the first sack and withdrew a demon.

Ham watched, fascinated and not a little alarmed, as Lucy spoke to the demon in a foreign language — and offered it a prize bit of liver from her pocket.

The demon gobbled the liver — cooking it in the process — and almost at once began to glow a little brighter in the nether regions. More speech between them produced the extraordinary spectacle of the demon presenting its gleaming rear end to Lucy, who fanned it rapidly with her large webbed hand.

When the fanning had brought the glow to its brightest and hottest condition, Lucy then instructed the demon to stand *just so* against the jamb. She helped it by supporting it with her fingers.

The result of this was the picture of a red hot demon leaning forward in a squatting position, with its behind hard up against the door jamb, while Lucy held its paws in much the same way a mother might hold the hands of a child who was having a difficult moment on the pot.

But however domestic the image, the effect was precisely as Lucy had predicted: the wood flared and burned like a magic cinder, and very soon, there was a hole in the door jamb the circumference of a broom stick.

By the time Mrs Noyes had returned with her pail of water, Lucy was on her second demon and the first was lying exhausted on the step, being careful to lie on its belly, so as not to set fire to the stairs. The burlap sack containing the demons of the other kind was smoking away like a campfire and Mrs Noyes lowered it into the pail, where it made a satisfying *hiss*.

⟳ Each demon had to be applied twice to the job of making a hole that would be large enough not only for Lucy to get her arm through, but — once it was through — to allow her enough mobility to draw the bolts on the far side. This was finally accomplished, though not without difficulty — most of it caused by Lucy's attempts at silence. The bolts were rusty — and wanted to squeal — which meant that Lucy had to work them very slowly. But, at last, with hardly any sound at all, she succeeded.

"*Done!*" she whispered — withdrawing her arm triumphantly. "We're free!"

The Revolt of the Lower Orders was about to begin.

∞ Slipping the sacks of demons over their backs — very slowly, so as not to produce any squeals of delight — Lucy and Mrs Noyes picked up their paring knives and pitchforks and stood aside.

Ham, who was wearing a burlap cape around his shoulders, stepped to the door with his spears in one hand and his pitchfork in the other. His knife was secure in his belt.

"Here goes," he said, and pushed the door open with his toe.

What greeted them was a sight that none had thought possible.

It was snowing.

"Oh — how beautiful!" Mrs Noyes whispered — staring wide-eyed at the scene before her.

"It won't be beautiful once we get out there," said Lucy. "Be careful," she said to Ham. "It will be icy." But Ham had already gone through.

The air was full of milky light, in spite of the fact it was two or three in the morning, and — otherwise — pitchy black. Every inch of the deck — including the Castle, the Pagoda and the Armoury — was covered with a thick, wet layer of white, and there was not a breath of wind. The snow was falling straight down, in flakes the size of copper pennies — and its thickness produced an eerie but comforting silence.

The demons, intrigued by the smell of the snow, pushed their heads up out of the sacks and stuck out all their tongues to catch it, producing a sound like drops of water thrown into a frying pan.

Turning towards the Armoury, Mrs Noyes caught a glimpse of all the birds on the railings, huddled under their capes of snow — and some with their beaks grown longer where icicles had formed at the tips. It wasn't long, in fact, before icicles began to form on the ends of her hair as the snow started to melt and run down her neck.

Ham was lying — as had been prearranged — on the roof of the Armoury above the door, from which position he would ambush Japeth. Lucy, with her glowing sack of demons, marched to the door and gave it a loud *thwack* with the handle of her pitchfork.

There was no response except that some of the birds woke up and began to shift along the railings to get a better look at what was happening, shedding their snow as they went and bumping into other, less inquisitive birds.

Lucy gave the door a second *thwack*.

One or two birds looked up — bad-tempered at having been disturbed. But Lucy paid no attention and battered at the door three times in succession.

Still nothing happened.

Then — all at once — there was a movement near the Castle and a figure stepped forward, behind the conspirators.

"Are you looking for me?" it said.

It was Japeth — armed and armoured from head to toe — and wearing a bright red cape against the weather.

Furthermore, he had with him his two wolves on their brass chains.

Lucy's only terror was of dogs and wolves — and she was frozen in her tracks, as Japeth let the chains fall from his wrists and barked; *"attack!"*

The wolves, immobilized by a terror of their own, stood stock-still, their eyes fixed on Lucy. For several long seconds, no one moved. And then Japeth took another step and raised his sword.

∞ Fifteen minutes later, Lucy, Ham and Mrs Noyes were seated on the deck with their backs to the Armoury wall and the sacks of demons hissing in the snow beside them.

Ham was disconsolate.

"We never even thought he wouldn't be in there." he said. "We never even thought of it!"

"Next time, we *will* think of it," said Lucy.

"Next time?" Ham raised his bound wrists and made a hopeless gesture. "What next time?"

"The next time and the next time and the next," said Lucy. "However many times it takes to win. If you're wise — you'll regard what we've done tonight not as failure, but as a rehearsal. And one we can turn to our advantage . . ."

"Oh, yes," said Ham. "Turn it to our advantage. And just how do you propose to do that?"

"I don't know yet. But I'm thinking about it — which, I might suggest, would be a much more profitable way for *you* to spend *your* time, ducky, than wallowing in defeat."

At this moment, Japeth reappeared from the Castle with Shem and Doctor Noyes in tow.

"There they are," he said. "Over there."

Noah — looking very old and as if he had risen from his grave in a winding sheet, rather than from the warmth of his bed in his shawl — came across the deck and peered at the prisoners through the falling snow.

It was the first time he had seen his wife in over a month, and he barely recognized her, thin as she was and filthy, in spite of the snow. He certainly didn't recognize Lucy, what with her copper hair and bony face which seemed to have so little to do with the face he remembered: white and round and beautiful. His son, dressed in burlap and slush, with long straggly hair and bound wrists, was utterly unknown to him.

"Who *are* these people?" he said to Japeth. "Another boarding party?"

"No, father. I've told you: it's Ham and Lucy and Mother."

Noah blinked. And sniffed the air.

"Are they on fire?" he said.

"No, father. That's the demons."

Noah regarded the burlap sacks and the glowing eyes with a mixture of distaste and alarm.

"Are they dangerous?" he asked.

Shem said; "no," and Japeth said; "yes."

"Then get rid of them," said Noah.

Japeth stepped forward and took up the sacks and threw them over the side of the ark.

∞ It happened so quickly that none of the conspirators could even protest. And the demons — not at all recognizing what was happening to them — thought they were just being hoisted and slung — so that, as they whirled out over the rail and into the sizzling storm of snow, they cried with delight.

Long after they had sunk beneath the waters, Mrs Noyes came out of her shock and looked at Japeth as if he might still be striding towards the demons, and the deed still undone — and she said; "please don't, they're our friends. . . ."

Lucy bowed her head in what appeared to be grief, but in fact, it was anger. Very slowly, the ropes on her wrists began to smoulder, though no one but Ham appeared to notice.

Japeth had moved away from the railing and was trying to untangle the chains attached to the collars of his wolves, who were becoming restive, their eyes still on Lucy.

"What's the matter with you?" he said. "Be still." Japeth was still annoyed with them for having refused to obey his order to attack.

The wolves, however, seemed not to hear him. They were sniffing the air and grew more nervous, still. The female, especially, was pulling very hard at her chain, which made it next to impossible for Japeth to gain control of them. The male had lowered his tail and was trying to hide behind Japeth — while the female continued to tug in the opposite direction.

Ham watched Lucy's wrists with growing fascination as the ropes gave off more and more smoke and began to turn red — then orange — then yellow as the heat increased. All the muscles in Lucy's arms were straining — and she made and unmade fists of her hands with her head still bowed and her shoulders and back piling deeper and deeper with snow.

Mrs Noyes was being lost beneath a drift because she could not — or would not — move, and Ham became fearful. His mother appeared to be falling asleep — and he knew from all his winter nights spent watching the stars from the cedar grove, that sleep and snow can be a deadly combination. He had seen some tamarins die that way — ichneumons, wombats and other beasts who should have been in the wood but who had strayed to the Hill and been trapped there by blizzards. Now, he wanted to warn his mother — call to her — but he was afraid of drawing attention to Lucy, whose wrists might at any moment burn free of their bonds — in which case, she might be able to untie them all and revive his mother.

Japeth's wolves put all Ham's fears to rest. They could smell the burning ropes and would not be still — and at last, they became so entangled that they both sat down and began to howl.

"Stop that!" said Noah.

"Stop that!" said Japeth.

"Stop what?" said Mrs Noyes, coming awake all at once — and sitting up with such violence that all the snow around her fell away like a discarded garment.

The wolves howled and their howling brought Hannah, cloaked in white blankets, to the door of the Castle. She had obviously been asleep and was, at first, disoriented. But when she took in the snow and what was happening, she retreated into the lantern-lit interior.

"Was that Emma?" said Mrs Noyes.

"No, Mama," said Ham — his voice lowered. "And try not to draw attention over here."

"Why not?" said Mrs Noyes. "I *want* attention. I'm freezing here — aren't you?"

"Yes, but . . ."

Mrs Noyes called to Shem; "come over here at once and undo your mother!"

But the Ox did not move. He was much too busy rearranging his garments to keep the snow from falling down the inside of his shirt.

Japeth stepped — at last — from the bindings of the wolf chains — lifting one leg and then the other — with the chains still caught around his right wrist and lower arm.

Noah said; "what's that?"

"What?" said Japeth.

"Over there. Over there . . ." Noah was pointing vaguely in the direction of the prisoners — trying to hold his shawl in place at the same time. "Smoke . . ." he said.

Japeth looked.

Hannah appeared behind them — innocently advancing with the black umbrella raised above her.

Suddenly, Lucy raised her head and cried; "look out!" and she flung her arm at Japeth and Shem and Noah — all of whom turned on pure reflex, as if the sky might be falling behind them.

"Look out!"

Shem drew his cloak across his face, thinking Hannah was the Angel of Death — all white as she was, with the black apparition above her — and a muffled cry was heard from behind his arm. Noah had to look more than once to see who was there — but Japeth was given no chance to look for more than a fraction of a second.

Just as he turned, and just as she cried; *"look out,"* for the second time, Lucy leapt at Japeth — even in spite of the wolves — and threw him to the deck.

Ham thought — oh, if only she had freed me first!

But Lucy was not, it turned out, seeking to continue the revolution. Otherwise, she would indeed have freed not only Ham, but Mrs Noyes as well. All she wanted in that moment was Japeth himself — and the chance to avenge the death of her demons.

Japeth did not know what was happening to him. All he knew was that his wolves had turned on him and were slashing at his legs and feet with their teeth — while some other creature (who could have guessed it was Lucy?) sat on his shoulders and pinned his arms to the deck with its knees. And a great bronze palm came down above his face and smothered him, while the web and fingers of this gigantic hand were wrapped like a cabbage leaf about his head, shutting out all sound and all sight, and he felt a dreadful searing pain he could not identify running through his whole body.

Rescue was not necessary.

Lucy rose to her feet as soon as her gesture was completed and she stepped, quite willingly — almost docile — back to her place beside Mrs Noyes and Ham.

When Japeth staggered to his knees, he was sure he would never see and never hear again. But what Lucy had effected was nothing like blindness — nothing like deafness. It was simply her seal upon a curse: *that Japeth would never know a moment's peace from his flesh as long as he lived.* Where the wolves had bitten him, he would fester forever. And no wound received in any future encounter with an enemy — whether human or animal — would ever heal. He would smell, henceforth, of every death he inflicted and the proof of this was that he already smelled of fire, the result of having murdered four demons.

Shem, who by now had recovered from the shock of Hannah's appearance — and realized he was not going to die — went forward and released Japeth from the chains around his wrists — and moved the whimpering wolves to one side.

Hannah stood near Noah's shoulder, holding the black umbrella above the old man. She had thrown the tails of her shawl around her neck and drawn its cloth up over her mouth and nose, so that only her eyes could be seen. These remained downcast.

Noah peered through the falling snow at Lucy as if she were an apparition (*Yaweh?* . . .) and he said; "who is that man?"

Shem said; "it's not a man, father. It's Lucy. *Lucy* — Ham's wife."

"It's a *man*," said Noah. "You think I don't know a man when I see one?"

Shem looked at Hannah. Clearly, his father was either seeing things, or had slipped completely into senility.

"I beg to differ, father," he said, with a formality born of fear and exhaustion. "Perhaps it is just a trick of the light . . . the snow . . . the lateness of the hour."

"It's a *man*," said Noah.

Hannah touched the old man's shoulder. "Come, Father Noyes," she said. "You must return to your bed. You will catch your death out here."

Noah turned. "It's a man," he said, quieter now.

"Yes, yes," said Hannah — taking his elbow to guide him — leading him towards the Castle. "It probably is a man. You're right."

"Another boarding party . . ."

"Yes. Yes."

"Pirates."

"Yes."

"But we won again — didn't we."

"Yes. We won. Again. Now you must go to bed."

"Will you. . . ? Are you. . . ?"

"Yes. I will come with you until you sleep."

At the entrance to the Castle, Noah half turned back to the others and said; "deal with them."

"Yes, sir," said Shem.

Japeth said nothing.

Noah went away into the Castle and Hannah, letting down the black umbrella and giving it a shake, went after him and closed the door.

∞ As the snow continued to fall, the wind began to rise. By daybreak, the ark was in the thrall of a full-scale blizzard — perhaps the worst storm it had encountered since first being cast adrift.

Japeth and Shem herded the prisoners below and Shem, with the wolves, stood guard as Japeth made the rounds of the entire three lower decks, smashing all the lanterns and throwing all the candles into a sack.

"There will be no light for you from here on," he had said. "You will live in perpetual darkness until we come to land."

When he came to the Stable, he seized several lambs and, looping a rope around their hind legs, he strung them all from his back, and with his sword drawn, made his way with the lambs and the sack of candles all the way to the top of the stairs.

"This door will be barred in ways that you will never defeat," he said. "You may starve, and we may starve," he added; "but at least *we* won't starve in the dark."

Then he was gone — leaving Shem to bring up the rear with the wolves.

When Shem got to the top of the stairs, he looked incongruous in his spotless clothes, with the two great wolves at his feet and the snow blowing in around him. Perhaps he was aware of the incongruity, because he looked down and pulled the skirts of his nightshirt awry, as if he were making a ruin of his neatness on purpose — and then he looked rather sheepishly at his mother and his brother and at Lucy and he said; "I'm sorry. . . . "

After which he turned and walked through the door. And for a moment while the door stood open, the snow blew in and drifted down the stairs and over the floor towards Mrs Noyes's feet as she watched the little patch of sky up above, and then the sudden darkness that came with a *bang*—and the sound of hammers and nails and chains.

∞ In this darkness, while Lucy was removing the ropes from Ham's and Mrs Noyes's wrists, Mottyl came and stood at Mrs Noyes's feet and cried.

Mrs Noyes was alarmed.

"You should never have left your nest while Japeth was about," she said. "I've told you that."

But Japeth was not the problem.

The problem was Mottyl's and Mrs Noyes's favourite kitten, Silver.

All the while the Revolutionaries had been on deck the door had stood open, and during that time, Silver had disappeared.

∞ Noah sat at the great long table in the saloon, waiting for Sister Hannah to bring a bowl of hot rolled oats. He was chilled from his adventure with what he still insisted was a boarding party "under the leadership of a red-headed buccaneer." But he was also exhilarated, and chattered, toothless, at Sister Hannah as she puttered and pottered in the galley, preparing his porridge.

Japeth and Shem, all this while, were sealing the great double doors to the lower decks — battening them in place with cross bars and chains and boarding them over with an X shape of planks and spikes.

Sarah was already in Noah's lap but Abraham — for the moment, at least — was absent. Probably making scat in the box of sawdust kept in the passage outside the latrines.

Noah's wooden teeth lay on his handkerchief before him — freshly painted only two days ago, and looking almost alarmingly youthful, on the one hand, and not unlike all that remained of a human skull, on the other.

"What sort of ship were they on?" he asked. "A three-master? Two? Square-rigged or jibbed?"

Hannah did not answer — even though she heard him. Best to let him ramble. Feed him and bed him — get him to sleep and pray that his mind would clear itself with dreaming.

"There's not a pirate ship on the Seven Seas we can't defeat," said Noah. "Believe it. With Yaweh on our side — *nothing* can beat us! Not even this storm can beat us, I tell you. Yaweh has promised . . ."

The ark gave a sudden lurch, which sent the lanterns spinning and Noah's teeth careening to the floor, while — in the galley — several pots fell down with a crash. Noah was almost thrown from his chair — and Sarah, grabbing at whatever would save her, caught the back of the old man's hand with her claws, though Noah hardly seemed to notice — perhaps because of the violent motion of the furniture and lamps around him.

His first thought was that Yaweh might be announcing His presence. What better way could He choose to re-enter their lives than by lifting the ark in His hands and shaking it, as in a greeting?

When Hannah came to the door to see if he was all right, she found him on the floor on all fours, looking for his teeth.

"Were you thrown down there?" she said. "Are you hurt?"

"I'm praying," said Noah. "Praying. Didn't you notice? Yaweh just spoke to us. . . ."

Hannah did not dare answer this — knowing full well that only the storm had battered the ark, but knowing equally that Noah would never accept the argument that every gesture did not come from God.

Noah found his teeth and palmed them.

"Help me up," he said.

Hannah got him to his feet and seated him back in his chair.

"I'll bring your rolled oats now," she said — and went back to the galley.

"Where's that child we have?" Noah called to her.

Silence.

"Sister Hannah? Daughter? . . ." Noah called.

Hannah was standing frozen above the porridge pot in her hand — the wooden spoon poised at her lips — and the galley swaying all around her. *What had he said?*

"Where's that child we have, I say!" the old man called.

Hannah slowly lowered the spoon and laid the back of her hand against her forehead — closing her eyes.

"Emma!" Noah roared. "Where is she?"

Hannah's eyes flew open.

Emma.

"Oh," she said — and then, calling back to him; "Emma is in her cabin. Sick." (She dared not say what the sickness was — that Emma had fallen silent and would not eat, like a grieving animal.)

"You work too hard," said Noah, whose mind had begun to wander away from the storm and the pirate ships and into the future (possibly hand-in-hand with Yaweh) where there would be houses again and kitchens the size of arks and nurseries full of children — a fitting way to end one's days — with Sister-Daughter Hannah, all in white, presiding. Noah would sit beneath the newly planted but already thirty-foot-high walnut tree; and the newly planted, already ancient orchard behind its sacred gate would fill the air with the scent of wisdom and blossoms — apples, pears; and the newly appointed angel would be seated, too — but in the branches of . . .

"Daughter?"

"Yes, Father Noyes?"

"Was that my wife on the deck, with her hair all white and dressed in sack cloth?"

"Yes, Father Noyes."

"Not Pirates, then?"

"No, Father Noyes. Not Pirates."

"And who was that man beside her. . . ?" (*Angel. Angel. Was that not an angel's face beside her — angel skin and angel hair? . . .*)

"Ham, Father Noyes. That was Ham, your son."

The vision flickered on and off — swaying with the lamps, in and out of reach. Another face — not Ham's — but . . .

"The *other* man."

Hannah came and stood in the doorway, porridge pot in hand, prepared to serve the rolled oats.

"The other man?"

"He was an angel, Daughter." Noah turned and flashed his gaze at Hannah — on and off, like the vision. "You think I don't know an angel when I see one?"

Man. Pirate. Angel. What could Hannah say? To remind the old man that all he had seen was Lucy would enrage him.

"Yes," she said. "Perhaps an angel. Yes . . ." And she went back into the galley and began to fill two bowls with porridge, dark brown sugar and the very last of the clotted cream.

When she had rolled two silver spoons, each one in a wide, white napkin, she picked up spoons and bowls and went back into the saloon — aware, all at once, of a draught.

Noah was standing — not sitting — and he was staring at the door to the deck, which the storm must have blown open. It was swinging to and fro on its hinges — never quite closing — never quite opening all the way.

Hannah set the two bowls down on the table and advanced around the long end, making for the outer door in order to close it. But before she had got even halfway there, she spied the male cat, Abraham, looming out of the darkness — with snow on his back and something in his mouth.

She tried — and succeeded outwardly, at least — to control her revulsion at the prospect of yet another rat brought home by the enterprising Abraham. He never ate them, merely beheaded them — and left the residue for her to pick up and throw overboard. Sometimes, she found the heads staring up at her from the seats of chairs and the drawers of cabinets and the covers of her bed. No matter that she locked all the doors between herself and the rest of the ark — somehow, Abraham found his way in.

This time, she stepped around him and closed the door before she turned back to face the inevitable — already planning that if she could avoid it, she would not have to deal with the rat until she had eaten her porridge.

But Noah had already seen that the thing in Abraham's mouth was not a rat — but something else — and of silver.

∞ Abraham stepped to Noah's feet and bowed — with the thing still hanging from his mouth. Then he leapt — all grace and surefootedness against the rocking of the storm — first onto Noah's chair, where he bowed with the thing to Sarah and then to the table top — where he laid the thing out, broken-necked and dead, for Noah to inspect.

Abraham sat down before his prize.

Noah was less intimidated by the dead than Sister Hannah. She retreated — but he stepped forward — already reaching with his fingers.

"It is a silver kitten," he said — each word pronounced in utter astonishment.

Then he looked — mad, already with the promise of a miracle flowering in his brain — across the table at Hannah.

"Whose kitten can this be," he said; "but God's. Was Sarah pregnant? Never. And have we other cats aboard with us?" He swept the room with his arm. "Not any — not one anywhere! Whose kitten, then? Whose *child* is this?"

He stared at it — laid out perfect before him.

"A miracle," he whispered. "A true and absolute *miracle* . . ." He fell all the way to his knees — holding the table with both hands and touching the table top three times and three times more with his forehead. "Oh, All The Names Of God . . ." he prayed; "oh, Every Name Of All The Ten Thousand — hear me — see me — witness my gratitude. Witness even my drowning out of The Explicit Name . . ." Here, Noah pounded the table with his fists with such a furor of banging that Hannah feared for his hands. But she could not and did not hear the Explicit Name — forbidden to all but Yaweh Himself — as Noah uttered it in his frenzy of ecstasy — touching and touching and touching his head at the table's edge, where the body of the silver child was laid.

Hannah could not resist the fall to her knees, since Doctor Noyes was convincing her by the fanaticism of his own belief, that this could not be other than a miracle — because Sarah had certainly not been pregnant — and there was not another cat on the ark — and males do not give birth, or subdivide. . . .

What else could it be?

What else could it be?

What else could it be?

Three-times-three. A miracle.

Abraham confirmed it by lying down in front of the silver kitten. And he did not touch it. Not even the head.

∞ The disappearance of the little silver male had caused a great search to be made of the lower decks. Between them, Crowe and Mottyl asked every animal in every cage and pen if the kitten had been seen and Mottyl called for him in every gutter and every drain. She also called for him in all the most dreaded places — the cisterns, the latrines and the rain barrels.

All this while, the storm was increasing in intensity and there was a good deal of agitation amongst the animals, who could not keep their footing. The storm, under any circumstance, would have been difficult to bear — but in the dark and with all the animals in an undernourished, weakened condition, it was appalling. The eternal dampness, the chill produced by the sudden drop in temperature, plus the icy wind that blew through every crack and crevice, moaning in all the drains — it was all especially hard on the newly born and the very old. But the greatest enemy was darkness.

Crowe, whose powers of sight were as sharp as those of any creature alive — was bereft of these powers in the dark, and therefore her flights up and down the aisle and corridors were hazardous, to say the least. She kept flying into open doors and wire mesh. She developed a dreadful headache.

Mottyl was running low on adrenalin. She had been from

top to bottom of the lower decks — even so far as the dreaded pit — and, in the process, had given up one feeding of her kittens. At the best of times, these days, she was finding the feedings increasingly difficult. Normally, her kittens would have been weaned long before this — perhaps as long as three weeks ago — but because of the growing shortage of mice and rats and the larger insects, she had been forced to supplement their diet with milk she could barely produce. The nipples at the long end of her milk lines had completely dried up and the kittens had to be crowded as close to the source as she could manage, which meant that her remaining nipples were now almost raw with too much suckling. Besides which, the kittens now had rather sizeable teeth, and Mottyl waged a continual war against these teeth — biting the kittens' ears and pushing hard with her claws against the undersides of their jaws — sometimes even having to pierce their lips. Her own diet, too, was suffering from the dearth of mice, and she found she was increasingly weak and prone to colds and running sores.

By the end of four or five hours of continuous searching, her brain was frantic but her body almost immobilized from exhaustion. Her drops into the resting position were becoming more and more frequent — until, finally, she could barely rise to make the journey back to her own corridor.

Bip remarked; ''if you could get us out of here, we could help you.''

But Mottyl could not even rise to this offer. Bip and Ringer were all the way around on the other side of the Well and the thought of the long trek to free them made Mottyl cringe.

Why can't I move?

You are twenty years old. You are starving. You have worms, fleas, mites and an abscess behind your ear and another on your hip. You have a cracked rib that won't knit. You have a torn tendon, a twisted bowel and a total depletion of vitamins. You are blind. You are going deaf. You have stepped on a nail. Can't you hear yourself breathing? Possible pneumonitis is setting in. You are partially dehydrated and we would suggest that the first thing you do — if, as and when you are able to rise — should be to drink water. You are distressed, depressed and short on red blood cells. You are also suffering from oxygen depletion and you have a heart condition. Lastly —rheumatism of the left rear leg and a liver condition we cannot describe because it is not yet fully declared. And you ask why you cannot move? We suggest you are also crazy.

Thank you for the dissertation. Now tell me how to rise.

We cannot tell you how to rise. The simple fact is, you can't. What you can do is call for Crowe.

Why?

Do not ask wasteful questions. Call for Crowe.

"Crowe!"

Mottyl's voice was much too weak to be heard any further than a few feet on either side of her — but it did carry out across the Well. Bip heard her.

"Crowe!" he called — and with his innate ability to sound over distance, Bip managed, very soon, to have the whole deck ringing with his voice. Mrs Noyes, on hearing him, thought she had been transported back to her porch overlooking the valley.

"Crowe! Crowe! Crowe!"

Soon enough, Crowe arrived, her wings creaking and her headache at its worst.

"Get us out of here," Bip called. "Just Ringer and me. We can help — and so can the ones who can see in the dark."

Crowe immediately got busy at the lemur's cage. A few snakes — the wombats — and the nightjars were also released and soon the corridors had many scurrying feet and busy wings. The owls, however, whose night vision would have made them superb detectives under the circumstances, were rejected because of their voracious hunger. The silver kitten might have been located by the Great Horned or the Snowy — but Mottyl and Crowe were not looking to find a corpse.

∞ In the meantime, Lucy, Ham and Mrs Noyes had gathered in the galley, where the glow of the stove provided, at least, a little light and a good deal of warmth. They had spread their outer garments—burlap and homespun—over the backs of their chairs and turned the chairs to face the heat. The galley smelled like a winter kitchen—with a brewing pot of tea—a large pot of cornmeal and all the wet smells of hemp and wool and scorched cotton.

Lucy had become intrigued, over the last few weeks, with the hives of dormant bees. These hives, which had been woven by Hannah, were made of straw plaits the thickness of rope and their shape was conical—each hive rising to a height of four feet. At the bottom of each there was a small, semi-circular opening through which the bees could enter and exit. Inside, the bees themselves had constructed several layers of honey-comb and separate levels for eggs and pupae and nurseries for the young who must be fed by others until they emerged from the cells to assume their roles in the scheme of things. Each hive had its own Queen—and each its own store of food. But Lucy's interest in the bees was in the heat they made, and in the deep, urgent sound of their awakening.

Ham had suggested the hives be brought to the warmth of the galley, since the bees could be killed by cold. Their own warmth could not sustain them. Lucy had set the hives on the table and every once in a while she pressed her ear against them—and she would *hum.* "So stimulating," she said. "Quite extraordinary . . ." And her expression became quite intense.

Gradually—and unhappily—the search for the kitten was abandoned, and as the searchers admitted defeat, they gathered one by one and in pairs with the humans huddled around the stove.

Bip had simply picked Mottyl up—as he might another lemur—and carried her into the galley, where she presently lay beneath the stove, half asleep and wheezing badly, while Ringer returned to the secret nest and brought the remaining kittens to be fed from a bowl of thin, watered goat's milk.

The wombats and nightjars sat overhead, avoiding the smoke from the stove, and the snakes crept into the corner as far away from the heat as they could get. Crowe perched on the washline which Mrs Noyes had strung in happier times—and on which she had hung her gaily coloured tea-towels and dish mops, waiting for Emma's return.

For the longest while, there was silence — aside from the various sounds of feeding: porridge bowls and spoons — tea mugs and — milk lapping. In Crowe's case, the sounds came from pecking at raw cornmeal offered in handfuls by Ham and Mrs Noyes. The nightjars and the wombats fed on flies — while the snakes were content to doze — like Mottyl — merely dreaming of food.

Lucy had fallen into a trance — her ear pressed to the beehives — her porridge spoon hanging down — in danger of falling from her fingers — and her bowl tipping ominously. Ham — having just turned away from Crowe and about to sit back down to finish his own porridge — saw his wife's predicament — and gently removed the bowl from her hand. But she would not give up the spoon — clutching at it when he reached for it, though saying nothing and not even looking at him. Ham retired to his chair — and watched her intently as he ate.

Lucy was sweating, but the more the sweat broke upon her brow and coursed down over her face — dripping from her chin and nose — the more she refused to move her chair away from the stove, even when her garments began to smoke and steam. Her eyes, as she listened to the hives, were wide open — and her lips were parted — and from time to time, the shapes of words appeared and moved like ripples and spasms over her mouth and under the skin of her jaw.

Mrs Noyes said; "are you listening to those bees?"

Lucy did not reply — but Ham said; "this isn't the first time this has happened. It began when she was feeding the other insects. I went in one day to see what was wrong because she hadn't come back to the feed bins and she'd been gone over an hour. There she was — just like that — crouching beside the beehives and I thought she'd fallen asleep. I spoke to her — just the way you did — and there wasn't any answer. I spoke again and the same thing happened. Then, I walked around in front of her and *called* her — and saw that her eyes were open and she was wide awake. Except she was in this sort of trance . . ."

"It reminds me of Mottyl," said Mrs Noyes. "Of a cat-trance. You know the way she stares sometimes? Just like that, eyes wide open — as if she's watching something I can't see — or listening to something I can't hear. But I've never seen a person do it. Not before Lucy, anyway . . .''

Both Mrs Noyes and Ham had been talking in whispers, their voices humming in the heated galley — sibilant as pots on the boil.

"She's so still," said Ham. "That's what alarmed me the first time. Even when I called her name — it was as if she wasn't there. And then, when I called it again — she looked right through me — but she did not speak. 'Wait,' she said. 'It isn't over yet . . .' And later — when, apparently, it was over — I asked her what she'd meant by it and all she said was; 'the voices.' ''

"The *voices*?" said Mrs Noyes. "You mean the bee voices?"

"I don't think so," said Ham. He looked at Lucy — who was now so tense that she was soaking wet. And the steam from her clothing rose about her more like smoke than steam — the sort of smoke given off by burning incense — wisps of it rising towards the ceiling . . .

And when she spoke — which she presently did — it was not in her own voice — but another voice — deeper than her own.

"*Crowe*," she said. "*Crowe will save us.*"

And then — in her own voice, but still inside the trance — she said; "how?"

"*Crowe set the lemurs free,*" said the other voice from Lucy's mouth. "*Crowe set all these others free from their cages to help us look for Silver.*"

"Yes," said the Lucy voice. "Go on."

"*What we need is another Crowe on the upper decks. A Crowe to set us free. A Crowe to undo the locks that hold us here in our cages . . .*"

"Yes?"

But the voice had ceased. Lucy, still in her trance, had fallen silent again — but she was leaning, now, away from the hives of bees and she began to tap against the chair with her spoon. It was not a conscious thing — just a reflex — as if she could beat her exhausted brain to sharpness — drum it to action as armies were drummed. And trumpeted.

All her revolts had failed. Paradise was behind her forever. Her refuge in the Morning Star and, later, in the Cormorant had only proved that she could not fulfill herself in any other form but the one she had been given. Her sojourn in the orchard had only proved that the orchard — as she had long ago suspected — was empty of anything but an unjust fear of beauty and the tyranny of apples. Her only success had been her marriage to Ham which had secured her survival aboard the ark — but in the end, that, too, had failed. She was kept in this dungeon — consigned, yet again, to the depths — and she had failed to revive the Unicorn — she had failed to invent the electric light — she had failed to save the demons — she had failed to gain the upper hand over the forces of evil that reigned on the upper deck under the protection of Japeth Noyes, just as she had failed to gain the upper hand in Heaven, where the forces of evil reigned supreme under the protection of Michael Archangelis. It was hopeless. And all her powers were failing, one by one. She had been unable to burn down the Castle. All she could manage was to burn through her ropes and lay a minor curse on Japeth.

She felt pathetic.

Her spoon went on tapping — and she was tapping it still when Mrs Noyes rose to her feet and went about collecting the porridge plates and the porridge pot and the tea mugs and the kittens' milk bowl and dropping them one by one into the wash tub. . . .

The wash tub.

Tap-tap.

The wash tub.

Emma.

Suddenly, Lucy rose to her feet, knocking over her chair and speaking in the other voice; *"Emma,"* she said. *"Emma will be our Crowe!"*

∞ A gutter was removed, and this provided space enough for Crowe to crawl through and reach the outside. Her mission was very straightforward. Find Emma — and lead her immediately to unbar the doors that led to the upper deck.

This time, they would not — could not — fail.

Without light — without weapons — their strength depleted and their chances of victory ridiculously low — they had nothing, now, with which to win but the will to win. And the need.

∞ In the Chapel, Noah had laid the silver kitten upon the altar.

Sister Hannah knelt and pulled her shawls around her.

Abraham and Sarah crouched in the doorway.

Noah thanked Yaweh for the gift of miracles — and he drew the knife through the lifeless flesh. Squeezing the meagre drops of blood onto his fingers, he presented them to Sister Hannah and commanded her to drink.

When she had done so, and released his fingers from her lips, he dabbled them yet again — and drank from them himself.

He then fell forward — prostrate — and pressed his face against the floor — where he began, beneath the howling of the wind, to recite all the prayers of sacrifice and redemption.

Hannah, for her part, began to pray — but soon gave it up in a dreadful surge of pain.

"I'm not well," she whispered. "I'm not well. Help me."

But Noah was praying to his God and did not hear her.

∞ Finding Emma was relatively simple.

Crowe, having lived so long in the Pagoda, was well aware of the layout of all the cabins in the Castle and of all the ways in, both secret and obvious. She knew as well as Abraham the tricky latch on the saloon door.

Japeth — overconfident of barricades and suffering dreadfully from hives as a result of Lucy's curse, as well as from all his unhealed wounds — was desperately trying to sleep in the Armoury. Shem was nowhere in sight. Slipping into the corridor beyond the saloon, Crowe could see Doctor Noyes and Sister Hannah at prayer and — alas — she also saw the object of their adoration on the altar: Mottyl's silver son — her prize.

But there was no time for sorrow — no time even for rage — and she flew on towards the rear of the Castle,where Emma's cabin was located beside the latrines.

Crowe beat against the door with her wings.

"Go away," said Emma.

Crowe went on beating — afraid to speak for fear Shem might be nearby and hear her.

"*Will* you go away!" said Emma.

Crowe stopped beating. What could she do?

If she could not raise her voice, she must try something else.

She sat on the floor and regarded the door. There was a crack at the bottom — presenting perhaps an inch of space. Crowe thought about it and thought about it and received no answer — except the obvious answer that an inch was not enough to allow her passage.

In the Chapel, Noah's voice droned on with its endless prayer — and Crowe tried not to think of what was on the altar. The smell of the incense brought other bitter thoughts — of how she had been driven from her hiding place above the chimney and . . .

Driven from her hiding place above the chimney.

Incense.

Smoke.

Crowe flew back down the corridor — looking for a lighted candle or some other source of fire and found one in the galley.

∞ When Emma saw the smoke curling up from beneath her door, she immediately tried to climb from the port hole.

"Oh, oh, oh!" she said — but quietly — mercifully subdued by her horror of fire to an almost voiceless panic. "Oh, oh, oh . . ." And she scrabbled at the door handle.

When, at last, she got the door open, she had already thrown a blanket over her head in preparation for the flaming furnace she fully expected to greet her. But when there were no flames — no sound of them and no heat from them — Emma slowly pulled the blanket back and stared out into the corridor.

"What are *you* doing here?" she said.

Crowe had no time to explain. She only had time to beckon; *"follow me."*

∞ The snow had drifted into corners where sheets of ice were forming over it, creating a landscape of treacherous slides and curves. Birds had been frozen to the railings. The deck was a roller coaster rink and the sky above it was a mass of jet black clouds without shape or division. What now fell from them was less snow than sleet and the wind that drove it was merciless.

Crowe had to aim her flight far over the waters in order to maintain her place above the ark — and Emma, terrified of every kind of instant death, clung hard to the ropes with both hands and closed her eyes and simply *went.*

Like a skier on a mountain slope, she was spun down the length of the deck, never letting go of the rope, never so much as changing the position of her feet. Halfway to her destination she opened her eyes, and by the time she was approaching the portico shelter above the barricaded doors, she was wailing against the storm's great voice; "look out! Look out! Here I come!" As if the barricade might rise and step aside.

But the ice journey had also been exhilarating — and, as she picked herself up, Emma was already hoping there would be time to take another ride.

There was little hope of that, however, in the face of what she must do.

Crowe had managed to secure a place that was more or less out of the wind in the furthest corner of the portico and she sat there shivering, urging Emma to; *"hurry, Hurry."*

Emma regarded the mass of boards and bars and chains and could not begin to figure out how she was meant to remove them. Looking to Crowe for instruction, all she got was: *hurry, hurry* — and there was not much help in that.

The wind was no great help, either, whipping her blanket over her head — blinding her, and lifting her skirts so that her legs began to freeze. Finally, the precious blanket that was meant to have kept her warm became such a menace to her eyes that she tore it from around her shoulders and was about to cast it aside when she saw that its windblown tails were in tatters. The idea occurred that she could rip these tatters off and wrap them round her hands so that at least some part of her extremities would be warm.

The cloth of the blanket — woven long ago by Sister Hannah in the sun-drenched yards on the Hill — was tough and difficult to tear for a mere mortal — though the wind had had no problem. The strength of the tatters themselves gave Emma another idea — or rather, they reminded her of an ancient device that had been used by her mother to carry heavy objects when the heavy objects were either too awkward to be held by human hands — or too sharp. Slings had been made and Emma had been taught how to carry rocks in the slings and pails full of scalding water whose handles would have cut her childish fingers.

Emma looked at the boards which formed the outer face of the barricade. Selecting a place up close to where they had been nailed, she looped what remained of the blanket through and around the top board — and, bracing her feet against the door, she began to pull.

At first, the boards did not respond. But Emma was strong. She had played all those years at being an axeman, emulating her tall blond brothers. Over and over again she braced herself — each time applying the full weight of her body and every ounce of strength in her arms, her shoulders and her legs, until — finally — one nail gave and then another and another. The first board was free at one end — and soon she had it free at the other.

Once she had the first board off, the second was easier because she not only had the blanket to pull with, but also the board to pry with.

Two boards down and only the chains and bars to go.

∞ Inside the depths, Mrs Noyes, Lucy and Ham crouched on the top step ready to push whenever the order came from the other side. All the while, they called encouragement to Emma and Emma called back that she was "trying."

Mottyl, Bip, Ringer and the others sat on a lower step and

waited for freedom. It did not matter, any longer, that—if this revolution ended as the first, in defeat—they would be thrown, as the demons had been thrown, over the side of the ark. Certainly, it no longer mattered to Mottyl that she should be hidden—or that her kittens should be hidden. *You cannot hide forever*, she decided. Doctor Noyes and Japeth would be there beyond those doors no matter who opened them—and a person might as well face that now as later.

Bip and Ringer had not been free since the voyage began and the sensation, at first, had been somewhat intimidating. The ark's great size had overwhelmed them. "We could almost grow trees in here," Bip remarked. "We could almost start another wood—right here on board."

"I'd rather have a real wood, thank you," Ringer replied. "I'd rather see the sun."

By now, Emma was down to chains—and she was using one of the iron bars as a kind of windlass, turning it through the chains, turning it hand over hand, until the chains pulled so tight that she could feel a shift in the spikes with which they had been driven at either end.

"I've got it! I've got it!" she called through the doors. "They're coming free! They're coming free!"

But at this precise moment—so close to victory that she could see the chains being flung through her mind and far out over the waters—disaster struck.

Japeth, rising from his bloodstained, itchy bed with a desperate need to urinate, had barged out into the weather in his filthy tunic and was already hoisting its skirt and starting to sprinkle the wind, when he caught sight of Emma and came, with a great, skidding *whoosh* across the deck—barefoot skating on the ice.

He had no weapons but his hands—though these would normally have been enough for Emma. However, given the circumstances of the storm, the sleet, the ice underfoot and his essential nakedness, he was very much at a disadvantage.

Nevertheless, he attempted to tackle her and pull her—slide with her—away from the doors. But he failed to catch her—and slid all the way to the opposite rail where he very nearly went overboard. His wound-covered legs and his hive-covered arms and back made him scream with pain as they struck the railing and the ropes.

It was a dreadful struggle to return to Emma for the next attack — but he found one of the discarded boards and, with it, managed to clamber back to his feet and get into a position behind her from which he could strike with the board at her shoulders.

Crowe flew down, in this moment, and made straight for Japeth's eyes, beating her wings, lying slightly on her side against the air and raising her feet so that she could attack him with her claws as well as her beak. But the wind was against her and she was blown back towards Emma.

Japeth came forward — raising the board again — not above his head, but towards one side, as one of Emma's brothers might wield an axe — and this gave Crowe her second chance to go for his face — which was perfectly exposed. Japeth was still yelling — both in pain and rage — demented.

Crowe flew up above him, this time, and then she fell like a great black stone, folding her wings and extending her yellow claws.

Bam!

The board hit her.

Crowe.

∞ Emma screamed — and raised the newly released chain in her hands above her head and brought it round with a wide swipe, striking Japeth on his left side and sending him down to the deck with a great crash, where he slid again off towards the open railing, crying out; *"HELP!"*

Emma slid back towards the doors and yanked them open, not even knowing she was wailing, not even knowing she was bleeding from wounds she could not remember receiving in her struggles with the barricade — only aware that she was safe again with the only people in the world she loved.

∞ Ham and Lucy managed to save Japeth from drowning and locked him with all his pain and weapons in the Armoury.

Then they joined Mrs Noyes — who was holding Crowe in her arms and folding the great bird's wings and drawing in her yellow feet and shutting her eyes.

"Let me take her down to Mottyl," she said. "Please."

Lucy glanced at the Castle and saw there was no sign there of any activity and then she nodded at Mrs Noyes, but said; "quickly. We mustn't lose our advantage."

While Lucy and Ham advanced up the ropes towards the Castle, Mrs Noyes and Emma went down into the hold and sat on the bottom step; Mrs Noyes with Crowe in her arms.

"Is she dead?" Mottyl's voice was as bleak as the words she spoke.

"Yes," said Mrs Noyes. "She is."

"May we have her, then?"

"Yes."

Mrs Noyes got up and went with Crowe into the relative peace and warmth of the Stable.

"I'm sorry," she said. "I cannot stay to mourn with you — but, one way or another, whatever the outcome is, I will be back, Motty. We will all come back."

She knelt then and laid Crowe down in the meagre straw near the cows, thinking they would keep her warm — in that odd, irrational way that people think of the dead as not being dead — but in some kind of need for warmth and gentle gestures.

Mottyl came forward, led by Bip and followed by Ringer and the wombats — and she sat down in front of Crowe, who might just have been in her nest, with her tail sticking up to show where she was. Mrs Noyes touched Mottyl tenderly on the head and began to walk away.

"What news is there of my son?" Mottyl asked, her voice a monotone.

Mrs Noyes said; "none."

"Please bring him back," Mottyl closed her eyes.

"Yes," said Mrs Noyes. "I will bring him back." And she hurried away to join the others.

"Will you come with me?" she said to Emma. "Or do you want to wait here?"

"I want to wait here," said Emma. "But I will come with you."

∞ Mottyl wished fervently for even a moment's sight of her friend. But there was nothing before her eyes — open or closed — but the black of her blindness.

"Is she there, Bip?"

"Yes."

"Is she really dead?"

"Yes."

"Have they hurt her very much?"

"There's a mark all along one side of her head."

Mottyl thought about it.

"Are her wings still whole?"

"Oh, yes."

"Is her tail still there? Sitting up?"

"Yes. Yes."

"Are her eyes still in her head?"

"They are."

"And her beak? Is it broken?"

"No."

Mottyl now allowed herself to hunker all the way down in the trance position, facing her dead friend.

"There's been a lot of dying," she intoned. "Hasn't there."

"Yes." Bip spoke softly.

"Do you think my child is dead?"

"I can't say. I don't know."

"I think he is dead."

"I'm sorry."

"Don't be sorry," Mottyl told her friend. "It is what we are given here. After all — we are only animals."

Then she went into a trance and grieved beyond the reach of her body and her mind.

∞ In the Castle, the Great Revolution of the Lower Orders was won with a single gesture.

Lucy — who had gone in first — found that Noah and Hannah

were still in the Chapel, together with Yaweh's cats.

All she had to do was close the door and bolt it.

As for Shem, he seemed — by all that could be discovered —
to have disappeared.

∞ Watches were appointed.

Ham took the first and established himself in the saloon with
a blaze of welcome candles and one of his father's double-
layered woollen shawls.

"You aren't going to sleep?" said Lucy. "You look too
comfortable, to me."

"I swear," said Ham. "I only mean to revel in all this light.
I wouldn't dream of closing my eyes."

∞ Lucy told Mrs Noyes and Mrs Noyes told Mottyl. The
little silver male was dead.

All that Mottyl could think was; *another experiment, thank
you* . . . and the hand of Doctor Noyes reaching down into her
nest — into all her nests forever — removing this one and that
one — this eye and that eye — these ears and that tail — the
brain of this one and the testicles of that one — the head of this
one, the intestines of that — this colour, that colour, white and
yellow, silver and calico . . . never, never, never, never . . .

Never to end.

Mottyl stood up — slowly — painfully — like one too long
asleep.

"Where are you going?" said Mrs Noyes — very quiet and
only afraid, not demanding.

Mottyl paused — more than a little lost — suddenly overwhelmed by the strangeness of the space around her.

Where was the porch? Where was the yard? The field? The
wood?

We have just left Crowe in her nest. Where are we?

Nothing.

I say — where are we, *whispers*? Are we not in the wood?

Nothing.

"WHISPERS?" Mottyl howled. *"WHISPERS!"*

Nothing. Not a single response. They were gone.

∞ "Mottyl?" said Mrs Noyes. "Motty?" She was more than alarmed. She was terrified.

Bip went over past the woman and sat on his haunches beside the cat.

"Is that you, Bip?"

"Yes."

"I'm trying to get out of the wood and back up the Hill. I have kittens there."

"Yes. I can tell. You've been feeding them."

"Which way, then? I'm in a hurry. Hurry."

"I can take you," Bip told her. "Come along. I will show you."

Then he walked in front of her, raising his tail very high — straight up — so that Mottyl would be able to follow by his scent.

As she went away, Mrs Noyes held the lantern higher (stolen from the saloon) and saw that all around her, the Stable was filled with silent animals — watching.

∞ Mottyl was in her nest.

Her kittens were asleep.

Bip and Ringer sat waiting.

Ringer whispered; "do you think she's going to die?"

"She may."

Ringer wondered; "shouldn't we leave her, if she's going to die?"

"No. We must watch with her—because she is blind. And I don't think she knows where she is."

Mottyl could hear these words, but it barely mattered. She was drifting — the way all animals do when they are close to death—when the death is not violent—when there is space to drift through — and time.

She was lying in the sphinx position — paws extended — head very slightly lifted—her blind eyes open and staring. She had drawn her tail in tight along her side and her body was taut so that every nerve and every trail along which her *whispers* had once travelled was pulled into focus. She waited for them. But they did not come.

What came, instead, in Mottyl's drifting, was a concert of white noise and shivers. Bip could see the patterns of movement flickering under Mottyl's skin—some of them spasms—some of them long, thin messages sent through the whole circuit of routes from one end of Mottyl's body to the other. And then, all at once, with a final flick of the muscles on her back, as if she were discarding a pest — she fell still and began to sing.

The singing was gutteral and rich and the song had a pattern to it, and many notes. Bip and Ringer had never heard such singing before, though they recognized at once the meaning of it, since almost every animal has a song it sings at death — and some would have said they were songs addressed *to* death.

The content of Mottyl's song was only known to her. Her children, her Crowe and her *whispers* had all died before her. And now, the world would die. Her song described that world — the world into which Mottyl had been born and in which she had lived. It also described all her kittens and all their various births over time and all their colours and their markings. It described Mottyl's mother and Mottyl's own birth and Mrs Noyes and the porch where they had sat on summer evenings. It described the rocking chair, its size, its smell, its age and the noise it made. It described the place where Mottyl had lain through most of her evenings, in the shadow of the trumpet vine, and it described the smells that surrounded her there — the smell of dust — the smell of gin and the smell of flowers and herbs. It told of all the mice she had killed and eaten. It told of milk she had drunk — and broth and water. It told of the wood and the place where the catnip grew up high above the chamomile and it told of broken fence rails and whole ones — places to avoid and ways of entry to and from the wood. It told of Crowe. It told of Whistler. It told of the Vixen and the Porcupine. It told of Japeth's wolves at their gate. It told of demons, dragons and other dangers and it told of the greatest danger of all: it told of Doctor Noyes.

The world—whose litany of praise and sorrow was the subject of her singing—was also the world she watched inside her mind beyond her blindness. Bright with light and thick with shadows, it was the world of green and yellow life that she had seen from the day of her birth. It was filled with dusty yards and high green fields and other fields that were mown and yellow. It was white, overhead, and all the places in the wood were silver and blue and brown. It was teeming with life — all of it vital — all of it in motion — all of it crying to her:

Wasn't it wonderful here!

Goodbye. Goodbye.

The tall grass parted—and there before her was the whole of everything: alive. No one would ever know what she had seen—that she had seen the last of the world that was: of the world that could never be again. In blind Mottyl's mind was the last whole vision of the world before it was drowned.

Gone, now.

Under.

Forever.

∞ "Mottyl?"

It was Lucy.

"Mottyl?"

Bip and Ringer hung in the shadows and waited.

Lucy put her hand into the nest and touched Mottyl's side.

"Wake up."

There was a stirring.

"Chicken broth, Mottyl. Here."

Mottyl muttered; *"hello."*

Bip sat back on his haunches.

"Well," he offered. "She's still there."

Ringer curled up — and slept.

Mottyl, very slowly, lowered her chin to the dish and drank.

It was good.

∞ When the storm abated, it left behind a residue of scudding winds and thick yellow clouds slinking off in the direction of where, in other times, the mountains of Aleph, Beth and Gimel had made a recognizable horizon. Now — on every side — there was nothing but a thin, dirty line waving between the waters and the skies, as if the horizon itself was in search of definition.

Below decks the lanterns that had not been lit for so many days were now re-hung along the ceilings, and Lucy moved from lamp to lamp with a taper, creating aureoles of dust amidst the darkness.

Mrs Noyes, having waited with Emma until the child had told her story and fallen asleep, closed the door of the tiny cubicle behind her and stood in the narrow gangway, one hand raised against either wall, trying to maintain her balance. The exhilaration of victory was fast giving way to the old exhaustion and Mrs Noyes longed to drop where she stood — sag all the way to the floor and sleep with her back to the wall for a week. But this could not be. She knew she had to stay on her feet and maintain her vigilance. Shem had still not been located and — so long as he remained at large — they were still in danger, though she had to wonder what they might have to fear from the Ox, he had become so docile.

Still: *safety first*.

Whatever *"safety"* might mean.

Well — at least we can light the lamps, she thought, watching Lucy. And at least we can drink fresh water and breathe the air again — walk about, upright, on the upper decks and speak to one another aloud.

And Mottyl . . . We don't have to hide her any more. Though now she had taken to hiding herself. We must keep an eye on her, Mrs Noyes decided. She must not be allowed to go the way of The Lady, out of grief.

Mrs Noyes went blundering down the corridor, passing under the lamps and reaching up to touch each one of them out of sheer pleasure. "Hello! Hello! Hello!" she said.

To the lamps. To the light.

∞ The dark of the lower deck was dreadful, as it always was — and as she passed the various pens and box stalls, Mrs Noyes put out her hand for the animals to smell, so they would know who was passing. "It's only me," she said in her lightest voice. "It's only me. . . ."

Even with her lantern she could barely see — but it didn't really matter. She had them all by heart, after so much time and so many visits — so many hours spent feeding and reassuring and telling stories and listening to the woes and worries of all these beasts in the dark.

"Lucy's coming — with light for everyone," she said, as she touched the nearest faces and felt the breath of monkeys on her wrist. "And then there will be a special feeding; everyone will have fresh peanuts and hay. And we'll open up the stores and have whole oats and corn and sunflower seed. . . ."

Turning the final corner, she slowed her pace before she came to Mottyl's nest.

∞ "You up there?" she asked, climbing up on the boxes and trying to see inside the nest.

"*Yessssss . . .*"

"You very tired?"

"*Yessssss . . .*"

"I wondered if you'd like me to take you up on deck. Breathe some real air; feel a real breeze. It's calming down quite nicely, now."

Mottyl was hunched up — sitting in the sphinx position — with her blind eyes staring and her lips drawn back.

"I'm sorry," said Mrs Noyes. "I know you probably want to be alone — but it isn't good for you to stay down here in the dark. Do you understand?"

"*Yessssss . . .*"

Still, Mottyl didn't move.

Mrs Noyes reached out and smoothed the cat's sides with the palm of her hand.

Mottyl struggled to her feet — arched her back and pushed at all her aching bones and muscles.

"Here," said Mrs Noyes. "I'll make a sling for you — tie you round my neck so you won't even have to hold on."

Mottyl said nothing. She let Mrs Noyes lift her down and into the sling of her shawl — and then she rested in against the breast where she had rested all her life. Her breathing was so laboured, Mrs Noyes had to fight very hard to hold away the thought of death.

∞ The sea — when they reached the upper deck — was calm as a dooryard pond. But more than that, the sky was clearing and a star could be seen: the first star seen since leaving the earth.

"Star, Mottyl . . ."

Mrs Noyes could not believe it.

More clouds passed — and there, almost directly above them, was the moon.

Very slowly, barely able to move at all, Mottyl raised her head above the woollen edges of the sling and sniffed the air.

"Moon, Mottyl. The moon . . ."

Mrs Noyes held her up.

"*Yessssss* . . ." Mottyl could feel it.

All the way through the dark, they stood. Till dawn.

∞ The moon and the stars had not been seen in all the nights at sea. And while the moon descended and the western stars went out, the Wolf-Star rose where the sun would be.

The Wolf-Star was red.

Mrs Noyes remembered Ham's excitement, all those countless years before, when he'd spent the night in the cedar trees above the sunflower terrace and come running down through the early morning light — and thrown all his bits of paper on the kitchen table — jumping up and down and barely able to contain himself.

"I've watched it now every day for a week, Mama; and every day for a week it's been the same! Red! Red! Red! More beautiful than anything you've ever seen. And every day — every morning — just as it blazes up, in the east — all of Japeth's wolves begin to sing! So I'm calling it the Wolf-Star."

"Oh, is *that* why they're singing?" Mrs Noyes had said to him, amused at this huge new enthusiasm that had replaced the huge new enthusiasm of the week before, when Ham had finally decided the moon had *phases* — and the phases could be calculated. Next week . . . the sun would rise in the south, no doubt. Or something equally outrageous. Nonetheless, you could not ignore, you could not refuse to be infected by, the child's enthusiasm: by the wonder of it all — of everything — and by the wonder of his wonder. Every leaf that fell and every new egg that got carted down from somewhere and laid out tenderly on the kitchen table (*"Please — don't touch! It has to go back where I found it!"*) — and all the story of its finding, told. *Everything* told. The whole world — *told* — and written down.

And there — right now — precisely as it had been told — precisely as it had been written — was the moon descending — and the Wolf-Star rising.

"Wolf-Star, Mottyl. Red . . ."

But Mottyl slept.

∞ And then, the sun.

∞ The sun — so it seemed — did not have to rise.

Instead, the waters gave way — and it was lifted from their depths — as the dead are raised from graves.

Mottyl awakened.

And Mrs Noyes said; "yes. It came back."

∞ When Lucy had finished lighting the lamps, she went back up to the top of the stairs and looked out over the deck. There was Mrs Noyes, the smallest woman that Lucy had ever seen. She was standing against the railing with Mottyl slung around her neck in a cradle, and every once in a while her lips moved and she pointed at the sky.

The sun, the moon and the stars, Lucy thought. *Well, well, well. It all begins again.*

Then she turned back and went along the corridor to her

cabin. When she had gone inside, she locked the door and sat on the bunk. Emma was snoring beyond the wall.

Lucy looked around her — bleakly, at first, and then with a modicum of tenderness. This is where she had slept with Ham. A man. And human. There were his tunics hanging on the wall — torn and worn and lonely looking. A person's clothes always looked lonely when the person wasn't there, Lucy thought. Not so in Heaven, she remembered. In Heaven, a person's clothes were always at the cleaners. *Being improved.* She smiled. Or else, *the person* was at the cleaners, being improved . . .

Ham was a nice enough boy. Immature — enthusiastic — brilliant. Mozart would have liked him, she thought; for the games they could have played. Shelley would have liked him for his pockets full of books. Whitman would have liked him for the walks they could have taken. Einstein would have adored him — what a pupil! All his answers were *yes* and *no* — and all his questions equally terse: *why?* he would say — and *what for?*

Nothing more.

He's been my *"husband,"* here. The games; the pockets full of books; the walks; the answers and the questions have been mine . . . for a while.

And now?

What for — the human race?

And *why?*

I heard a rumour — didn't you — another world. . . .

Where? she wondered. When?

When?

When?

∞ Ham heard noises in the Chapel.

His father and Sister Hannah had been there many hours — and it occurred to him that people had to eat. They had to drink water — go to the latrines — breathe air they hadn't breathed for six hours and more.

But he must be careful. No mistakes — no rashly opened doors through which the prisoners could escape. If they wanted to use the latrine — they would have to do so under his eye. If they wanted food — he would feed them in moderation. If they wanted air — he would have to think about it. . . .

"Oh!" said Hannah — her voice rising. Possibly in pain.

What if she's started having her baby? thought Ham. It would never do to cause its death by leaving Sister Hannah alone without another woman to help her.

He had already risen from his father's chair — with its sheepskin cushions and its woollen shawls — and he strode down the hall past the galley and past his father's stateroom and study.

Standing before the Chapel door, he very distinctly heard Sister Hannah groaning.

He knocked.

There was instant silence.

"Are you all right?" he said.

"Yes," said his father. "Yes."

Then there was whispering — whispering and more whispering until, at last, Hannah's voice spoke aloud and she also said; "yes."

"Do you want the latrines?"

"Not yet," said Noah. "No."

"Do you want any food?"

"No."

"Water?"

"No."

"Nothing, then?"

"No. No. Nothing."

All of these answers were Noah's. Sister Hannah said nothing.

Ham went away then and visited the latrine. After that, he came back down the corridor, pressed his ear — to no avail — against the Chapel door and went on into the galley, where he made himself a cheese on rye.

∞ Hannah was lying on the floor. The water had broken and was spread beneath her and between her legs.

The silver kitten was still laid out on the altar — shrivelling — slowly disappearing under the concentrated heat of the incense bars that Noah had set around it in honour of its miraculous appearance.

The altar lights — some red, some gold — were burning low and soon would require fresh candles.

Noah was halfway between the altar and the woman on the floor, seated on the velvet headrest of an ornate *prie-dieu* — riding it rather like a side saddle, with one leg hooked around its corner.

Hannah was perspiring — almost soaking wet — and she was holding onto the legs of a chair, with her arms thrown back on the floor behind her head.

"I need help," she said. "I need help. I cannot do this alone."

"I will call for help as soon as the child is born," said Noah.

"But the child is dead. It is dead. And I cannot be rid of it alone. . . ."

"Mrs Noyes gave birth to a dozen dead children, Daughter. I know it can be done. All you have to do is *do it*."

"But — I want someone with me."

"You have someone with you."

"I'm afraid. . . ."

"All women are afraid."

"But, if it's dead, why can't I have *help?*"

"Because we must see the child."

"I don't understand. . . ."

"It's very simple. We must see the child before there can be help."

Hannah resigned herself. The old man was adamant. There would be no help. Even if she were to die, there would be no help. She must do this alone — present him with the corpse — and, if she lived, go free.

Noah said; "I will pray for you, now — and you will deliver the child."

He spoke with such icy calmness — behaved with such appalling cruelty. Yet, she knew he was frightened as she was. But why, she could not tell. Unless there was some mark upon the child he dreaded — something that would show its lineage — something that would prove it was his.

She pushed.

Noah prayed.

Equally fervent in their desire — both the pushing and the praying ultimately brought success.

And when Hannah finally saw her child, she screamed — though not because it was dead. Its death had long been known — and all her mourning for it had passed into time. But nothing had prepared her for the shock of seeing what she had carried all those months — nothing, for the horror of what it was in which she had invested all her ambition and all her secret love.

Noah was determined, of course, that the child's deformity was her responsibility alone. As he cut the umbilical cord with the altar knife, he said; "I feared it. Though in every prayer I uttered, I begged it would not be so — that you, like all the others, would not be contaminated with this curse. . . ."

He seized the child in an altar napkin and began to wrap its limbs, to cover them from his sight. One — and then another — then another altar cloth — but he could not seem to cover the thing — to hide its monstrous shape.

Hannah had just begun to recover her strength and was pulling herself into a sitting position when the door flew open and Ham stepped in with a knife in his hand.

"I heard you cry out," he said. "But I could not come till I had found a weapon. . . ."

He stopped in mid-sentence — staring at his father, all too clearly seeing what it was that was held, half hidden — half encumbered in the altar cloths in his father's arms.

Noah stood stock-still.

Hannah rose, with the help of the chair, to her knees and then to her feet. Her pristine gowns were soiled with dust and blood — and the child was gone from her belly.

She sank into the chair and said to Noah; "give it to me. I will bind it in the winding sheet. . . ."

Ham was speechless.

And then he fell.

Shem, at last, had emerged from his hiding place in his father's larder. But he did not see the child that was not his. He was too busy striking Ham — too busy saying to Noah; "you are free now, father."

Noah's eyes flickered briefly — seeking the thing in Hannah's lap.

He smiled.

It was true.

He was free.

The little ape was gone beneath its winding sheet forever.

"Let us pray," said Noah.

But Hannah would not pray.

In spite of weakness — and in spite of rage — she was able to rise from the chair and take her child and go.

∞ Mrs Noyes still stood alone by the railing, looking out over the sea — since "the sea" was all she could think to call it. Not that she'd ever seen the sea, and the only awareness she had of oceans was what she had heard in shells. And this that she called the sea did not sound like that: like an ocean. Perhaps there was no coined word for what these waters were — but "the sea" would do.

The ark was, at last, becalmed — and the only movement came from the huge green swell that lifted it, from time to time, as if from the pit of the earth itself.

Mrs Noyes looked down.

There below her was all the world: its valleys, hills and woods as she had never dreamed they could be seen. Not even birds could have seen the world as she saw it now — with all its movement stilled and all its features perfectly limned and shadowless: all its trees — each one — leaning up through the green depths — and the furthest reaches of all the hills untouched by clouds or mist or distance — everything equal — valleys and mountains drowned in the same viridian deep — the great, jade bottle of these waters, under which Noah had placed the penny of the world and turned Yaweh's mind with the wonder of its "miraculous" disappearance.

There were the farms — and all the white stone buildings — all the winding ribbons of the cowpath geography that had defined the place where she had lived her life. There were the terraced fields and the white stone walls and the tumbled fences over which and through which all the drowned cattle and all the drowned goats had finally managed to find their way — and the pastures on the hillsides where the sheep had learned to sing and the sacred orchards where the elders and the rabbis and the chosen women would never walk again or dream their sacred dreams. There were the drowning pools made one with harmless ponds — and the bridges fording meaningless river-beds. Roads that led to towns and villages and all the houses where all the people had lived, lying emptied now of noise and commerce and community — and only fish to pry the gossip loose that lay behind the walls.

And there were the altars — put down forever.

"No more fires," she whispered. No more bloodied falls.

It was the world she had always dreamed of.

Real.

∞ As the calm extended beyond all the visible horizons — there were no clouds anywhere and nothing in the sky but the sun. Two days before it had snowed — and all the birds had been frozen to the railings. Today, all the birds were sailing around the ark in dizzying circles — calling and crying and mew-ing in a myriad of rejoicing voices. Some were seated on the waters — floating in perfect contentment — unafraid of losing their places on the ark, since the ark had neither wake nor bow wave.

At the entrance to the hold there was a sound that at first could not be identified. Something — or someone — was hum-ming, and the noise of it was in the stairwell, rising.

A tall gaunt woman wearing a gown of heavily pleated raw cotton slowly made her appearance — looking over her shoul-der into the pit, as an actor might who makes his entrance through a trapdoor — backing upwards into the limelight.

The humming sound that accompanied this woman's entrance grew very loud — and soon it was clear exactly what it was, when the woman lifted two large, woven beehives onto the deck and set them in the sun.

For a moment the woman looked about as though she might find a more suitable place to set her hives — but, aside from a very slight adjustment which moved them out of the way of the doors, she finally settled for the place she had, and stood away to admire them.

At first it had not been clear this woman was Lucy. Only her great height was reminiscent of her other incarnations. Now, her hair was neither black nor red—but honey-coloured—and neither rolled and set in piles on top of her head, nor close-cropped and wavy. This hair was long and straight and it hung down her back as far as her shoulder blades. The face — this time — was neither round nor angular, but wide and flat, with extraordinary eyes of an almost golden colour: animal eyes, fierce and tender. The eyes of a prophet whose words, like an animal's warning cries, would be ignored.

When, at last, she had settled the hives and spied for herself a suitable place to sit, Lucy removed the woven lids. Releasing the bees into the air, she went and sat above them, high against the sky, on the portico over the stairway to the hold. Once seated, she became a kind of beacon for the bees, and they rose up around her in a column and at first appeared to engulf her. But they soon flew above her and made a cloud to shield her from the sun.

Just about the time Lucy settled, another figure as white — though bloodied — appeared from the Castle and walked towards the side of the ark about ten paces from where Lucy sat.

Nothing was said. Lucy evinced neither anger nor surprise that one of her prisoners was walking freely on the deck, and Hannah gave no sign that she was alarmed by the presence of so many bees. Neither woman greeted the other—both maintaining their long established coolness. It was barely obvious that one existed for the other, so discreet were their reactions— a tilt of the head — a pause before movement: nothing more.

Hannah, who had wept, but who was done with her weeping, was carrying her child in its winding sheet. Her whole demeanour was so severe — so formal — that she might have carried nothing more than a package — an object only — nothing that might have lived or been, in any sense, a vessel for life. But Hannah could not ignore the fact that she had been its vessel. Whether wittingly or not, whether rightly or not—the

thing was hers. Therefore, she did it this much honour: that
she held it, very briefly, close against her breast and kissed
the top of its head and caressed its back as though it might
have been human — and then she threw it into the waters —
upon which it floated for a good while before it drifted away
from the ark some distance and disappeared from view, presumably beneath the surface — though Lucy, for a moment,
thought she might have caught a later glimpse of it. This could,
however, have been a sea bird, since there were several out
on the water in that direction.

Hannah walked very slowly back to the Castle — not looking
over her shoulder — not even hesitating before she went in
beneath the canopy; simply walking in a straight line and passing from Lucy's view.

∞ If Lucy could bring the bees on deck, then why not
others?

It was Mrs Noyes's inspiration to bring her sheep up top
where they could see the sky and breathe the air and maybe
sing a song.

The ram and all his ewes and lambs stumbled up the stairs,
blinded by the brightness of the sun and intimidated by the
size of the sky — which they had forgotten. Some of the lambs
had never seen the world, because they had been born on board
the ark, in the darkened Stable.

All this was quite a revelation — the air and the water — the
great, wide deck — and all the sheep and lambs just stared.

Mrs Noyes picked up the smallest, youngest lamb of all and
she spoke to its parents and to all the sheep whose numbers,
aboard the ark, had grown from seven to twenty — and that in
spite of all the lambs that had been taken for sacrifice and to
feed the lion.

"It's time this youngster learned to sing," said Mrs Noyes.
"And what better song to learn at the beginning than *Lamb of
God?* . . ."

At once, having said this, Mrs Noyes regretted it. *Lamb of
God* had taken on such a dreadful meaning since they had
learned it first before Yaweh's arrival. "No," she said. "Let

us not sing *Lamb of God*. Let us sing some other, happier song. I know! We'll sing *I'll Take You Home Again, Kathleen*. That's one we all used to sing together. . . ." And she began the song herself — addressing it to the lamb in her arms.

> *Oh, I will take you home, Kathleen,*
> *To where the . . .*

She stopped. "Isn't that funny," she said. "I forget the words!"

"Baaaa . . ." said one of the sheep at her feet.

"What?" said Mrs Noyes.

"Baaaa . . ." said the sheep.

Mrs Noyes began to laugh. "What a curious sound," she said, "*Baaaa.*"

"Baaaa . . ." said the sheep.

"I know," said Mrs Noyes. "Much, *much* better! We'll sing the *The Skye Boat Song*. All right?" And she began:

> *Speed bonnie boat,*
> *Like a bird on the wing*
> *Onward, the sailors cry!*

"Come on! *Sing!*"

> *Loud the winds howl,*
> *Loud the waves roar,*
> *Thunder clouds rend the air . . .*

"Aren't you going to sing with me?" she said.

"Baaaa . . ."

Mrs Noyes turned to the ram.

"You remember this song. We used to sing it as a duet. Come on, now . . ."

> *Baffled, our foes*
> *Stand on the shore.*
> *Follow they will not dare . . .*

"Baaaa!"

"Baaaa!"

"*Baaaa!*"

They were all saying it. All of them — the ram, the sheep, the lambs . . .

"Baaaa!"

And none of them was singing.

Mrs Noyes set the lamb on the deck and knelt down.

"Please sing," she said. *"Please."*

She knelt directly in front of the oldest sheep of all, whose name was Daisy. Daisy had helped her to teach the others, out in the lambing fields back home. There was not a song in Mrs Noyes's whole repertoire that Daisy could not sing.

"All right, Daisy. You and me together. Here we go:

> *Speed bonnie boat,*
> *Like a bird on the wing . . ."*

"Baaaa."

> *"Onward, the sailors cry!"*

"Baaaa."

> *"Carry the lad, ·*
> *That's born to be king . . ."*

Mrs Noyes picked up the lamb and held it to her breast. She was weeping.

"Please," she said. *"Over the sea to . . . Skye . . ."*

Silence.

Not a word.

Mrs Noyes sat down on the deck. Tears poured down her cheeks.

"Oh," she said. "Oh — no," she said. "Oh, please — *please* sing. . . ."

"Baaaa."

Mrs Noyes just stared at them — and she sniffled, using her apron as a handkerchief. The lamb wanted down — and she let it. And it rejoined the rest of its kind.

Mrs Noyes sat watching them — all the sheep and lambs — huddling together — excluding her. Her mouth hung open. No more songs and no more singing . . .

"Baaaa."

Only baaa.

The sheep would never sing again.

∞ It took a while for Ham to recover from the blow he had received — as much because Shem had delivered the blow as because of the instrument used, which had been nothing more than the plate from which Shem had been feeding.

Technically, the situation between the two factions might have been called a draw. Since Japeth was still incarcerated in the Armoury and only Ham knew how to set him free (an ingenious sequence of knots) there was no one to do battle. And without battle, there could be no decisive victory.

There were, however, defeats on both sides. Ham had been overpowered — and had lost control of his prisoners. Shem, Hannah and Doctor Noyes were free. But so was Ham free, and his mother and Lucy and Emma.

Noah was darkly (and rightly) suspicious of Ham — being certain his son had not only seen the ape-child, but had drawn the correct conclusion about its parentage. Nothing was said of this, though the fact of it hung like a knife between them.

Noah's way of gaining the upper hand was to reassert the unshakeable supremacy of the Edict.

Yaweh had decreed thus and so.

Two by two they had come on board.

Two by two they had survived the voyage thus far — and obviously, given the present sky and the sun's return, the worst of the voyage was behind them.

Two by two they must abide. If they did not, then all would be lost: for all. The ark and its animals could not survive without Ham and Lucy and Mrs Noyes and Emma—and Mrs Noyes and Emma and Lucy and Ham could not survive without Doctor Noyes and Sister Hannah, whose prayers and intellect and intimacy with Yaweh had guaranteed the survival of all. (Strangely, in this litany, nothing was said of Shem or of Japeth.)

Ham went out, after hearing all this in Shem and Hannah's presence, and sat in the shade of the portico, behind the beehives and below his wife. She asked him what had happened—

and he told her. He did not, however, tell her about the ape —
he only said that Hannah's child had been born and was dead.

"Yes," said Lucy. "And she threw it overboard. Just as
they will go on throwing all the apes and all the demons and all
the Unicorns overboard for as long as this voyage lasts. . . ."

Squinting, Ham looked up, but all he could see was his wife's
webbed feet and the hem of her dress — and the lintel, crawling with bees.

"You make it sound as if the voyage will last forever," he
said.

"Perhaps it will," said Lucy.

Ham was quiet for a moment. Then he could not resist the
question any longer and he said; "why did you say they would
go on throwing all the apes overboard, besides the Unicorns
and demons?"

"Because they will."

"But — why apes?"

"Because that is what Hannah threw into the water . . .
while I watched."

"How did you know it was an ape?"

"I knew it would be an ape from the moment it was conceived."

Ham thought it best not to ask any more about the ape, lest
Lucy trap him into saying what he did not want to say.

"Do you love your father?"

(*She knew!*)

"I respect him. I must."

The bees buzzed and Lucy said; "I wish I could teach you to
be more afraid."

"*You* aren't afraid," said Ham.

"Yes, I am," said Lucy.

"Are you really?"

"Yes. With all my heart."

Mrs Noyes came out through the portico and stepped around
Ham.

"Where is your father?" she said.

"I think he may have gone to pray."

Mrs Noyes said nothing, but went and sat on the step that led to the poop deck and drew her apron over her head against the heat of the sun.

Emma came then and sat — completely silent — on the upper step leading down to the hold. She was holding a large white Dove.

No one spoke.

Every one of them was watching the Castle: wondering — and waiting.

What would Yaweh say to Noah?

What would Noah say to them?

∞ In the Chapel, Noah shut the door and was utterly alone.

The silver kitten was still on the altar.

Miracle, my foot!

It was that wretched cat of Mrs Noyes all along!

He glared at the Icons; glared at the altar; glared at the Great Red Boxes of Wisdom.

"Where are You?" he said. *"WHERE ARE YOU?"*

The Icons — the altar — the Boxes were silent. Only the incense made any effort to answer, gently collapsing and ceasing to smoke.

"Everyone else is dead," Noah whispered. "Why not Yaweh?"

He looked at the Icons.

There.

Very well. If that is where He had gone — that is where He would stay. Bearded; old and ruby-eyed. Gold-skinned and black-robed. Smelling of crumbled incense. Sounding of bells and prayers. Leaving His friends to rot — alone . . .

Noah sat down and drew his robes around him.

He waited half an hour.

In half an hour, he stood up.

He walked to the nearest Icon — an Icon that showed Yaweh wide-eyed and angry. Noah took Him to the altar and he pushed aside the silver kitten and he laid the Icon in its place.

Then he drew out more incense and lighted it and he threw

Chinese powder onto the Icon and he set it on fire and he began to ring the Bell.

Then he went outside to tell the people what Yaweh had said.

∞ Everyone was gathered on the deck beneath the sun.

Noah stood with a Raven on his arm and he told them all about the Covenant between himself and Yaweh: the promise that there would never be another flood; the decree that all should go forth and multiply upon the face of the earth; and that everything that lived and breathed and moved had been delivered into their hands — *forever*. And he pointed — and he showed them the symbol of the Covenant and he said to the Raven; "go and be free. When you have found what we seek, return."

And everyone watched and everyone listened and some were dubious and some believed.

And Japeth battered on his door.

It was Noah who set him free.

∞ Emma said; "I thought the rainbow was awfully pretty, didn't you?"

Lucy said; "yes. As pretty as a paper whale."

∞ The Raven did not return.

They waited.

One whole week.

It did not come.

Noah sent forth a Dove.

And they waited.

It was Emma's Dove.

One whole week, they waited again.

And it did not return.

So Noah sent forth another Dove. And another. And another.

And none of them returned.

One week — two weeks — three weeks.

At last, he sent forth a Dove of his own — better trained than the rest had been.

And this Dove did return. With an olive branch in its beak. And Noah said; "you see?"

"Yes," said Lucy. "We do."

∞ Mrs Noyes brought Mottyl with her onto the deck of the ark and they sat, one night, beneath the moon. The old cat was very still as it lay in the old woman's lap. Seven hundred and twenty-one years between them.

Mrs Noyes thought about Noah's paper rainbow — his Covenant with God and the olive branch that had once been the olive branch on which the Dove had sat in its cage, where Emma had fed it. And she thought; it will never end. The voyage will never, never end. And if it does . . .

She laid her hand on Mottyl's head. Here was this cat, whose sight had been taken by Doctor Noyes, and down below them all was the world that had been destroyed by Doctor Noyes (with some help from his illustrious Friend) and all that remained of that world was what, to all intents and purposes, had been seen by this old blind cat and by herself — sitting long ago and rocking on their porch above the valley. And now, Noah wanted another world and more cats to blind. Well — damn him, no, she thought.

"No!" she said.

Mottyl heard her — and stirred.

Mrs Noyes said; "I didn't mean to wake you. I'm sorry. Sorry — but not sorry. Watch with me, Motty — you blind and me with eyes, beneath the moon. We're here, dear. No matter what — we're here. And — damn it all — I guess we're here to stay."

Mrs Noyes scanned the sky.

Not one cloud.

She prayed. But not to the absent God. Never, never again to the absent God, but to the absent clouds, she prayed. And to the empty sky.

She prayed for rain.